# THE SIXTH OF JUNE

## Books by Lionel Shapiro

*Novels*
### THE SIXTH OF JUNE

### TORCH FOR A DARK JOURNEY

### THE SEALED VERDICT

*Reportage*
### THEY LEFT THE BACK DOOR OPEN
*(A chronicle of the Allied campaign in Sicily and Italy)*

*Play*
### THE BRIDGE
*(The Old Vic Company, Theatre Royal, Bristol, 1952)*

# The Sixth of June

## BY LIONEL SHAPIRO

DOUBLEDAY & COMPANY, INC.

*Garden City, New York, 1955*

*THERE IS A LAND blest with the heritage of knowing intimately her British kinsmen and her American neighbors and of loving and in a sense uniting both. The land is Canada, and it is to this precious heritage that I dedicate gratefully this book.*

## Author's Note

A DECADE is so short a passage of time in the sweep of recorded history that the use of the word historical in connection with this novel seems at first glance a literary impertinence.

Nevertheless I like to think of this as a historical novel. The fact that most adults now living recall World War II as a personal experience does not, in my opinion, apply as a disclaimer. This is certainly a historical novel from the standpoint of the methods of warfare here described which are not dissimilar to those employed at Ypres, Belleau Wood, and even Bull Run, the only differences being the numbers of men involved, the speed of their machines, and certain imaginative advances in the efficiency of essentially ancient forms of weapons. One need only consider that the great operation code-named Overlord would have been pricked like a child's balloon by a single strike from any one of a score of modern weapons.

There is another point. The trauma into which we have been flung by the advance of science has endowed our memories of 1942, '43, and '44 with an incredibly romantic aura which is the vital element of the historical novel.

It is therefore scarcely necessary to add that the persons depicted herein, and the units and staff sections, belonging as they do to so simple and sequestered an epoch, could have been rallied into the structure of this novel only by use of the author's imagination. Except for certain names long recognized by history, these persons do not and did not exist.

# Contents

*BOOK ONE*

Two Farewells

*1*

A later call on President Roosevelt and Prime Minister Churchill, a guest at the White House, was no more than an informal chat. . . . Tobruk, in the African desert, had just fallen to the Germans and the whole Allied world was thrown into gloom. . . . General Clark and I, with a few assistants, left Washington in late June 1942. This time the parting from my family seemed particularly difficult although it was, in a sense, a mere repetition of previous instances covering many years. Our son came down from West Point; he, my wife, and I had two days together, and then I left.

—*Crusade in Europe,* by Dwight D. Eisenhower.

S O  M A N Y were leaving, so many and mostly so young. They poured out of their homes and moved urgently to the last barricades, for the war was nearly three years old and the lesser barricades had already been overrun. They were all sorts and sizes and shapes, these men who were to be twisted into a solid mold of olive drab and khaki; the eager, the laggard, the brave, the sensitive, the frightened, the kind, the cruel, and the noble, in such myriad variety and combination that the important personages who pondered global charts and issued global orders must have felt a trifling of what it means to be God. So many paths were to be crossed, so many were to die, so many to live and perhaps learn.

From where Lieutenant Brad Parker stood, on the railway platform at Malton, Connecticut, his global view was somewhat constricted by a group of thirty relations and friends.

His handsome wife, Jane, stood beside him neither snugly nor coldly but with a sure sense of possession, and the first semicircle that faced him was composed of his father-in-law, Damien Lakelock, who was publisher of the Malton *Daily Star,* his mother-in-law, Grace Lakelock, and his own mother, Delilah Parker. The other people, as though sensitive of the occasion's protocol, had arranged themselves in distinct waves. Behind Brad's immediate family stood his distant relations, then close associates from the business and editorial offices of the *Daily Star*, and in the rear, intimate friends. Standing on the edge of the group were two men who didn't quite fit into any of these categories. They were Sanford Jaques, the congressman for Malton and district, and old Abe Maxted, a typesetter who was president of the newspaper's Quarter Century Club of which Brad, as prince consort, was an honorary member.

The two fifty-one for New York was already ten minutes late. Everything that needed to be said had long since been said. The mid-afternoon sun, slanting beneath the platform's roof, set the men to perspiring and the women to fanning themselves with their handkerchiefs. Since no one dared, for fear of betraying boredom, to peer down the track in search of the train, they all looked at Brad in a solemn and respectful way that might have thrust upon a stranger the impression that the personable young lieutenant was unique among Malton's 215,000 population in leaving "to take his place of duty on a far and lonely rampart."

The phrase had appeared that morning in the *Daily Star's* leading editorial and had been composed more or less in honor of Brad's departure for Britain although it was circumspectly used to cover all of Malton's young men who had gone or were preparing to go to war. Its eloquence was only part of the tribute arranged for the occasion.

There had been a luncheon in a salon of the Pentland Hotel, across the square from the station, and this, like the editorial, was privately savored by Brad's family and a few friends. Congressman Jaques was present and also Ben Carver, the *Daily Star's* venerable editor. Damien Lakelock had gone so far as to instruct the city desk that no mention of the event was to appear in the paper, not even in the society notes, thus breaking, though not seriously, the distinguished journal's sixty-year tradition that the executive tower does not meddle with the content of the news columns.

The luncheon had gone off well. By and large, its bittersweet atmosphere could hardly have been improved upon. It had progressed with a murmur of conversation sparked now and again by polite laughter as if all present were conscious of a duty to be normal and cheerful. There had been a hush when Ben Carver raised his voice slightly to deliver his opinion that the choice of an unknown general

to command in Europe was another of Roosevelt's gambles with the
nation's destiny, but Congressman Jaques promptly responded that
under the American system a leader was only as effective as the effort
behind him, and when Washington assigned young men of Brad
Parker's caliber to the headquarters staff in London, nothing much
could go wrong with the effort there. Ben Carver grumbled "Hear,
hear" to this, and the proper atmosphere had been restored. Brad's
mother held her handkerchief significantly high, but not too high,
on her cheek as she whispered something to Mrs. Lakelock. She
managed, however, to smile when she turned around to glance at
her son. Then a waiter served brandy along with the coffee and an
expectant silence fell on the gathering. Damien Lakelock turned
quite informally to Brad. He said, "Well Brad, the publisher is going
to miss the assistant to the publisher, and so, I'm sure, will all the
rest of us. Godspeed, good luck, good hunting, and come back safe
and sound when the job is done."

That was all. Brad nodded his thanks, his mother jabbed hurriedly
at her eyes, Ben Carver managed to catch the waiter's eye for another quick brandy, and then it was time to walk across the square
to the station where a group not invited to the luncheon awaited the
final act of farewell.

Now, as they stood on the platform, the bittersweet flair was being
undone by a blazing sun and a laggard train.

Brad scanned the faces that looked upon him with such well-
behaved glumness. He felt a curious elation, soaring but secret, and
he had to withhold himself not to parade it openly. Being a sensitive
man, he knew that elation was a wrong, even a sinful way to approach war. But he was also an honest man. The war had come at
the right time for him, exactly at the right time. Five years ago would
have been too soon; at twenty-one he was too young, too ambitious,
and there was gamble enough in reaching out blindly for a career.
Five years hence might well be too late; a mature marriage, perhaps
children, and the tentacles of the Lakelock dynasty might have
smothered any urge for a fling with adventure. At twenty-six, for
reasons he dared not admit to himself, the time and the war fitted
perfectly.

His Aunt Ellen, of the Parker side of his family, had unwittingly
put it into words at the luncheon when she whispered, "Don't you

feel grand, Brad? You *must*. First Lieutenant Bradford Gamaliel
Parker, United States Army—it just sounds *so wonderful!*"

It *was* wonderful to a man who hadn't enjoyed a real chance to
flex his muscles and was already weighted down as assistant to the
publisher, heir apparent to the executive tower, president of the
Junior Chamber of Commerce, and a director of the Country Club.
The thought that he might be killed in the war occasionally entered
his mind and he dreaded it, but there was also comfort in it for the
greater the risk the less guilty he felt for being elated.

His gaze fell on his father-in-law's gray, distinguished face. He
thought he detected a wry smile. Their eyes locked for a moment
and he knew that Damien was sharing his secret, that the wry smile
was a smile of envy, of chagrin for a long ago chance that was lost.
Damien had been in the same position in the first war, married to
Grace, the only child of Everett Bolding, founder of the Malton
*Daily Star*. But Everett had been a tough old puritan, a power in
New England politics in a time when power could be nakedly
wielded, and he saw to it that Damien's uniform carried him no
farther than a desk job at the Boston port of embarkation.

He too had felt something of that frustration when they called
him up as a reserve officer just after Pearl Harbor. He had volunteered for the Special Service Force, training in Helena, Montana,
in parachute and winter warfare, but Jane had gone along to live
with him in married officers' quarters and there were monthly leaves
home and constant telephone conversations with Malton, and at least
the suspicion that he might remain stateside as an instructor. Now,
inexplicably, the War Department had given him a fortnight's embarkation leave and had reassigned him to London. He was going to
have his war at last.

He could almost hear Damien murmuring, "You're lucky, Brad.
You're lucky I'm not old Everett. I didn't fix it. There'll be time
enough when you come back, a whole lifetime, to be chained to the
women who surround you, and to the paper and to the community."

A crusty voice called out, "Careful, folks!" and they all moved
aside to make passage for a mail cart moving to the head of the
platform. Then a train whistle sounded. The faces peering at Brad
became animated.

Jane whispered, "Thank heaven. I thought it would never come."
She lifted herself closer to his ear. "Don't forget to fuss over your

mother. I think she's furious about not coming on to New York."

They had broken ranks now and were all around Brad, slapping him on the back and making brisk, jocular remarks, but most of what they said was drowned in the roar of the engine as it rumbled past them.

Brad kissed his mother on the mouth and then on the cheek. She said, "Brad—Brad—it's not the war or the danger. I know you'll come through all right. It's your health. You give yourself so much to anything you undertake——"

He kissed her again. "Just take care of yourself, Mother, and don't worry about me."

Then he kissed his mother-in-law. He thought he detected a furtive note as she said simply, "You'll write Jane often, won't you?"

Damien didn't say anything. He shook hands with Brad and smiled the same soft envious smile.

The Lakelock chauffeur was already handing up Brad's baggage and Jane's overnight case to a Pullman porter.

"Good-by, everybody," Brad called out. "Write you from Berlin around next Thursday. Might be a day or two late." They all laughed. He took Jane's arm. "Come on, dear. Up you go."

Standing on the platform of their Pullman as the train moved slowly out of the station, they appeared to the farewell party as fine and decorative as the American dream itself.

Brad wore a tan summer uniform, exceedingly well cut by his own tailor, and his blouse already bore a metal parachute insignia above two efficiency decorations. Moreover he looked the part. His lean, well-shaped face was virile rather than handsome; he was attractive (as Grace Lakelock described him to her friends when he was courting Jane) "in a wholesome way—no airy-fairy foreign good looks but solid New England." His nose was certainly New England, straight but neither thin nor small, and his blue eyes, when they looked straight at you, were inclined to hardness. He had healthy black hair, a determined mouth, and a distinct cleft in his chin. He carried his six feet so well it was hardly noticeable that his shoulders were disposed to roundness in the manner of a man hurrying toward success.

Jane was big for a young woman, something over five feet seven and inclined to be fleshy at the hips and bosom. The features of her face too were generously large but she carried herself with style and no little verve. From the time she was a child, her parents had taken an honest view of her developing ungainliness, and they pushed her through years of planned exercise and ballet and dancing classes until she had attained an unusual degree of gracefulness. This, in addition to her finely shaped legs and a lavish budget for clothes and coiffeur, had made her into an extremely desirable woman. Now, at twenty-four, she was at her best. On this day she wore a silk print dress expertly tailored to amend her less attractive lines, and her thick brown shoulder-length hair swept daringly to one side, her right, setting off her better profile which was her left. Altogether she looked a magnificent companion piece to the officer who was her husband.

They waved and waved, and when the train had passed the head of the platform she said, "I'm sorry, darling. It was all too precious. I need a drink—a real big fat drink."

The parlor car was a madhouse of activity and high spirits. Businessmen, tourists, and soldiers and sailors of all ranks up to brigadier general filled every seat and overflowed into the passageway. On a writing desk in a corner two Wacs had set up a portable gramophone. A cluster of GIs joined them around it and all gestured to the music with their hips and their hands. Every ash stand was equipped with a serving rim and these were covered with drinks and dollar bills. Two Negro waiters, grinning and perspiring, ran a marathon between the pantry and their demanding clients. Like every other corner of America at war, the car was shot through with a sense of animation and well-being.

Brad congratulated himself on having had the foresight to reserve a drawing room. When he and Jane had seated themselves in the quiet, air-cooled room, he rang for a waiter.

"I want service," he said to the breathless Negro, handing him two dollar bills.

"Service you'll get," the man replied. "Jes' give the order, General."

By the time the train reached New Haven, Jane was on her third whisky. Brad, still toying with his first, watched her quizzically. She didn't like liquor. At parties she usually sipped at a single drink the whole evening and then only because the young married crowd in Malton drank freely and she wouldn't have them think she was better or more respectable even though she was the Lakelock heiress.

Now she had taken a gulp out of her third drink and her eyes, still clear, stared out of the window. The pose was handsome, decorative, and full of hurt.

Brad reached across the table, took the glass out of her hand, and played with her cold finger tips.

"What is it, Janie? Come on, dear. Out with it."

She gave a little shake of her head. He waited. Then, still staring out of the window, she said, "Our three years together have been good years, Brad. I've been happy."

He smiled. "Don't try to jinx me, honey," he said deprecatingly. "They've been wonderful years and there'll be a lot more—so many more you'll be damned good and tired of me. I can just see you about thirty years from now, saying, 'What did I see in this goat when I could have married Cary Grant or somebody like that?'"

She turned and looked at him squarely. It was an honest and affectionate look. There was a nakedness in it she rarely brought herself to expose even in the act of love.

"I'm not unhappy about your going, not desperately unhappy, not the way I suppose a wife should feel when her husband is off to war—and I'm not trying to jinx anything, Brad. You'll come through all right. I was never surer of anything in my life. But—oh I wish I hadn't had these drinks. I'd explain myself better——" She snatched her glass and took another gulp and pushed the glass away distastefully. "It's just that I'm losing you. *I'm losing you, Brad.* I've had the feeling during the whole two weeks of this leave that you can't wait to get away, to get away from everything, from Malton and from the paper—and from me."

He was shocked by her perception. In their three years of marriage they had been honest enough with each other, although the true depth of their honesty had never been tested. There had never been need for it. They had been happy in the glare of attention that played on the early years of a brilliant match, and this happiness carried over adequately into their private lives together. She had been a proper, even a delightful wife, possessive in a way that complimented rather than imprisoned him, proud of his achievement though it had been mostly the gift of the dynasty he had wedded, and charmingly boastful, in the subtle ways young matrons have of communicating these matters among themselves, of his virility.

Now, in their first emotional crisis, she was showing a depth of feeling he had never suspected in her.

He said, "You're my whole life, Janie, and so in a way is the paper. You know me well enough. I don't run out on anything. I never have. I'll be honest with you——"

She squeezed his hand impulsively. "I don't want to hear it, darling. Whatever it is you're going to say, I don't want to hear it."

He knew he hadn't struck the right note. He had hurt her. He said quickly, "I love you, Janie, and I also want to get off to the war. You've got to be a man to understand it. Look, darling, war happens to an American once in a lifetime. I don't want to read about it in the papers, even if I'm wearing a uniform. I've got to see it and be a part of it, and be lucky enough to come out of it. That's why I fidgeted when they were trying to make me out some kind of martyr. I'm no hero. I'm just curious."

She pulled her hand away gently and took another sip of her drink.

She said, "I'm glad they're sending you by plane. It'll be nice and symbolic seeing you off flying tomorrow. Then I'll come back to Malton and wonder how it will be years from now when you come back. I'm getting good and tipsy now, darling."

"Years from now?"

"Yes, years. The Germans have got everything from Leningrad to Spain and the Japs are sprawling all over the Pacific. We'll win it—but years, darling."

The train rattled across the Connecticut countryside. Brad finished his drink and ordered another for himself. They didn't speak for a time.

Then he said boyishly, "How did you know I wanted to go so badly?"

"I knew it"—she smiled a sad, wise smile—"because I know you."

"Come on, Janie. You can't know me that well. Not in three years."

"Think you know me?"

"Not completely."

"But I know you. That's because I love you. Shhhh! Don't argue. I haven't been this gay in my life so let me talk. It's your going-away present to me. Let me talk. You didn't marry me, Brad. I married *you*. It couldn't happen any other way. I couldn't marry Cary Grant or some band leader. I had to marry a man who would someday be publisher of the *Star*. And then you came along and I fell in love with you and it was too good to be true because I wanted you and you fitted. You fitted perfectly and on top of it I loved you. What came first, the chicken or the egg? Did I love you first or did I know you fitted and then fell in love with you? *I* knew. So I blitzed you. You didn't know I blitzed you, did you? I never intended you to know, and you never would have known because the years were going to be so full and fast you wouldn't have time to realize what had happened to you, and when we were old it wouldn't matter any more because by that time you'd really be in love with me. Oh, I had it planned, beautifully planned. And then the war has to come along and the Parkers have always gone to war, always, back to '76 I suppose, and Janie's fifty-year plan goes bang after three little years. I feel silly and wonderful and I'm making a ridiculous spectacle of myself. Forgive me, darling. Don't say anything. Please don't say anything."

She pushed her glass toward him. Her eyes were shining. She smiled and said, "Don't look so shocked. You drink it, darling. I hate the stuff. I really do. You see what it's gone and done to me."

He took her drink and smiled at her, and like embarrassed children, their smiles became too abundantly gay. He leaned across the table and puckered her lips with his fingers and kissed her lightly.

She said, "Don't let me drink any more. And no more weepy conversation—oh, I almost forgot. I'm supposed to tell you that you're to sign the bill at the Waldorf. It's Daddy's gift. And the dinner at "21" is mother's, and your mother got us the tickets for the Gertrude Lawrence show. Wasn't it sweet of them?"

"Terrific. I suppose though I'll have to shell out for the checkroom."

"And Brad——" She looked away quickly. "I've got a gift for you too but let's wait till later. I'm almost afraid to give it to you now."

The train was rolling through Greenwich and her eyes found refuge in a row of billboards advertising the Broadway shows. It was coming up to four o'clock as the train passed Greenwich Station.

## 2

IN ENGLAND it was coming up to nine o'clock in the evening.

The sky over Lincolnshire had been overcast all day, and now dusk brought with it a gentle rain that whispered softly as it fell on the eaves and gardens of the village of Burlingham. Along High Street, which stretched a quarter of a mile between the railway station and the common, blackout curtains had already been drawn. The only light to be seen was a tiny red glow which marked the entrance to the village pub, The Stag at Bay, and even this minuscule break in the blackout pattern, although permitted by the authorities, disturbed the elderly residents of Burlingham because German planes lately had been prowling the skies in the vicinity of the R.A.F. Bomber Command station at Belnorton, four miles to the east.

Burlingham's middle class, in large part retired merchants who had fled the bustle of Lincoln, population: 70,000, lived in houses which ringed the common. These were mostly two-story dwellings, low, wide, stolid, and so encrusted with pampered plant life that one might suspect they were never built by man but grew naturally out of the soil of England. Unlike the homes on High Street which were identified by number, these on the common bore only a charming and usually illogical name plate. "The Cottage" was in fact the finest and largest house in the village, and "Hillview" and "The Moors" had no visible connection with hill or moor.

On this evening, as the day's last light glistened feebly on the wet fields, an ungainly, mud-spattered military vehicle called a 1500-weight rolled into Burlingham, traversed the deserted length of High Street, circled the common, and came to a halt in front of a house, half hidden by trees and wrinkled with ivy, which bore the name plate "Darjeeling."

Captain the Hon. John Wynter sprang from the vehicle.

"I'll be about half an hour, Bailey," he called back to the driver. "I'll try to arrange tea for you."

"Thank you, sir," the driver said.

The captain pushed open the gate of "Darjeeling," passed along a path rimmed with rosebushes and violas, and pulled at a bell beside the blacked-out door.

He had a slim figure, even wearing the coarse cloth of British battle dress, and he appeared taller than his five feet, nine inches. His blond hair bulged thickly from under the headband of a green beret, and his eyes, pale blue and inordinately mild, looked out rather sadly from a face that was tanned and weather-beaten. His features seemed a bit too finely shaped, the nose too thin and the mouth too sensitive, for the rough masculinity associated with his shoulder patches which bore the legend Commando. He looked younger than his twenty-seven years.

He pulled off his beret as the door was opened by a tiny, dark-skinned woman with hair of pure white. She wore a severe black dress, and from her left shoulder flowed a section of bright maroon cloth which gave the impression of a sari.

"Good evening, Mala."

"Captain Wynter! Do come in out of the rain."

John hesitated. "I'm afraid it's a rather impolite hour, but I couldn't get through on the phone——"

"I am sure you will be welcome. Do come in." Like all Indians who speak English well, she articulated her words with quiet authority which was altogether pleasant. She closed the door behind him and pushed aside the blackout curtain which cut off the vestibule. "The brigadier is always pleased to see you," she said with a faintly proprietary air, "to say nothing of Miss Valerie."

"Oh good. Then she's here too."

The tiny woman led the way through an entrance hall to a living room which was neatly but inexpensively furnished. She said, "I daren't disturb the brigadier while he's listening to the news——" She smiled obliquely. "But I'm sure Miss Valerie won't mind."

Her guile was lost on John. He nodded solemnly and said, "Mmmm, I hope not." He added hastily, "By the way, we've done about two hundred miles today and my driver is out there. I—I wonder——"

"I'll see to it, Captain. Tea?"

"That would be splendid."

She left, and a few moments later Valerie Russell came into the room.

"What a wonderful surprise, John," she exclaimed. She came across to where he stood and extended both her hands. He took them in his hands, and his face was so modestly happy it was almost sad.

He said, "It's good to see you, Val, but I think I should explain. We left Inveraray this morning and when the colonel gave me permission to break out of convoy at Doncaster, I tried to get you on the phone but the trunks into this area seem all tied up, and— well——"

"Bother the trunks," she said lightly. "It couldn't matter less. It was grand of you to come." She gave his hands an extra little squeeze and went to a sideboard for a sherry decanter and glasses. "You look absolutely fit. Commando training must suit you." She placed the sherry and glasses on a serving table. "Now do sit down and tell me all your news."

He didn't sit down, nor did he speak at once. His pale blue eyes studied her as she concentrated on pouring two glasses of sherry.

She was the loveliest girl he had ever known; indeed, the loveliest he had ever seen. Middling tall, she possessed both suppleness and carriage in unusual harmony. Her light brown hair, which contained a slight tint of red, swept back severely from her forehead and was gathered up in a tight bun at the back. John felt this was just as it should be. When she allowed her hair to fall into its natural waves, as she had on one occasion early in their acquaintance, she was too strikingly beautiful for his taste. This hairdo, to his way of thinking, was just right. It was severe enough to lend a classic line to her features, and it rather offset her lips, which were generous with a most un-English fullness, and her deep, darkly brown eyes which were foreign to her pink and white complexion. It was as if the place of her birth, which was Darjeeling in India, had invested her with something of its agelessness. At twenty-two her face possessed a maturity and strength of one who has lived a long time and has witnessed much.

The gray cardigan and tweed skirt she wore on this evening failed to make her look typically English. She defied classification, John thought.

She handed him a glass of sherry. "You must excuse Father for a few minutes. He still marks up his war maps, the poor dear, according to the BBC reports."

"How is he, Val? Really."

"He seems improved—at least physically. Even the scars are healing over. The trouble is, the stronger he gets the deeper he falls into his peculiar bitterness. I don't know——" She looked into her sherry glass. "They've really retired him, haven't they?"

John said, "He's still on the sick list—officially, that is. But—well, things have changed. War isn't the same and Britain isn't the same." He looked up and smiled sadly.

She said, "You mean old Indian army officers are no longer in style."

"More or less. Pity. He's a wonderfully brave soldier."

They fell into silence. Then Valerie said brightly, "Do forgive me, John, nattering about Father. Are you happy with the Commandos—you certainly look as if you are—and how did you ever manage to break off convoy at Doncaster?"

He didn't want to look at her when he told her the news. His eyes fixed on a brigade pennant framed over the fireplace.

"It was a sort of embarkation privilege. You see, Val, I'm off."

"John! On operations? So quickly?"

He nodded. "It's really grand news."

She said slowly, "But it isn't true! The division hasn't been training more than a month or two."

"Oh, the division isn't going. Just a reinforced company, sort of small Commando. That's what makes it so splendid. They picked my company, Val."

Valerie stood. She took a step toward the slim young man, then walked slowly away toward the fireplace.

"Yes, it *is* splendid." She smiled briefly. "I suppose you can't tell me where or when."

"Wish I knew," he said cheerfully. "We rendezvous at Aldershot tomorrow afternoon and—well, I suppose it's safe enough to tell *you*, Val—we proceed to a southeasterly port for embarkation. You know what that means."

"Then it isn't a coastal raid."

"I'm sure of that. It's overseas operations."

"The Middle East?"

"Good guess, I imagine. We won't know till we break open our orders a hundred miles, or some such figure, out to sea."

John brought his head up and allowed himself to look squarely and unashamedly at Valerie. She came across the room and sat on the arm of his chair.

She said, "How long can you spend with us?"

"I should be off in ten or fifteen minutes."

"But John! You may be away for months!"

He took her hand. "I know it's a bit of a rush, but I'm luckier than most chaps in the company. They can't get home at all. The orders came through only last night."

"It's not fair! It just isn't at all fair. It's a filthy way to run an army."

He smiled shyly. "It's not really bad, Val. Between Bailey and myself, we can drive all night and make London early enough to give him a couple of hours with his wife. Then we'll pop down to Tunbridge so I can see my father for a bit, and we should hit Aldershot dead on time. Works out rather well."

Valerie said, "Then we'd better go in and see Father."

"Won't he mind being interrupted?"

"He's very fond of you."

They passed through the hall and paused at the door of the brigadier's study. The nine o'clock news was still on. ". . . at this afternoon's press conference, a spokesman for the War Office made no attempt to minimize the loss of Tobruk, but he appeared to take a much more serious view of the effectiveness of the new 88-millimeter cannon the Germans are using on our tanks. Their firepower from positions of almost perfect concealment cost the Eighth Army fifty-seven tanks in the last two days of fighting. According to our correspondent in the desert . . ."

John whispered, "Oh Val, do you think, afterward, we might pop across to the pub? One drink. Just the two of us."

"Of course, John. I want to." She knocked lightly on the study door and opened it.

The brigadier paid no heed to the interruption. He sat stiffly in an armchair and stared ahead at the blackout curtain which covered a full wall of the small, square room. He was a tall man, three inches over six feet, thin and big-boned, and his cropped, steel-gray head framed the face of a born warrior. It was a lean, knobbly face with a steel-gray brush mustache and eyebrows and a chin which jutted belligerently as he listened to the wireless. Only the eyes betrayed the warrior. They were small, spiritless eyes which stared dully from dark circles of discolored skin. On the right side of his face, a pattern of ugly keloid scars scampered across his chin and neck and was lost beneath the collar of the tropical bush jacket he wore.

". . . As a result of our evacuation of Tobruk, the Afrika Korps under Field Marshal Rommel now controls the entire stretch of Mediterranean coastline as far east as Alamein. However, as the enemy does not control the sea or the air, his overland supply line is vulnerable to the type of raid——"

"Father."

"For God's sake, girl, can't you see I'm listening?"

"John is here."

"Well, can't he wait? Shush——"

". . . Commenting on the fall of Tobruk, Reuters correspondent observes that while the situation is serious, it is by no means devoid of hope. The arrival of increasing supplies of American Sherman tanks with their high speed and improved maneuverability——"

"He has only a minute or two."

"Dammit, Valerie, I don't see——"

"Father, he's off overseas. To the Middle East."

The brigadier reached a long arm to the wireless on his desk and turned it off. "Serious but by no means devoid of hope," he scoffed. "These piddling experts! What do they know about it?" He turned about and when he saw John standing behind Valerie he nodded and his mouth lost its scowl.

"Come in, Wynter."

"Thank you, sir." John dropped his arms stiffly at his sides for a quick moment and entered the room. "You look fit, sir."

"I'm quite all right." Brigadier Russell smiled narrowly as he studied the junior officer. "Sit down and tell me about this Commando of yours. Is it any good?"

John glanced at his watch, then at Valerie. He sat on the edge of a chair and detailed his company's stiff training schedule. Encouraged by the brigadier's approving nods, he brought himself to say, "We've got beach assaults down to a pretty fine point, sir. I put a stop watch on my engineer platoon at Inveraray yesterday. From the fall of the ramp to the laying of a bangalore thirty yards up the beach took them exactly nine seconds."

"First class. Absolutely first class." The brigadier's eyes took on an unaccustomed sparkle. "And now, Valerie tells me, you're off to the Middle East."

"We've had emergency embarkation orders. I can only guess it's the Middle East."

The iron-gray face clouded over.

"Are you in the habit," he thundered, "of spouting emergency embarkation orders to your friends? By God, Wynter! I thought I taught you better."

John said, "I see what you mean, sir. But it's rather difficult to be going off for months or years——"

"What's difficult about it?" the brigadier demanded. His chin came up and the keloid scars on his neck stood out inflamed and ugly. "We've become a bunch of ninnies. That's the trouble. Ninnies!"

Valerie said, "Oh, come now, Father. It's my fault and it's not at all serious."

"You keep out of this, Valerie." The brigadier's mouth hardened and he clenched his fists as if trying to control an emotion that was overtaking him.

"Ninnies!" he growled. "The whole damned lot of us! Can't do this, can't do that! Sit here and pinprick the Hun with a bomber or two! Fall back on the desert like a lot of cowards! Beg the Americans to come over and help us! The Americans, by God! I remember them in the last party. Running up three divisions to attack on a brigade front! Can't die. That's the trouble with the Americans. Never could. Always had to raise the odds on dying. Ninnies! Every last one of them!"

The iron-gray man took to staring at the blackout curtains and his eyes blinked incessantly. John looked to Valerie. She made a hand gesture as if to say, Let him go on, don't try to stop him.

"We should be standing up to the Hun," the brigadier grumbled harshly, "standing up to him and driving him back. You remember St. Omer. You decoded the order yourself. You did, didn't you? Fall back on Dunkerque. What nonsense! Fall back on Dunkerque! I said, stand and fight! Attack! Cut off their damned line at Béthune! Or die! When the British can't stand up to the Hun, then die!"

He kept staring at the blackout curtains.

"If I hadn't caught their shrapnel, I'd have gone on ignoring the damned order——" Now his voice turned faint and strangely plaintive. "But my 2IC was a ninny. Bundled me up and rolled me back. Didn't have the decency to leave me there—leave me there with the men who obeyed my order to stand and fight—didn't have the common decency."

He blinked his eyes faster.

"You know, Wynter, why they're keeping me on the sick list. Two years and still on the sick list. When I go back they've got to give me a division and they're afraid to give me a division. They're afraid I'll fight. You know that, Wynter. You know it, don't you?"

John said, "I hope you get your division, sir. I'll be proud to serve with you again." He glanced anxiously at Valerie. She went to the back of her father's chair and passed her hands softly across his shoulders. He was panting like a spent bulldog.

John got up. "I'm afraid I have to leave now, sir."

The brigadier didn't look at him. "You've the makings, Wynter. I haven't forgotten St. Omer. Get out there, wherever you're going, and come to close quarters with the Hun. Close quarters, you understand. It's the only way. A bit of the bayonet is better than ten thousand of these playthings that take off from Belnorton every night."

"I understand, sir."

"All right. Good luck." The brigadier shook off Valerie's hands and stood up. He towered over the captain as they shook hands but his gaunt frame swayed slightly and the steel-gray head with its black eye sockets was a shell.

Outside it was black as pitch, and silent except for the feather whisper of rain. Valerie and John walked blindly down the cottage path until their outstretched hands touched the gate. They could barely make out the hulk of the 1500-weight parked in the roadway.

John called out, "Are you there, Bailey?"

"Right here at the wheel, sir."

"Had your tea?"

"And sandwiches, sir."

"We'll have to drive all night. Feel up to it?"

"Piece of cake, sir."

"That's the spirit. Pick me up at the pub along High Street in fifteen minutes. And mind your lights. Just the pinpoints. There's a raf station over the fields."

Valerie took John's hand and conducted him across the walk and the roadway. She broke the even rhythm of her progress only to make certain she had negotiated the open gate which gave entrance to the common. Once on the path which cut diagonally across the common to High Street, she resumed a normal pace but she did not let go of John's hand. The press of his fingers on hers was inexpressibly shy and tender. She felt like weeping although she could think of no urgent reason for it.

She didn't know him really well. They had met in the military hospital at Watford. It was on a Sunday, sunny and warm and deathly quiet. The defeat at Dunkerque had stunned the people of Britain into a haze of unbelief as if they were all asleep and the dream was unpleasant and one had to walk quietly because it was impolite to disturb a dream no matter how unpleasant.

She had come down to London from the A.T.S. station at Lincoln on compassionate leave along with a score of red-eyed girls in khaki who sought word of the fate of husbands, brothers, and fathers in the British Expeditionary Force. She had waited with the others in a hostel on Sloane Street for six miserable days while the survivors were sorted out in countless ports and beaches on the southeast coast, until that Sunday the War Office called her to say that Brigadier Frederick Hassard Russell was to be found in the military hospital at Watford. She had stood looking down at his unconscious eyes which were the only part of his face and neck uncovered by bandages, and in the welter of frantic visitors in the forty-bed officers' ward she had scarcely taken note of the haggard young man in filthy battle dress who hovered near the brigadier's bedside. And then an M.O. had come by, saying, "By the way, Miss Russell, Lieutenant Wynter can tell you what happened. He was there. Matter of fact, he escorted the stretcher all the way from St. Omer until we had your father safely on the operating table."

She saw him again several weeks later, after her father had returned to "Darjeeling" on convalescent leave. John had arrived to fulfill his last duty as the brigadier's aide. He spent two concentrated days compiling an official record of the ghastly defeat at St. Omer. It was then that she first noticed the man's inordinate shyness. He seemed like a schoolboy in the first flush of puberty, unwilling to look directly at her, and when they passed in the narrow hall she had the impression he shrank against the wall to avoid contact by the widest possible margin, a practice which amused her and to some extent engaged a latent protective instinct in her.

During the next twelve months he had showed up several times, whenever his military journeyings brought him remotely into the area, and he seemed quietly content with tea or a meal and the evidences that the brigadier was gradually recovering from his wounds. But in the summer of 1941, when he decided to volunteer for the Commandos, he had asked her to come out for a walk in the fields and it was to her that he haltingly broke the news of his decision.

His subsequent visits became as frequent as the stern regimen of Commando training allowed, and although he spent most of the time chatting with the brigadier about the new daredevil corps which was to spearhead Britain's return to the offensive, an understanding, unspoken yet vivid, came into being that the purpose of his journeys to Burlingham was to see her. He had family of his own, of course. He was the second of Viscount Haltram's three sons but he apparently derived scant warmth from a leave spent at Smallhill, the rambling manor house near Tunbridge Wells in Kent. His mother had been dead for years, his older brother Derek was with the Royal Dragoons in the desert, his younger brother Bertie a fighter pilot, and his father was old, introverted and bookish, a dedicated historian, amateur archaeologist, and terribly inept manager of the tax-ridden estate.

As the months passed she came to realize that she had unwittingly penetrated the fabric of his life to a depth she could not fathom, for he spoke very little of himself and not at all of his emotions, and yet she was conscious of an intensity in him her instincts were defenseless to resist. In the Britain of blood and tears, the only softness left to life was a woman's softness and she was urged to extend it to this gentle, diffident soldier. She often wondered how much of the urge extended to the symbol and how much to the man himself.

Indeed, his very diffidence constantly puzzled her. She had not been surprised to know that he had fought fearlessly at St. Omer, for she had been brought up in military stations and coolheaded bravery was to her a normal attribute of the British soldier. Yet she was completely unprepared to hear that in his first action as a Commando, the raid on Vaagso Island the previous November, he had won his captaincy and an immediate award of the D.S.O. for breaking the hard core of resistance by closing on the two senior German

officers and killing them with knife thrusts in the throat. She would
not have believed it of this spare, shy man if her father had not
read to her, with appetite, the War Office report on the action.

Even now, as they made their way through the gloom of the common, she could scarcely believe it of him. The feel of his hand holding hers was like that of a small boy being led to school.

She said, "I shouldn't have mentioned the Middle East to Father.
You got a ticking off."

"I don't mind really. Probably made him feel like old times, ticking
me off. He used to do an awful lot of it."

A few steps later she said, "John, why are they sending only a
company?"

"Can't tell about the War Office. Odd blokes."

"Will it be raids? Like Vaagso?"

"Something like that, I imagine. Are you sure we're going the
right way? I can't see a thing."

She said, "High Street is just ahead. Will you be on the planning
staff or—or on operations?"

"We all do a bit of everything." He chuckled quietly. "You do have
the most remarkable eyes, Val—I mean, they give us all sorts of vita-
mins and eye exercises so we can operate in the dark, and I can't
see anything but absolute pitch. There's one chap in my company
though, Glenning. He can spot a Bren at fifty yards in visibility zero
—hallo! What's this?"

They stopped, puzzled. A faint, diffused light had broken over
the common, giving black definition to the buildings ahead on High
Street. In almost the same instant the scream of a multi-engined
plane, still distant but rising in volume, broke into the silence. They
turned about swiftly. A cluster of searchlights had speared the dark
across the fields a few miles to the east, moving back and forth, now
crisscrossing, now singly, in an urgent, relentless search along the
gray-pink underside of a cloud bank.

John said incredulously, "A raid?"

"A fighter-bomber, probably." She listened intently. "It's a German,
all right. Hear that rhythmic crump?"

"Cheeky of him."

"They try to shoot up the runway at Belnorton pretty regularly——"

The wail of Burlingham's siren shattered their ears. It rose and
fell in pitch for a long, sickening minute, and when it petered out

the sharp rattle of Belnorton's light ack-ack filled the night sky. Streams of orange tracers leaped up between the shafts of light. The German was climbing and banking and diving. The labor of his motors receded behind the rattle of ack-ack, then came roaring through over it.

"God, Val, it's wonderfully exciting," John cried. "What's this now?"

A new vibration, full-throated and straining with power, convulsed the night air close at hand.

Valerie said, "Our night fighters taking off." She raised her head as if she could see them and murmured, "God bless them." She added quickly, "I've seen them afternoons in the pub. They're awfully keen but they're boys. Children, really."

Suddenly the roar of motors came down almost upon them, shaking them physically. A furious gust of wind tore at their clothes and drove the rain hard into their faces. They held to each other to keep from being blown off their feet. Then they saw the raider, its exhausts glowing crimson, swoop across a corner of the common like an enormous black hawk. It pulled up gracefully and thundered back into the night sky.

They half ran the rest of the way to High Street. As they reached the cobblestoned thoroughfare, a blinding flash lit the countryside, nakedly revealing for a brief moment the outlines of the village. Then the crack of an explosion rolled across their ears and a fire sprang up in the fields over near Belnorton.

Now the air was filled with the coarse shrieking of many swiftly banking planes and the shattering crack of the big anti-aircraft guns and the incessant chatter of small ack-ack. The searchlights still wildly crisscrossed the sky, revealing nothing in their beams but soft and innocuous gray-pink clouds.

John shouted to make himself heard. "Come on, Val. We've only about ten minutes and—well, I've got something I want to tell you."

They hurried over the cobblestones toward a tiny red light which marked the entrance to The Stag at Bay. The street was deserted but here and there among the windows of the old houses a white face could be seen peering upward into the lacerated heavens.

## 3

A MAKE-BELIEVE firmament on the arched ceiling of the Waldorf's Starlight Roof twinkled almost as prettily as the summer sky outside and cast a mellow light on a great throng of dancers swaying to the soft rhythm of a song called "I'll Be Seeing You."

Uniforms of all ranks and branches abounded. Some couples, encouraged by a battery of alto saxophones, hummed the popular tune as they moved within the narrow restrictions of the overcrowded floor, and the sweet music of farewell invested their faces with an entirely touching sadness.

Jane danced closer to Brad than she would have dared in Malton. She pressed her cheek against the slightly stubbled curve of his jaw, and she enjoyed her awareness of his hard, slim body as if this were a rare and clandestine rendezvous with the man she loved. Brad responded in full measure. His fingers pressed against the nape of her neck, persuading her closer, and the rhythm of his dancing was smooth and exciting.

The saxophones faded out and a cute girl with blond upswept hair slid to the microphone on the bandstand to sing the lyric.

> *I'll be seeing you*
> *In all the old familiar places*
> *That this heart of mine embraces*
> *All day through . . .*

Jane whispered, "I'm glad we came."

He said, "The show was good but this is better."

"I think so too."

"You never danced like this before."

She said, "I feel sad and sort of wonderful."

"Last time I danced this close was at Dartmouth——"

"I don't want to hear about it."

"Forgotten her name. Some chorus gal Glen Van Melder brought to a frat dance. Terrific."

She said, "I'm not interested in your flaming youth."

He pressed her still closer.

"Didn't dream I'd marry someone even bitchier."

"Brad!"

"Had to find out sometime. I'm glad we came."

"So am I, darling."

He wanted to remember her this way; her ardor, her decorativeness, the comfort of her. It made the leaving of her harder, and the return greatly to be wished for. Somewhere deep in his mind it compensated for this other urge to leave his set-piece civilization behind him, to plunge headlong into the war. The sweetness of this moment made it somehow easier to go.

The saxophones slid into a new and higher key, and the singer reprised the last eight bars of the song.

> . . . *I'll find you in the morning sun*
> *And when the night is new*
> *I'll be looking at the moon*
> *But I'll be seeing you.*

They glided to a halt and remained a moment locked in each other's arms.

He whispered, "Will you miss me, Janie?"

She said, "I'll manage, darling, as long as you miss me—terribly."

It was a few minutes later that Dan Stenick broke briefly into their last evening.

They were mooning at their table in a remote corner of the crowded room when a roll of drums caught up their attention. The band leader stepped to the microphone. "Ladies and gentlemen," he announced, beaming, "as you have read in the papers, six members of the armed forces selected from camps all over the nation are here in New York to inaugurate the war-bond drive. We are proud and happy to have these fine young Americans as our guests tonight——" A ripple of applause rolled across the room. "If the spotlight man will be good enough to pick out table thirty-nine, I'm sure you'll all want to give them a real big hand!" A spotlight fitfully roamed the room and came to rest on a large table decorated with flags and summer flowers. The six—an ensign, a marine, two army privates, a lieutenant, and a Wac—stood up, blinked, and sheepishly waved their hands. The room thundered with applause and cheers.

Jane touched Brad's arm. "Isn't that Lieutenant Stenick? It looks awfully like him."

Brad had turned his head casually to glance at the party. Now he swung full around.

"I'll be damned! Dan Stenick——" He chuckled richly. "Wouldn't you just guess it, darling? About a million first louies around the country and Dan has to snag himself a trip to New York! We've got to get him over——" He beckoned a waiter.

Jane said indecisively, "Do you think we should?"

"Of course, Janie! We've got to buy him a drink. Imagine running into Dan!" He was chortling as he wrote a note on a table folder.

Of all the junior officers he had served with at Fort Harrison, only Dan Stenick had stimulated him. Dan was old for a lieutenant, thirty-two, stubby and robustly good-looking as a prize fighter (which he was for a time in the depression) might be good-looking, and he possessed a sharp intelligence and disposed so many moods and parts in such surprising profusion that he constantly intrigued all ranks up to the commanding general. Jane didn't much care for him —for the same reasons (Brad suspected) he found him stimulating. Dan was different from anyone they had ever met. He seemed to revel in having neither background nor breeding. His life had been a patchwork of bizarre jobs, poverty, bursts of prosperity and high adventure, in the course of which he had picked up an amazing amount of knowledge on matters both scholarly and mundane. But (to Brad) nothing about him equaled in importance the wondrous fact that he was a completely free soul. He had no family he ever spoke of, his experience had taught him few scruples, his moods knew no consistency, and his spirit admitted no restraints.

His mood of the moment was clearly evident as he held aloft a whisky glass and dodged between tables toward where they sat.

"As I live and laugh," he whooped as he came up to their table, "it's the printer and his doll! H'ya doll!" He grabbed at Brad's hand and at the same time planted a kiss on Jane's cheek. "H'ya Brad! What the hell you doin' here? I figured you over with the Limeys helpin' Whoosenhauer or Ossenpoofer or whatever his name run our show—and here you are livin' it up——"

Brad held up a protesting hand.

"Whoa, boy—hold it! Don't go throwing questions at me. You're the witness on the stand. How's C platoon? They hit the LZ on the last jump?"

Dan shook his head soberly. "Bellenger's got your platoon, Brad. Okay, good boy and all that, but he isn't you, tootsie. Your boys are pinin'—hell with it. Let's do a little drinkin'." He drained his glass and before he had put it down he was wildly snapping his fingers for a waiter.

Brad said, "I figure out of three-four million defenders of our country you belong down around the last half dozen. How come you rate this trip?"

Dan rolled his eyes conspiratorially and brought them to rest on Jane. He said, "Confidentially, your printer husband is eminently correct. I wouldn't have made corporal in Coxey's army but——" He muttered to Brad in a mock whisper, "If you'll buy me a drink, I'll let you in on the secret. Cheap at half the price. Scotch."

When the waiter came, Jane held her hand over her glass. Brad ordered drinks for himself and Dan.

"It's a long story," Dan said, "but I'll give it to you in one pregnant sentence. I heard about the Treasury organizin' this junket and fig-ured I could use six pretty days in New York, all expenses paid, models provided and no holds barred for a hero, so I sat down and wrote my congressman. Get it?"

Brad said, "No, I don't get it."

Dan frowned. "Say doll, the printer isn't very bright tonight. You been wearin' him down since he got sprung from the outfit?" Jane shuddered but managed a cursory smile. She loathed being called "doll" and his oblique reference to her private life with Brad was akin to Japanese torture which she accepted as part of her war sacri-fice. Brad had long since become hardened to the consequences of having a wife as decorative as Jane living with him on a military post.

"It's this way," Dan went on, swinging around to Brad. "My con-gressman's a real combination—native intelligence of Barney Baruch and moral fiber of Al Capone. He's got bodies buried everywhere. What's more important, he knows that I know, so what's a little thing like callin' up some joker in the Treasury and droppin' a little word in favor of a hero, name of Dan Stenick? Now you get it?"

The drinks had come. Brad lifted his and said, "No question about it, Danny boy. Someday you're going to make a great politician."

"And to you, kiddo. Turns out you didn't do so bad yourself."

"Me? What do you mean?"

"What the hell. Let's do a little drinkin'." He waved his glass. "Happy landings!"

"What do you mean, Dan?"

Dan hesitated. Then he sang out, "Okay, but the doll will have to excuse us." He cupped his hand around Brad's ear and whispered swiftly, "We're droppin', brother. Next month. The real thing. Don't know where yet but I figure the Aleutians. Place called Adak. Now for Christ's sake, forget it." He turned to Jane. "Okay, doll. Everythin's fixed. Let's start livin' it up again. Dance, sweetheart?"

She said, "Sorry, Dan. I've only got a dance or two left in me and this is Brad's last night." She glanced anxiously at her husband. The cleft in his chin made a deep furrow. She knew the symptom.

Dan knew it too. He swallowed his drink in big gulps, bit his lips, essayed a smile, then fell into a long silence. Suddenly he got up.

"I been thinkin', Brad. They know what they're doin' down in Washington. They're no fools. You were the best in the outfit. Real class. They need guys like you where it counts most. That's why they reassigned you. Me? Give me two and two and I'll come up with three and a half. Not 'cause I don't know better, 'cause I always got to figure my percentage. Any mugg can jump. That's why the big brass reached out and grabbed you for the London job. I wanted you to know because I love you, tootsie. You don't mind, do you, doll? G'by and God keep you. Real good."

He ruffled Brad's hair and, giving him no time to reply, pranced away.

Brad watched him until he was lost behind some couples coming off the dance floor.

Jane said, "Was it important?"

He wished he could tell her about his old outfit going into action. She would be more content about his reassignment to London.

He said, "There's no telling. He was drunk."

"You were angry for a minute."

"No one on earth can stay angry with Dan for more than a minute. He's quite a guy."

She pressed across the corner of the table that separated them. "I'm finding out you're quite a guy too, darling."

They finished their drinks slowly, oblivious of the festive air and the music and goings and comings of people around them. They knew the time had come to go down to their room. He signed the bill and they walked hand in hand to the elevator.

The moon over East Forty-ninth Street played around their wide-open window and cut sharply into the darkened room. Somewhere, probably still on the roof, the music of a dance band was faintly heard in counterpoint to honks of taxicab horns in the street far below.

She lay in the curve of his arm. Idly they watched the curtains billowing before a light warm breeze that penetrated the room and refreshed their bodies.

After a time she said drowsily, "Darling——"

"Yes."

"Little confession——" She hesitated. "When I saw Sanford Jaques at the luncheon I thought you'd arranged something."

"Arranged what?"

"And when you got so angry with Dan Stenick I thought about it again."

"Arranged *what*, Janie?"

"For you to get a transfer overseas instead of staying at Fort Harrison."

He thought, She must have a lot of old Everett Bolding in her. Never loses sight of her point. Not Janie—lovely, soft Janie. She had to chase down every doubt, and know, and be reassured.

She said, "Wasn't it awful of me?"

"Terrible."

"But he didn't have anything to do with your reassignment, did he?"

The notion had never entered Brad's mind. He vividly recalled the G-1 at Fort Harrison saying, "We're sorry to lose you, Parker. Real sorry. And it's my own fault. I laid it on too thick on the staff side in your fitness report. Unfortunately it happens that General Eisenhower's real hungry for staff, especially junior staff, in this new London setup of his. You were a sitting duck for those War Department sharpshooters when they riffled through our fitness reports. Guess I'd better start lying if I want to keep this outfit together."

He said, "No, Janie, he had nothing to do with it."

"Forgive me, darling?"

"Forgiven."

After a time she murmured, "I'm heavy on your arm, dear. Come down here with me."

Her breathing became measured. His urge for sleep seemed to have fled. He listened to the subdued cacophony of early morning in Manhattan. He had been lucky. He was going to London instead of Adak. It was a pity in a way; he honestly believed his platoon was the best in the outfit; he would have liked to jump with it in action at least once. But going to war was to him more than going into battle. It meant people and emotions, a civilization in turmoil. There were probably only a few Eskimos in Adak; no emotions, no civilization in turmoil. London! London! He warmed to the thought of tomorrow and the plane to Britain. He had wanted so much to go all his life. He had planned it for their honeymoon. But they married in July of 1939 and the papers were filled with stories of American tourists scrambling for cattle-boat space to flee the European crisis. He had said to Janie, "Let's go anyway. I don't think war's going to happen. Even if it does, we're Americans, we're neutrals, we'll get out of it. And what an adventure to remember the rest of our lives —to be caught in a war on our honeymoon! What do you say, Janie?" She had been willing, but their mothers were aghast and Damien adamant, and they went to the Chateau Frontenac in Quebec. Then in 1940 when bombs were falling on London and people in Malton were saying how gosh-darned lucky they were to be Americans, he sat listening on the radio to the sound of bombs and Edward R. Murrow deeply intoning, "This is London——" and Quentin Reynolds making frolic and excitement out of bravery and death, and he yearned to be there, bombs and all.

Now he was on his way. He was going to miss Janie, but there was no connection between this strange elation and Janie. It was possible to be faithful to both dreams.

He felt her hair brush across his ear.

"Brad——"

He whispered, "Shhh. Go to sleep."

"Brad, I forgot something."

"It can wait."

"No," she mumbled, half asleep.

He said nothing.

"Brad, I forgot to give you your present."

"In the morning."

"No. Now. Must, simply must."

She heaved a deep, weary sigh and pushed the sheet aside. She groped at the foot of the bed for her negligee and swung her feet to the floor. More asleep than awake she maneuvered across the room to a dressing table. When she returned she handed him a tiny box.

"Open it, darling." She dropped her negligee on the floor and crawled under the sheet.

It was a round gold medallion glittering on a thin gold chain.

"Can you see what it says?"

He dangled the medallion until it caught the flooding moonlight. Engraved on the face of it were two semicircular arrows, each pursuing the other to make a perfect circle. Inside the circle were their names, "Brad and Janie."

"Can you make it out, darling?"

"Yes, Janie. It's a lovely thing."

"It's for your dog tags. Let me put it on you."

She unclasped the steel cord he wore, removed the identification discs, slipped them on the gold chain and hooked it around his neck. "There," she said, and slid deep into the bed.

He kissed her.

She said, "Promise me something."

"What, darling?"

"Never take it off."

"Never?"

"Not until I take it off myself the first night you come back. Promise."

A sense of premonition gripped him. He looked at the medallion and at her tousled head half buried in a pillow, and he wondered what myriad and measureless moments, what tests and dangers and challenges must pass behind him before they might come together again.

"Promise, Brad."

"I promise."

She sighed contentedly and shifted toward him and soon her breath blew warm and even against his shoulder.

## 4

T H E percussive rattle beyond its threshold scarcely un-
settled the Victorian stolidity of The Stag at Bay. Its great oak beams
encased in Northumbrian rock denied entrance to the noises of war,
especially into the musty saloon bar which was to the rear and since
the bombing started had come to be called "Gladstone's shelter" in
recognition of the Prime Minister in whose time and stout tradition
the establishment had been founded.

Occasionally a thud like a bass drum being thumped in a far part
of the village penetrated the room and caused the ornamental pewter
mugs hanging from the low ceiling to shiver on their hooks. Neither
this nor the chatty voice of Mr. Pepper, the publican, who was be-
moaning to three dour clients how Home Guard shenanigans on
the common were ruining the finest cricket pitch in the Midlands,
was capable of impinging on the remaining minutes John had sal-
vaged for his farewell drink with Valerie.

He had less than ten minutes if he was to keep to his schedule.
Mr. Pepper, sensing a special occasion, had surreptitiously produced
two pink gins, but a penalty was attached to this rare privilege. They
had to listen to a pronouncement on the scarcity of pink gin and the
reasons therefor. This consumed a full two minutes of John's diminishing time.

He had so much to say and wanted so much merely to look at her.
Being incapable of doing both at the same time, he studied the grain
of the heavy oak table at which they sat. Even denying himself the
sight of her, he couldn't seem to find the words or the proper approach.

She watched him over the rim of her glass and slid a reassuring
hand across the table. "What is it you wanted to tell me?"

"It's—rather complicated."

"Why not say it flat out?"

There was a pause. "You see, Val, I do care for you tremendously."

"Don't think I'm dreadful, but I'd feel hurt if you didn't—after two years."

He said, "That makes it easier," and once more took to groping for words. "Now—at the moment it isn't important if you care for me——"

"But I do, John, and why isn't it important?"

"It *is* important, naturally. What I mean is—it isn't *pertinent* at the moment. You see, Val, it's unfair of me to bring anything up at all because I'm leaving for a sticky show and we're all inclined to be a bit emotional and to feel sorry for ourselves and for others. You know what I mean."

"I know."

"Besides, you've had a devilish time of it staying at home with the brigadier."

She said, "That's quite another matter."

"No, Val. It's all to do with the same thing. Do you intend to keep on staying here?"

"Now that you ask—no. Father is getting well enough so Mala can take care of him. I'd intended to go down to London in a week or two. Lady Gantling at the War Office asked me to see her whenever I felt I could come back to the forces."

He said, "I hope she finds you a posting that's a bit gay."

"I hope so too. I've hardly been a mile beyond the common for two years. Like a yearling rather grown up and still tethered."

"That's just the point. I know how difficult the brigadier can be; I had a year of him. You deserve a bit more out of the war than that. I hope you get a posting in London. You'd be amazed how gay it is. Oh, the Jerries send over odds and sods, just enough to keep the place on its toes. I honestly think London is better now than ever before and—you see, Val"—his eyes were avidly scanning the table—"I wouldn't want anything I said or even thought to give you the feeling of being tethered."

She wondered why he always made her feel years older.

"Come, John, what are you trying to say?"

"I told you it was rather complicated. In the first place God knows what will happen in the desert, rather silly to think of anything beyond the fighting. Besides, I'm a younger son. You know what that means. Derek will inherit Smallhill one day—I *am* looking forward to seeing him in the desert; wonderful chap, I wish you could know him—and there'll be precious little left for Bertie and me. With taxes and all, Derek will be lucky if he can keep Smallhill in one piece. I could stay in the army if they'll have me, but I imagine I'd go back to Threadneedle Street and begin learning all over again about gilt-edged and Kaffirs and that sort of nonsense. The point is though, I'm really not up to much. Afraid I never was."

She tugged at his hand.

"You sly old thing! Now don't try to crawl out of it. This sounds terribly serious."

His eyes came up, earnest and mournful.

"It isn't, Val—honestly. I do adore you but I wouldn't dare——"

The pewter mugs on the ceiling began to shiver as if they'd suddenly come alive, and a thud somewhat heavier than the others pushed through the dimly lit room. A worried little man at the bar said, "That one was close."

"That one," Mr. Pepper announced, "was just about over at Ernie Ballantyne's place. Ernie's cabbages'll go cheap tomorrow, that's if you don't mind a bit o' shrapnel in your stew."

John got up. "I'd better bring Bailey inside. I won't be a minute."

She knew the primary attributes of a good officer. John was a good officer, brave and above all thoughtful of his men. Watching him stride to the door, his slight body erect but rather lost in battle dress, she found herself fighting back tears. Junior officers of John's character had a combat life that was measured in minutes. Not even hours, she thought bitterly. She was not in love with him; this she knew with the certainty of one who has dreamed on love and has prepared a place for it in the unfolding pattern of her life. Yet she wondered if in the end he mightn't turn out to be the man. He had drawn himself closer to her, gradually, shyly uncovering new and gentle facets of his character. One day all the facets might suddenly merge into a single dazzling portraiture and she would be in love with him. But there hadn't been time for the miracle to occur in her laggard heart and she wished only that they could have more hours together. She knew a desperate urge to give herself completely to this man who, going into battle, asked so little. It was no more sinful, she thought, than the bleak, rigid orders of commanders like her father that sent men advancing to their deaths with the blessings of their country and under the signs of God. It was less sinful, much, much less sinful.

She heard him say, "I shouldn't have bothered. Bailey's in the public bar on his second mild and bitter," and he was facing her once more, the shy, adoring look unchanged and unchangeable.

"It's getting quieter," he said. "Just the light ack rattling away." He glanced at his watch. "We've only a minute or two and I haven't begun to tell you what I'd hoped."

"I wish you could stay a little longer."

"I wish I could."

"Take another minute—please, John. And tell me quickly."

"It's just this, Val. You see, when I went off to France in '39 it wasn't anything like going away now. It was a lark then. Some of the lads I'd gone to school with were along and every now and again in that winter we used to tear around Lille on a bender. We didn't feel sorry for ourselves. No worries, everything found, and lots of Saturday-night spirits. Then when the party really began we had our hands full and there wasn't much time for thinking, especially at St. Omer, and——" He paused. His mouth had begun to twitch slightly.

"And then at Dunkerque, standing out in the water and waiting —it was about forty-eight hours before we were taken off—I did begin to think. It may have been the shock, I don't know, but for a bit there didn't seem much point in coming home. It sounds silly now but I remember quite distinctly thinking something dreadful's happened, we're beaten, and England won't be the same. And it wasn't, Val, it really wasn't. Father seemed to have got suddenly terribly old worrying about Derek—Derek's always been his favorite—and Bertie was down at Malta with the raf and there seemed nothing much to come home to. I think that's why I transferred to the Commandos and more or less attached myself to you, Val. Unlucky you! I know I'm talking an awful lot of tripe but you did ask for it."

She said, "Go on. Please please go on."

"Now I'm pushing off again and—in an odd way I need you. I'm sorry about it but I do. You know, grousing is the most wonderful pastime in the army. You grouse, grouse, grouse about everything. It's good for the nerves, lets off steam, but you can't grouse about the army when there's nothing *but* the army in your life. That's what I mean by needing you. I'd like to be able to think about you, and to write to you and"—he pursed his lips and his fingers played rest-lessly on the oak table—"that sort of thing. I've made an awful hash of it."

She was glad he wasn't looking at her. Her mouth quivered and she wasn't sure she was able to speak.

He said, "Does it make any sense at all?"

Suddenly her voice came flooding out. "Don't you understand, John? I need someone overseas just as badly as you need someone at home. The war is empty and ridiculous without someone to be proud of and frightened for. There's nothing I'd like better than to have you think of me and to read your letters as often as you can send them, and of course I'll write you, and whatever happens I'll be at the dockside waving madly when you come sailing home."

He got up nodding as if a most unpleasant task had been at long last accomplished and went to the bar and settled his bill with Mr. Pepper.

It was quiet outside. The searchlights had been snuffed out. The rain falling on the village made a velvet sound in the blackness.

The 1500-weight was parked close in to the curb a few yards beyond the red glow of the pub's light.

"Bailey?"

"Ready, sir."

"Be right with you."

John held tightly to Valerie's hand and they walked into the road-way to the right side of the vehicle.

"I'll run you home, Val."

"Please not. I'd rather walk."

"Sure?"

"Quite."

He took her other hand. "Then this is it. Good-by, Val."

She felt the warm pressure of his hands. In the darkness she could barely see his face and the sensitive line of his mouth.

He said, "I'd like to kiss you, Val. May I?"

"Please do."

His kiss was light and tender as if her full, un-English mouth had not been made to be violated. She disengaged her hands and drew his head down. She parted her lips and kissed him long and shame-lessly. Tears welled up from the corners of her eyes.

At length she found his hands once more. She whispered, "God bless."

"God bless——" he echoed.

She didn't know whether he intended to say more. The "all-clear" suddenly shrilled over the village. He looked chagrined for a moment, then pressed his lips against her cheek and left her quickly.

She stood in the roadway and watched the rear light of the vehicle move off into darkness. The siren was still sounding clear and triumphant as she buttoned her mackintosh and turned reluctantly toward the common.

She was grateful for the rain that refreshed her face. Her cheeks were burning and the noise pierced and paralyzed her brain. After a time the siren petered out with a low grumble, and she was able to think clearly in relation to the violence that was coursing through her.

Walking over the cobblestones she wondered on the strange affliction that comes upon women in war, at least in England in this war, and, she imagined, in every country in every war. She felt indescribably lost as if the darkness about her were endless. The bitter, dried-up man sitting in his study at the cottage would be of no help to her. She reflected on how much easier it would be if she had a mother to give her direction and example, but she had long since become accustomed to the void. Even in her childhood in the garrisons of India she had learned to accept the circumstance that she was unlike other officers' children. They all had mothers as well as Indian nannies; she had only Mala.

It was when she was nine, the year they left India for England, that her father mentioned the matter for the first time. He had called her into his study and had said stiffly that it was his duty to tell her that her mother was dead. She remembered asking him with a child's appetite for exhibitionism if Mala would buy her a black dress, and he had shaken his head and said her mother had been dead a long time.

She had learned the full truth of the tragedy later on. In 1919 young Lieutenant Russell, fresh from the war, had been transferred to the Army Staff College in India and had married Lauriel Beech, the daughter of a wealthy British jute merchant of Calcutta. Less than two years after Valerie's birth, a scandal shook British garrisons from Rangoon to the northwest frontier. Russell's beautiful wife had decamped with a brother officer, a Major Keeling. There had never been a divorce, for Hassard Russell had determined if the fugitives must live together it would be in sin. Seven years later, Lauriel and her lover, driving from Nice to Monte Carlo, had lost control of their car and plunged over an embankment into the sea near the town of Beaulieu.

Hassard Russell had never mentioned the name of Lauriel Beech to his daughter until she was fifteen. He had arrived one day at her boarding school in Bath to inform her that her grandfather Beech had died in Calcutta and had left her a trust of a thousand sterling a year. It was the first time that Valerie had heard emotion break through her father's enigmatic voice. The telling of this episode had hurt him deeply, and she concluded at once, being at that ignorant, noble, and wonderfully honest age when all of life turns on true love, that her father must be spared further pain. She rejected the legacy out of hand. He had kissed her (it was the first time he had done so except on arrivals and departures and birthdays) and had suggested that he would instruct the solicitors in Calcutta to hold the legacy in abeyance until she grew old enough to weigh these considerations for herself.

Here the matter had rested all these years, except that the semi-annual letter from Tamarga and Boland, barristers and solicitors, inviting her to make a final disposition of the legacy, served as a constant reminder of a dreaded incursion of wild blood that must lay far buried beneath the maturity and balance of her emotions.

The rain came down harder now. It soaked the kerchief she wore over her hair and she could feel the cool wet seeping through, but she did not quicken her pace. All the way across the dark common she wondered on the mother she had never known and on herself —and on John.

A dim light came weaving toward her through the gloom and she heard a dog barking in a crisp, well-behaved way. She knew Mr. Sargenter was doing his round of the village, a duty he performed after every air raid in fulfillment of his position as Burlingham's honorary air-raid warden. He was the perfect choice, a portly, white-haired widower whose huge jowls moved like pontoons along the sides of his neck and gave him an air of authority in such matters as a crack of light showing through a blackout curtain.

His fox terrier reached Valerie first and nuzzled happily around her shoes. Mr. Sargenter braked his bicycle at the curb and beamed his light along the walk until it had located both her and the dog.

"It's Sargenter here," he said apologetically and turned the light on himself. "I hope I haven't frightened you, Miss Valerie."

He wore a rain cape and a steel helmet. The chin strap cut into his jowls, causing them to burgeon, and gave him the appearance of a fat comic in a Christmas panto.

She said, "Not at all, Mr. Sargenter," and ruffled the terrier's dripping ears.

"Devilish night but somebody simply had to see where that hundred-pounder dropped. A report has to be made, you know."

"You're much too conscientious, Mr. Sargenter. Wouldn't tomorrow have done?"

"I volunteered for this job and—well, there you are."

She allowed him a moment to enjoy his spinsterish air of sacrifice. "Did the bomb hit anything?"

"Not much really. It took the door off Mr. Ballantyne's tool shed and flattened a few of his gladioli."

"No damage at Belnorton?"

"I asked the lads at ack four. They said the Jerry didn't come within a mile of the runway."

"Thank God for that."

"Slippery chap though. He got away. Still"—he added pensively —"I can't say I'm unhappy about it. Brave lad, hedgehopping through the sort of barrage we threw up at him. I say, you *are* wet. Been visiting?"

She said, "Madly drinking. Over at Mr. Pepper's."

The raid warden balanced his great bulk astride his bicycle and tossed his head to shake the water from his helmet.

"Ah yes, dear Pepper. Doesn't know what he's in for. Have you heard, Miss Valerie?"

"I don't think I have."

"Mind, it's not official. Most certainly not. But the wingco over at Belnorton was telling me yesterday there's a chance they may be pulling out. Bomber Command fancies turning over the station to the Americans. Now then!" He shook his head and repeated darkly, "The Americans, Miss Valerie."

She said, "I should think Mr. Pepper will be very happy to have them. All he needs is a frig. I hear they like everything cold."

"It's very disturbing."

"Come now, Mr. Sargenter!"

"Mixed races the Americans, very mixed races," he said ominously. "I don't know, I really don't know. Ah well——" He swung his bicycle pedal to a starting position. "My compliments to the brigadier and a very good night to you, Miss Valerie. Come along, Trixie, that's a grand girl. Come along!"

## 5

S E V E N hours out of New York the full-bellied B-24 suddenly dipped its starboard wing. The twenty-seven men who had been dozing on bucket seats in the converted bomber came nervously to life and peered through the windows. From seven thousand feet they saw Labrador's endless succession of bald hills separated by valleys of green scrub and chains of tiny lakes. Behind the tail structure the sun lay low and red.

As the plane swung level and then banked sharply on its port wing, cigarettes were lit all over the cabin. Some of the men took to staring at a forward door marked "Crew only." Eventually the door opened and a staff sergeant poked his head out.

"Cigarettes out!" he bellowed over the racket of the engines. "We're in the approach pattern for Goose Bay. Refueling takes forty minutes and there's a canteen on the field. Better eat good. There'll be nothing more till we hit Prestwick. That"—he added knowledgeably —"is in Scotland."

Someone barked, "What about this parachute harness, Sergeant?"

"You don't need it on the next hop, sir." The sergeant noted that his questioner was a full colonel. "Can't do anybody much good over the ocean."

Brad twisted his chest buckle, slapped it with the flat of his hand, and the parachute harness fell away. He put on his trench coat. Under New York's blazing sun the plane had been a furnace; now the air was sharp and thin and cold. He noted for the first time that he was the only junior officer in the cabin. There were two civilians; a gaunt, elderly State Department courier who carried an oblong canvas pouch chained to his right wrist, and a curly-headed young man who had identified himself as a war correspondent for *Time.* The others were field officers, majors and both ranks of colonel, ac-

companied by a sprinkling of staff sergeants; clearly administrative
people who probably didn't know a Garand from a grenade.

The plane had begun to lose altitude. The steady pitch of the engines gave way to gasps and surges, and the wings shuddered in the
bumpy air. As a veteran of eight jumps, Brad enjoyed watching the
body gyrations and paling faces of the others, especially the full
colonels who had looked so formal and fearless on boarding the plane.

Brad was not given to vanity. Yet in this company of civilians and
desk soldiers he liked the distinction of having been combat-trained.
The men of the Special Service Force regarded themselves as elite
soldiers; it was an integral part of the course that they should, for
they were at once parachute, raid, and winter troops, and many a
recruit who would be acceptable in an ordinary infantry outfit had
been washed out during the first two months at Helena. He had
made the grade, had won his parachute wings, a first lieutenancy,
and command of a platoon. It had been the first triumph of his life
because it had been all his own; he could recall no other real achieve-
ments that had not been the gift of the Lakelock connection.

He wasn't braver than the next man. This he could admit to himself, although the Special Service Force, being fully volunteer, had
tried to nurture in him the notion that he must be. He hadn't volunteered in the same spirit that Dan Stenick, for instance, a born ad-
venturer, had deliberately sought out an extra hazardous duty. He,
in truth, had stumbled into it.

It happened a week after Pearl Harbor. He had been summoned
before a white-haired colonel in the Evaluation and Assignments
office at Hartford. The man, thumbing through his R.O.T.C. and reserve record, had said, "Hmm, so you're Bradford Parker. You know,
Parker, if there's one thing we need right here in this headquarters
it's a public-relations officer. The establishment calls for it but we
haven't got one, and we're going nuts with these reporters crashing
our offices as if they owned the place. Now you must know the newspaper business. Want the job?"

The notion of spending the war in Connecticut appalled him. He
turned it down flatly.

"All right," the colonel said, returning to the record, "let me see.
It says here you made the cross-country ski team at Dartmouth.
Right?" Right. "Well, we've got a brand-new outfit organizing out at

Fort Harrison. Going to specialize in winter warfare. They need skiers. How does that strike you?"

Fort Harrison was at Helena, Montana, half a continent distant from Connecticut. That struck him fine.

The colonel's eyes twinkled in a blank face, like a born practical joker. He said, "Looks like a pretty hot outfit. They prefer volunteers. Might even be some parachute jumping involved. Still strike you fine?"

He remembered how the challenge had given him pause. Thinking it over, he had heard the colonel murmuring, "We sure could use a good public-relations officer at this headquarters——" and that had done it. The day after Christmas he was on his way to Helena.

The family had been shocked. Although it was beyond question that the *Star's* heir apparent, being of military age, should get into uniform, this seemed too much. His mother tearfully mentioned a foolhardy streak in the Parker blood which she had been praying would not become dominant. Grace Lakelock stared at him unbelievingly and retired from the living room, apparently in anguish. Even Damien brought himself to say, "Your sense of judgment was one quality I thought I could always depend on. I think in this case you've made an unfortunate decision."

Only Janie seemed to understand exactly what had happened. "Listen, darling," she said to him that night, "you don't want to be a parachutist. I know you too well. You're not the kind that goes looking for trouble, but you're not the kind that steps away from it either. You did what you had to do and I'm proud, but I hope they wash you out at Fort Harrison."

Dear Janie! She knew him better than he knew himself. She possessed that sixth sense of behaving exactly as she knew he would want her to behave. This morning was the perfect example. She had accompanied him to the door of the Military Transport Office at La Guardia Field. In the corridor a throng of excited wives and sweethearts and children waited while their men went inside to present their travel orders. There were tears and lingering kisses and an occasional sob.

"This is as far as I go," she had said. "Good-by—good-by, Brad. Don't be too brave or too foolish. Just remember I want you back exactly as you are." Then she had kissed him and walked away swiftly. He had watched her as she moved with long, graceful strides to the end of the corridor. There she had turned and looked back over the distance of fifty or sixty yards, and, seeing him still watching her, she had smiled widely and waved. Then a group of new arrivals had cut off their line of vision and she was gone. She had been fine—fine and brave and neatly disciplined, just as he had hoped she would be.

"For God's sake, Lieutenant! Fasten your seat belt!"

He looked into the terrified face of a colonel sitting next to him and grabbed at a pair of canvas straps hooked into the bucket seat. The plane was teetering like a tightrope walker off balance. Not more than a hundred feet below, wild wooded terrain was rushing past. The engines surged and the plane lifted sickeningly, then dropped with a thump into an air pocket.

The colonel muttered, "I don't like this . . . I don't like this one bit."

The plane continued to career downward. Suddenly the treetops gave way to stumps in an open field and the engines cut back and a wide, clean runway miraculously appeared beneath the landing gear.

"This fellow," the colonel grumbled, "must have learned his flying in a jujitsu school."

It was dark when they filed out of a Nissen hut which operated as a combination lounge and cafeteria. A stiff wind nipped at their ears, and the stars seemed tiny and very dim in an inhospitable sky. They passed a hut which advertised a movie called *This Gun for Hire* and they stopped to watch station personnel going into the movie as if it were an intriguing sight.

When they reached the B-24, the pilot, a frail young man who seemed to have hardly any chest, was meandering under the starboard wing eying the engines. He paused before No. 3 engine and his tongue played inside his cheek. They stood around and contemplated the pilot.

A colonel called out, "What's the matter, Lieutenant? Anything wrong?"

"Naw. Cowling got loose coming in. They fixed it. We're all set." He smiled self-consciously and edged his way through the group and climbed into the plane. He called down to them from the head of the ladder. "Pile of blankets here, one to each man. The idea's to roll them around, Indian-style, and lie down crosswise on the floor. We can't give you much heat but it won't be long. Nine-ten hours. We got a tail wind right across. All aboard now."

As they climbed into the plane someone said, "He sounds like he's made the trip before."

Brad found himself stowed between the correspondent and a fat staff sergeant who burped with alarming regularity. Somewhere down the line of bodies laid out like jam pancakes someone mumbled, "This is a hell of a way of transporting key personnel." Then the ceiling light went out. One by one the engines swirled into action and the plane bumped toward the runway. Someone cracked, "Well, g'night folks."

The correspondent said uneasily, "My name's Kennelly."

"Parker."

"Noticed your parachute wings. I guess this is old stuff to you."

"It's my first ocean hop."

"Can't be as bad as a jump. Pilot friend of mine flies these kites." Kennelly spoke in short, nervous bursts. "Says the thirty seconds after take-off are the toughest. I mean at the controls. If the engines don't cut out in the first two hundred feet of climb you're away to the races."

Brad said, "We made it out of La Guardia."

"Yes but if—if anything happens out here you're gone. For good. Look at us bundled up, in the dark too. We wouldn't have a chance."

The plane pivoted on its undercarriage and came to rest. The engines were revved up one by one, then in pairs, then all four. The plane shivered against its brakes.

Kennelly said, "Imagine a kid lieutenant flying a four-engine job across the Atlantic. It's lousy organization as far as I'm concerned."

"The war's young," Brad said.

"So am I." The correspondent sat up. "Why do they have to shut the lights? Gives me the willies."

Brad pulled him down firmly. "Look, Kennelly, light reflections out of the sides confuse the pilot's visibility. Besides, we can't sleep with the lights on and you yacketing. If you're scared you shouldn't be here."

The correspondent lay silent. After a time he said, "I'm sorry."

Brad listened to the roar of the engines. It must be two or three minutes, he thought. He felt nervous too, but he was tough compared to the man lying next to him. The engines were idling now. The pilot was awfully young, probably plenty nervous up there. He wondered what the co-pilot was like.

Kennelly said, "What do you think?"

"I think we'll be in Scotland in the morning——"

A full-throated roar cut him off. The plane shuddered and swept forward. Brad listened to the rumble of the wheels racing over the runway and tried to estimate the distance. His temples hurt and he became aware that he was clenching his teeth. He felt the plane waggle. Suddenly it surged upward, banked steeply for a few seconds, then straightened out in a steady, shallow climb. He listened to the engines, high-pitched and powerful, and the pressure came away from his temples. Farther down the cabin people began to sit up. The sergeant next to him emitted a burp which gave hope of being the climactic one.

Kennelly said, "I think we're all right."

Brad nudged him. "Thanks for telling me."

He lay back on the floor boards, his head pillowed against his folded trench coat, and gazed at a cluster of dim stars trapped in the circle of the plane's window.

Over the curve of this night, England and the war awaited.

The thought set him tingling, for he knew with the certainty of a man who habitually takes a long look fore and aft over the years that this night's journey must mark the second climacteric of his life.

He knew it with the same certainty that had gripped his mind on the night of the other climacteric, the night he first entered the silk-paneled living room in the Lakelock mansion. Damien had come forward to receive him, but his attention had been speared by the dark-haired girl who sat carelessly on the arm of a chair and watched his approach with large, appraising eyes. Before the evening had ended he remembered knowing he was going to marry the Lakelock daughter and that, at twenty-three, his life was suddenly brand new.

He remembered it well, even to the date—February 12, 1939.

It snowed that night. His small Chrysler roadster, a relic of happy years at Dartmouth, churned in drifts which billowed on the pavement of Hamilton Terrace Drive. He had neglected to put on chains —they weren't necessary down near the center of Malton where he lived—and he wondered if the driveway into the Lakelock grounds would be clear. He didn't fancy walking through snow in his dress shoes. Besides, he was late.

His mother had come into his bedroom while he was doing up his black tie and had said, "Don't think it's any compliment being asked to the Lakelocks for dinner——"

"There's nothing social about it, Mother." He suspected that she resented not being asked along with him. "I suppose Damien Lakelock wants to discuss the ad with me. He's really sold on it."

She had settled herself firmly in his reading chair by the window.

"If anybody should be complimented, it's the Lakelocks. Your grandfather always regarded Everett Bolding—that's Grace Lakelock's father—as a particularly uncouth man. He *was*, you know, an ordinary typesetter up from Bridgeport."

"He managed to build up the best newspaper in the state——"

"And as for Damien Lakelock—well, he's acquired some polish, I must admit, and that's to his credit because his father Barney, everybody called him Barney, never Mr. Lakelock, he was an ordinary shoemaker."

"Oh come, Mother. The Lakelock business was sold to National Shoe for over two million dollars. Even in the boom of '27 it was fair enough for an ordinary shoemaker."

"That's what he was."

"Have it your own way. Blast this tie, it never ties right. If some of us had worked like Barney Lakelock, maybe I wouldn't have to be tootling through this snowstorm for a business dinner."

"You shouldn't say that, dear. You've never wanted for anything. You've had a good education, good clothes, a car at Dartmouth, and when I die you'll have this house and maybe a little income from the corner property if the city really buys it for a community center. Only yesterday the real estate people——"

"What brought this up, Mother?"

"It's just that you seem to forget you carry the finest name in Malton, none better in the state, and I don't want you to think the Lakelocks are doing you any honor. You just remind Damien Lakelock that you're Delbert Parker's son. Why, when your father was courting me, the very thought of Barney Lakelock's son moving in our circles was ridiculous. If your father hadn't died a young man, things would be different . . ."

While he struggled to get his tie neatly placed under the wings of an excessively stiff collar, she went on reminiscing rather sadly about an era that seemed to him a million years removed.

He had heard it many times before, almost since childhood. The truth was that for two generations the Parkers had lived comfortably by selling parcels of land from what had once been the Parker farm. (The street was still called Farm Street and had become an outmoded residential district on the edge of the city's business center.) During his own lifetime his mother had sold three parcels of land and had acquired as neighbors an A&P supermarket, an undertaking establishment, and a bowling alley. Now she possessed only her own house and the corner lot, hardly enough for him to take up the traditional Parker career of managing the estate.

On his graduation from Dartmouth with an A.B., he had taken a job as a junior account executive with an advertising firm called Debeney, Fancourt and Smith. Arthur Fancourt, luckily, had been a boyhood friend of his father. In 1937 too many Dartmouth graduates could get nothing but sales jobs on commission.

He had done well in his year and a half with the firm. Malton was coming out of the depression with a rush. Shoe and textile factories were reopening on the quickening pressures of the tense situation in Europe, business on Pentland Street ripened fast, and his personal client list grew steadily. But the high point of his career had just been reached.

Mr. Fancourt had thrown open to all twelve account executives an assignment to lay out a series of promotion ads on the Malton *Daily Star* itself, to be run in newspapers all over its circulation area, and Brad's idea had won out over the others.

The display text in 72-point italics across the page read: THE MOST EXCITING EVENT OF THE DAY—YOUR FRONT PAGE! Below was a reproduction of the *Star's* front page of that morning, detailing the recurring crises in Czechoslovakia, Ethiopia, Spain, and the Polish Corridor. Along the side, the text read: *From Danzig to Addis Ababa, from the Moldau to the Pyrenees, the world is striking fire! Is a movie more exciting? A novel? A stage play? Everything pales before the pulsating drama being written by men and by nations in today's world! Read it in its most thrilling narrative form— the* Star's *front page!*

Only that morning he and Mr. Fancourt had been invited to lunch with Damien Lakelock in his private dining room atop the *Star's* executive tower. There had been a number of *Star* executives at the lunch and he hadn't figured much in the conversation. But when the lunch broke up Mr. Lakelock had maneuvered him into a corner and had said, "Sorry we didn't have our own little chat. Would you like to come out to the house tonight? I don't know if my wife has anything else planned but I can promise you a drink and a reasonably good dinner. Let's say seven-thirty—12 Hamilton Terrace Drive."

A stiff wind whistled through the celluloid side curtains of his roadster as he turned into the gateway of the Lakelock estate. Snow had blown onto the driveway from the open gardens. He swung into low gear and moved carefully along the circular drive to the canopied front entrance.

Walking through a spacious front hall toward the living room, his mother's bitter chant rang in his ears. He saw himself somehow unfaithful to his forebears but only for a few minutes. On the second sherry, Damien smiled his soft, charming smile and said, "I even remember your grandfather, Gamaliel Parker. He once caught me stealing apples from his orchard on the farm—that's where the Y.M.C.A. stands now. I'll never forget it though it must be a good forty years ago. I was nine or ten. He demanded to know my name and then he bellowed, 'If you're Barney Lakelock's son you've no need to go stealing my apples.' He had a real foghorn voice. You know, I was surprised he didn't say Barney the shoemaker. That's what most everybody used to call my father, behind his back that is, to the day he died."

If he intended the remark to disarm his visitor, he succeeded perfectly. Brad felt easy and warm and a little proud. He glanced toward Jane to see how she was reacting to her father's remark. There was no reaction. She was watching him as if politely interested in the conversation but she obviously wasn't listening.

All through dinner she remained inconspicuous and quiet—unusually so, her mother pointedly remarked several times—and when her father suggested she might not be feeling well, she eagerly confessed to a headache and asked to be excused.

Driving home that night Brad felt wildly prescient about her curious behavior, and he was confirmed in his theory, at least to his satisfaction, three days later. Another invitation came from the Lakelocks. This time Jane was decorative and excessively gay and there were several young people present. Later, when they all piled into cars to go dancing at the Pentland Hotel, he found that he had been paired off with Jane. After that they saw each other almost every day, and six weeks later their engagement was announced.

Mrs. Parker received the news with reserve, but Brad understood perfectly that much of her secret happiness lay in playing the aggrieved party. At the wedding she was unquestionably the *grande dame*. In her eyes the scion of the Parkers was ascending his rightful place at the pinnacle of the little empire that was Malton, Connecticut.

The B-24 came down steeply through layers of thick white overcast, and when the mists finally scampered away from the wings Brad had his first glimpse of the Old Country. The plane crossed high above a gray coastline and he saw what looked like a shuttered resort hotel built long and narrow on an escarpment facing an angry sea. Behind the hotel the fields were bare and despondent.

Banking for its approach run, the plane passed low over a solid expanse of rust-colored roofs each thrusting up uniform clusters of chimneys. Rain began to fall as it taxied to a halt before a duncolored shack which bore a sign, "U. S. Army Air Forces, Transport Section."

Chilled and hurting with weariness, Brad nibbled at a lunch of franks and beans (it was a few minutes past noon in Scotland) and blindly followed a transport officer down a hall to a waiting room, unpainted and unfurnished except for a scattering of wooden chairs.

The T.O. said, "I know you're all dying to get to your billets, but Croydon's fogged in right now. Take it easy and we'll do the best we can."

Their best turned out to be three unbelievably long hours of waiting and then a rocky ninety-minute flight in a C-47 through pelting rain as far as Bristol. The rain was still slanting down when they landed. Brad was too wretchedly tired to put on his coat. While the others dashed across an open space to an administration building that looked as if it had been put together with old doorframes, he straggled behind and got thoroughly wet and couldn't care less. Yesterday's neat uniform, like his eager spirits, had become a shambles.

He saw no American personnel at the field. A gray-haired R.A.F.

officer with a rigid way of carrying himself checked their numbers against a passenger manifest and herded them into a bus.

"This is the form," he said crisply. "Your train to London leaves in an hour and eighteen minutes approx. You'll be driven to the Grand Hotel where you can have tea and sandwiches, coffee if you like, and a wash. Train time to London three hours fifteen minutes if you're lucky. Any questions? None? Right-e-o, we're off. And gentlemen— when we drive into Bristol, those open spaces you see will be—uh —Bristol. Taken some pretty hard knocks."

Brad looked at the man through half open eyes and decided he didn't like him.

The bus moved into the city at a faster clip than seemed safe for so noisy a vehicle. Brad had an impression they were traveling on an overpass through fields of rubble. As far as he could see through the rain, bricks and doors and windows with shreds of curtains still cling- ing to them were strewn everywhere in crazy heaps. There were no other vehicles on the street, and no pedestrians. In the midst of this desert the bus screeched to a halt for a traffic light, then moved along past a massive brewery which stood intact and a burned-out church which retained its steeple somehow balanced atop a single scorched wall.

They turned sharply into a narrow street lined with military vehi- cles and pulled up before a solid brick wall. This on examination proved to be the entrance to the Grand Hotel.

"Sharp right, gentlemen," the R.A.F. officer called out muscularly, leading the way into the hotel.

The lounge was large, dim, smoky, crowded with British officers, and deathly quiet.

Brad sank into the deepest chair he could find. Two British officers, a lieutenant colonel and a captain, who sat stonily in the same circle of chairs made no move to speak to him. He dozed until a waitress brought him coffee and a sandwich. He didn't taste the sandwich, two slices of brown bread stuck together by a ketchup-colored smear, and, after a sip, abandoned the coffee.

He was thoroughly miserable. He hated the room with its air of despondency, the British officers who seemed smug and self-pos- sessed, and the thought of a long train trip before he could stretch out on a bed.

The colonel was ruddy and had an enormous nose which overhung a receding mouth. He resembled a pointer, especially when he took quick neat nibbles at his sandwich. The captain badly needed a barber. His blond hair curled behind his ears and he held his teacup with a delicate hand.

Brad closed his eyes and wished devoutly he were back at Fort Harrison.

After a time he heard voices.

"The convoy is ready to load aboard, sir."

"Thank you, Bailey. Be right out."

"I say, Bailey, have you seen my servant?"

His *servant!* Brad pried open his eyes.

A private standing by the table said, "No, sir."

"Dash it all," the colonel muttered, "hasn't anybody seen my servant?"

"He may have gone aboard by this time, sir."

"Dammit, he's never around when I need him." The colonel snatched up his beret and stalked away.

The private watched him go. He grinned and said to the captain, "Shall I take your haversack, sir?"

"Thanks, Bailey. I'll manage."

"Better put on your coat. It's pouring out."

As the captain reached for his coat, Brad caught a glimpse of a Commando flash on his battle dress. He opened his eyes a little wider and scrutinized the sensitive face and the curling blond hair and wondered how long this joker would last at Fort Harrison.

"Glad to be off, Bailey?"

"Yes, sir."

"That's the spirit. Let's go."

Cheerleader type, Brad scoffed, and went back to dozing.

Someone shook him and said it was time to go to the station.

The journey to London was a nightmare of bone weariness and exhaustion and disappointment, suffered in snatches of awareness. He had impressions of a crowded train, of drawn shades and a tiny blue lamp, of being driven from Paddington through caverns of rain and pitch darkness to a billeting office and thence to a room that was sickeningly cold and smelled of dust. He fell asleep thinking it was a strange June and how terribly far he was from Malton.

The morning was wonderfully fresh and sharp with slanting sunlight.

On Grosvenor Square uniformed Americans converged from all directions toward a huge red apartment building which housed ETO headquarters. Some yawned and were laggard, some brisk, some savored the weather and seemed loathe to go indoors; they were, Brad thought, very much like men passing into a factory gate on any summer morning in Malton.

But here, too, were scorched wrecks of Georgian residences, and blast walls of brick and cement protecting each doorway, and above the roofs in the distance barrage balloons glinting in a crystalline sky. He spied a flight of tiny fighters, undoubtedly Spitfires, pass high over the sprawling city. In a few minutes they would scream across the Channel where the enemy, droning in the sky, awaited combat.

This was the brink of war and he a part of it at last. He strode across the square in a tremor of exhilaration.

An image of Dan Stenick fell into his mind. He, like Dan, was footloose at last, disentangled from the Lakelock dynasty, delivered out of the bondage of being Brad Parker. He felt fresh and strong and indescribably free as if his spirit had been ransomed by Pearl Harbor. He wondered what the first Parker, who sailed from Devonport more than two centuries ago seeking adventure in a dangerous new world, would think of the last Parker who had returned to the Old Country on the selfsame quest.

Inside headquarters a Wac captain, bored and impersonal as if she were working in a bargain basement, glanced at his orders, checked his name on a long document filled with names, and flipped over the cards of an index file. He watched her capable hands as a man watches a bouncing ball on a roulette wheel. Her fingers paused at a card, then flipped it over and paused at the next—and the next. ETO headquarters was just building up; there were hundreds of junior officers arriving to be placed among hundreds of staff sections. Would his name be paired against a vacancy in Operations? Or Special Services? Or, God forbid, Supply? He watched the nimble, unpainted fingers and enjoyed the brief gamble as if they were fingers of fate.

Finally the fingers stopped decisively. He was directed to report to Lieutenant Colonel Timmer—in Operations! He offered up silent thanks and went off briskly lest she found she had made an error.

He could not know that the selection of this card lying among hundreds was the first of a series of accidents, tiny but inexorably chained, that was to lead him to a meeting with Valerie Russell.

# BOOK TWO

Valerie

## 6

THE 8 A.M. train for Peterborough, Doncaster, and Hull hadn't left King's Cross Station and here it was nearly nine o'clock. An air alert had hit London just after midnight, and although the main enemy thrust had been blunted halfway up the Thames estuary by a heavy barrage and the fierce resistence of night fighters, two Heinkels managed to squirm through to the city and a stick of bombs looped down over the northwest suburbs.

A brakeman passing through the corridors of the stalled train saw an American lieutenant sprawled in lonely grandeur in a first-class compartment.

"Won't be long now, mate," he said, leaning into the open door. "The Jerry left a bit o' fuzz on the track. Up near Hendon, it was."

Brad said, "How long?"

"Oh, give 'em another ten minutes," the brakeman cajoled. He was a sallow, gangling man. Dark creases ran down his face, denoting a lifetime of poor nourishment. He said, "We're pretty slow here compared to America." He pronounced it *Ameyrica*.

Brad said, "Will I miss my connection? I've got to change trains at Newark."

"Going up to the bomber station?"

"Wherever I'm going, I've got to change trains at Newark. Will I miss the connection?"

The brakeman winked. "That's the spirit, mate. I know it and you know it and the Jerry knows it. But"—he cupped his mouth and his voice fell to a whisper—"no use letting the bloody Mesopotamians know it. No, sir, your connection will be sitting nice and pretty on the track waiting for you. About fifty Yanks back in third class, they're all changing at Newark. All pooped too." The brakeman chuckled.

Brad sat up.

"Can I get coffee on the train?"

"Buffet three carriages back——" The train suddenly jerked and moved forward slowly. "Well, wadd'ya know," the brakeman said in a poor mimicry of the American idiom, "the slowpokes ackchelly got the track fixed."

When the brakeman left, Brad glanced over the *Daily Express* he had bought in the station. The headline read: AUSTRALIANS SMASH AT ROMMEL'S FLANKS and the dispatch beneath was a highly colorful descriptive by Alan Moorehead of moonlight fighting in the desert near a place called Sidi Barrani. There was also a long report on a debate in the Commons about the feeding and housing of 18-B internees on the Isle of Man. A small item near the bottom of the page hinted at a major naval battle in the Solomons but there were no details. He searched the paper for a report about last night's air raid and found only a three-line item: "An alert sounded in London at 12.33 A.M. Anti-aircraft fire was later heard in most districts of the city. The all-clear sounded at 1.48 A.M."

The train gathered speed along an overpass. He put away the paper and glanced out at the rust-colored rooftops of north London, drabber than ever beneath an overcast sky.

Last night's air raid had been his first. After three weeks in London it had finally happened. He had looked forward to the experience, and now, thinking about it, he felt singularly chagrined. Of all the nights to pick for a bender! It was a pity, for he had promised Damien he would write a chatty letter describing his first air raid, the intention being to publish it, anonymously of course, on the *Star's* feature page. There was nothing he could write. His only recollection was of a frolicsome night, some wonderfully gay bravado on the streets, and innumerable drinks in a variety of places. He hadn't been so drunk, he recalled mournfully, since a night in his freshman year at Dartmouth when, suddenly free of the maternal influence, he had indulged his awareness of man's estate by guzzling four quarts of Canadian beer with rye chasers and disgracefully passing out. He hadn't passed out last night but he couldn't remember much of what happened. He wouldn't even write Janie about it, let alone the *Star*.

A minute or two later the train slowed abruptly. On the side of the track scores of workmen stood watching the wheels pass over the roadbed. Barely crawling, as if the engineer was himself taking a good look, the train chugged past the place where a bomb had struck.

Brad saw, fenced off from the right of way, a series of vegetable gardens belonging to a row of uniform two-family dwellings. The bomb had exploded in one of the gardens, completely shattering the rear wall of a house and shearing off the corners of two adjoining houses. A scramble of brick and timber had cascaded into the garden, and above it a bedroom lay open and naked. A red and blue patchwork quilt, a washbasin, and some framed pictures lay halfway down the fall of rubble. Steel-helmeted men, their hands on their hips, stood at the base of the rubble. They appeared to be looking up idly into the bedroom. An L.C.C. ambulance was parked in an adjoining garden, and women and children grouped around it in a respectful circle, except one little boy who had climbed on its fender and was peering inside.

Once past the wreckage the train picked up speed. Brad's New England conscience, a relic of an astringent, God-fearing ancestry, prodded at his torpid brain. He wondered where he had been at the time the bomb had struck. He tried to remember.

It had all begun at four in the afternoon when Lieutenant Colonel Timmer summoned him into his office.

For three weeks he had been waiting for the summons, three interminable weeks of idling at a desk in a large office in which everyone else, about twenty staff officers and enlisted specialists, worked with speed and a certain air of excitement on a great mass of documents. He had heard the word "Sledgehammer" whispered about and he guessed it was the code name for an operation, but he knew better than to ask. His duties consisted of reading the London papers and clipping everything pertaining to the American forces, seeing to it that the colonel's staff car was brought around from the motor pool whenever it was needed, and acting as a courier to other offices on the same floor. He was clearly on probation even with the other junior officers. He spent the evenings wrestling with his lonesomeness in the American Officer's Club on South Audley Street and the weekends wandering the unbelievably empty and quiet streets of Mayfair and Whitehall. He wrote ardent and descriptive letters to Janie. The days passed slowly.

Now the summons had come.

He was followed into Lieutenant Colonel Timmer's private office by a pfc. carrying a pot of coffee.

The colonel waited carefully until the pfc. left the office.

Then he said, "I don't know how *you* are, Parker, but I work hard and I play just as hard as I work. I've done it all my life. Might cut a couple of years off my old age but that's all right with me. Working or playing, I give it everything I've got. But"—he compressed his lips and poked his index finger forward in regular strokes—"the minute I walk out of this office nights, I don't know any more about the war than my youngest kid back home and she's going on four. It's a sort of reflex action. You get that way when you've been working in Plans awhile."

Brad could believe it, at least the part about playing hard. Alex Timmer would command equal attention at a cocktail party or in a room full of wrestlers. He had a hard, square, handsome face and a low rasping voice that was absolutely without shading. His black mustache was neatly trimmed, his shiny hair fitted close to the scalp, and everything about him, his small stabbing eyes and his darkly shaded jaw, leaped with virility. The head, set upon a pair of enormous shoulders, was reminiscent of a silent-movie star well past his prime. The middle buttons of his blouse were bursting tight across his stomach. He looked and talked like a composite of the dedicated professional soldier, but he happened to be, Brad knew, a Minnesota automobile salesman in civilian life, one of the few non-professionals who had made good in an exacting staff job.

Brad said, "I've been fully briefed on security, sir."

"Where?"

"Fort Harrison, sir."

The colonel grimaced. "Kid stuff."

"And naturally I've studied the regulations here very thoroughly."

Timmer drew deeply on his cigarette and snorted two sharp streams of smoke out of his nostrils. He picked up a folder from his desk.

"You've had the course all right," he said. "A lot more than you realize. We've made a full field investigation of you here and back home." He turned the pages of the folder. "Good family line, good life history, fitness reports okay, and you look like you can stand the gaff." He tossed the folder aside. "The Department's cleared you a hundred per cent. But you've certainly got a couple of doozies—Bradford Gamaliel. What do they call you?"

"Brad, sir."

"All of this doesn't mean a thing, Brad. You've got to live security, breathe it, sleep it. And even *that's* not enough. Security has got to become like a steel door in your brain, shuts automatically even if you get falling-down drunk or talk in your sleep alongside some fancy bitch. Tell you how *I* do it. To me this office means work—plans —secrets. Minute I step out of this office I don't know a goddamn thing. If I've got work to worry over, I worry over it right here. All night if necessary. So, rule number one: No homework, mental or material. Understood?"

"Understood, sir."

Timmer poured a cup of coffee and swallowed half of it in a single gulp. He said, "Where are you billeted?"

"I'm still in transient, sir. I thought I'd better wait until I knew where I stood."

"Smart." Timmer swallowed the rest of the coffee. "Billet's important. Don't kid yourself there aren't any German agents in this town. Plenty of 'em."

Brad said, "Captain Boyce has offered to let me share his apartment." Captain Boyce occupied the next desk to Brad's in the outer office.

"Boyce is all right. Where does he live again?"

"Arlington Flats, sir. Just along Grosvenor Street."

Timmer nodded. "Good enough. Our secret service keeps it covered."

"Thank you, Colonel."

He let Brad get as far as the door. "But remember, the fact that Boyce works in this section doesn't mean he knows everything you're going to know. Understood?"

"Understood, sir."

"That's all." Timmer barked. "Consider yourself on the team. And good luck." He was reaching for the coffeepot as Brad left the office.

During the next two hours a whole new exciting world was opened up to Brad. He was allowed to learn that Operation Sledgehammer was a plan to pinch off the Cherbourg peninsula before the end of summer. The objective was twofold: to seize the area as a launching platform for an eventual full-scale drive into northwest Europe, and to relieve the mounting political pressures for an immediate second front. Seven months after Pearl Harbor, the people back home were impatient to start winning the war. They didn't know, as he had just learned, that the total American strength in Europe was two incomplete and partially trained divisions, and that Sledgehammer would be fought mostly by British and Canadian troops. He thought of Ben Carver bending over his ponderous war editorials back home in Malton, and how little he knew. How little they all knew.

It was well after six o'clock when Brad moved his gear from his transient billet to a handsome six-story apartment house called Arlington Flats at 37 Grosvenor Street.

The hall porter, a frail old man with hollow cheeks and exceedingly sad eyes, led him through a richly tiled lobby to an elevator and brought him to the fourth floor.

"Captain Boyce sends his compliments, sir," the porter said, "he left word he'd be back shortly." He opened the door with a passkey and they entered a large living room which was tastefully and expensively furnished. On the far wall a set of french doors opened on a tiny balcony.

Brad thrust open the doors. The sun had disappeared from Grosvenor Square but in the sky the barrage balloons were still shining crimson. He caught himself up wishing there would be an air raid. After three weeks he was impatient to be tested.

He said, "This is a very nice room. Captain Boyce has expensive tastes in furniture."

"Well sir, this is Mrs. Ecklin's flat. Lived here going on eight years. She's at her cottage in Surrey for the duration."

Brad had no idea where Surrey was. He said, "It's safer out there, I suppose."

"Indeed it is, sir."

When Brad closed the french doors, the porter came forward and drew the blackout curtains.

"Think we might get a raid?" Brad asked.

"I wouldn't think so, sir, unless it clouds over. The Germans like cloud cover these nights. This way, if you please, sir."

They passed a dining room which, the porter explained, was used to store Mrs. Ecklin's bric-a-brac and certain especially valuable pieces of furniture. Two bedrooms were located at the end of a long hall. Boyce had taken possession of the master room, a large and feminine affair in pale blue and pink. The other was considerably smaller and more severely furnished but exceedingly comfortable.

Brad said, "This'll do fine. Was it Mr. Ecklin's?"

"Young Mr. Ecklin's, sir. Mrs. Ecklin is a widow."

"He in Surrey too?" Brad asked flippantly.

"Oh no, sir," the porter said. "Young Mr. Ecklin was taken prisoner at Douai. That was in '40, sir."

Brad was angry with himself for having asked the question; the reply hit hard against the sense of happy excitement he had been enjoying. He walked about the room, casting critical glances at the wide, comfortable bed, the handsome chest of drawers, the scatter rugs, seeking something to complain about, to suggest, anything to erase the subject of young Mr. Ecklin. He groped without success for an appropriate remark.

"It seems only yesterday young Mr. Ecklin went off to war, although I dare say, sir, it's a bit different to him. Two years is a long time in a prison camp. You see, sir, I was taken in the last war . . ."

Why did he have to go on? It was the one thing about the British that annoyed him. Their talent for understatement was admirable when it reached across an ocean but sharp and excruciating when it was rammed into you at close quarters. He didn't need to be reminded that the British had fought since 1939 nor had he asked to come over and sleep in young Mr. Ecklin's fine bed while young Mr. Ecklin languished in a prison camp.

". . . They can be correct the Germans, sir, but being their prisoner is no music-hall turn. I found that out . . ."

He went on and on, maliciously it seemed to Brad. And then Boyce burst in, his arms wrapped around a paper bag which contained his monthly liquor ration—one rye, one scotch, and one sherry—and loudly suggested that the occasion called for a celebration.

"Two celebrations!" Boyce cried. "Your graduation *summa cum laude* from Timmer's patented probationary course—proves you're untainted, untarnished, unpolluted, uncorrupted, and a hundred and ten per cent American." He dashed into the kitchen and came out brandishing a corkscrew. "And then there's *my* celebration. Billets had a knife at my throat to fill this extra room and I was dead scared they'd foist some pinhead on me. Drink, Middleton?"

The porter said, "Oh no, sir. Never on duty." He backed toward the door. "Anything else, sir?"

"Nothing, Middleton, except when is Anny going to get rid of that pink chiffon drape in my bedroom? Makes me feel like a daffodil. Anny"—he explained to Brad—"is our *daily*. Half sister to Dracula but she has her own peculiar charm."

Middleton said vacantly, "I'll jog her, sir," and left the apartment.

The captain poured two drinks of scotch. "Come on, Brad. You look like the last act of *Hamlet*." He lifted his glass. "Bless this house and all who float in her!"

Brad swallowed his drink like a man gulping unpleasant medicine. The notion of sleeping in young Mr. Ecklin's bed still rankled. The second drink was a lot better. He began to count himself lucky to have so fine an apartment and so superior a companion. He felt complimented that Ray Boyce had selected him to share this de luxe location. Junior officers usually had to live a subway jump from headquarters.

Raynold Boyce was clearly a mettlesome fellow. He carried his honors carelessly (a master's degree from Oxford and a Northwestern Ph.D.), but this did not prevent his colleagues and even his superiors from standing slightly in awe of his learning. He was a political adviser attached to Lieutenant Colonel Timmer's section. His direct commission (by order of the War Department) had interrupted a brilliant career as a lecturer in political science at Georgetown. A narrowly built man in his early thirties, his pleasant, youthful face leaped with awareness and intelligence. Patently he enjoyed the army although he made no pretense of being a soldier. His tie was invariably askew, his blouse fitted as if he'd picked it off a rack at a bargain sale, and he wore his overseas cap squarely on his head like a toque. He never returned an enlisted man's salute; instead, he responded with a nod and a cheerful "Good morning" or "Good afternoon." In the evening he took no notice of salutes. "Off duty," he always explained.

"Absolutely amazing Timmer's agreeing to let you share this apartment," he said over their third drink. "I'd an idea he doesn't completely approve of me."

Brad said, "Timmer's passion is security. He apparently decided you're safe."

"Did, did he? Well, he's wrong. I'm a man rent by three passions. I'm gregarious, blindly trusting, and hopelessly talkative. Also I drink. Not passionately, only pleasurably. I've found that hangover is the finest brain sharpener in existence. I'm absolutely brilliant the morning after. Feel wretched but absolutely brilliant."

On the fourth drink they took to comparing notes on their respective wives. Brad dug into his baggage for a photo of Janie, and Boyce produced a snapshot of a petite, vivacious girl balanced precariously on a hammock, a glass in one hand and the middle finger of her other impishly thrusting upward. "Last year's commencement party," Boyce explained. "I had a terrible time keeping her from goosing the dean of arts."

In a burst of unanimity they determined that the occasion called for a meal and a fine bottle of wine. There was only one place, Boyce decided, and that was the Savoy Grill. They piled into a taxi.

The atmosphere at the Savoy was quiet, distinguished, and somewhat ludicrous. It required the services of three waiters to serve them a boiled leg of chicken. But the bottle of Montrachet which Boyce had pried out of the wine list was absolutely magnificent.

"Timmer? Wonderful machine, Alex Timmer," Boyce said, mooning over the last of Montrachet. "Plays bridge Sunday, Tuesday, and Thursday nights, reads military history Mondays, Wednesdays, and Fridays, goes on the town Saturday nights and gets horribly boiled. Sees his girl every morning at six. Brilliant organizer."

Brad said incredulously, "Sees his girl every morning? At six?"

"Certainly. Rather handsome girl too. I've met her. She's a V.A.D. Runs a first-aid station in an underground shelter till five-thirty every morning. Visits Timmer at six and goes home at seven. Suits him perfectly because he's a very ordered man. Work, study, sex, bridge, and drink in precise proportions. He's a perfect push-button individual who someday will be a perfect push-button general fighting a perfect push-button war. If you have any ambitions in the military, hitch your star to Alex Timmer. He's going way up, he and electronics."

"He doesn't look like the bridge type to me."

"He isn't," Boyce replied. "He's bursting to get a star on his shoulders and bridge has become a mania among the professional staff officers. The word's gone 'round that Eisenhower is a bridge fiend. Timmer would break into the Reichs Chancellery with his bare hands if it brought him favorably to Ike's attention. That's how ambitious he is. He knows he's got to be twice as good as the West Pointers at practically everything or else he'll never get that star. Lieutenant colonel is about as high as a civilian can go on the staff side."

They began drinking brandy after dinner.

How they got involved with the war correspondents in the residents' lounge of Savoy was never quite clear to Brad. He faintly remembered that Boyce and a correspondent of the Chicago *Tribune* tested each other's conversational mettle, found it happily explosive, and proceeded to clash on the subjects of Roosevelt, Britain, and Senator Burton K. Wheeler. Somehow a virile character from New Zealand inserted himself into the group and insisted on betting a round of drinks that he could sing all the verses of "John Brown's Body" which was more than any American he had ever met could do. He proceeded to prove it with a lusty rendition.

That was when the Savoy's night manager, his blanched face tweaking with anguish, interrupted to say that an air raid was in progress and would they kindly proceed to the lobby or down to the shelter.

Instead, they grabbed their caps and frolicked out into the Strand. The muffled, distant gunfire was no match for the New Zealander's uninhibited singing. They marched down the black, deserted street to the beat of "John Brown's Body," and when they came into the open space of Trafalgar Square they could see the searchlights tracking the sky over the estuary and the tracers and the rocket shells exploding orange darts.

It was here that they heard a series of cracks and saw a sudden burst of distant light. They all squealed, feigning terror. Then, for no apparent reason, the *Tribune* man took careful aim, kicked the New Zealander squarely in the pants, and the two closed in, scuffling like a couple of spaniels.

> "Glory, glory hallelujah . . . glory, glory, hallelujah
> "His truth goes marching on . . ."

All four of them were singing now. They marched up the Haymarket into Piccadilly, bowed with extravagant gallantry to each prostitute who came up to them out of the darkness, and finally piled into a huge bottle club on Old Bond Street which was crowded with American officers and their girls. They drank the *Tribune* correspondent's scotch and took to singing "A Lovely Way to Spend an Evening" to the annoyance of everyone around them and Brad didn't recall how or when he got back to 37 Grosvenor Street.

He was awakened by a persistent telephone at six in the morning. It was the night duty officer in Timmer's section.

"Report in at seven," he said, "you've got a courier job. Better bring a musette bag. You'll be away overnight."

The train raced north across the open countryside. Under rain-laden skies the fields looked wonderfully green, a deeper and richer color than Brad could ever remember in Connecticut.

The bomb tragedy, he thought, was something he would have to get used to. This was war and people got killed in it. He might die too but so far he was having fun. Dan Stenick was going to drop on Adak, while he lived in a luxury flat in Mayfair. That was the luck of the draw.

He felt extraordinarily good. He was, he suspected, still a little drunk. Later in the day he would feel wretched but it didn't matter. There would be no need to pull himself together for the editorial luncheon, no company for dinner, no chiding glances from Janie. He was free, free, free—and, back home, a hero to boot.

The breathless rhythm of the train on the rails was in tune with his spirits.

## 7

F O R a time after she had read the letter, Valerie held it in her hand. She wondered what *he* would think about it. From the open window of her upstairs sitting room she cautiously observed her father.

He sat ramrod straight in the front garden, his khaki tropical jacket buttoned up to the neck despite the enervating heat of a humid, cloudy afternoon. He seemed to be staring at the dogwood growing along the fence. His tea lay untouched on a wicker table beside him. His only movement was the flick of his swagger stick against his calf in regular, dispirited strokes.

Nevertheless, she believed, he was making progress. For the third successive day now, he had let himself be persuaded to take tea in the front garden instead of moping in the privacy of the rear lawn. It was Mala who had persuaded him; she had always been able to exert the greater discipline on him. As so often happens with devoted servants, she had long since obscured the line between service in and mastery over her little domain.

The inspiration for the shift devolved from Mr. Sargenter, who, in addition to being chief air-raid warden, was captain of the Burlingham company of the Home Guard. He had suggested to Valerie that the brigadier might agree to favor the company with a few crumbs, as he put it, from the great supply of his battlefield experience.

"You see, Miss Valerie, we're facing rather an emergency," he had explained darkly. "Now that Bomber Command has gone, what protection have we from a parachute attack? Not the Americans, I'm sure. They salute one another, I'm told, with their caps off. Quite extraordinary the number of Italians among them. Spend their days sitting around something called a 'jook box' which may be all very well, mind you, but is it facing up to it? No," he had answered himself mournfully, "I'm afraid we've ourselves to depend on now. I've extended our training sessions to five a week. Simply must. And if you could persuade the brigadier . . ."

Dear old Sargenter! He was so English she often felt like a foreigner in her own country. However, the notion of encouraging her father to take an interest in the life of the village had long been exercising her mind. Here was an opportunity. But how to approach it? Certainly not by suggesting to a man who still dreamed of taking a division into combat that he command a group of elderly merchants.

She had discussed the problem with Mala.

"There is only one way, Miss Valerie," the servant had said in her precise voice. "He must be nudged toward it like a kitten to a saucer of milk."

Thus had begun the campaign to shift the brigadier's tea to the front lawn while the Home Guard exercises were in progress.

Watching from her window, Valerie could perceive no sign that he was even aware of the training session. He was at his tea now. He had leaned his swagger stick against the table and was gazing into his cup and occasionally taking a sip from it.

On the common some sixty assorted gentry were lined up in two meandering rows and held their first war Lee-Enfields at the slope. Mr. Sargenter walked slowly and sternly between the ranks, sniffing at each rifle. He wore battle dress and a steel helmet, and his stomach bulged handsomely although no more handsomely than most of the others. On the grass in front, the company's prized possession, a Bren gun, rested on its bipod alongside three wooden facsimiles.

"The exercise for today is exceedingly important." Mr. Sargenter's piping voice carried across the common. "An enemy ground force is attacking from the north, or Lloyd's Bank side, of the common. Occasional parachutists are dropping on the east and west sides——"

A train whistle shrilled across the village.

The connecting train from London was nearly an hour late, Valerie noted. The BBC morning news had mentioned a seventy-five-minute alert in the metropolitan area, and she had fallen into the habit of guessing at the severity of the raid by the lateness of the train. During the Battle of Britain the train sometimes hadn't arrived at all.

Thinking about it, her mind fell to London and to the letter she held in her hand.

"Dear Valerie," Lady Gantling had written in a neat hand on War

Office stationery. She had known Valerie since childhood, Lord Gantling having been a subaltern in India during the early twenties.

"I have been thinking about you rather often since your visit last week. It was good to hear that the brigadier, of whom my husband and I have such fond memories, is better. What an extraordinarily brave person! Both as a soldier and a man." (Lady Gantling could not resist this oblique reference to the family scandal.)

"Your request for termination of compassionate leave has been referred to the proper quarters and has been granted, although I must say there are no immediate postings for section officers. For quite some months now we have stopped accepting officer candidates in the women's services.

"We would like to second you for special duty with the American Red Cross. The A.R.C. has forwarded a request for a number of British girls of breeding and ability to assist in a liaison capacity in their clubs and leave centers, which are springing up all over London.

"I don't want you, my dear Valerie, to think of this as light or unimportant duty. Mr. Churchill, Mr. Bracken, and the new U.S. commander, Major General Eisenhower, have spent many hours in conference over the problem of meshing a million or more Americans into the life of our island.

"I consider you particularly suited for this assignment. I am enclosing your travel order and look forward to seeing you in London as quickly as possible . . ."

She knew the parting wouldn't be difficult. Her father regarded sentiment with a certain distaste. Indeed, several times recently he had questioned her indeterminate leave of absence from the A.T.S. "Damned poor staff work," he had called it. But the nature of the duty would certainly roil him and she toyed with the notion of keeping it a secret.

Down in the garden the brigadier had moved out of his chair. His angular frame leaned against the gate and he was at least noticing the Home Guard exercise. The portly men were distributed all over the common, some clicking their rifles, others squatting behind the Bren gun and its facsimiles. Mr. Sargenter whirled about in the center, shouting, "No, chaps, no! Let's do it again. This is a perimeter defense, not cricket fielding. Mr. Pepper! You wouldn't have a ghostly in that position! Mr. Clifton! Where is Mr. Clifton? Oh, there you are! Good heavens, man! What are you doing there? . . ."

Several American soldiers, walking from the railway station, had drifted along the edge of the common. They watched, grinning broadly, as the men panted under Mr. Sargenter's stern commands.

"I sigh, chawps," one of them mimicked, "this ain't cricket, doncha know?" The others thought he was uproariously funny.

"The top kick looks like my gran'ma the day they buried her."

"Hi, gran'ma!"

The Home Guard was by now lined up in two ranks in the center of the common.

One of the Americans whooped, "You know something? It looks exactly like the St. Patrick's Day parade in Passaic."

"Passaic, hell! The geezer on the end stands just like my old man when he's got a skinful."

Mr. Sargenter turned about and looked at the youngsters with pained and infinite patience.

"Ooh, the man's mad. You mad, pop?"

"Wait a minute, fellas. There's the guy who owns the bar. He might put a mickey in our beer."

"That *gotta* be an improvement!" This remark seemed to convulse the Americans. They rolled about, doubled up with laughter.

Valerie watched Mr. Sargenter walk grimly across the grass toward the Americans. She glanced anxiously at her father. He had pulled open the gate and was standing in the roadway. His swagger stick, tight in his fist, whiffed the air.

She hurried downstairs.

In the office of Major Allan Mills, adjutant of the 632nd Bombardment Group, Brad shifted restlessly on an exceedingly hard chair. He was wretched with lack of sleep and hangover, as he knew he would be. He had delivered a thick, double-sealed envelope to the adjutant, and the latter had taken it into the group commander's office. Now he waited.

He wished the man would return with a signed receipt and dismiss him. He was furiously hungry. (He had fought his way into a crowded buffet on the train but had been turned back by the filth of the coffee cups and the grime on the fingers of the steward who handled the sandwiches.) He could use a drink too, but most of all he needed sleep.

Major Mills finally reappeared. "It's pretty damned ridiculous," he

kept muttering, "pretty damned ridiculous." He was a compact little
man with a neat, worried face. "You fellows down at Plans sure have
it easy. An office and a mimeograph machine and you're operational.
We're not so lucky. We've just inherited this pigpen and few half-
trained crews, and right away they want us to suggest feasible targets
for Sledgehammer. Who're they kidding? Sledgehammer! On the
target date they've got here, we couldn't dent a tin can."

Brad said, "I don't know anything about it, sir. I've been ordered
to bring back a set of tracings."

"We'll have it for you in the morning."

"Thank you, sir. Can I be put up on the station?"

"I guess we can fix you up——" The telephone rang. "Mills here
. . . Yes. . . . Yes . . ." He listened, scowling into the phone. "For
God's sake, Dennis, why bother me with it? I'm trying to get this
post set up. Do I have to handle the provost's work too? . . . Oh
. . . Oh, no!" He glared at Brad and grimaced broadly. "You say a
brigadier? . . . A wounded brigadier! Oh God, I'll be right out. Yes
. . . Yes . . . YES!" He slammed down the telephone.

He said, "I've got to go, Lieutenant," and reached for his cap.

"My receipt, sir."

The adjutant scrawled his signature on a form, flung it toward
Brad, and made for the door.

"And you were going to arrange to put me up."

Major Mills stopped short. "Oh dammit, yes. Look, Lieutenant,
officers' quarters are in block E—that's three huts over and turn left.
You'll find——" He paused and glared at Brad. "By God, we'll leave
that till later. I want you to come with me. You can drop your musette
bag on the chair. It'll be safe enough here."

Brad, crestfallen, said, "Are you sure, sir, I'm required to come?"

"*I'm* requiring you. Come on, snap into it."

The adjutant led the way out and climbed behind the wheel of a
jeep. Brad reluctantly took the seat beside him.

"It's time you people down at ETO knew exactly what's happening
up here," the adjutant muttered. He swung the jeep roughly around
a bend and raced down the station's main roadway. The sign said:
"5 m.p.h. Strictly enforced!"

"Spaatz wants us to be operational, twenty-one Forts, by the end of
the month. With what? A wireless net Marconi must've built with
his own hands and a bunch of half-baked kids from Brooklyn and

the Ozarks. We get a scorcher from Eisenhower. A real sermon-type
guy. Demands urgent measures to maintain ideal relations with the
civilian population. Maintain! That's the joker. Hell, we've been
lepers from the word go. Our men go into the pub for a beer and the
place clams up and the beer mysteriously runs dry. Look at a girl
and she screams rape. Anyway most of 'em are so buck-toothed a hill-
billy wouldn't touch 'em with a barge pole. It's all right for you fellows
to go fancy-danning around London where they're civilized, but you
can tell the brass for me not to send us rockets until they know what
goes on. Even *I* sometimes wonder what the hell we're doing over
here and I'm supposed to have a better than average I.Q. You can
imagine how these kids react."

They were delayed at the gate by a convoy of trucks. Once clear
of the station they hurtled along a country road. The trees, the
hedges, even the verges were excessively neat and almost humanly
proud.

Brad commiserated only with himself. Of all the days fate could
have chosen to involve him in something that wasn't remotely his
business, this was the worst.

He said, "What's happened now, Major?"

"I don't know, but it's sure got our provost all excited. Some mish-
mash about a scuffle with the Home Guard, only this time a British
brigadier got mixed up in it, a wounded brigadier no less," he
groaned. He glared through the windshield as if scanning the road
ahead for a land mine. "I know what's biting Dennis. This one will
get to the War Office and wham! another rocket from ETO and he
wants to be covered."

Brad said weakly, "I'm in OPD Plans, Major."

"Makes no difference. I've just about decided that every ETO
officer who sticks his nose around here, even a louie, is damned well
going to get it rubbed into this situation."

The adjutant looked about as the jeep rattled over the cobblestones of High Street. The complement of villagers seemed normal
except for a long queue of women standing quite still before a shuttered butcher's shop.

For a moment after they reached the common they could see nothing remotely resembling a disturbance. The Home Guard stood in a
haphazard semicircle watching Mr. Sargenter struggle with the
breechblock of a Bren gun he was trying to dismantle.

"There they are," the adjutant said. He stepped on the accelerator and roared around the common to the opposite side where seven American enlisted men stood easy in the roadway looking glumly at a captain wearing an MP brassard.

When he reached the group, he and the MP captain walked a piece down the road and stood talking earnestly for a few moments. Then they returned. The adjutant scanned the line of seven assorted faces.

He said, "Don't you men like three-day passes?"

"Yes, sir," they chorused. "Sure do, sir."

"Well, remember 'em fondly. They're souvenirs as far as you men are concerned."

He walked along the line, his sleeve almost brushing the men, and stopped before a dark, wiry youngster who carried three chevrons under his AAF patch and silver wings on his chest.

"What's your version, Gerbett?"

The sergeant blurted, "The rest of the fellas will tell you, sir——"

"I asked you to tell me."

"All I have to say is I don't have to take a whipping from anybody, sir, I don't care who it is." The sergeant was neither timid nor contrite. His crafty eyes burned with indignation. "The other fellas'll tell you. I didn't even see him coming. That guy there"—he pointed out Mr. Sargenter, who was still concerned with dismantling the Bren gun—"he came over trying to give me a line of crap and before I know it somebody is whipping me from behind, right on my neck too, so I turned around and grabbed the stick and let him have the same, just one, sir, and I broke the stick and threw it on the ground and then a girl came rushing over and broke it up and took the old man away. That's the truth. The other fellas will tell you, sir."

Major Mills looked at him painfully. "You in the habit of hitting old men?"

"I told you, sir. I didn't see him till after he hit me. Anyway, I don't care if I get broken back to private for it, sir, I'll hit anybody who hits me first. I'm an American soldier, sir. My own officers can burn me down to the nub and I'll take it, but I don't have to take any whipping from any limey and nobody can make me."

Someone along the line said, "That's the truth, sir. That's exactly what happened." The others chorused, "Yes, sir."

Mills said, "What were you men doing here anyway? There was a vehicle at the station to pick you up."

"We weren't due back on post till 1800, sir," the sergeant replied. "We figured we'd wait around till the pub opened and have ourselves a beer before we went back."

"So you decided to pass the time riding these men who are doing what they can to help win the war. Is that it, Gerbett?"

"We weren't riding them, sir. We were making some remarks among ourselves. There's no law against that, sir."

Mills said, "You're lying. You were riding them loud enough to be heard all over the place."

"No more than they ride us, sir," Gerbett burst out angrily. "They been giving us the silent treatment ever since we got here like we were Japs or something. We're human beings too. If we're not good enough to talk to, why can't they fight their own wars? All the fellas feel the same way. We didn't ask to come over here and——"

"That's enough out of you, Gerbett." Mills turned to the provost. "Take 'em back. Confined to post until further orders, all of 'em, and no club privileges."

He watched the men being marched around the bend of the common. He said to Brad, "All right, Lieutenant. What do you think?"

Brad said, "The sergeant seems to have a case. He missed his calling. He's a real barracks-room lawyer."

"Notice the Home Guard?" Mills asked bitterly. "Just look at 'em. Not even coughing in our direction. You'd think we weren't alive. That's the real trouble."

Brad tried to look lucid and concerned, but he was thinking of a drink, a meal, and bed. He edged toward the adjutant's jeep.

"Not yet, Lieutenant. I've got to look in on the brigadier. Maybe if I rub his fine English fur the right way, he'll let it pass." They walked slowly along the road. "Hate it. Between ourselves, I feel exactly like Gerbett."

"You think he's telling the truth?"

"Do you?"

Brad said, "I think so."

The adjutant grimaced. "He's lying like a thief. These country English can murder you with a glance but they don't go smacking you from behind. No, Gerbett provoked him. He's a tough kid. From Jersey. Tough and smart but a damned good turret gunner. All the same——" He let the sentence dangle and pushed unhappily through the gate of "Darjeeling."

Mala showed them into the living room with a proud, baneful look about her. It seemed to Brad the French must have looked like this when German staff officers arrived to take the surrender of a town.

"I will inform the brigadier," she said. "I'm not sure he cares to see anyone." She walked very erect out of the room.

The adjutant tossed a glance toward Brad. He mumbled, "Brace yourself, Lieutenant. She's only the servant."

A hum of rain falling on open fields came abruptly to their ears. They watched through the window as the Home Guard trotted off the common toward High Street, shielding their rifles inside their jackets. Mr. Sargenter remained alone. He addressed himself to the task of pulling a canvas cover over his precious Bren gun.

The adjutant muttered, "It couldn't have happened half an hour ago. We wouldn't be in this lousy fix."

After a time they heard low voices in the hall. Brigadier Russell entered the room alone. He closed the door carefully behind him, acknowledged his visitors with a brief nod, and walked to the fireplace with a briskness which did not quite carry all the way across the room. He swayed slightly and steadied himself against the mantle. His gray face was blank and stern, but there was a twitching around the muscles of his mouth and the keloid scars on his neck glowed red. In the failing light his small eyes were scarcely visible in their great, dark sockets.

"Sorry to have kept you waiting," he said in a low, controlled voice.

The adjutant stepped forward. "I'm Mills, group adjutant at Belnorton, sir. This is Lieutenant Parker of ETO headquarters."

The brigadier came away from the mantle and lowered his gaunt frame into an armchair. Mills, who had anticipated a handshake, flushed and glanced at Brad. They sat down. Brad had forgotten his lethargy. He was transfixed by the clear signs of struggle inside the man to hold together the loose packaging of his pride and bearing.

"Yes, gentlemen?"

The brigadier's crisp inquiry belied his eyes, which blinked and were pale and lifeless.

Mills said, "Brigadier, I would like to offer my own very sincere regrets for the behavior of one of our men this afternoon——"

He paused for a rejoinder but the gray face remained impassive. He went on. "We'll have the man up on charges of course, and from what I know of the incident I think I can assure you he will be adequately dealt with——"

Again he paused hopefully. There was no response except for an accelerated blinking of the flaccid eyes.

"If there are any ill effects of the blow he struck you, we will be glad to entertain a claim for the discomfort you've suffered, and naturally for any medical attention."

The adjutant waited a moment. It occurred to him he might be talking to a deaf man for the keloid scars pushed close around the right ear. He leaned forward and said loudly but with deep concern, "Do you hear me, sir?"

"I hear you perfectly well, Major. You haven't told me why your men were loafing in the village."

The suddenness of the rejoinder stiffened the adjutant's back. He said, "Well, sir, they were simply on their way from the railway station. They'd been on leave."

"You still haven't told me why they were loafing in the village."

"The village is not off limits to our men."

"Then I suggest you consider putting it off limits."

The American said slowly, "It's a pretty drastic thing to do way up here——"

"I can think of rather harsher orders I have issued without the slightest difficulty."

Major Mills compressed his lips. He wondered if he had struck the right note, whether he should have taken an aggressive attitude from the start. He wasn't a belligerent man and, besides, it was too late now. He would have to swallow more pride. He was sorry he had brought the lieutenant along.

He said, "I don't blame you, sir, for feeling bitter. The fact that you were struck by one of our enlisted men——"

"The fact that I was struck by one of your men has nothing to do with it. He had every right to strike me. I thrashed him thoroughly before he could get his wits about him."

"Surely you gave him a warning, sir!"

"I am not in the habit of parleying with street urchins."

The adjutant's eyes blazed.

"The street urchin, as you put it, sir, is an American airman who's over here to fight a war."

The brigadier's mouth worked for control before he spoke. "The war has been going on some little time now. I suggest he begin fighting it."

Mills sprang to his feet. "I can see there's no point in continuing, Brigadier. That man is three thousand miles from home and the odds are five to one he'll never see it again. He happens, sir, to be a turret gunner and when we start our daylight bombing his life is worth about ten missions—if that!"

The brigadier looked sternly toward the window.

"You are entitled to slop over your men, Major. We in the British forces don't fret about life expectancy when there's a war to be fought."

Mills shot out a quivering finger. "That urchin will die all right! He'll die to defend you, Brigadier, and I'm goddamned sorry it's got to be this way! If you people hated the Germans just half as much as you hate us, maybe we wouldn't have to be over here at all. Do anything you like! We'll stand up to it. Yes, and win the war for you in the bargain." He swung around to Brad. "Come on, Lieutenant. Let's get out of here!"

The brigadier's eyes, blinking rapidly, now fixed themselves on the ceiling. His fingers plunged into the leather arms of his chair. His mouth opened as if to speak. Nothing emerged.

Brad came slowly to his feet, fascinated by the man's immense struggle for control of himself.

The adjutant paused, frowning, at the door. He looked at Brad and then at the silent old man. He shook his head in anguish. He said quietly, "I'm sorry, Brigadier. I came here with the best intentions but—damn it, we've got to run our own show in our own way."

The Americans waited. Russell slowly lowered his head. He didn't look at them. He said, "Will you please go, gentlemen." The voice was almost inaudible.

Mala was at the front door to let them out. They doubled through the rain to their jeep, swiftly pulled up the canvas top, and climbed in. The adjutant lit a cigarette and leaned wearily against the wheel. He said, "Friendly, eh? That'll give you some small idea."

Brad said, "He's a sick man."

"What the hell," Mills said defensively. "They're all sick. They were licked in '40 and they're still taking a walloping. They won't admit that they're dead pigeons. That's the trouble with 'em. They need us inferior Americans who've got no manners but a lot of power and know-how and it's killing 'em."

Brad said, "We've got our troubles in London too." He was thinking of Middleton, the hall porter, and his stiletto thrusts about young Mr. Ecklin.

"So what are we supposed to do?" Mills growled. "Do we borrow a piece of their crying towel and sit around telling them how wonderful they are? Or do we start fighting this goddamn——"

Brad cut in. "Wait a minute, Major. We've got company."

Valerie had come up on the driver's side of the jeep. She was breathless as though she had run. Her light brown hair was darkening in the rain and her blouse clung wet to her shoulders.

The adjutant swung around in his seat and looked up quizzically at her.

She said, "I won't keep you a moment, Major. My name is Valerie Russell. You've just seen my father."

"Miss Russell——" Mills groped for words. "It's just one of those things, Miss Russell. There's nothing we can do about it except hang on, I suppose, and hope for the best."

"There *is* one thing, Major," she said. "You had the men marched off. Will they be punished?"

"Do you think they should?"

"Most definitely not. My father was clearly in the wrong."

The adjutant looked at her a long time as though to make sure he had heard her correctly. She didn't seem to be aware of the pelting rain. The corners of her mouth turned up and made a half smile that was both anxious and sweet.

He said, "Say, Miss Russell, you're getting wet. Why don't you climb in for a minute."

"I don't mind the rain. I rather like it——" She smiled broadly now. "You see, we think even rain, our own English kind, is something quite special. We're a most peculiar people, Major. We take a lot of knowing."

Major Mills was clearly charmed. He shook his head from side to side and said, "I wouldn't say you were peculiar, Miss Russell. No sirree."

"I gather you didn't have a very pleasant interview with my father."

"That's where I suppose I've got to be sorry. I didn't realize he was so badly wounded."

Her face turned pensive. "That doesn't excuse the village, Major. We haven't been hospitable to your men or gracious about our partnership or even thankful. We're not very good at being thankful because we've not had occasion to be thankful to anyone, except possibly to God, for several hundred years. But we'll learn, Major, really we will. Do be patient with us."

She spoke the words crisply and with a content of warm humor. The front of her blouse was sodden now, clinging like a bathing suit.

The adjutant said, "You'd better be getting back. You're good and wet. And thanks a million, Miss Russell."

"Good luck, Major."

She hurried off. Mills swung his head around and watched her progress as far as the gate. His face was wistful, quizzical, and a good deal happier than it had been.

He murmured, "Holy Moses," and stepped on the starter.

Brad recalled that she hadn't noticed him. He sipped at his scotch, his third, at the bar in the Nissen hut they called "the club" and watched the clock creep toward nine and listened to the rain rumbling on the tin roof. He was lightheaded and sleepy. He dreaded the run through the rain to his billet, which was a good quarter mile away.

He wished she had noticed him. He wished it wasn't raining and he wasn't so tired. He might have driven into the village and called on her. It wouldn't be hard to find a pretext. They might have gone to the local pub for a few drinks.

He had been thinking about her since supper. Now it was nearly nine, too late to call on a strange girl in an English village as suspicious as this one. But he found it pleasant to think about her.

A poker game had been going on all evening. It must have developed into a big game because it had been gay and noisy at first, and now it was quiet and the remarks were tersely spoken.

"Raise."

"Jump you once more."

"I'll buy a look."

There were eight in the game. Major Mills was among them and also the group commander, a bullet-headed man with an extraordinarily thick neck. He wore his colonel's eagles on his shirt collar as well as on his epaulets. A few officers, strewn about the room, had their noses dug into paper-backed books. A young captain played a slot machine, feeding quarters into it angrily. The rain drummed steadily on the roof.

There was no harm thinking about the girl, now that it was nearly nine and too late to do anything about it. There was nothing else to do.

He had met prettier girls, though not many, and none with such deep and luminous eyes; certainly none with so expressive a mouth, certainly none as strangely beautiful. She looked warm and aloof, a very odd combination. He wondered if he would meet someone in London like her. If there was one hidden away up in this village, there must be hundreds in London.

He ordered another drink. This would be the last. He listened to the rain coming down, harder now. The harder it came down the sooner it might stop and he'd make a dash for his billet.

He wasn't so sure there would be hundreds like her in London. Not quite like her. Her voice was soft and yet it was crisp. And she was obviously intelligent. He wondered how old she was. She was probably married, but he remembered she had introduced herself as Valerie Russell. Maybe she was engaged. One way or another she wouldn't be running around loose for long, not with three or four hundred American fliers prowling around the village.

The rain slackened off suddenly. He swallowed the rest of his drink, grabbed a detective story from a pile of paperbacks on the end of the bar, and dashed for his billet.

Lying between ice-cold sheets, the rain drumming on the roof which curved just above the head of his bed, he remembered how she stood in the rain. Odd creature, standing in the rain and being quite comfortable about it. He realized that he hadn't enjoyed the luxury of thinking about a pretty girl for a long time. Thinking about Janie was different; he never thought about Janie in the way a man ordinarily thinks of a pretty girl. He wondered what Janie would expect him to do about girls; he didn't know but he had a fairly good idea. Certainly Damien anticipated that he would acquire a light romance; it was practically written in his quiet, envious smile that day at the station. Besides, it was traditional for a soldier. If he *had* to have a girl, someone like her would be his choice. She had breeding and intelligence and a strange quality he had never before encountered.

The whole thing was ridiculous. The girl was up here and he was stationed in London. He would never even meet her. But it was amusing to think about it and he tossed aside the detective story and turned off the light.

Valerie was scarcely aware of the rumble of rain on the slanting roof above her bedroom.

Her two suitcases, already packed, sat open on the bed. Both were crammed to the top and she wondered how she could find space for her evening frock. She knew it was a waste of effort; no one in England had dressed formally since 1939. But the uniforms, sweaters, tweeds, and utility underthings looked so drab and the pale beige taffeta so decorative. She had bought it in Paris the summer before the war when her father had let her accompany him on a weapons mission to the French. She had never had a chance to wear it. Taking it along now represented a hope. John had said that London had become wonderfully gay. It had been so long since she danced.

Surveying the cases, she abruptly removed two sweaters and a thick tweed skirt, replaced them with the Paris frock, closed the suitcase, and snapped shut the locks. There! She felt she had scored a lilting victory over the whole dreary war.

One more chore remained, a chore she had dreaded and delayed all evening. Now it had to be done. She picked up Lady Gantling's letter and went downstairs to her father's study.

She found him standing before his wall map of the Middle East, studying a conglomeration of red and blue pencil marks he had drawn in the area between Benghazi and Alexandria.

"I'm all packed, Father."

The gray man nodded amiably. "That's good and snappy for a woman," he said, still contemplating the wall map.

He had been calm, even cheerful since dinner, as though the incident with the Americans, which had not been mentioned in the household, had reacted on him like a powerful tonic.

She hated now, on the eve of her departure, to tell him of her new posting. But there was no other way. She couldn't bear to have

him think, when he found out, that she lacked courage to tell him
face to face.

He looked at her pleasantly. He said, "Do you realize, my dear,
that it's been nearly two years? That's more time than we've spent
together since you first went off to school."

"I've liked it, Father."

"Don't be silly, girl. You've had a miserable time. When does your
train go in the morning?"

"I believe it's nine-fourteen."

"Get hold of Ballantyne?"

"He's sending around his pony trap."

"Fine." He nodded and smiled. "Much as I'll miss you, anything is
better than having *two* spivs in the family."

"That's simply nonsense."

He glanced longingly at the map on the wall. "I feel somehow I'll
be back in action very soon. The medical people are coming up, you
know, to give me a once-over. I don't see how they can possibly
reject me. Can you?"

"When did you hear, Father?"

"Oh, I get letters from the War Office too," he said jocularly. He
was in rare good humor. "I rather imagine they might send me out
east. There's a big offensive building up. I was thinking they might
even post *you* out in Cairo."

She said, "They won't. I'm sure of it."

"You can't tell what will happen when you report tomorrow. Don't
forget young Wynter is out there. You're keen on him, aren't you?"

"They're not sending me, Father. They've already told me what
I'm to do."

She handed him Lady Gantling's letter.

She watched him as he read it. He blinked and frowned deeply,
pushing the gray fur of his eyebrows together into a ragged line.
When he finished the letter he handed it back without looking at
her.

He said, "Don't you think you'd better be off to bed?"

"Do you mind terribly, Father?"

"Mind?" he snapped. "What the devil are you talking about, girl?
This is an order."

The brigadier turned abruptly to survey the battle lines of the
desert war, his lifeless eyes blinking rapidly.

## 8

O N   T H E next morning, crystalline clear and warm, Valerie arrived at the station platform in Mr. Ballantyne's pony trap. Among a scattering of persons waiting for the train was Brad.

He didn't recognize her at once for her identity was briefly obscured by the bizarre spectacle of her arrival. Mala, wearing a modified sari over her black dress, sat erect and tight-lipped at the reins as the pony trotted briskly alongside the platform. Her passenger, in the uniform of an A.T.S. officer, clung to her dignity from a precarious perch on the open side of the trap, her tight khaki skirt revealing a good deal of her legs, which were encased in coarse utility stockings and low-heeled shoes. Her khaki collar and tie fitted trimly on her narrow neck and her tiny peaked cap sat ridiculously atop her hair which shone red and gold in the clean morning sunlight.

Brad felt warm laughter welling up inside him. He wished he had brought along a camera. In this war of gargantuan machines (since breakfast his head had been bursting with the roar of four-engined Forts practicing take offs and landings on Belnorton's short strip) the quiet spectacle of this British lady going off to the wars was ludicrous and singularly touching.

The stationmaster tipped his cap and came forward to lift her luggage from the trap. Brad heard her crisp, pleasant voice say, "Isn't it a glorious morning, Mr. Dulcram," and he realized with a start of sheer delight that she was Valerie Russell and that she was obviously going to take the same train. He hurried toward her.

He didn't expect her to remember him. He saluted informally and explained the circumstances of their meeting yesterday.

She smiled warmly. "How nice of you to remember me. How really nice!"

Her eyes, deep and unbelievably lucid, looked up at him with genuine pleasure. He knew he was staring impolitely. He couldn't help himself. It would require more effort than he could muster to turn his head away from its fixed position.

He said, "Perhaps we can find two seats together."

"I do hope so. It's a miserably dull trip alone."

No guile, he thought, no airs, no affectation. And yet she was beautiful. Standing in yesterday's rain in her thin blouse, she had given him an impression of softness and grace, and now, though she wore the shapeless khaki the British regarded as a proper uniform for girls, her face was completely beautiful in a way he was sure he had never before experienced. It shone with compassion and honesty. The girls back home, he remembered, practiced variations of mood and behavior which he came to recognize as standard feminine tactics. Not this girl. There was wisdom deeply imbedded in her eyes, as if she understood a great deal more than she could possibly know. But there was no guile.

"Let's promise," she was saying, "not to talk about the wretched war. I wonder if I've forgotten how to talk about anything else. We'll try, shall we, Mr. Parker?"

She turned to say something to Mala whose tight-lipped, proprietory air was clearly tinged with suspicion.

He knew he was still staring. A train whistle hooted across his ears and he twisted away from the sight of her and reached for her baggage. Out of a corner of his eye he watched her embrace Mala and then she rejoined him. They walked to the head of the platform where the first-class carriages would stop.

"Let's make believe it's five years ago," she said. "You're visiting over here and I've let myself be picked up shamelessly. What do we talk about?" She smiled wistfully. "Do you know, I can't remember what I talked about to young men five years ago? Not a clue. Are those cases very heavy? You should have let Mr. Dulcram carry them."

He said, "They're not heavy. All right, it's five years ago and I've picked you up——"

"Quite shamelessly."

"Brazenly. Where do we go from here?"

"I imagine, Mr. Parker, into the train."

He had been staring at her again and didn't notice that the train had come to a halt and that most travelers had already climbed

aboard. They laughed together as if a beginning of understanding
had been created. Then they ran for the nearest carriage door.

"Oh Lord," Valerie groaned. "No war."

The first-class carriage was jammed. In each compartment the
armrests had been lifted and four or five passengers squeezed into
seats designed for three. An overflow almost filled the corridor from
end to end. They were mostly British airmen and Waafs.

Brad struggled along the corridor with the suitcases. "To think," he
panted, "the train was nearly empty when I came up yesterday."

She said, "I should have remembered. The morning run is always
filled with Coastal Command people down from Grimsby."

They found a space at the upper end of the corridor. He put down
her cases and they both sat on the larger and sturdier one. It was
warm. She took off her tunic and laid it across the smaller case. He
was careful not to stare at her. He fixed his eyes on the green and
shining landscape passing across the window frame.

"Well now, Mr. Parker," she said brightly. "Isn't England doing
wonderfully well for our tourists this summer?"

"Trouble is," he said, trying to enter the spirit of her banter, "you
people can't cook."

"Do you think there'll be a war?"

"No!"

She said, "Neither do I. It's too ridiculous. We simply can't afford
one, and besides, Mr. Chamberlain is so much cleverer than this Hitler person."

"Have you read *Gone with the Wind?*"

"I'm just reading it now. It must make you terribly proud to be an
American."

"I'm a Yankee from way back."

"Oh dear. What do you people really think of your Mrs. Simpson?
I think she's charming . . ."

The whistle hooted and the train raced south across the countryside. She talked of India and how dearly she had loved that gentle
gray old lady of a land, of her fourteenth birthday when her father
took her to her first evening theater performance and Mala abruptly
began to call her *Miss* Valerie and couldn't be persuaded otherwise,
of a trip to Paris and her first dance at the embassy with a shy, almost
terrified boy who was the son of the air attaché.

Brad told her about Dartmouth, and skiing trips to Mont

Tremblant in Quebec, and the first Parker who sailed from Devonport. He liked the way she listened with intensity, and he liked her remark when they talked about the Revolution: "It was the only war we ever lost, but then it was British fighting British." He told her about the Parker farm, how a city ringed it and finally devoured it. She thought it was a pity and couldn't imagine it happening in England.

When the train stopped at Peterborough they dashed out on the platform, bought tea and buns at the station kiosk, and just managed to clamber back as the train was pulling out. They settled themselves breathlessly on the suitcase and applied themselves to the food.

A group of Waafs squatting in the corridor began to sing "*J'attendrai.*" They sang it squeakily, their Yorkshire accents faltering and slurring over the French words. Afterward they sang "The White Cliffs." Almost everyone up and down the corridor joined in.

> *"There'll be bluebirds over the white cliffs of Dover*
> *"Tomorrow, just you wait and see,*
> *"There'll be love and laughter and peace ever after*
> *"Tomorrow, when the world is free . . ."*

The voices were mechanical and sad, and when the song petered out the carriage was quiet except for the click of the wheels on the rails.

Valerie said, "We British don't cry very well, do we?"

She had been dreamily looking out the window, her chin cupped in her hands. A narrow river flowed parallel to the tracks and a row of tired old willows on the bank drooped its branches almost into the water.

He said, "We weren't going to talk about the war."

"I think we've done well. You've been sweet listening to my chatter which couldn't possibly interest you."

"It couldn't possibly," he said blankly, "but it has."

"You're very sweet."

"The last person who called me sweet was an aunt of mine when I was about twelve. I remember I reacted by going out and getting good and muddy."

"I can't imagine you muddy. It's one thing I've noticed about the

Americans. Our troops look so scruffy compared to them. Do you hate the war as much as I do?"

He said, "I deplore it but I can't say I hate it. Of course I've got what they call a cushy job. The fellows in the Solomons or Tobruk probably have other ideas."

"I hate it. I've lived through it for three years and I hate it for what it's done to me and to everything and everyone I love."

He said, "It doesn't sound much like Mr. Churchill's finest hour."

"My father was part of the finest hour. You saw him."

"It's better than being defeated."

She said, "Sometimes I wonder. We had another finest hour—on the Somme in the first war. Sixty thousand of our men died between dawn and dark on the one day."

"It hurts—but the important thing is the victory."

She shook her head. "We can't afford such victories in a country as small as ours. It may be different in a big and growing country, but not in ours. I sometimes think the man I might have loved was never born because someone fell on the Somme, and someone else I might love will die in the desert, and I think to hell with Britain's finest hour! What about mine? And then I feel selfish and cowardly and I hate the war for having done it to me."

For a time they were silent.

She thought how lucky it was that he was stationed in London. He was so very brisk and alive and he probably danced well. She thought of the three years she hadn't lived at all, the best three years of her life, the years between nineteen and twenty-two spent in an A.T.S. signal station in Lincoln and watching over her father in the flower-ringed little prison of "Darjeeling." She thought it was splendid she had come to know someone in London so quickly and that he was an American who had not forgotten how to be gay. She thought it must be the youngness of America that she and this man could come to know each other so blindly and yet so intimately in so little time. She thought of John, who must have arrived in the Middle East by now, how sweetly he had urged her to do exactly this. She wondered if she had reached for it too quickly. She must put a checkrein on herself.

Brad thought of this girl who was different from any girl he had ever met, who could speak of India and of Paris as if she held them in her hand and stroked them, who was romantic in a way that was completely removed from her loveliness. He thought he had never heard anyone speak so crisply and beautifully, who was so plainly sincere and yet so fugitive. He thought it was damned lucky she was going to be in London. There were girls readily available for Americans around the officers' club and the bottle parties. A lot of them were attractive and well-bred, but they were eager and this made them cheap. He knew he would eventually have to reach for a girl. If he could ever reach her, which he doubted, it would be something not to be ashamed of. He thought of his twenty-six years filled with a sense of duty, first to his mother and then to Janie. He thought how only yesterday he felt fine to be free and irresponsible, and now he was sure he wanted to see no one else in England except this girl; yet he could never remember feeling quite so alert to life and warm and magnificent.

They began speaking again. She told him about John and he told her about Janie, and they talked with studied earnestness about the people to whom they owed their primary loyalty, as if it was necessary and urgent to do so.

The train raced into the outskirts of the city, across factory sites and emergency-landing strips with a few tiny planes on them.

He said, "I'd like to see you in London."

"I'd like you to, if you can put up with me. I'm afraid I'm not terribly cheerful."

He said, "I can put up with you."

They spoke very little more until the train rolled into King's Cross Station.

## 9

FOR several days Colonel Timmer had been in a state of tension which even his unyielding exterior could not entirely disguise. An unusual tightness played around the muscles of his massive jaw, and when he spoke of routine matters his small eyes stabbed and sparkled as if he was enjoying an exciting secret bubbling deep inside him.

On this mid-August afternoon the whole staff watched his orderly and driver, Pfc. Arkinson, pass into his office with a steaming pot of coffee. It was the third pot since lunch. Ray Boyce leaned across the space which separated their desks and whispered, "Come on, Brad, what is it? There's something more than coffee brewing up in Timmer's skull."

Now Captain Marcus and Lieutenants Gibbs and Halloran, who occupied a cluster of desks at the opposite end of the large outer office, came across to Brad's desk.

"Let's have it, Brad," Captain Marcus said in his dry, Midwestern twang. "Won't be much work done unless we know. We're beginning to make book on the coffees goin' in."

Brad shook his head in honest ignorance. He said, "It's elementary. The man just likes coffee."

He had become the section's recognized authority on Colonel Timmer. In the month since his formal induction into "the team," as Timmer liked to call it, he had found himself drawn more and more into the position of the colonel's personal aide, a duty he didn't especially relish but could do nothing to avoid. Some of it was interesting; he carried Timmer's brief case into conferences of staff section chiefs, sitting directly behind the colonel and handing him pertinent documents as the conference ranged over various facets of an operation. But he had other functions; attending, for instance, Timmer's cocktail parties for his opposite numbers at the War Office and the Pentagon, and being inevitably cast in the role of executive flunky, and occasionally running furtive errands to Timmer's girl friend to deliver a bottle of whisky or a box of nylons which had arrived imbedded among documents in a courier pouch from the Pentagon.

Although this development favored him with a quick importance, especially among the section's junior officers, he felt a certain rebellion against being adopted by Timmer as his trusty faithful. The man was generous enough by character, even thoughtful in a gruff, calculated fashion, but he savored the prestige and privileges of his rank to a degree that labeled him as not quite the *grand seigneur* he pretended to be. The building of a personal staff, which thus far consisted of Brad and Pfc. Arkinson, was clearly designed to create an aura of the full professional soldier. Brad resented being party to it but he kept his feelings well in check. There were established places of exile for obstreperous junior officers, one being the supply depots near Manchester and the other, for more serious cases of intransigence, a posting to Iceland. More than ever he wanted to remain in London.

He had been seeing a great deal of Valerie. The small spark they had ignited on their train ride had brought something gentle and warm and inexplicably new into his life. If he instinctively hated to be an adjunct to Timmer's ego, he counted it a cheap price to pay for the privilege of remaining in London.

When the other officers had left his desk, Boyce nudged him.

"You can tell *me,* Brad. Anything to do with Torch?"

For several days the section had been fully concerned with Operation Torch, an ambitious plan for an invasion of North Africa from Casablanca as far east as Tunis. Operation Sledgehammer had long since been shelved as being too perilous, even though the legend "Second Front Now!" was chanted by thousands every afternoon in Hyde Park and scrawled on every vacant boarding in England.

Brad said, "I wouldn't tell you if I knew, but if it will make you feel any better, I haven't the foggiest."

"Maybe Timmer's getting his chicken wings. I'll bet that's it!" Boyce drew himself up to strict attention. "*Hochwohlgeboren Oberst Timmer! Sieg heil!*"

"You're mad, Ray."

"My secret asset. Mad but delightful. My wife warned me: 'Come

back as mad as you are. Any glimmering of sanity and I'm off to
Reno.' Her exact words."

"Sentimental little thing."

Boyce said, "My idea of as beautiful a farewell speech as I ever
expect to hear. What do you say we get cut tonight?"

"Not tonight——"

"I've discovered a wonderful pub just off Greek Street. The
clientele's smack out of Dickens. Cypriote I got talking to is in the
pandering business. Guarantees nothing over fifteen years old. Also
he can let you have a pinch of cocaine for eight shillings. Wonderful
ale too. I think we should explore it tonight."

"Sounds terrific, but I've got a dinner date."

"Valerie?"

Brad nodded.

"Look Brad, there's a rule about soldiers' comforts. They're supposed to be physical, not emotional."

Brad turned abruptly to his work. He didn't care to discuss Valerie
with anyone, certainly not with Ray Boyce. The man's philosophy
was earthy and amusing on practically all topics, and he could not
bear to hear Valerie mentioned in this context.

"I'm serious, Brad."

"You don't know anything about it."

The afternoon passed slowly. Arkinson ambled through with still
another pot of coffee and the whole office studied his entrance and
exit. Brad applied his sluggish mind to a draft of an operations order
on the unloading, warehousing, and issuance of Net: Mosquito, anti-
malarial. The weather outside was sunny and warm and gave promise of a balmy evening.

"Brad!"

Timmer's voice cut clear across the room. The colonel stood at the
open door of his office, a cup of coffee in his hand. He gestured im-
patiently and Brad, feeling somewhat like a schoolboy being hauled
up on the carpet before his classmates, hurried to him.

Timmer closed the door carefully and went to his desk. He pushed
his powerful hands down hard on the arms of his chair, smiled widely
enough to bare his bottom teeth, and said, "We're taking a little
trip, one of the best damn little trips we'll ever take."

"Yes, sir."

"Have Arkinson gas up the car. We'll need an extra jerry can, maybe two, in the trunk. I want him ready and downstairs in fifteen minutes."

"Overnight, sir?"

"You bet your life overnight—and all day tomorrow." Timmer was restless with enthusiasm. "And nobody's going to know we're even gone, not even the bunch outside. Let 'em think we've gone AWOL. That'll be a hot piece of gossip, eh? The colonel gone AWOL."

Brad said, "I'd better run over to my billet and get some overnight kit."

"Not necessary. Anyway it's lousy security. I don't want anybody to know we've gone anywhere. Understood?"

Brad, thinking of Valerie, said, "I have a dinner appointment for tonight. Have I permission to cancel it?"

"Absolutely no."

"But sir, it might look suspicious if I didn't." He was curdled by the thought of Valerie waiting vainly for him to show up. "Don't you think it's better security for me to break the date on some minor pretext?"

Timmer made a spitting noise with his lips. "Let me tell you something about security. You cancel a date and a dozen other guys cancel a date and the first thing you know it'll be all over London that something's up. That info alone might cost a thousand lives. We walk out of here in fifteen minutes like we're going to the officers' club for a drink. Is *that* understood?"

"Yes, sir."

"Right. Get Arkinson to gas up the car."

On the highway, with the windows of the Chevrolet staff car wide open, the air was still close and lazy. They were heading south. On previous missions out of town Brad sat in front with Arkinson which made him feel uncomfortably like a footman to a parvenu, but this time Timmer had cheerfully motioned him into the back of the car. They sat together in measured silence. Timmer had his eyes inclined toward the yellowing fields but, glancing at him occasionally, Brad knew he was not seeing them. The rugged, mustached face was fixed in deep thought, the line of the mouth grim, wide, and apprehensive.

When Arkinson slowed at a traffic circle from which the directional signs had been removed as an anti-invasion measure, Timmer consulted a road map spread on his lap.

"Left fork," he instructed, "and when you hit Reigate pass on through and keep south."

They picked up speed on a four-lane highway which was deserted save for an occasional lorry with army markings. Brad gave no thought to the mission or its mystery; he was concerned with the mile markers whizzing past the hubcaps. London was falling farther and farther behind. When six o'clock came around Valerie would be watching for him at her Red Cross club. He wondered how long she would wait and what she would think. He listened miserably to the flat scream of the speeding wheels.

Suddenly Timmer said, "Aren't you curious, Brad?" The query came ludicrously from the gruff, powerful man.

"I didn't feel I should ask, Colonel."

"Right. Absolutely right. You're learning. You're going to make one hell of a fine GSO someday." He sat back expansively, like a man determined to put his troubles behind him. "You know the first thing I liked about you? Those parachute wings. My idea of fighting a war is to go out and fight it. Any Joe with an ounce of brains and a little pull can wind up behind a desk. I like it when a young fellow with connections goes out and does it the hard way. I was an infantryman myself until they shoved me into staff school and, believe you me, I didn't like it. The one thing the general doesn't know is that basically I'm a fighting man. Always was, always will be."

Brad wondered vaguely about the reference to his connections. He wanted to challenge the man and groped for a respectful rejoinder, but Timmer, chuckling heartily, gave him no opportunity.

"What time is the staff meeting tomorrow?"

"The one on Torch co-ordinates?"

"No, the one the general called."

"Nine-thirty, sir."

Timmer said, "Can you imagine how he'll scream when I don't show? Can't trace me? Timmer gone AWOL! He'll be burning all right. And you know who'll be the happiest man in the whole damn ETO? Ed Cantrell, that's who."

Lieutenant Colonel Cantrell headed up another of the sections in OPD Plans. A regular officer, West Point '32, he was regarded as the young hot-shot at headquarters and clearly earmarked for bigger things if one could interpret the rapt attention his opinions commanded at staff meetings. For Timmer he had become a primary symbol of regular army favoritism over the reserve.

Timmer kept chuckling as the car raced across the flat Sussex terrain. "Can't you just see Ed Cantrell trying on his chickens? Well, let him dream. I'd rather gamble. My friends always said Alex Timmer would come home a general or a corpse and I guess they're right." He chuckled a little more and then as if he realized the joke was growing thin he swung around to Brad. "What do you know about Jubilee?"

"Jubilee? I haven't heard of it, Colonel."

"You're about the only one. Lousiest security I ever heard of. Wouldn't surprise me one bit if the Germans were sitting up and waiting on the other side."

Brad's daydreaming about Valerie stopped abruptly. "What is it, Colonel? A raid?"

"Bigger than that. About half a division, Canadians, going across tonight, tanks and all. Strictly experimental, just to find out if the Jerry is on his toes in the port areas. Between ourselves, Brad, I think it's murder." Timmer compressed his lips and watched a trio of Land Army girls baling hay in a field far off the road. "Wonderful bunch these Canadians. You'd think it was a Saturday-night brawl they were going into. Pure bloody murder."

It was impossible, Brad thought, that they were going to take part in the operation. He hadn't been briefed. He had brought no equipment. And yet there was the evidence of Timmer's behavior, now clearly in focus; a curious blend of apprehension and bravado.

He said, "Are we going to observe, sir?"

"Not we, Brad. *Me.* Our Ranger battalion's got permission for fifty observers spread around the Canadian formations. Number fifty-one is a strictly unofficial crazy coot called Alex Timmer. Can't sit at a desk all the time setting up plans for other guys. Got to see a little action." His hard, square face was deadly serious now. "Can you picture Ed Cantrell's face when he hears about it?"

"What about the general, sir?"

"Sure I'm playing hookey," Timmer replied snappishly. "Sure he's got to give me hell when I come back, *if* I come back, but you know damn well he's going to be thinking a lot different. He's going to be thinking this crazy coot has got something these other bastards haven't got. Get what I mean?"

At that moment Brad liked the man. He knew it was sheer ambition that was driving Timmer into the adventure. Thinking back on it, he realized the man had been scared for days. But a challenge was a challenge; this was something he could understand and admire.

"How did you work it, Colonel?"

"Hell, it was a cinch. They're a mad bunch, these Canadians, my kind of guys. Play hard, fight hard, break rules like crazy. I put it up to a pal of mine. We drink Saturday nights in a club on the Haymarket. Wonderful guy from up Toronto way, a battalion commander. He fixed it."

They drove in silence for nearly an hour. There was no traffic at all on the road. It was as if all of Sussex had taken to slumbering on this hot sunny afternoon. Timmer kept his eyes on the fields. He looked tough and sad.

They passed through a pretty town called Lewes and on its outskirts they were halted by a roadblock, two 1500-weights spread across the highway. A Canadian captain wearing battle dress with full webbing, a steel helmet, and a pistol belt carefully examined Timmer's AGO card, asked a few sharp questions, then stepped two paces back and saluted smartly. One of the 1500-weights backed off the highway and the American car drove through.

Timmer said, "These Canadians sure show that old spit and polish. Wonder why our fellows can't do it right. Ever see our guard outfits in their full-dress uniforms back home? Always look like a lot of refugees from a costume ball. It's a funny thing."

The air rushed fresh and sharp through the car and now they could smell the sea. Just ahead the green countryside rose to a lofty horizon cleanly etched against a pale blue summer sky and they knew these were the headlands that faced the enemy across the Channel, the chalk cliffs that had not been conquered in a thousand years.

Brad said, "Can you tell me where the assault goes, Colonel?"

Timmer was peering along the skyline. Above the heights a flight of gulls made fine long spirals, rising effortlessly with the wind that swept upward and inland from the cliffs.

"Dieppe."

The road took a sharp turn and suddenly they were speeding down through a narrow gap shaded from the sun and cool with the brisk, salt air. The road wound down steeply and when they came into sunlight again the eaves and spires of a seaside town spread out before them. In dead center were the docks. The breakwater circled out to sea, two pincers almost touching to form the narrow harbor entrance. There were cement emplacements at each extremity and thick, ugly cannon thrust their snouts toward the enemy over the bend of the horizon.

On the calm and glinting sea beyond the breakwater an armada lay at anchor, fifty or sixty dull gray ships of assorted sizes. There were squat, square, tank landing craft, and infantry landing ships, and farther out larger ships which might have been excursion steamers except for their drab raiment and the guns on their afterdecks, and out to seaward there were destroyers looking sleek and graceful. They all lay comfortably on an amiable sea and they might have been painted there except for the motor torpedo boats which scampered about in wide circles, cutting white ribbons in the blue and shining water.

This was the negation of all Brad had ever imagined about war. Everything was too quiet and too orderly and too pretty. It seemed ridiculous that fifty miles across this becalmed sea a savage battle might be fought on the morrow, and not less ridiculous that the men he could see lolling on the decks might be dead at daylight. He always thought battle was a climax that had to be approached through stages of mounting fury. Here was no fury nor a beginning of fury.

The staff car descended into the town. The streets were empty, but from the gardens and windows of small, weather-beaten houses men and women peered respectfully as if they thought royalty might be riding in the car. Only the children playing along the side of the road cried gaily and waved.

When they reached the end of a narrow street which gave entrance to the docks, a Royal Navy chief examined Timmer's credentials and waved the car through. Arkinson maneuvered in low gear along the edge of a burned-out warehouse, followed the line of a railway siding, and reached an open, uncluttered landing stage with a clear view of the breakwater.

The loading had apparently been completed. Only a few small motor launches were lashed to the hards, and on the edge of the dock about twenty Canadian officers stood about conversing quietly among themselves. Brad could see the troops on the ships clearly now. They crowded the deck rails and every now and again someone waved at the pretty town on the shore.

As Arkinson braked the car, a Canadian officer detached himself from a group and came striding forward.

"Alex, you old fool!"

He was a lieutenant colonel, short, powerfully built, and handsomely mustached, and he looked oddly rotund for the thick battle dress he wore and the full webbing hung with ammunition pouches, a pistol belt, water bottle, commando dagger, medical pack, and several grenades.

Timmer leaped from the car and slapped his hand into the other's. "Hi'ya Dunc! You didn't think I was going to miss it."

The Canadian said, "It's going to be quite a party, brother."

"What the hell, we've had parties before."

"Not like this one, baby," the Canadian said, punching Timmer playfully on the chest.

The two men, talking with extravagant hilarity, walked along the dock. There were introductions, salutes, and handshakes as the Canadian conducted his friend among the groups of officers. Then Timmer came back to the car alone. He took a pistol belt and a helmet which had been lying on the floor boards in front.

He said to Brad, "Zero's at 0430. They tell me we should be back in the afternoon. Can't tell where though. They're operating out of Portsmouth too. If I don't show by six, go on back to London. Understood?"

"Understood, Colonel."

"And Brad"—his voice took on a gravel roughness—"if I don't show at all you'll find a couple of letters on my desk. Slip 'em into the mailbox." He looked away and his mouth grimaced in a crooked, thoughtful way. "I was just thinking. Wouldn't it be just like Ed Cantrell to walk off with the jackpot without gambling a dime?"

He paused to release a gurgle from the pit of his stomach as if he were genuinely amused. Then he shook hands with Brad, and after a moment's hesitation, reached into the car and shook hands with Arkinson.

Brad said, "See you tomorrow, sir."

"Yep. Tomorrow." Timmer turned abruptly and walked away hooking on his pistol belt.

"Good luck, Colonel!" Brad called out.

Timmer didn't turn around. He waved with the helmet he carried by its chin strap and strode to the dock's edge where a motor launch was already filled with Canadian officers. A naval rating grasped his arm as he jumped down into the bobbing craft. He stood well aft with his Canadian friend as the boat chugged slowly out toward the harbor entrance.

A small group of senior officers, one of them a brigadier with red tabs on his battle-dress collar, remained on the dock and threw waving salutes at the men on the launch. Long after the others had stopped, the brigadier kept throwing salutes. "Good hunting, men!" he shouted over and over again. "Damned good hunting, men! Remember, damned good hunting now!"

Brad leaned against the car and watched the launch chug beneath the thick barrels of the cannon at the harbor entrance. He could see Timmer standing a little apart from the others, looking out to sea. The launch cut around the breakwater and disappeared from view. He saw it again farther out and then it swerved behind a tank landing craft and was gone for good.

He remembered how Damien had wished him good hunting. It came to him like a blurred memory out of his earliest childhood, the feeling of pleasure and anticipation was more easily remembered than the event, and yet it happened only two months ago. It was hard to believe that two months ago his whole life was concerned with the *Star* and with Janie, with the rising cost of newsprint and staff salaries, with the problem of Ben Carver's retirement and whether Nate Schoenfeld would make a proper successor, with little things like Grace Lakelock's developing gallstone condition and his mother's long-time maid who suddenly decided to go to the aircraft plant at seventy dollars a week. It seemed so distant and so hazy. Even Janie had receded into a tiny crevice of his mind and wasn't really alive. All in two months! He realized with a start that he hadn't written to Janie in a couple of weeks.

Somewhere back of the docks a clock was chiming off the hour. He counted seven strokes.

Valerie would have been waiting almost an hour now. He was revolted at the thought of her waiting and wondering. To reach her

by telephone would be the grossest breach of security, even if the
trunk lines were operating out of this port. Whatever remained of his
New England conscience (precious little, he was beginning to suspect) rejected the notion.

He tried to concentrate on the vessels lying beyond the breakwater, on the men crowding their decks and gazing inshore. He recalled
Sledgehammer and the estimate, scientifically arrived at, of twenty-
seven per cent assault casualties before a beachhead could be established. The men out there on the decks didn't know that. He tried
to place himself among them, to think what he might think if he
were out there. He knew his luck wouldn't hold for the duration,
that someday he would be out there on a deck gazing inshore, and
the rule of thumb, twenty-seven per cent, would apply to him. It
was easier to think of Timmer, who was somewhere among the mass
of bodies pressed against the deck rails. He wondered how much he
would care if Timmer failed to return. He was shocked to realize
how little he would care. And then he knew it was no use. He wasn't
really thinking any of these things. He was thinking of Valerie.

Far out to seaward an Aldis light began to flash feverishly from
the bridge of a destroyer. A single chime sounded from the clock in
the town. It was quarter past seven.

She wouldn't have given up hope yet. She would be sitting at her
desk in an alcove marked off by a little gate in the lobby of the Park
Street club and she would be watching the door each time it opened.
Scores of officers came in at this hour. She would have her cap on, a
kepi with a Red Cross badge which set off her expressive profile. He
remembered the first day she wore her A.R.C. uniform, how delighted she was with its neat tailored lines and how she laughingly
suggested she would desert rather than be forced back into the bulky
A.T.S. uniform. Thinking about it, he resented every officer who
walked into the club and exercised the privilege of talking to her.

He hadn't seen her in four days. She had used her weekend
leave to visit her father in Burlingham, and now it was Monday evening. They had never been apart for so long a period, not since the
day they arrived together at King's Cross. In the beginning they met
every evening simply because there was no reason why they
shouldn't. They enjoyed the newness of each other, the novelty of
the alien worlds each had lived in, and the fascinating discovery
that the genuine London had to be explored and excavated like the

treasures of ancient Egypt. It was all jolly and harmless; they had
learned to know each other's primary loyalties and could talk about
them easily and sometimes sentimentally.

He watched several ships flashing their Aldis lights, angrily it
seemed to his distant mind, in reply to the destroyer, but the flotilla
remained motionless under the magnificent patronage of a great red
sun.

He wondered at what precise moment his evenings with Valerie
stopped being jolly and harmless and became a desperate joy. He
wondered what had happened and when.

There was no precise moment he could remember. Whatever had
happened seemed to have happened precipitously but strangely
without spur or incitement. One evening they had gone to a movie
on Oxford Street. It was a pre-war French film starring Raimu and
they found it disappointing. When they came out, the night had
clouded over and there was a feel of rain in the air. Oxford Street
was pitch black. Feeling their way along a turning off Regent Street
they were halted by a sound of quiet but sprightly music and they
pushed through a blackout curtain into a restaurant. It was a garish
room and clearly Middle European as to clientele. Most of the tables
were occupied by women who sat nursing a pot of coffee and their
faded pride as they waited to be asked to dance by the few men
in the place. Val and Brad felt conspicuous for their uniforms. They
drank half a bottle of Tokay while a violinist, a fattish, dark-
haired Viennese with startlingly white fingers, stood by their table
and played the "*Fiakerlied*" to the accompaniment of an accordion
and a guitar. They wished the man would move off because he spot-
lighted their contagion of quiet happiness in an unhappy place, but
he persisted and played the theme melody from the "Warsaw Con-
certo." When they finished their wine they made their way slowly
through a complex of streets to Berkeley Square and then to Hill
Street where Valerie lived.

They had stopped outside the blacked-out door of her apartment
building.

"It's too late to ask you in," she had said. "Poor Bridget needs her
sleep. She'll be getting up soon." She shared a flat with Bridget
Felton, a wealthy school chum who was up at five every morning
for work in a factory that produced shell casings.

She had taken his hands. "Thank you, Brad. I loved every minute of tonight."

"Bad picture too?"

"Bad picture, bad violinist, I loved every minute of it."

"Tomorrow then?"

"Tomorrow, of course."

"Pick you up at the club." He gave her hands a little squeeze and walked quickly away in the darkness. He heard her voice when he was a short piece down the street.

"Brad!"

He traced his way back. She was still standing at the door.

"Brad——" In the dark he could barely make out the little smile, half sweet, half anxious, that played on her face. "Brad, don't you think we'd better make it day after tomorrow?"

He knew exactly what she meant. The same bitter, soaring, helplessly joyous note was sounding inside him.

"Perhaps we'd better."

"It's a good idea. Isn't it? Honestly?"

"It's a bad idea but I think you're right."

"Bless you."

"Good night, Val."

He knew she was still standing there when he reached the turning. He paused and then moved on resolutely across Berkeley Square.

After that they saw each other every second night and it seemed to him a useless sacrifice, worse than useless, for despite the bright chatter of Ray Boyce's intellectual cronies and their hardy sociological forays into the nether regions of Soho, he thought of her constantly and was infinitely more eager when they met. But they fought a valiant and adult battle and made believe it was all jolly and harmless as it had been at the beginning. Only once had she broken discipline.

They had returned to Hill Street late and as they stood in the blackout in a little lingering ritual of good night, a long moment materialized between them. It was not only London that had blacked out. The whole world seemed to recede into a distant darkness and they were alone in it. It was a long frightening moment suspended out of time. "We mustn't believe it, Brad," she had said, fighting the moment and driving it back into the scheme of their lives, "it's the war." She was looking up at him unflinchingly as she might have faced an enemy. And he had said, "It must be. The war does funny things to people," but he knew he was lying for her and for himself.

That's the way it had gone. And now, because he hadn't seen her in four days, it was worse than ever.

Somewhere in the town he heard the clock strike eight. By this time she would have telephoned his apartment, but Ray wouldn't be able to enlighten her. He didn't like the notion of Ray talking with her. He didn't like the notion of anyone talking with her. He wondered if she felt as miserable as he did . . .

"This your vehicle, sir?"

A ruggedly built Canadian RSM stood before him.

"Yes, that's mine."

The Canadian said, "Would you mind removing it, sir? We've got a casualty clearing station setting up here."

Brad looked past the man out to sea. The flotilla had begun to move. It was spread over a wide area and some of the forward ships were already mere specks glimmering in the low-lying sun. The destroyers raced proud and impudent along the flanks of the convoy.

"All right, I'll move her." He climbed in beside Arkinson. The latter put down his western-story magazine and said, "Where now, Lieutenant?"

"Back off and drive along the sea front. I guess every hotel is a requisition job."

All of the townsfolk seemed to have drifted silently down to the sea wall. They stood, shielding their eyes against the horizontal rays of the sun, and watched the ships steam lazily toward the far horizon.

Brad was disappointed. It was not that he expected to find the people of the south coast shaking their fists toward the enemy. But there were men, still faintly visible on the decks of the tail-end ships, who would be storming a German shore at the dawn, and on the docks surgical tents were being set up, and there were long convoys of ambulances moving down to the jetty. These people, watching silently, might have been weekend trippers enjoying a pretty sunset.

Arkinson stopped before a huge, dilapidated structure which bore the title "Hotel Beaurivage" and a cheerful captain belonging to a British anti-aircraft regiment assigned Brad a room and directed the "other rank" as he called Arkinson to a smaller hotel which was infinitely more dilapidated.

When Brad forced open the weather-beaten shutters in his room, dusk had fallen over the sea and the convoy had been swallowed up. The people along the sea wall peered out as if they could still see the ships. The British, Brad thought, had a peculiar talent for standing motionless when excitement was running highest. He admired them but this did not make him understand them any better.

For Valerie it had been a mercifully busy evening. American fighter wings and bombardment groups were arriving in England almost daily now, and the young airmen, piling into London on leave, made the Park Street officers' club their first port of call. On this evening the groupings around her desk proved unusually heavy. Although her workday normally ended at six-thirty it was not until well past seven that the olive drab queue began to thin out.

She surveyed the lobby, crowded and leaping with high spirits. It seemed odd not to see Brad waiting in his usual chair near the entrance to the reading room. She surveyed the room once more, then turned her attention to a lieutenant, a pilot with a baby face who had been standing patiently before her desk. He explained as delicately as possible that he understood there was a "lively, sort of girlie show" in London and would she by any chance happen to know where it was. She jotted down street directions to the Windmill and savored his youthful self-possession as he said, "I'm greatly in your debt, ma'am," with a solemn gallantry she thought existed only in fiction of the Old South.

The myriad types of America constantly intrigued her. There were those like this youngster who called her "ma'am" with aplomb, and others who called her "dream girl," "baby," and "cutie" which amused her most of all. Although her name was conspicuously displayed on the desk she was seldom called Miss Russell except by senior officers, usually elderly colonels. The variety of accents and gamut of requests proved fascinating to her. She would never cease to enjoy the experience of a cracker-barrel voice asking for directions to the Abbey or wondering if she knew whether the Goya exhibition was still at the gallery.

She had long since concluded there was no America as the English thought there was an America. The nation was an agglomeration of varied types and nationalities and mentalities loosely held together by a contagious and undisciplined spirit of freedom. She found that

the only inhibited Americans she met were Jews and this discovery
came as a surprise. She had never before come into contact with
Jews, not even British Jews, and had known about them only by
reading and hearsay. For a long time she puzzled over the wide
divergence between her fixed impressions and the experience of talking with them.

Now at last there were no more inquiries. She turned off her desk
light and closed the gate that gave entrance to her corner of the lobby.
Brad was nowhere to be seen. She went back to her desk and
dialed his number. Ray Boyce answered against a background of
spirited conversation.

"That's damned curious, Val," he said. "He left the office with the
*Obergruppenfuehrer* around four but he expected to be back. Matter of fact he told me he had a dinner date with you."

She said, "I know you can't answer this, Ray, but I wondered if
—if——"

"It so happens I *can* answer it," he cut in brightly. "There's nothing
happening, at least that I know of, if that's what you're getting at. I
guess they picked up a flat somewhere and are stuck in an elfin
glade not yet invaded by the invention of the telephone. Why don't
you come over here and wait? I'm entertaining a couple of majors
who have phony intellectual pretensions and are basically lechers
and I think you'd do a lovely job of breaking their black hearts on
both counts. What say, Val? Lots of scotch. Wash your feet in the
stuff if you like."

"Thank you, Ray, but I'll be at my flat if he gets in at a reasonable
hour."

She closed the phone. All afternoon she had been sensitive about a
sudden upsurge in the war, about raids and death. The war had
been quiescent a long time, especially *her* war. It couldn't go on this
way forever. She stole another glance at the *Evening Standard* which
had lain on her desk since the lunch hour. The item hadn't dissolved
like a bad dream. It was still there, small and innocuous among the
bulletins on the front page, and the sight of it set her mouth to quivering.

### COMMANDOS IN DESERT?

In his regular commentary over Radio Berlin this morning, General
Dittmar put forward the claim that British Commandos attempted a
demolition raid on Tobruk during last night. According to Dittmar, the

bodies of twenty-three Commandos, including four officers, were found in
the dock area or washed up on nearby beaches after a sharp action which
he described as "a disaster for the foolhardy raiders."

(This morning's Allied communique makes no mention of a raid on
Tobruk and there has been no corroboration from Eighth Army sources
that British Commandos are operating in the desert.)

Of course she didn't believe Dittmar any more than she believed
Haw-Haw although everyone listened to him. It was his job to chip
away at morale, to darken British minds with anxiety, as he was
darkening her mind.

But the British too were being untruthful, at least by default. The
Commandos *were* operating in the desert. Only that morning she
had received a letter from John.

"Dearest Val," he had written, "What a lovely, lovely way to finish
off the evening—I mean, writing to you. It's the sort of evening I can
almost see you, almost touch you. We're bivouacked on an escarpment overlooking the Med and there's a yellowish moon playing on
the water. Pity, isn't it? We must remember someday to visit here
together. Something to dream on. All my men are asleep and I'm
more than ready to climb into the old bedding roll. We've had a
devilish day rehearsing to singe old Rommel's hair, went all out at
top speed. I don't blame the other chaps for snoring away but I
feel rather sorry for them. They don't know the wonderful joy of having you on the tip of my pen . . ."

This was the third letter from him in a week. Each had been bolder
and more ardent than the last.

"I must tell you about running into Derek yesterday. It was the
most fantastic luck what with most of England and all of the Anzacs
milling about in the desert. I'd been to Corps and driving back I
spotted the markings of Derek's regiment—must remember the dear
old censor!—on a tank. I was really excited. I raced to the head of
the column and there was Derek, looking brown and splendid, on
the turret of his command tank. We had a grand old reunion. Really,
darling, you'd hardly believe we were brothers. Derek looks every
inch a general and I've no doubt he'll be one soon. When you've got
a battalion command at the start of a big party, you need just a bit
of luck and talent to make brigade—and all his life Derek's had
plenty of both.

"But he's not as lucky as I am in one rather wonderful way. It's grand news that they've posted you to London. Do make up for all those miserable months in Burlingham. Permission granted for a big, wide tear—whale variety! All for now, darling. Must bed down. The major's got us going again *before* dawn so we can rehearse our cat's eyes. Damnable nuisance, the war! But the sooner we get at them, the sooner the end. So—with all my love, good night—John."

She sat in her darkened corner and read the letter again by a fringe of light from a great chandelier overhanging the boisterous lobby. It was dated two weeks ago. She studied every word, feverishly seeking a clue which might reassure her that John hadn't been on the raid, if there *was* a raid, but her eyes always moved back to a single line: "We've had a devilish day rehearsing to singe old Rommel's hair."

She tried to fight down the fears that flooded her mind. The Germans were always making fancy claims. Perhaps there had been no raid at all . . . perhaps a unit of marine Commandos had made the raid . . . perhaps other Commandos had followed John's company to the desert . . . perhaps, perhaps—there were so many conjectures, but her mind remained tortured by a piercing sense of logic: John's unit had been bivouacked near the sea, it had been rehearsing a raid, and now the Germans claimed a raid had been repulsed with twenty-three dead.

She put on her cap, opened her shoulder bag, looked at herself in the flap mirror. Her mind raced on remorselessly. There were about one hundred and twenty men in his company. If there were twenty-three casualties, the chances would be one in five. But everyone knew German claims were exaggerated. If there were only fifteen casualties, the chances were still one in eight.

It was providential, she thought, that Brad had been delayed. Over the whole weekend she had counted the hours that separated them. But now the war bore down heavily upon her. She was a child of England's misery, as was John. A month ago she would have hastened madly to Brad, spilling her hopes and forebodings. Not now. That magic period had passed. They were no longer friends. By every honest appraisal she was capable of, they were in love.

The lobby, crowded with Americans, had become suddenly alien. She edged quickly through, fleeing across snatches of conversation. "—I tell ya she's got a friend. What we need, brother, is a crock—" . . . "—on Orange Street. Steaks *that* thick. Like back home—" . . .

"—you haven't seen any yet? You kiddin'? Scads of 'em on Piccadilly—"

Outside the day's last light hovered over the quiet street. It was
going to be a dark and moonless night. She walked slowly toward
Brook Street.

"I beg your pardon, ma'am."

She had heard the voice before. The baby-faced pilot came up
beside her and saluted with the gravity of a general at a march-past.
"I didn't go to the Windmill, ma'am. I thought it over and decided
against it."

"So I see."

"I do hope you'll forgive me, ma'am, but I happened to notice you
seemed sort of undone back there in the club."

"Good heavens, I didn't know I was being observed."

"No intention of being rude but I couldn't help remarking you are
an astonishingly handsome lady."

Her heart went out to the youth in his struggle to maintain an
old world self-possession. "Well, Lieutenant, what am I to say? You
leave me rather speechless."

"Allow me to introduce myself. I am Lieutenant Clayfield Binns,
Jr., ma'am, and I would be greatly honored if I could entertain you
at dinner. Let me assure you I am not a flippant person."

She smiled. "I'm sure you're not. You're very nice but"—it hurt her
to see his eager, young face turn anxious—"I'm afraid I simply can't."

"I'm very sorry, ma'am." He saluted gallantly. "I hope you don't
consider me too bold."

"Not at all, Lieutenant. Good night."

"Good night, ma'am."

She walked slowly into the heavy darkness that had fallen over
the city. When she came to Hill Street she paused, knowing that she
dreaded to go home.

She heard a stir. Somewhere close a woman's voice, soft and delicate, whispered, "Kiss me, darling—hard—hard!" and in a doorway
there was the outline of a man's back and a pair of slim white hands
pressing fervently against the khaki of his battle dress. She walked
on. The war, she thought, and what it has done to all of us!

She walked aimlessly in the refreshing night air and after a time
she found herself on the Mall. She could see the black outlines of
the palace. Approaching closer, she heard the measured tread of the

sentries marching from their pillboxes. It was curious, she thought, how she found herself urged to walk near the palace whenever the war was too much to bear. She had walked there on the Sunday of Neville Chamberlain's dull voice proclaiming, "We are at war with Germany . . . We will be fighting evil things," and a few months later, coming away from her father's bedside at Watford, she had walked there once more. She didn't know why. The palace was old and forbidding but when the standard flew from the center mast and she knew the Family was there she found a strange comfort in its Victorian ugliness. It made her feel a kinship with all the other British, those who were apprehensive and those already weeping. Many thought it was foolish, but it was so. And if it was so, it couldn't be foolish.

The moment she turned the lock of her flat her premonitions came violently alive. The lights in the living room were ablaze and Bridget was standing there in her dressing gown.

"Thank heaven you're here, Val. I've been calling the club and calling Brad and calling everywhere——"

"What is it?"

Bridget, a big, ungainly, warmhearted girl, attempted a carefree smile. "Nothing, I suppose." She took a blue envelope from the pocket of her dressing gown. "This cable came about ten minutes ago. I— I didn't open it."

Valerie snatched it from her. She read her name and address on the face of the envelope and examined the censor's stamp on the reverse side.

"Gee, Val, aren't you going to open it?"

She ripped it open, glanced at it, and sank into a chair and fell to weeping.

Bridget took the cable from her hand and read: FEET BIT WET OTHERWISE GRAND ALL MY LOVE—JOHN.

"Honestly Val, you're nutty as a fruitcake. What in heaven's name are you crying about?"

Valerie didn't answer. She sat in the room long after her roommate had returned to bed. She was utterly exhausted. It didn't occur to her until very late in the night that Brad hadn't called. But she had been thinking of him in her weeping, and of John, and of the emotional trap she had fallen into, and as happened so often lately, of the mother, dead and disgraced, she was only now beginning to know and love.

## 10

I T  W A S as though the light breeze weaving in off the Channel had been whispering ominously. The atmosphere on the docks was heavy with foreboding.

Medical officers, nursing sisters, and orderlies stood about in small silent groups in the warming sun outside the three huge tents of the casualty clearing station which had been set up during the night. Senior officers, some with red tabs on their lapels and wearing handsome Glengarries, peered out to sea from the edge of the landing stage. The townsfolk were lined along the sea wall, their faces scrubbed and solemn as on a churchgoing day. Even children frolicking in the streets behind the sea wall seemed to understand they must not laugh or shout.

Brad moved restlessly about the docks. It was five hours past 0430 zero and there was no news, at least they were giving out none.

At a signals unit, which had established itself in a shed, a rosy-cheeked lieutenant simply shook his head. "Nobody really knows anything," he said. "The wireless net is all balled up."

A Canadian brigadier, tall and slim and crisply handsome, shaded his eyes as he looked out to sea. "The battle is still engaged," he said curtly, "heavily engaged." He walked a piece down the landing stage in a clear maneuver to avoid further inquiry.

Toward eleven o'clock a new convoy of ambulances rumbled down the gap into the town and parked behind the ambulances which had come in during the night. Everyone turned to watch the drivers slide their vehicles into disciplined rows facing the casualty clearing station. Two jeep-loads of war correspondents and photographers roared in, looked about, and roared away, but not before they had left a rumor in their wake that the first news would soon break on the wireless. By the time it came almost everyone in the dock area had converged on the signals shed.

"The Prime Minister has just informed the House of Commons," an immaculate BBC voice announced, "that shortly before dawn this morning a strong Canadian force joined by small elements of British troops and escorted by ships of the Royal Navy drove onto the French coast in the vicinity of Dieppe. Beyond specifying that no permanent beachhead is being attempted, Mr. Churchill provided no details of the action, but a dispatch just received from Ross Munro of the Canadian Press indicates that some tanks have managed to get ashore and very fierce fighting has developed in the beach area near the Dieppe casino . . ."

Brad went up into the town and searched out the post office. It was a small, well-ordered room staffed by an elderly woman who was brewing tea on an electric burner behind her wicket.

He said, "Can I get through to London?"

"It depends, sir. All the trunks are reserved by the signals people. I can put you through to them. If it's official business I should think they'd have a line open."

He said, "It's not official business."

The woman poured boiling water into a pot and dropped a cosy over it. "I'm ever so sorry, sir."

He didn't have to wonder what Valerie might be thinking. It knifed at his brain. "Are you sure I can't get through? A very short call?"

The woman said, "Oh yes, sir, quite sure. I couldn't possibly."

Making his way back to the docks he remembered about the fierce fighting on the beach and he thought of Timmer. It came as a discovery that, in the crisis, he liked the man enough to worry about him. He moved around the silent, waiting groups of Canadians and sat on an ironhead and smoked. The Channel was sparkling calm; wisps of white cloud made the sky interesting. It was a perfect summer's day and indescribably sad.

The first wounded came in a few minutes after the clock in the town struck noon.

A flight of Spitfires roared low over the docks, banked steeply, and screamed back out to sea as if to herald an approach of importance, and a little later two ships appeared on the horizon. Gradually they became identifiable. One was a tank landing craft, low and stubby, and on its port side a sleek corvette moved slowly in escort.

As the ships passed under the breakwater cannon, a murmur rose from the folk along the sea wall. The LCT was holed and scarred above the waterline and a portion of its bridge had been blown away. A blood-red flare, discharged from the corvette, hung in the air a brief moment. On the landing stage a space had been cleared for medical officers and a host of orderlies hugging stretchers.

The moment the craft was tied up, the orderlies scrambled aboard and carried off the wounded. When all the stretcher cases had been brought into the tents, the walking wounded hobbled off, slowly and with a certain dignity, but their rough stubbled faces were yellowish pale and tense and they spoke not a word until they disappeared inside a reception tent. The last were the dead, eight stretchers bearing bodies snugly rolled in khaki blankets with only their scuffed boots protruding. These were carried to a great empty warehouse at the back of the docks.

The small ships came in all during the afternoon. They arrived in groups of three and sometimes four under escort of a warship and canopied by a flight of fighters. No one asked how the battle had gone. There was no need when an LCI came in under tow, its steel sides twisted and holed, its decks almost awash, its passengers lying in grotesque positions, lying dead; or when battle-shocked soldiers, their faces darkened by terror, were led faltering like whipped children into the reception tent. The crisply handsome brigadier paced a section of the dock, his swagger stick flicking nervously against his thigh.

In the CCS orderly room, a businesslike sergeant allowed Brad to consult the lengthening list of dead and wounded. There were names from Edmonton and Windsor and many towns in the province of Quebec. His eyes lingered on one from Bridgeport, Connecticut, a lieutenant belonging to the 1st U. S. Ranger battalion. There was a French-Canadian name from Ste. Agathe, Quebec. He had often passed through that pretty town on his way to the skiing hills, and he thought how little the man must have dreamed he would wind up wrapped in a khaki blanket on a dock in the south of England.

After a time he wandered to the back of the surgical tent. A medical officer, his rubber apron flecked with blood, sat smoking on a stool.

"Bad?"

The medical officer said, "Bad. Mostly amputations."

"Any idea how the casualties run?"

"Rough guess would be fifty per cent. Maybe more. A lot never got off the beach. We won't know about them until the Germans tell us."

A nurse appeared at the flap of the tent.

"The patient is ready, Major."

The surgeon tossed away his cigarette, looked distastefully at the mess on his rubber apron, blinked up at the sun, and went in.

Brad found himself at the warehouse where the dead lay on stretchers. A three-ton truck covered by a tarpaulin had backed up to the entrance and the dead were being loaded. The boots protruding from each wrapped blanket held him in terrible fascination. As each stretcher was lifted into the truck, the boots jiggled.

He counted the dead being placed in the truck. Eighteen bodies exactly covered the empty space and then the tarpaulin was fastened down and the truck moved off. Another truck backed into position. He was unable to keep his eyes from the operation, yet he was strangely unaffected by it. Death in khaki was a most simple event, final, factual, and trivial as a penny transaction. He studied the boots jiggling as each body was lifted and he remembered the men on the decks of the ships peering inshore. Before the war ended he too might be lifted into a truck, his boots jiggling, and he found he could consider even this possibility without high emotion. But he was too honest not to realize he was safely on England's south coast and that the nearest enemy was fifty miles across the water. He watched the loading and after a time he thought of Timmer and he felt a sudden, terrible urge, like a barbarous cry rising from deep inside him, to run off, anywhere, away from this place.

By late afternoon he began to doubt that Timmer had survived. More than forty ships had put into the harbor, most of them carrying a complement of dead and wounded, but there were a few that arrived unscathed, the troops aboard fresh and cheerful. These belonged to a floating reserve that had not been committed to battle because the situation on the beaches had become hopelessly beyond repair.

The docks surged with troops, some tattered and glassy-eyed, some defiantly happy as if they had proved to their own satisfaction that they were sufficiently tough and unafraid. Most chattered excitedly to anyone within range. Non-coms, seeking to form up the remnants of their units, added to the din, and over everything a loud-speaker crackled out countermanding orders to all ambulance drivers to take their loads to No. 6 General "and not—repeat not—to No. 5." A bedeviled Red Cross girl found it difficult to get anyone to accept the gum and cigarettes she carried about in a cardboard box and seemed grateful when a war correspondent in a spanking new uniform took a handful.

On the strength of his alien uniform, Brad managed to gain the attention of a full colonel who had just come off a destroyer in company with a lot of important-looking naval officers.

The colonel, panting and harried, said, "If he went in on the flanks, at Berneval or Pourville, he may be all right. If he went in at Dieppe, chances are he's been hit or a prisoner. Sorry, old man," he said and hurried off.

At six o'clock Brad shouldered his way off the docks in search of Arkinson. He found the driver perched on the running board of the car polishing a long-barreled pistol.

"What do you think, Lieutenant?" Arkinson called out, displaying his acquisition. "German Luger for twenty bucks. Bet I can get fifty for it in London. Any sign of the colonel yet?"

Brad said, "We'll give it another half an hour. If he doesn't show we'll have to figure he landed at another port."

"Or he's a dead pigeon," Arkinson volunteered, still admiring his Luger.

They watched a flight of Spitfires circle over the Channel and soon a lone destroyer appeared on the horizon. Brad hurried back to the docks. The clamor had subsided and everyone strained toward the water's edge as the warship steamed slowly toward port. Both of its forward turrets were heaps of blackened, distorted metal. Its deck railings hung like ribbons over the sides. A multitude of uniforms, soldiers and sailors, jammed the afterdeck.

A tug was required to push the ship's stern toward the dock and then the debarkation proceeded in the regular order—the wounded, the walking wounded, the unscathed, and last, the dead. Timmer was not among them, at least not among the living.

There was no point in waiting any longer. It was nearly seven. Brad walked among the milling, excited survivors on the landing stage and tried to convince himself that Timmer had been brought to another port. He couldn't imagine him dead or captured. The man was too strong, too ambitious, too calculating, and though a fragment of shrapnel was neutral in its flight, he wouldn't believe Timmer had fallen when so many lesser men had succeeded in getting away. Whatever else Timmer might be, in the business of being a soldier he was more professional than the genuine article.

He made a last check in the CCS orderly room. The sergeant on duty, weary of the repeated inquiries, shook his head in advance. "No luck, sir. All we got in the line of Americans is a couple of Rangers, a lieutenant, and a W/O. One dead, one wounded. No colonels."

Then, on his last look around before quitting the docks, he caught a glimpse of Timmer.

For a moment he wasn't quite sure. He had spotted him in a break between two platoons of Canadians marching toward a column of trucks. The man sat on a packing case, his body bent forward and his hands circling his eyes like blinkers. He wore no recognizable uniform; a faded khaki shirt open across the chest, and blue, grease-smeared trousers, and white sneakers. But there was hardly any mistaking the rugged shoulders, the shiny black hair, and the square, stubbled jaw.

Brad scrambled across the line of march.

"Colonel!" he called out. "Colonel Timmer!"

The rugged man brought his hands down wearily from his face. He looked about frowning, his mouth agape, and when he caught sight of Brad, his frown deepened.

"I'm glad to see you, Colonel. For a minute I——"

"What are you doing here?" The gruff monotone had taken on a new, almost plaintive quality.

Brad was mystified by the query. The man's face clearly bore the pallor of exhaustion but he appeared in full possession of himself. His arms were crossed on his hairy chest and he was looking away distastefully.

"I asked you what you're doing here?"

Brad said, "I don't know what you mean, sir."

"What time is it?"

"About seven, Colonel."

Timmer was still looking away. "What were my orders?"

"You said to wait till six but I decided to stick around awhile longer——"

Timmer growled sharply, "What were my orders?"

"Six o'clock, sir."

"God damn it, why don't you follow orders?"

Brad said, "The way this thing was going, I was frankly worried——"

"To hell with it." Timmer got to his feet. "Let's get to the car."

His sneakers lacked laces and were too big for him. They flopped on the pavement as the two men made their way between trucks and ambulances and columns of marching soldiers to where the car was parked.

Timmer didn't return Arkinson's smart salute, nor did he seem to hear the driver's cheerful, "Oh boy, Colonel, am I glad to see you!" He half stumbled as he entered the car and sat heavily in a corner of the back seat.

Brad said, "Would you like to stretch out, Colonel? I'll sit in front."

"Stop fussing, God damn it!" Timmer growled. "Come on in here." His mouth worked angrily. "After this be goddamn sure you follow orders."

As the car moved slowly forward and merged with the stream of military traffic chugging up the gap, Brad studied his chief. The man's jaw was tense, his teeth tightly clenched, his eyes fixed straight ahead as if trying to spear Arkinson's back. There were signs of traumatic shock but not to be compared with some of the helplessly wailing men who had been led off the ships.

He couldn't credit the first explanation that entered his mind for Timmer's strange attitude of resentment. It was hardly possible that the man had wanted him to return to London alone and report him missing, in order to create as profound an impression as possible on the high command. Thinking back on the sequence of events, he decided it *was* possible. There had been, after all, only one purpose in Timmer's mind.

Progress was slow. The highway was jammed with trucks, troop carriers, ambulances, and huge tank transporters. The latter, most of them vacant, covered almost the whole of the road. Arkinson weaved the light car in and out among the slower vehicles but there was always another lumbering convoy around the next bend.

Timmer remained silent, his small bloodshot eyes open but introverted. After almost an hour he muttered, "I didn't get ashore."

Brad said carefully, "From what I hear, Colonel, perhaps it's just as well."

Timmer didn't seem to hear him. He said, "Our LCI took a direct hit a hundred yards out. Holy Christ, the mess!"

"You were lucky."

For the first time some animation came into Timmer's face. His forehead creased over quizzically and he said, "A lot of guys weren't."

He lapsed into another silence and his tired eyes concerned themselves with Arkinson's driving. The truck convoys were thinning out and the staff car gathered speed as it leaped ahead into the dusk.

Night came swiftly. Timmer sat motionless in his corner. He might have dozed off. Then suddenly, from behind the shield of darkness, he began to speak.

"Twice," he said, picking up a train of thought as if there had been no interval. "I was exploded into the goddamn water twice." His voice retained only a portion of the gruffness he had always affected. Now it was shot through with a nervous, tremulous intensity.

He said, "First time a torpedo boat fished me out and it swung inshore to pick up a couple other guys and then *that* boat caught it smack on the button. Christ! Those German gunners! Had the beach and the approaches taped with enfilading fire. Artillery was deadly —deadly. Second time I hit the water I was naked as a baby. No Mae West. Nothing. I flopped around a hell of a time. They were machine-gunning me out there. Then this sub-chaser picked me up. Christ!"

Brad remembered seeing a sub-chaser tie up a piece down the docks. It hadn't shot a red flare, there seemed to be no troops on its deck, and he hadn't checked it.

Timmer wasn't finished. "Know what I was thinking out there? Get Timmer! That's what I was thinking. Get Timmer! Like the Jerry gunners had an order. The way they were gunning for me that's what I was thinking. Christ!"

That was all. The car rumbled through the darkness. Now Brad understood the man's resentment. He understood it clearly. The key was Timmer's vanity. The man who knew he was better than the professional had discovered he wasn't.

Brad leaned back against the seat and closed his eyes and listened to the wheels singing on the pavement. He laughed to himself. They weren't singing Valerie but he imagined he could hear it. Just a year ago, he remembered, he had been nominated Malton's "young man of the year." His picture had been in the paper, stern and scrubbed, the epitome of civic responsibility. He wondered how it had come about that he needed her so much. He wasn't that young, nor that unhappy, nor that lonesome. Yet he needed her. The very fact that the wheels were spinning toward her brought into play emotions he neither understood nor had ever experienced. For the first time he couldn't analyze a problem involving himself. The trustworthy look fore and aft over the years was failing him. He was living on a level of excitement and Valerie was part of the excitement and he wouldn't know until the excitement was spent what was her real place in the fabric of his life. Meanwhile the wheels were spinning and they were singing Valerie.

He heard Timmer's voice cry, "Pull up here!"

They were passing through a city. The night was black, but there were tiny flashlights weaving on both sides of the street, as though a great many people were strolling, and subdued signs marking the entrances to places of business.

"Pull up! Pull up, Arkinson!"

The car came to a halt and the sudden silence was dominated by Timmer's quick, heavy breathing. He said, "Got any money, Brad? Couple of pounds?" Brad handed him two pounds and he thrust the money at Arkinson. "We just passed a pub. Run back and see if they'll sell you a bottle."

The driver said, "What kind, Colonel?"

"Anything."

"You mean liquor, sir?"

"God damn it, I said anything!"

When Arkinson had gone, Timmer muttered, "They gave me a swallow of rum on the sub-chaser. Water was freezing."

Brad said, "I can understand, Colonel. That and the shock."

"What shock?" the other demanded. "I don't know what the hell you're talking about. Stop fussing! God damn it, stop this fussing!"

Arkinson came back with a bottle. "It's Irish whisky, Colonel. That's all they'd sell me. Came to twenty-six and six."

Timmer held out both hands for the bottle and the change. "All right, let's get going." He pressed the change into Brad's hand. "Swig?"

Brad said, "Not now, Colonel. I'm not up to it."

There was a grunt in reply. Timmer thumbed off the cap and, leaning back to steady himself, took a long drink, gasped, and took another. During the next half hour he took frequent swigs. Between swigs he rested the bottle on the seat between his thighs and stared out the window into the darkness.

He said, "They got guts, those Canadians. Jeez, they got guts. All kinds of guts." The monotone was gruff and virile now as Brad first knew it. "I don't mean only the troops going in. Hell, the poor bastards *had* to have guts. What else have you got?—going in with the Germans sitting behind their emplacements pretty as you please and mowing 'em down like dry hay. Christ, you never saw anything like it."

He chuckled inexplicably and took a long, gurgling drink.

"It's the boyo in command I'm thinking of. The battalion commander. *He* had guts. I tell you, Brad, you got to have it to take your battalion in there when it's pure murder. Going in there and getting shot up—that's all right, but the guy who's got to give the command when there's hardly a hope in hell, *that* takes guts, and whoever it was I take off my hat to him."

He chuckled again. "I know 'cause I was there, right in it. I couldn't believe it when our LCI's began moving into the beach. I knew we'd never make it. I kissed myself good-by a dozen times. Every reason, Brad. I guess there's no more'n half that battalion alive right now. No more'n half, prob'ly less. Takes guts to give orders like that. You got to have it. In the military business you just got to have it. Here's to the baby who gave the order——"

He drank again, but this time only a sip, for the bottle dropped from his hand and fell to the floor boards. Brad grabbed it and handed it back. Not much liquor spilled. There wasn't much left to spill.

The car slowed down and moved in a stream of traffic through a narrow street.

"What's this, Ark'son?" Timmer asked. His voice had become furry.

"Not sure, Colonel. I think it's Croydon."

Timmer said, "Say, boy, that's nice going. We're almost in. Almost in," he repeated. He turned to Brad. "Well, I guess Mister Ed Cantrell didn't win his gamble after all. This crazy coot Timmer went to France and got back in one piece. Whadd'ya think of that? Whadd'ya think of that, eh, Brad? Crazy coot goes to France and gets back. In one piece too. That'll shake Mister Honor Cadet. Eh?"

He took a swig out of the bottle and handed it to Brad.

"Here, take it. Lousy whisky. Plain lousy."

Brad took the bottle, which was nearly empty. Timmer's hand dropped to the seat between them and the big, handsome, stubbled face twitched and rolled from side to side until the car reached Brook Street where he lived.

Brad half ran toward Berkeley Square. The night was moonless but the sky bright with stars and he could make out the line of the curbstone and could hurry without fear of stumbling.

The moment he rid himself of Timmer, he had darted into a pub on Davies Street and had called Valerie.

Their talk had been brief and breathless. "Where are you?" she had asked, and the emotion in her voice had cut across his chest like a tightening rope.

"Just got back, Val. I——"

"You weren't at Dieppe?"

"No——"

"Thank God! Thank God! Come quickly."

"I'm on my way."

"How long will you be?"

"Three minutes," he had said. "Make it two."

He was panting when he reached the traffic island at the entry into Berkeley Square. In the pinpoint of shielded light he saw a woman's skirt and legs and he heard her lazy voice: "What's your hurry, Yank?" He said, "Sorry," and darted on. The gentle habit of a lifetime which bade him respond when spoken to asserted itself even in the case of a prostitute's solicitation.

"So am I, Yank," she called after him as he strode across the roadway to the south side of the square.

The emotional drive that was urging him on almost took him past Hill Street. He forced himself to slow down. He hadn't seen her in five days and he was wildly impatient, but he had always been emotionally mature even as a youth. He mustn't surrender now. He paced himself to a steady walk and his footsteps, still zealous, echoed in the quiet, narrow street. Then he heard her voice inquiring from a distance.

"Brad?"

He called out, "Val!"

Now he could hear her footsteps hurrying toward him. The street was impossibly black and he stopped to listen to the crisp sound of her walk. It seemed to him an exquisitely beautiful sound, ordered and graceful, a true echo of the woman herself. Then he darted forward.

They came out of the dark into the sight of each other and stopped. She was three or four feet from him, her hands thrust forward as if to touch him, and he thought he would die for the breathless compassion that played out of the upward curve of her mouth.

He took her hands and they stood looking at each other across the length of their arms, the fine discipline they had always practiced delicately balanced on the night air, but doomed.

In that blank and tremulous moment they were driven together by a force more compelling than they could know. He had seen her and that was power enough. Here, all about her, were comfort and tenderness and respite and also the roaring urges of life as it surely was intended to be lived. Here too were burying and forgetting. Here was the barrier flung up against the bulky men with full webbing, grenades, ammunition belts, and steel helmets, against the men peering inshore from the ships, against the scuffed jiggling boots, against the smell of ether at the surgical tent and the blood on the major's rubber apron as he sneaked a quick smoke between amputations, against the brigadier standing on the edge of the dock and calling out, "Damned good hunting, men, damned good hunting now," as if they could hear him or cared.

She had looked at his face, his eyes shining as if he were beholding miracles. Here was escape from the wasted nights and years of her young life, escape from the prison walls of "Darjeeling," from the hurt of reading John's letters and knowing he is going to die and sometimes, in a secret and tortured way, wishing he would die so the pain might at last cut hard and begin to recede. Here was escape in the face of a man she adored and who adored her and was here and wasn't going to die.

They clung to each other in the great black privacy of the night.

Presently they began to walk. They walked around the edge of Berkeley Square, up Hay Hill and along Dover Street, and then back toward her flat. The streets were deserted for it was past mid-

night, and they swung their linked hands and every now and again
each beheld the other in wonderment. London at war was a city for
lovers. The faint luster of stars penetrating the narrow streets provided the perfect light. They could behold each other as lovers
should, enough obscured, enough seen.

Timmer strode into the office the next morning, brisk, handsome,
and aware that every eye was upon him. As he passed Brad's desk
his lips spread in a grim, confidential smirk as if to say he was expecting trouble and was in great shape to meet it. Arkinson brought
in the day's first pot of coffee almost immediately.

Precious little work was done in the section that morning. Ray
Boyce had already heard as much as Brad proposed to tell, but
Marcus, Halloran, Gibbs, and the others clustered about Brad's desk
and pestered him for details of the escapade. There was broad spec-
ulation as to what might happen to the colonel. A number of outside officers visited Timmer during the first two hours and each face
was studied for hints and portents.

Then Timmer's door opened.

"Brad!"

Inside the office Timmer stood at the window idly surveying
Grosvenor Square. "What are they saying out there?"

"They're all dying for details, Colonel."

"Oh." Timmer tried to look displeased but didn't quite succeed.

Brad said, "I'm playing it close to the chest."

"Good boy. What do they know?"

"Apparently they knew last evening, Colonel. Somebody in the
building got a report you were missing."

Timmer laughed comfortably. The man was apparently as rugged
as he looked. There wasn't a sign of trauma. His face was fresh and
hard and lively. He went to his desk, poured half a cup of coffee,
and knocked it back in one huge swallow.

"Missing, eh? Well, nothing's happened yet. I'm still waiting for
the big chopper to hit me."

"An officer from Colonel Cantrell's section came in here yesterday
to check on the rumor."

"You bet he would." Timmer mused on the thought a moment. "By
the way, Brad, I wouldn't say anything about the bottle—I mean—
I don't want you to lie, it isn't that important and anyway I wouldn't

ask anybody to lie for me—but if the I.G. or somebody like that questions you officially, I'd appreciate it if you didn't volunteer the information. I was all right last night, wasn't I?"

"Yes, sir."

"I needed a couple of snorts. Canadian M.O. on the dock wanted to get me into a hospital for a couple days' observation—afraid of delayed shock or something—but I lost him quick. I knew a couple of snorts would fix me up fine." He chuckled quietly. "Missing, eh?"

"It was just a rumor. Apparently reached here about four yesterday. Somebody thought he heard it on a broadcast as near as I can put it together."

"All right, that's all. Just don't talk too much, Brad. I know you won't."

When Brad got to the door, Timmer said, "All hell should break loose any minute now. Don't worry about it. I can handle it."

Brad said, "I'm sure you can, Colonel."

But as the day wore on, nothing happened. Timmer grew restive and snappish. Late in the afternoon an order was distributed cautioning all ETO personnel against unauthorized visits to units engaged in active operations against the enemy. It was a general order; no names or specific incidents were mentioned. Brad realized the colonel was being deliberately ignored.

Timmer's ill-humor was comparatively mild until Part Two orders came down just before six o'clock. A paragraph at the bottom of a mimeographed page contained an order assigning Lieutenant Colonel Edward Cantrell to the headquarters staff of II Corps with the temporary rank of colonel.

Nothing at all happened to Timmer, not even a reprimand. Someone among the top brass had handled the situation neatly, cleanly, and with a murderous scalpel.

Only Brad knew how deep the colonel's disappointment was. "They're running a closed corporation," he growled, "but that's okay with me. It's still a long war."

## 11

MALTON was enjoying the best summer within memory. As Jay Elphinstone of the department-store Elphinstones told a war-bond rally, the city was forging ahead not because of the war but *despite* the war. Most of his listeners, recognizing a self-evident truth, cheered.

The weather had been warm but not burdensome; rainy enough for banner crops in the outlying districts and sufficiently sunny to encourage a veritable invasion of New Yorkers who, despite sharply increased prices, filled the resort hotels at nearby Lake Whitehead and whooped it up with an abandon befitting war-harried workers. The once-moldering shoe and textile factories worked two full shifts six days a week. Thousands of new residents, pouring into the city to man the freshly built aircraft plants, worked three shifts around the clock including Sundays, paid outrageous rentals for clapboard huts on porous foundations, and spent the rest of their pay in the Pentland Street shops. The *Star's* advertising linage often ran to more than seventy-five per cent of the available white space, and although Damien Lakelock fought hard to maintain an honorable balance for the news columns, the merchants demanded and got the space.

Damien, at dinner with his wife and daughter, spoke sorrowfully of the trend. He said, "We've got to give the people the news. Advertising is fine and necessary but a newspaper lives and breathes on the news it prints."

The publisher might have been talking to himself. There was no reaction whatsoever on the faces of his family. He addressed himself resignedly to his lake trout, it being a meatless day.

Grace Lakelock certainly wasn't listening. She was ruminating on the fact that it was not only people fighting in the war that got hurt. A mother's intuition told her that Jane was going through a crisis. The girl wore a taffeta cocktail dress altogether too decorative for an ordinary week-night dinner in the hot and windless weather. Grace recognized the symptom for what it reflected; Jane was seeking to bolster her confidence in herself as a woman. Moreover, she had very little to say, and Grace knew that symptom too.

When Jane excused herself after dessert and asked that her coffee be sent into the library, Grace waited an appropriate interval and then decided she too wanted coffee in the library.

She found her daughter curled up with a book.

"Aren't you feeling well, dear?"

"Perfectly well."

"It must be an interesting book you're reading."

Jane said, "It's a new one called *This Above All.*" She looked up, irritated. "You're not going to let Daddy have coffee all by himself."

"Oh, he's probably on the phone by now. He's on for hours these nights with that silly advertising manager. It's maddening the way they argue." Grace meandered along the bookshelves. "Oh, here's this new Smith book, *The Last Train from Berlin*——"

"Mother!"

"Good heavens, Jane. I was merely looking over the new——"

The girl sat up. "I know perfectly well, Mother, you haven't the faintest interest in the new books. Now what is it?"

"If you must know, you've been moping. It's upsetting your father." Grace, at fifty-one, belied her handsome, patrician appearance. She scarcely ever asserted herself except with the servants and had become addicted to expressing her anxieties in terms of Damien.

Jane said, "Did he tell you that?"

"He doesn't have to tell me. Lord knows I've lived with him long enough to know when he's upset."

"I've never felt better in my life and I'm not moping. My husband happens to be away at the war. I'm human enough to miss him and therefore I'm not terribly gay. Is that explanation enough or would you like me to go into detail?"

Grace, congratulating herself on having opened the desired vein of inquiry, picked out a comfortable chair.

"Good heavens, dear, I was a young married myself once. I understand these things. Have you heard from him lately?"

"Mother, I told you on Thursday I had a letter. Why don't you let me read in peace?"

"You didn't tell me what he wrote."

"There's really nothing to tell. He seems to be well and busy. He's still fascinated with England and with his work and why shouldn't he be? He's in the middle of things while I spend my days at the auxiliary with a lot of old crones who think they're winning the war when they bring sandwiches for the girls."

Grace said gently, "They're doing what they can. Is that all he said?"

Jane dropped her book and walked to the window and looked out. "Yes, that's all."

"Does he miss you?"

"How would *I* know?"

"Didn't he tell you?"

There was a pause. "Naturally."

"Then you *do* know," Grace said. "That's fine. Now there's something else I have on my mind——"

"Oh, Mother!"

"It won't take a minute, dear. Your father and I are thinking of going on a holiday trip after Labor Day so he can rest his mind before the election campaign. You know how conscientious he is about the *Star's* endorsements and how he worries over every editorial old Ben writes. I often wish we were straight Republican or Democratic; it's such a bother being an independent—especially this year with Brad not here to help. I think he should have a clear rest before the campaign really starts. Don't you?"

"Of course he should."

"I adore Mexico," Grace said brightly. "What do you think?"

"Perfectly fine."

"And I think in your present mood it would do you a lot of good too."

"I don't want to go."

"Your father would feel much easier in his mind if you did."

"Oh, Mother, you know it won't make a speck of difference whether I go or not."

"He'll worry about you."

Jane turned full around. "And therefore he won't have a good rest and he'll come back and have a nervous breakdown. So it's up to me. Is that it, Mother?"

"You're heartless, Jane. It's not too much to ask—that you come on a lovely holiday to Mexico."

"Are you and Daddy having spasms of conscience about me?"

"I simply must say I don't know what you're talking about."

Jane said sharply, "I'm talking about my idea for London."

"*That*. It was too ridiculous."

"I still don't see why. There were two—not one—*two* by-lines by women correspondents from London in this morning's *Star*. It would be the simplest thing for Daddy to send me over."

"Oh dear. I thought your father explained it to you quite thoroughly. You know the *Star*, Jane—or you should. We have a tradition. We're respected—good gracious, when your father attends the publishers' convention he walks like a god among the cheesecakers and the comic-strip Johnny-come-latelys. You must understand it, dear. The *Star* couldn't send the daughter of the publisher to London. Imagine going through the motions of getting permission from Washington, and think of the thousands of *Star* readers who are just as lonesome for their husbands as you are, why the whole state would be scandalized. Surely, dear, you can see that."

Jane approached her mother purposefully. "Daddy didn't mind using the *Star* to get Brad off to London."

"Whatever do you mean?"

"I happen to know, that's all."

Grace Lakelock was shocked by what the girl said but even more so by her grim, almost masculine attitude. She saw traces of old Everett Bolding's sclerotic features in her daughter's lovely face, and disturbed by it, she lost the thread of the discussion.

She said, "There's another reason, dear, and we might as well talk about it. You haven't had a child and both your father and I have been concerned."

"I don't see what one thing has to do with another."

Grace said gently, "I'm not prying. You needn't discuss it if you don't want to."

Jane took a chair directly facing her mother.

"I don't mind in the least. For the first couple of years I made sure. We didn't want a child quite so soon. And after Brad joined up it just didn't happen to us. We weren't lucky."

Grace nodded understandingly. She said, "Don't you see, dear? It's bad enough that Brad is in a place of danger. To have you both there would be unthinkable. You must remember, Jane, that you're something far more than another wife. You're a princess in a way—

and the last of the line. Family direction is the lifeblood of the *Star*.
You wouldn't want to imagine it running someday under the direction of a committee on behalf of Yale or the Malton General Hospital. It would die. You understand that, dear, don't you?"

When Jane replied she made no attempt to cut her sarcasm.

"Of course I understand, Mother. It doesn't matter too much if
Brad gets killed——"

"Oh, Jane! How can you——"

"—I can always marry someone else and breed a publisher for the
*Star*. Well, I happen to be in love with a man called Brad Parker
and I want his child or none at all! And Daddy might as well understand I'm not the *Star's* foal mare——"

"Jane!"

"—to be sent to any suitable stud farm. And as long as you're telling
him you might as well add that I know all about how Brad *just happened* to be transferred to London!"

It took Grace a little time to recover from the shock. She looked
strangely at her daughter and said, "You keep harping on that and
I simply don't understand. The army sent Brad. What did your father
have to do with it?"

Jane was waiting and ready with the answer. "Elsie Jaques sat
next to me at the auxiliary this afternoon. *She* told me—not in so
many words, but the meaning was clear. You know the way Elsie
Jaques talks—in rings with that airy fairy Boston accent. Well, she
told me."

"But what, dear?"

"That Sanford, as a member of the Armed Services Committee,
was glad to do it for Daddy despite the fact that the *Star* has endorsed his opponents in the last three elections."

"I still don't understand. To do what?"

"To have Brad transferred to England from Fort Harrison. I suspected it from the beginning when Sanford showed up at Brad's
luncheon."

"Jane! This is ridiculous! Surely you don't believe your own father
deliberately arranged to send Brad overseas. Surely, Jane!"

"Brad is a man. He's all man. He couldn't wait to get into the war,
to get overseas, and Daddy knew it. It's just like Daddy—he's so fond
of Brad. You know how many times he's joked, but seriously, about
not getting overseas in the last war. Well, he did it for Brad."

"But if, as you say, he's so fond of Brad, why would he want him overseas?"

Jane retorted bitterly, "Why don't you ask Daddy?"

It was all too complicated for Grace Lakelock. When she left the library she thought mostly about her daughter's fierce passion for Brad. She thought about it ruefully, for her placid life with Damien had never been more than discreetly emotional. She was sure he had made no such arrangements with Sanford Jaques. It sounded so unlike Damien to ask a favor of a politician. She wondered what could be turning poor Janie's mind against the world and her own father and mother.

In the living room Damien was on the phone. She waited through his long harangue to the advertising manager and then told him what Elsie Jaques had said. She muddied up the recounting because it was not clear in her own mind, and she was relieved to see Damien smile charitably and murmur, "Utter nonsense."

A moment later his brow clouded over. He picked up the phone and made a lunch date with Sanford Jaques.

They ate at a leisurely pace in the pleasant knotty-pine dining room which was part of the publisher's suite atop the *Star* tower and talked in a general way about the war. The Dieppe raid had been the big story in the *Star* that morning.

Damien speculated, "It might have been a stab at the establishment of a second front——" He observed that Jaques had begun to shake his head slowly and wisely. "If so, it must be counted a failure, I'm afraid."

"I know all about it," the congressman said. "It was supposed to go way back in June. Weather messed it up. No, Damien, we've heard from General Eisenhower on this whole subject of a second front. It's months off, years maybe. And maybe never. Churchill's dead set against it. He wants an African drive that'll fountain up into the Balkans. Great for England all right, but that's Churchill. Always in there punching for the Empire. FDR, I can tell you, has other ideas. No American boy is going to die to defend England's imperialism or Europe's rotten politics. He wants to hit the Nazis smack on the button, right across the Channel."

Jaques never used German when referring to the enemy. Nazi was safer. South Malton was filled with voters of German stock.

They conversed effortlessly through dessert. When Damien asked the waitress to bring an extra-large pot of coffee, the congressman was secretly pleased. This meant that Damien had something serious on his mind. It could be one of two things—Brad or the November election—perhaps both. Either subject could well turn out to be profitable. He had been waiting a long time for an opportunity to talk about Brad. If it turned out that Damien wanted to talk about the election, that was even better. It was not that he had any fear of losing; the recent industrialization of Malton had made the seat absolutely safe for a regular Democrat. But he harbored larger ambitions, the Senate or the governorship someday, and for this he needed the kind of state-wide prestige the *Star's* endorsement would give him. He awaited the coffee with some impatience.

Damien was trying to reappraise the congressman in the light of the touchy subject he was about to bring up. He had never been on intimate terms with the man although they had fallen into the practice of calling each other by their Christian names. Sanford Jaques was neither the kind of person nor politician he could instinctively approve. Damien was at heart a Democrat but the *Star's* congressional endorsements every two years scrupulously avoided a party inclination. Each candidate's personal qualifications and legislative record, if any, were carefully weighed against his opponent's. Jaques had never been endorsed by the *Star* since he first ran, successfully it turned out, for Congress on the Roosevelt ticket in 1936.

It was not that Damien regarded him as an evil or dishonest person. He had first captured public attention as a young attorney when he had won acquittal for seventeen union members up for manslaughter as a result of Malton's bloody labor riots in 1934, and although he had been investigated on charges of subornation of perjury he had never been indicted. Moreover, he had managed with such artfulness to charge persecution by Big Business that he was able to grab off the New Deal nomination in 1936. Even his political opponents grudgingly gave him credit for turning the brink of ruin into political victory.

In those days he possessed undoubted talent and few scruples on the hustings. When the *Star* endorsed his opponent he countered by reminding audiences that his father had been a lathe hand in Barney Lakelock's factory. "I didn't inherit the money to *marry* the *Star*," he cried, "but I inherited the *guts* to fight it!"

That was a long time ago, Damien mused. Six years in Washington had done something for Sanford. He had become almost a conservative, at least personally. He had taken off the chubby fat that used to squeeze his neck out of his shirt collar, his graying hair had given his face a certain distinction although his mouth was still large and loose, his voice had descended to quite pleasant levels, he ran a well-ordered home, and he was clearly veering toward the right wing of the Democratic party. Damien was the kind of man to understand that Jaques had been forced to play rough to pull himself out of his meager beginnings. Not everyone was fortunate enough to have had the upbringing Barney Lakelock's son enjoyed.

From the tower window they could see the noon-hour war-bond rally being conducted in Revere Square. The attraction was a bathing-beauty contest abetted by the charging music of the Malton police band. They looked out idly until a waitress arrived with a large pot of coffee.

Damien said, "Have we got everything? Cream? Sugar? Good." He nodded to the girl. "On your way out, Amy, tell Miss Grant I'm not to be disturbed. Thank you."

He opened the discussion abruptly. He said, "Tell you what's on my mind, Sanford. I want to clear up a little mystery about Brad's army assignment. Did you have anything to do with it?"

So this was it. Jaques was fully prepared. "What's the matter? Isn't he happy?"

"I've had no complaints, but that's not the point. I'm terribly disturbed about a story I heard." Damien went on to recount in somewhat more logical order what his wife had told him, and he added, "It first struck me as nothing more than coffeehousing until I remembered how I heard about Brad's new assignment. I think you called me from Washington a full day before Brad phoned the news from Fort Harrison, and now I'm wondering whether you just happened to see it in some army document or——" He stopped and looked steadily at the other.

Jaques smiled. "Elsie told me about it last night. Frankly, I didn't like it but apparently your daughter brought up the subject and persisted. She's a very determined girl, that daughter of yours."

"Sanford, you haven't answered my question. Did you have anything to do with Brad's reassignment?"

The congressman shook his head more in wonderment than denial.

"For me to answer that question, Damien, I'd have to dig into classified information you are not entitled to know."

"Then you did have something to do with it."

"Whatever I did or did not do, I followed my own best judgment. Why don't you let the matter drop?"

"Does Brad know anything about this?"

"Why don't you let the matter drop?"

"Sanford, I want an answer. I demand one."

"Of course not. Give me credit for knowing what kind of a man your son-in-law is. He hasn't the faintest idea. And let me assure you of something else, Damien. There is absolutely no waste manpower in General Eisenhower's headquarters. If Brad hadn't been assigned there, someone else, not nearly as qualified perhaps, would have been sent."

Damien's face clouded over.

"In other words, you had Brad reassigned."

"Oh come, Damien. What is this really all about? I'll give Elsie hell. She should have known better, no matter what the provocation. Now let's forget it."

"I'm not going to forget it. Brad volunteered in one of the most dangerous, certainly the toughest, branch of the army. I thought he was foolhardy but secretly I was proud of him. The fact that you gratuitously had him pulled out into a safer assignment leaves me no alternative but to let him know what happened so he can decide what action he should take. I owe it to him, to his record, and I also owe it to the *Star*. You understand that."

"If you'll pardon me for saying so, Damien, I think you're being foolish about this whole thing."

"I remember a campaign speech once about my money and your guts. You don't think I'm going to let you do the same kind of job on Brad someday."

Jaques sucked his loose lips in against his teeth. The line of discussion wasn't moving quite in the direction he had anticipated.

He said, "All right, I'll let you have the facts. You seem to think I was trying to get ammunition on the *Star*. That didn't enter my mind, nor, if you please, did I have any notion of doing you a service. I've managed to win my three campaigns without the *Star's* backing and, God willing, I'll continue to do the same. But you'll remember in my victory statement I promised I would represent *all* the people

of Malton, those who voted for me, those who voted against me, those
who——"

Damien cut in. "I'm waiting for the facts, Sanford."

"What I'm trying to bring out is that you and Brad happen to be
my constituents. I feel the same kind of duty toward you as I feel
toward my own campaign manager." He paused to peer into
Damien's face. He judged he had made no impression yet. "I regard
Brad as an outstanding young man, one of several outstanding young
men from my district who are in the service. I take an interest in
them. I follow their careers and assignments as closely as I can. Well
then——" He suddenly smiled. "Damien, I'm about to dip into classified information. I know you haven't anyone listening in."

The publisher said, "I don't want to hear anything I'm not entitled
to know."

"Damien, there are hundreds of people in Washington privy to
this information whose loyalty I wouldn't vouch for. I certainly feel
I can give it to you in strictest confidence. Whatever our political
differences I regard you as one of the best Americans I know."

The congressman felt he was back on the track. It wasn't often
he found a spontaneous opportunity to show his good will to the
*Star's* publisher.

He went on. "When Brad joined the Special Service Force I used
—well, frankly, some pressure to find out what the outfit was all
about. I found out more than even a member of the Armed Services
Committee should know. I found out——"

Damien said, "I don't want to hear any military secrets."

"It's past history. I assure you it's all right now. You'll remember
the force specialized in parachute jumping and winter warfare. I
found out it was organized for a specific mission—Operation Plough
it was called—to drop behind the enemy lines in northern Norway
and, listen to this, Damien, to destroy the power plants. If there ever
was a suicide job, this was it." The congressman said slowly, "The
surest kind of death or, if a few were lucky, capture."

Damien was silent. Jaques sipped at his coffee, feeling he had
gained complete control of the situation.

"The operation has since been cancelled, but I didn't know it then.
All I knew was that the chances of Brad coming home from the war
seemed pretty slim and *that* struck me forcibly. Brad isn't an ordinary
American boy. He's a coming leader. Malton is going to need him

after the war and so is the *Star*. I kept saying to myself, he's the only son of a widowed mother, he's the last of the Parkers, one of the real pioneer families of the nation, and if I may be so intimate, Damien, he also looks to be the last of the Lakelocks and the Boldings. I kept saying to myself, in war the best blood reacts first and flows quickest. Is the future of Malton going to be left to the 4-F's and the draft-dodgers?

"At the same time I knew the Pentagon's problem in connection with the build-up in England. They were hooking in all kinds of men with special talents, commissioning them directly. I didn't ask them to transfer Brad. I asked them merely to look over his record and if they, quite independently, thought him especially qualified, I *suggested* he be considered."

He bit the tip of a new cigar. "That's the story. Some day, God willing, Brad will come back alive and well, and the chances are he'll take off my britches on the editorial page of the *Star*. But I've got to do my duty as I see it."

He dropped his eyes and took a lingering sip of coffee. He knew he had made a fine little speech. He had scored like a ton of bricks. He had neatly maneuvered himself into the position of doing a priceless favor for the *Star*. But when he lifted his eyes, he was shocked. Damien's usually imperturbable face was hard with anger.

"You had no right to do this, Sanford, no right whatsoever!" The publisher's voice rose in pitch and intensity. "By whose leave, sir, did you interfere in Brad's life? I don't know what motive you had in mind but whatever the motive, you won't succeed! I promise you that!" His mouth quivered with anger. He hated being beholden to a politician. And there was more. He hated the prospect of writing Brad to tell him of this development. He was afraid of what Brad might do about it.

Jaques, dumfounded, said, "I swear to you, Damien, there was no motive. I do think you're being ungrateful——"

"Call me ungrateful if you like. I happen to know my son-in-law better than you do. If he heard about this, he wouldn't be grateful to you either. He'd be livid." Damien's anger came under control and he remembered that the congressman was his guest. "I'm sorry, Sanford. Perhaps I was too abrupt about motive. But you might as well know that's the way I feel, and I'm sure the way Brad would feel."

That night Damien went twice to his writing desk in the study, twice put pen to paper, and twice destroyed what he had written. He had always felt Brad was headstrong on matters of principle, perhaps overly headstrong. After all, the war was young. There could be no harm in thinking this out a little longer.

But there was one thing he needed to do. He put pen to paper a third time and wrote a memorandum so that Miss Grant could transcribe it first thing in the morning. It instructed Ben Carver that, no matter what the situation, Jaques was to be denied the *Star's* endorsement in the November election.

## 12

F O R Brad the autumn of that year of 1942 was singularly frantic and happy. The passage of those chill, wet months marked the last stages of preparation for Operation Torch. It was a time of overwhelming excitement in the closely secured war rooms at ETO headquarters.

The men in Timmer's section worked around the clock, snatching a few hours of sleep only when their senses refused to function properly, existing principally on coffee and, in certain extremities, benzedrine. They worked with urgency on a ponderous volume of operational orders designed to gather up the men and impedimenta of a great British-American force, to dispatch it in hundreds of ships of varying sizes and speeds over thousands of miles of ocean, and to fling it upon the North African shore on a schedule so tight that a delay of minutes might bring disaster. Timmer's section was an infinitesimal cog in the planning machine, yet the challenge fired each man with energy he could not dream he possessed and devotion the most dedicated would have denied.

Timmer drove them on, using his enormous vitality to set an almost impossible example. He had by no means abandoned his quest. The spectacular gambit having failed him, he was now determined to prove by sheer weight of work that he was the best staff officer in the ETO. He tongue-lashed the hesitant, derided the weary, flailed at the naval liaison for not keeping abreast of the pace he was setting, scoffed at the slowness of his British opposite number, and, so far as anyone in the section could divine, never slept.

Even Ray Boyce, who had been regarded as a chronic laggard behind the convenient façade of a thinking machine, even he fell into the spirit of the section. The political problems attached to an invasion of Vichy French territory were colossal. It was not unusual for him to enter a conference at eight in the morning and to emerge at midnight. At one point he disappeared for a fortnight under mysterious circumstances. When he bounced back into the office he was carrying what for wartime England was an unheard of delicacy, a bag of lemons.

He wouldn't divulge where he had been but winked a bloodshot eye and murmured, "I'm saving 'em. When this jig's over, we'll be the only people in England drinking real tom collinses."

As Timmer's personal aide Brad enjoyed a wider appreciation of the plan than most of the others. He was kept racing on a variety of assignments between his headquarters and Norfolk House in St. James's Square where the high command for Torch was barricaded. He was driven by the realization that this operation, if it could be successfully carried off, would mark the war's turning point, this in co-ordination with the British attack at El Alamein which was to be launched two weeks earlier. The effect on him was an exhilarating sense of purpose. Here were men's lives at stake and victory in the balance and a clean new world as the prize.

It was an altogether wonderful war. It had placed Malton and all its works in a conveniently tiny perspective. It had delivered him from the necessity of bleeding over carefully worded letters to Janie. He could truthfully scrawl a few lines saying he was well and furiously busy and would she forgive the brevity. And it had conferred sweet absolution on his meetings with Valerie, for the sheer physical strain of that autumn had transformed these from a clandestine delight into a fervent necessity. Exhausted as he was, he wished the war could go on forever this way.

They had discovered hidden in a mews off Park Street a nondescript little shop which showed an obscure figurine and an utterly inexplicable water color in its window but which turned out to be a tearoom. It was here that they met on such rare afternoons as Brad felt justified in taking a respite. More often they met at odd hours of the night. He would call for her and they would walk the dark, deserted streets, or when the weather was bad or the sirens had sounded, which happened frequently that autumn, he would stay a little while and she would cushion his head and they would be silent, more in blessed enjoyment of their nearness than for fear of awakening Bridget.

She had never asked what was happening but accepted the new regimen with such quiet understanding that he could have sworn she knew the plan. He began to suspect, in the lightheaded way of the exhausted and happy, that her Indian birthplace had somehow mystically touched her and that she was infinitely wise as well as hopelessly beautiful.

In early October she visited Burlingham for three days. She had been disturbed by the news that her father had presented himself to a medical board at Lincoln barracks and had demanded a final checkup.

Brad met her on her return to King's Cross Station. He had desperately missed her and managed to commandeer the time and Timmer's staff car.

"He's like a child," she said, as they drove back to her flat. "I mean in his sense of anticipation. He's put Mala to saddle-soaping his Sam Browne and he's got his Middle East map marked up exactly as if he were in command. Even his old Indian tropicals are cleaned and ready. He hasn't a chance, the poor dear," she said sadly. "I'm terribly afraid."

When they arrived at the flat she mixed a drink and talked of other, more pleasant things, as if realizing she mustn't send him back to work on a miserable note.

"I'm haunted each time I sit about 'Darjeeling,' " she said in a lightsome way. "I keep remembering you were once there—in our very living room—and I didn't know you. It seems quite impossible."

"Impossible nothing. Insulting," Brad grumbled. "You didn't even notice me in the jeep outside. I kept saying to myself 'Here's a dish' and practically stood on my head trying to catch your eye. Did you even know I was alive?" He shook his head in wide, sad sweeps.

She steadied his head and kissed him. "You're horribly vain and I hate you."

"And I hate you because you're so very ugly," he murmured. They kissed again.

"It's a pity you couldn't come with me," she said. "You'd love Burlingham now." She was speaking softly. The sound of Bridget's heavy breathing came like a metronome through the bedroom door. "It's not the same, not a bit. There's beer on ice in Mr. Pepper's pub and Council House runs up two flags now, the American as well. It took time, of course, time and casualties—that's the cruel part of it. The group are taking horrible casualties in their daylight raids."

He watched her mouth quiver a moment and then she smiled in reminiscence. "The most popular person in the village is a lad everybody calls Tex. He's the darts champion. They tell me there were forty people in the pub to watch him beat Mr. Clifton hands down in the final. The betting pool was fantastic. Our air-raid warden, they tell me, lost quite a packet."

Brad was content merely to listen. He thought he would never tire of the soft, ordered way she formed her words and the upward curl of her lips when she related something amusing.

"There's something else," she was saying. "I know it's a bit much but you simply must take my word for it. My dear, dear Brad, the Americans—are playing cricket! Mr. Pepper is coaching them and they've developed a star bowler, a warrant officer named Agostini. Mr. Pepper tells me he's a find, almost good enough for county, and they're all wonderful at fielding.

"Yes," she said, "everything has changed, everything and everyone. Everyone, that is, except Father."

As October wore on the pressures of Operation Torch became immense. This was the first massive American challenge of the war in the European theater and it was being mounted largely by men who had been unsuspecting civilians a year before. The word snafu became the commonest expression at headquarters. The men who used it to criticize their own work bore down all the harder.

Brad fairly reveled in the absorbing duties which fell to him. His moments with Valerie became more scattered and therefore more precious. He enjoyed being groggy for want of sleep because of the anxiety he saw in her deeply set eyes. He enjoyed her stern commands: "I insist you take Sunday off, and if it's fine we'll drive up to Richmond and spend the day doing absolutely nothing but look at the river." He even enjoyed her reprimand when he found he couldn't take Sunday off: "I don't think I ever want to see you again. Your head's going to pop and what good would you be to me addle-brained?"

Everything about that autumn was happy. Even the sirens which sounded regularly at nightfall made welcome music in his mind, pointing up the purpose and the drama. Best of all, he didn't have time or energy to ponder the direction along which the two of them were careening.

It didn't matter. The overwhelming circumstance of war obscured the future. In the desert and the Pacific, within the very borough of Marylebone, people were dying by enemy violence. Those who lived, lived for the present. The purview of his life extended to the target date for Torch. Beyond that the future was impenetrable to his mind's eye.

On the morning of November 8, however, the great British-American force swarmed ashore at Casablanca, Oran, and Algiers. The future into which he dared not look had overtaken him.

It is doubtful whether General Eisenhower and his personal staff at Gilbraltar awaited the first reports with more intensity than the men of Timmer's section. They gathered at the office as first light emerged hesitantly out of a rain-swept sky. Timmer was already there. They thumbed through the available Signal Corps reports, which contained nothing new except that an American cruiser had been torpedoed one hundred miles short of Algiers, and sat about with inordinate stillness through the morning hours. Timmer moved among his officers like a careworn impresario, dropping a word of appreciation here, a word of encouragement there.

Ray Boyce nudged Brad. "Nelson at Trafalgar," he muttered. "It'll break his heart if somebody doesn't shoot him. Go ahead, Brad, be a pal."

The first reports which arrived shortly before noon were garbled and inconclusive. Patton's task force at Casablanca had met unexpectedly stiff resistence from the French garrison and there were hints of a naval action in the harbor of Oran. The haggard, subdued men continued to pace the office. Then, in midafternoon, came the signal from the key point, Algiers. It read, in the graceless jargon of the military: D-day objectives secured, tactical surprise extreme, casualties light, scattered.

The men, huddling over the signal, began chortling about the biggest binge in history. Ray barked sternly, "Synchronize your watches, men. Rendezvous at four, 37 Grosvenor. Password, tom collins."

A few moments later, Timmer's door opened. "Will all officers please come in." His voice was surprisingly soft and weary.

They gathered about his desk and watched him rub his stubble in slow, thoughtful strokes. Ray, who was standing next to Brad, whispered, "Foch after the Marne."

"Men," Timmer said, his small eyes spearing the coffee rings on his desk blotter, "I want personally to thank each and every one of you. This section has done a horse of a job. We showed 'em. We won't get any credit for it—hell, we don't expect any—but I want you men to know how I feel personally."

He ranged the circle of faces around him. "Just one thing." His eyes fixed on Boyce. "That was lousy security, Ray, bringing back those lemons. You knew there wasn't a goddamn lemon in England. I'll pass it this time but you'll never know how close you came to a court-martial." Ray, it turned out, had been one of a party of officers that had scouted Spanish Morocco in search of a line on Arab political attitudes.

"All right, men," Timmer concluded. "Go and get boiled if you like."

Timmer's complaint served to make a merry party at 37 Grosvenor even merrier. Ray piled the priceless fruit on a platter, christened it "Boyce's folly" in a mock ceremony which included the anointing of it with a few drops of gin, and proceeded elaborately to mix the first "real, honest-to-goodness, genuine tom collins in the United Kingdom and to hell with the redundancies."

When everyone had been served, he lifted his own glass. "I give you Alex Timmer," he said gravely, "guardian angel of the security of these islands, high priest of the password. If you will examine these magnificent lemons, you will see that each is stamped with the deathless device Sunkist. I bought 'em in Portsmouth from a chief storekeeper of our beloved navy. Charged me five bucks, the larcenous bastard."

All present clicked glasses and proceeded to drink. Collinses were being passed out in such profusion that Brad felt it necessary to appropriate two of the lemons so that Valerie might enjoy the windfall when she arrived from work.

It still lacked an hour before she would be off duty. They had promised themselves a gala evening, drinks at the apartment, dinner at a French restaurant on Jermyn Street, and dancing at the Savoy. But, glancing about the apartment, he was troubled. The girls some of the men had brought along were questionable.

Boyce had invited a red-haired, somewhat overstuffed girl who was a barmaid on the Strand. Molly was her name and she had been

in the show business. On the urging of several drinks she proceeded
to prove she could shimmy better than Gilda Gray ever dreamed of.
Gibbs's girl, a brunette with a figure like a sapling in a high wind, let
it be known she was the granddaughter of an earl, then drained a
tumbler of neat gin and was rigorously silent thereafter. Ray had
made a special point of asking among others a tech sergeant named
Felder who did German translations for him. Felder, a small, sad,
bespectacled refugee whose parents had died in the ovens at
Nordhausen, had brought along a girl who was equally small, very
young, and grossly overpainted. She told them in a timorous Lanca-
shire accent that her name was Dolores but subsequently confessed it
wasn't really Dolores. She hated her real name which was Dora and
changed it the moment she got away from home to make her living in
London. On the sidewalks, Brad suspected. Marcus and Halloran
had started a noisy crap game in the hall.

The party roared along, silenced only for a brief interval when Ray
turned on the six o'clock news. The reports showed a rapid extension
of the Allied triumph. A note of excitement betrayed the flat neu-
trality of the BBC newsreader when he announced that Berlin had
reacted violently. Vichy France, it was rumored, was being occupied
all the way down to the Riviera.

"Perfect!" Ray chortled. "Absolutely perfect! What you are witness-
ing, ladies and gentlemen, is the emergence of America as a world
power. We were never really a first-class power, always kidded ourselves that we were but we weren't. Our foreign wars, especially the
last one, were piddling affairs but Torch is the breaking of the shell
and what is being hatched is a genuine world power. Mark this, I
tell you! There'll be bigger battles and Torch may be forgotten as a
military operation, but not by the historians. It's proved we've got
what it takes. From now on we Americans are *it*, God help us!"

Everybody yowled happily except the earl's granddaughter. She
crinkled her nose and knocked back another tumbler of gin. Brad,
increasingly concerned, managed to maneuver Ray into the kitchen.

"When do we break this up, Ray?"

"Never, old man, until the gin runs out."

Brad said, "Valerie should be along in a few minutes."

"Fine! Do whatever you like. I'm going to give Molly a snoutful of
gin and pop her into bed. This is the occasion. If there's one thing
that goes better than sex and war it's sex and victory."

Brad fought down the retort that came to his lips. He said, "You know damned well I can't bring Valerie into this kind of a rat race."

"Say, you've had the wrong kind of training," Ray said lightly. "My wife would adore a party like this."

"What I want to know is, how can we get rid of these tarts?"

"One, we can't, and two, why should we?"

"I won't have Valerie——"

"Oh, come now, Brad. Every now and again this New England stuffiness of yours gets out of hand. This is London and war and Valerie understands it a lot better than you think."

"You don't know a damned thing about it. Or about Valerie for that matter."

Ray said, unruffled, "What you need is a little perspective. You've gone hog wild over the war. It's just another experience. For those who don't catch a bullet, it's another trip out of town in a long lifetime. Someday you'll realize what a goddamn fool you're being at this moment and you'll reach over and kiss your wife a couple of times and she won't know what the hell hit you. For God's sake, pull yourself together. Hey there, Molly!"

Molly was doing her shimmy act again, this time holding aloft two tumblers filled to the brim. She moved in quick rhythm toward the two men. "You see, dearies," she shrilled, "it's all controlled from the shoulder muscles, all from the muscles. You don't have to move your shoulders a bit." Brad shuddered.

The moment Valerie arrived, Brad found that his apprehensions had been foolish indeed. Her presence seemed to have an immediate and sedative effect on the other girls. Felder's little friend squeaked, "Awfully pleased to meet you, I'm sure," almost curtsied, and shrank into a corner. Molly sat down for the first time. The earl's granddaughter shook herself out of her rigor and came partially to life, but her accent was so crisp it was unintelligible and after a time she gave up. Halloran and Marcus gathered up their dice and their money. By the time Brad had prepared and brought out her drink, the party had become focused on Valerie as if she were the guest of honor. She moved about the room easily, warmly, rekindling the merriment but on a new level. Brad observed the change with pride. It was simple, he thought; she's a queen.

Later, as they were riding to Jermyn Street, he said, "Turned out not a bad party. Ray of course is stark, raving mad. Can you imagine him lecturing to college students? I'm sorry though about those girls."

She smiled a contemplative smile. "I loved the sergeant's little girl. She's tarty and shabby and her face needs a good old scrub, but she's the war, Brad, just as surely as the raids and the rubble. When it ends we'll all have to pick ourselves up, all of us, and make ourselves clean—if we can."

He recognized the mood. He said, "You've heard from the desert."

She said, "You're wonderfully prescient. I wish you weren't." She looked out among the bobbing flashlights on Piccadilly. "Yes," she said, "I had a letter today. It's Major Wynter now. They've given him the company."

She didn't tell him that John's unit had been thrown into the line at Alamein and that the former company commander had been killed. She didn't need to tell him. From the tone of her voice he divined as much and more.

Fortunately for him, the French restaurant still maintained a prewar cellar. Mumm's '37 at ninety shillings the bottle was, in the circumstances, a wonderful bargain. It was not that he felt reproachful about being a non-fighting soldier. Torch had been a triumph of meticulous and imaginative planning. The men at headquarters had done the biggest part of the job, and he for one was content with his role. Movie heroics, he was convinced, didn't win wars. Nevertheless, the feel of parachute wings on his blouse was a distinct comfort. That and the champagne.

It was difficult not to be proud to be an American in the atmosphere which prevailed behind London's blackout curtains. For two weeks the divisions at Alamein had been toasted and prayed for, and officers in U.S. "pinks" had been looked upon as a species of spiv. Now the Americans were having their innings. Ray Boyce had expressed it exactly. America, overnight, had proved herself a world power.

They dined handsomely on mousse and steak (the restaurant kept hidden a larder for champagne drinkers) and talked foolish and wonderful talk which sprang from an abundance of wine and the joy of being carefree together. When dinner was over they fairly frolicked down the Haymarket and across Trafalgar Square to the Savoy and fell eagerly into each other's arms on the small dance floor on the embankment side of the hotel.

She was supple and danced beautifully, and the way she held herself as if she were a trifle afraid of him was part of the fugitive quality in her he adored. He knew he possessed her as surely as if she had surrendered herself. That was all he needed to know. There were moments during their dancing together when he felt a height of pleasure too dizzy to contemplate, and other moments when he was overcome with a sense of futility and helplessness. But these latter moments proved fleeting. A swallow of wine provided the perfect antidote.

They danced every dance, and for long blissful periods they were lost in each other. Then, suddenly, while the band was playing something lilting and innocuous from an Ivor Novello operetta, she said, "Please let's not finish this one. Please not, Brad."

They glided to a halt. She said earnestly, "I do apologize, Brad."

"Did we barge into some very special song?" he asked, as they returned to their table.

She faced him honestly. "Nothing like that, darling. Don't ask me why it happened. I simply don't know."

A waiter refilled their glasses, but now the magic had gone out of the wine. She did know, he thought, watching her over the rim of his glass. Her eyes were glistening. It was as if the whole structure of their lovely evening, like Cinderella's midnight, had come crashing down. She made no objection when he called for a bill.

They walked slowly and silently into the Strand, savoring the clear, crisp night. Presently they found themselves on Pall Mall. They stopped to peer at the bits of glinting sky showing through the skeletons of gutted buildings which once housed the famous clubs of a dim and distant England. Then they passed into Carlton Gardens and down the steps to the Mall.

From a bench along the walk they studied the squat lines of the old state mansions. They heard Big Ben strike two o'clock. Every now and again snatches of drunken laughter came out of the gloom and careened roughly across their ears. They sat close together, their hands tensely clasped, and for a long time they suffered the dishonest silence which had fallen over them.

Then she said, "What has happened to us, Brad?"

"Too easy," he said bitterly. "Give me a hard one."

"We can't go on this way."

"It's my problem. You're in the clear."

"In the clear," she echoed "It's sweet of you but it happens not to be the case." Her tone was soft and curiously impersonal as if she were whispering a brief to some third party standing on the walk before them. "I let it happen. There was no point at which I didn't know what I was doing. That is, until now. I can't go on and I can't stop. I'm hopelessly adrift. And don't blame the war, darling. The war has nothing to do with—with us."

A picture of Malton emerged out of a deep crevice of his mind and came vividly before him, merging with his awareness of the old state mansions and the snatches of drunken laughter.

He said, "I didn't come loaded for bear—believe me, Val. I remember too well how it was the first time I saw you standing by the jeep out there in the rain. You were pretty—no, you were beautiful. I'd never known an English girl before and I thought it would be nice if I could give this one a whirl, a nice romantic whirl for a nice well-bred English girl, something I could put down on the credit side of the war and think about someday when I'm full of business and belly. That's the way it started," he said, "but it didn't last long that way. A couple of days. Maybe just the couple of hours on the train."

He had been talking into the graveled verges of the path and now he lifted his head and turned to her. "I'm the villain in the piece. I'm married to a girl who loves me and I'm sure prays for me every night. And I'm married in a hundred other ways. It's my problem. You're way out in the clear."

She gave a little shake of her head and her face took on a look of compassionate authority as if she had lived a much longer time and was wiser. He didn't resent the look. It reflected a quality that made her so unlike any other girl, constantly elusive, constantly challenging.

She said, "If there's a villain in the piece, it's me——"

He began to speak, but she pressed her finger across his lips.

"It's me, Brad. Of course you didn't come loaded for bear. You see, I know what goes on inside you—I wish I didn't." She smiled fondly and distantly. "You're a strange intermingling of little boy and old man. It would be so much easier if I didn't know. I wish I could see you now as I saw you that first day on the train—gay, attractive, a bit fresh, not very endearing, very American. How simply it would have turned out! We would have danced and drank a little, and probably we would have had an affair, a happy physical thing with a little intelligent emotion tossed in for my benefit—to put me a cut or two above a Hyde Park pickup. That's the most we really wanted.

"That much I could have blamed on the war. I would be doing what thousands of Englishwomen who have men serving overseas are doing. A little bed has become something less than a sin in London. It doesn't matter if you are physically unfaithful as long as your emotions are under control. After our years of scars and discipline it was going to be fun to take over the perky, undisciplined Americans. It was going to be easy, a bit of wartime horseplay to cheer us up."

She looked at him and her eyes wept without tearing. "I didn't count on my emotions playing me false but they did. The process was reversed. And now it isn't horseplay at all. It isn't even cheerful, my darling. It's deep and hurting and I can't help myself. But I've got to try—I've got to try hard."

He thought, How wrong the English are about us. We Americans are the most disciplined people on earth. Especially this American. We got where we are because we're dumbly dedicated to home and career, to a routine that would drive us nuts unless, once in a lifetime, a war comes along and we can get up on our hind legs and holler and wear a holster low on the hip the way our grandfathers did and test whether we've still got the toughness they had. You, Val, were part of the hollering process for Brad Parker, American, dumbly dedicated to wife, mother, and career, but it didn't turn out that way, not by a long shot. I'm in love with you and I can't go on without you.

That is what he thought. He said, "Don't ask me to stop seeing you. I won't. I can't."

She said, "You're not helping me."

He shook his head and tightened his grip on her hand. A helmeted policeman emerged out of the dark, paused to peer at them, and passed on up the Mall toward the palace.

She said, "You dance well."

"I dance well with you."

"I wish you didn't."

After a silence she said, "I wonder if the standard is flying from the palace."

"What difference does it make?"

"It means the King is in residence. It doesn't mean anything to you."

He said, "I can understand what it means to you."

"I wonder——"

Suddenly the sirens began to scream sickeningly over the quiet city. Out in the open the sound came at them from many directions. When it died out they heard the boom of guns far down the estuary. It didn't seem important for them to move. They sat listening to the distant salvos with a dull curiosity as if the ruckus concerned people they didn't know or care about, and then searchlights speared up in the park all around them and a shattering blast of gunfire struck their ears. They scrambled along the Mall toward Trafalgar Square and reached the shelter of Admiralty Arch just as another blast shook them.

Now they could hear the roar of many planes. All the guns nearby thundered in quick succession. He pressed his hands over her ears and held her close against the wall under the arch. In the bizarre reflections of weaving light he could see her deeply set eyes gleaming with excitement.

The guns fell suddenly silent. Only the searchlights continued to scour the night sky. He loosed his hands from her ears.

"Frightened?" he asked.

She said, "No, darling. I was thinking it doesn't matter about us. The war will make it right. God alone knows how, but I'm sure the war will make it right."

She smiled in her half-sweet, half-anxious way and then the guns started up again.

## 13

W H E N Brad dashed into the office the next morning, half an hour late, a meeting was already in progress. Through Timmer's open door he saw the whole complement of officers grouped around the colonel's desk.

Trying to move as inconspicuously as possible, he edged to the rear of the semicircle and peered in over Halloran's shoulders. At first glance he judged that Timmer had enjoyed the championship binge of them all; his face was pasty and the flesh under his rugged jaw hung loose. He looked like a terribly beaten man. But his eyes were furtive as ever. Brad knew he had been spotted.

"Sorry I'm late, sir."

"Forget it, boy," Timmer said with a strange, dispirited amiability. "I was just telling the men it doesn't pay to break your back to do a job, it doesn't pay to show 'em how a section should work. Our reward," he said miserably, "just came down from on high."

He picked up a sheaf of documents stapled in thin batches, weighing it in his meaty hand. "Looks like a bunch of goddamn diplomas. No men, you can bet your sweet fanny they're not. They're orders. The goddamn team is broken up. How do you like that?"

His eyes roamed angrily across the semicircle of faces.

Brad didn't realize the full import of Timmer's bitter remarks until the man began to flip the pages disgustedly. "Crandall to II Corps, Oran . . . Marcus to OPD Plans, Washington . . . Halloran to AFHQ, Algiers——" He slapped the documents on the desk. "They're all yours, men. Come on and pick 'em out."

The officers closed in on the desk and rummaged eagerly among the documents, like women around a bargain counter. Each scanned the pages for his own name and then ran his eye down to see what his new duties would be.

Brad didn't go near the desk. He couldn't quite believe he might have to leave London and hesitated to make sure. He watched the other officers as they came away from the desk. Some were non-committal, most seemed disappointed. Ray Boyce waved his orders and winked happily. "Luck's holding, Brad. Free French liaison right here in dear old London. Me for the solid life. What did you draw?"

"I haven't looked."

"Might as well. It only hurts for a little while."

Brad said grimly, "Might as well."

He pushed through to the desk. Timmer, his chin resting on his fists, scowled about the room as if he was disgusted that no one had expressed regret at the breakup of the team.

"What happens to you, Colonel?"

"Me?" His voice dripped with indignation. "Operation burial, that's for me. I'm shifting downstairs to Movement Control. It's a doozie all right. Operation burial." He added in a low voice, "You know what I mean, Brad. The bastards!"

Boyce and Timmer—both remaining in London! Brad reached hopefully for the last remaining set of orders on the desk and quickly ran his eyes over the top page. His orders were to report for duty to the G-3 section, Allied Force Headquarters, Algiers. Travel authorized by first available aircraft. Priority two.

His mind fell to Valerie. The war *had* made it right. The war had made it so goddamn right! He wondered if this is what she meant, that the unpredictable paths of war would fix everything. It hadn't occurred to him last night. Now it flew shatteringly into his mind.

He scarcely heard Timmer's voice: "At least *you* feel it, Brad. I knew the minute I laid eyes on you you were a great team player. It's tough, boy."

He nodded briefly in Timmer's direction, not knowing quite what the man said, and walked out of the office to his desk. He wondered how he should break the news to her. There was time. The first available aircraft certainly wouldn't be organized for a day or two.

It was delayed that long and three days longer, but he never managed to see Valerie to tell her.

In the late editions of that day's evening papers, almost buried among the black headlines and detailed stories of the Anglo-American triumph in North Africa, a small item recorded the news that Brigadier Frederick Hassard Russell, C.B., D.S.O., M.C., had been found dead of a pistol wound in the head at his cottage in Burling-

ham. The chief constable, the story went on, stated that it was clearly
a case of death by misadventure while the balance of the mind was
disturbed. Except in *The Times* the following morning, there were no
details of his life history and military record. The news of America's
emergence as the ranking military power on earth filled all the available space.

The DC-4, though fully loaded with some fifty American soldiers
who sat in a bower of bedrolls, kit bags, rifles, a jumble of parachutes,
and at least three guitars, remained earth-bound on a hard-stand at
Northolt Airport.

The passengers, mostly enlisted men, had emplaned in high spirits
but now they had been waiting more than an hour for the aircraft to
take off. "Come on, Cap, let's go!" someone shouted. This set off a
cacophony of cries dominated by one iron-lunged soldier who kept
chanting, "Hey there! Gotta date in the casbah!" Then as if by signal
they all began to clap their hands rhythmically.

Brad was infuriated by the racket. It was impossible to concentrate
on Valerie's letter, which he had received just before he had left
London. He wished he were the senior officer on board; he would
have blasted them into silence. But he happened to be the most
junior of the four officers in the party. For purposes of the flight a
civil-affairs major had been appointed O.C. troops. He was a slickly
barbered man of middle age who worked an unlighted cigar up and
down in his mouth and made a pretense of enjoying the rowdiness,
probably, Brad suspected, because he knew no way of controlling it.

Brad tried once more to read the letter. It was impossible in the
aggravating racket. He wanted to study each sentence, each word.
Finally he shoved the letter in his pocket and made his way over the
litter and the bodies to where the major was sitting. He said, "You're
O.C. troops, aren't you, sir? Can't we get rid of this racket?"

The major removed the cigar from his mouth and looked at the
lieutenant's parachute badge and then into his face. He grimaced
uneasily. His own blouse was spanking new and bare of decorations.

"What the hell, Lieutenant. It passes the time. Let 'em enjoy themselves."

Brad turned away without a word. The noisy confusion rang in his
ears and he thought of London as if it were already a distant memory,
of the people who could stand quiet and motionless. He remembered

the trans-Atlantic flight and its frightened, whispering passengers. That was only four months ago. Americans sure learned fast even when it came to contempt for danger.

The cockpit door opened and the pilot, a youthful captain with a flattened nose and a crew cut, emerged.

"Attention, men! God damn it, I said attention!" He got immediate silence. "I want you to listen carefully, men. If you look around this airplane you'll see we got a lot of portholes. It's a transport airplane, not a bomber. You'll also see we got no curtains to black 'em out. Go on, look at 'em!" He paused belligerently. "All right. Our route takes us over the Bay of Biscay during the night. That's enemy air. The sky's full of German night fighters and they're lookin' for nothin' else except to shoot us down. So as soon as we level off in flight we'll have about half an hour of daylight. You men can smoke up during that half an hour. After dark the glow of a single cigarette will bring on the night fighters sure as God made little apples. You men understand? All right. Fasten up for take-off."

They climbed steeply and steadily through cloud for a long time. When they straightened out they were beneath a pale blue sky. Brad lit a cigarette, reclined against his overstuffed kit bag, and took Valerie's letter from his pocket.

She had written: "My dearest— The saddest of all duties is done and now I am back in my living room at 'Darjeeling.' I buried Father this morning. Looking back on it, to my memories of him as far distant as India, it seems that he really died two years ago in a place called St. Omer and only the great strength of his love for England carried him back for a spell so he could take a last look about before making it final. His one sin, if it be a sin, was his love of this island. It was not a gentle love, it was fierce and blind, a dangerous kind of love whether it be for a land or a person. I've never told you about my mother. She too loved fiercely and blindly but hers was a selfish love. She accepted all, gave nothing. Never the sweet ache of sacrifice as I feel it, knowing you are flying off, away from me. Someday, God willing, I will tell you about her.

"I had your sweet and troubling telegram yesterday, and my life was flung back suddenly into the old dreadful pattern. I'd forgotten how much I hated the war. Perhaps it is just as well that your news came to me yesterday, for in the presence of death it came easier than it would have otherwise. But that was yesterday. Now, sitting alone here, it is unbelievably hard to know you will not be in London when I return. Where shall I walk now? Which streets are open to me where we haven't walked together?

"I sometimes hate my own England. I sometimes think we have lived too long, we English, and are too content with our own wisdom. I thought of it yesterday when I heard our coroner, Dr. Feather-hulme, mumble the formula—death by misadventure while the balance of the mind was disturbed. I felt it was a poor tribute to a gallant soldier whose balance of mind was not at all disturbed. He had made his choice, and, having made it, he knew exactly what had to be done.

"His last day, as Mala described it to me, showed how clearly balanced his mind was. In the morning mail he had received notice from the War Office that the medical board had turned him down for active service. Later that morning he put on his service dress with decorations and attended a memorial service for the dead of 632nd Group. Do you remember me telling you about the American warrant officer named Agostini? The one who had turned out to be a star bowler? The village organized the memorial service when it was learned that the plane in which Agostini was bombardier crashed in flames while returning from a raid on Kassel. I can imagine what Father thought, what dark and curious feelings he must have had when he attended the service.

"He apparently went from the service to the bank and arranged with the manager, Mr. Baragray, to establish enough principal to provide a small pension for Mala. Then he came home and drafted a letter to Tamarga and Boland, a law firm in Calcutta, invoking a trust fund which had been left to me by my grandfather but which I had never claimed. In the evening he took a long walk about the countryside. He came back in time to listen to the nine o'clock news. After that he had tea. Mala thought it was unusual for him to ask for tea at that hour and inquired whether he was feeling well. He said to her, 'I rather fancy tea tonight if you don't mind.' When she came to his study to remove the tray he talked with her about India, about the early days. Mala tells me he didn't mention my mother but she noticed that the conversation was confined to the very short period before my mother ran off. (Yes, my darling, she ran off.)

"About a quarter hour later, Mala heard the shot. You and I were at the Savoy, as nearly as I can estimate, just at that time.

"I don't know what I shall do about 'Darjeeling.' I can't bear the thought of selling it. Of course Mala will come to London with me. I'll find a flat, with luck, where she can carry on. Dear Mala! The way she goes about the anguished business of clearing up after the dead, she is much more the tight-lipped Englishwoman than I will ever be. Yet she is Indian in the way she seems to understand that it is right and honorable to sacrifice oneself on the altar of one's forefathers. The link with the past is more important to her than the present or the future. She did her quiet weeping and now she is dry-eyed and very proud indeed of her master.

"What more is there to say? The war is like the sea. We cannot know it or control it. We can only pray its moods and tides may be favorable to our fate. I love you, my darling, and I am desolate. Val."

He read the letter over and over again. He could see her in the sitting room at "Darjeeling," her lips curling upward sadly and sweetly, and he could hear the velvet hum of rain on the common and the brush of her sleeve over the paper as she wrote. Then suddenly the roar of the plane's engines assailed him, and the tough happy talk of soldiers off to a strange and exciting bivouac.

The sky was darkening. Beneath the plane's wing, he peered down the cliffside of a huge gray cloud. They were over the sea but not far out, for there were tiny ships bobbing on the whitecaps and barrage balloons weaving and straining from their decks in the squally weather.

He looked down at this last bit of England and remained glued to the window until a black cloud bank moved irrevocably beneath the wing like a curtain being drawn across a stage. This was the end, the end of England. As he turned from the window he felt himself the first Parker crying farewell as if this were his home, his haven, his country, and Malton something dim and unreal.

He remembered there was another letter and he reached into his pocket. It was the regular letter containing tear sheets of the front and editorial pages of the *Star*. Miss Grant mailed them every day. The light in the plane was failing and he glanced idly at the front-page headlines. There was nothing of great interest. The Democrats had won the off-year elections and Sanford Jaques had scored a landslide. Who cared?

He lay back against his kit bag and listened to the high scream of the engines and closed his eyes in surrender to the galloping darkness.

He was bounced into wakefulness by a hysterical shout.

"That ol' eighter from Decatur, baby!"

The plane's windows looked out on a pitch-black night, but inside the cabin a diffused light rose from the floor boards. In the tail section the men were huddled close together. A pair of dice rolled happily in the beam of a flashlight. The well-barbered major, still chewing an unlighted cigar, was waving a fistful of bills in the center of the huddle.

Brad scrambled over the heaped-up baggage. "For God's sake, Major, do you want to get us all killed?"

The major kept his eyes on the dice until they rolled to a stop. Then he looked up and winked broadly. "Keep your shirt on, Lieutenant. There ain't a man here smokin'." The players howled with laughter.

It really didn't matter. Lying against his kit bag he thought that if the war ended tomorrow he couldn't go back to Janie. He couldn't be so dishonest. Let the Luftwaffe trap them. The way he felt about it, the plane could be a flaming torch plunging into the sea.

But no such clear solution presented itself. The DC-4 rumbled through the night, the crap game progressed noisily, and when the first streaks of dawn bounded across a clear blue sky they were still flying over water but the green-and-white coast of Africa could be seen lying off the wing tip to starboard.

## BOOK THREE

## The Challenge

## 14

BRAD came upon the code name Overlord toward the end of a miserable winter in Algiers.

In the months ahead he was to know the word in all its awesome significance and to pulsate to it as an ancient pilgrim might have pulsated before the Holy Device, but even the first time, when it was merely an unfamiliar code name in a top-secret dispatch which moved routinely across the communications desk, it held him in momentary fascination.

Code names were in common use that winter in the G-3 section at Allied Force Headquarters; names like Operation Husky which, if all went well, would send the American Seventh and British Eighth armies cracking into Sicily, and like Baytown and Avalanche which embraced the more distant prospect of an invasion of the Italian mainland. But these were ordinary code names selected from an approved list and designed to cover a logical extension of operations in the Mediterranean.

Overlord was something apart. It hadn't appeared on any approved list and it was clearly removed from the Mediterranean theater of operations. So much he knew. The rest was exciting conjecture, for even in the little community of men cleared to handle top-secret messages, Overlord was an enigma. Studying the word, he felt it had the sound and glow of *the big one*. The big one, as every staff officer dreamed it, was the inevitable dagger thrust across the Channel into the heart of Hitler's *Festung Europa*. Whoever had chosen the code name, he reflected, possessed a finer flair for semantics than for security. Overlord! It fairly heralded the massive and the climactic as if with a flourish of trumpets.

He pounced on the word each time it appeared thereafter. Eagerly and surreptitiously, as an enemy agent might, he examined the context for clues and portents and he fitted each flimsy detail into an imaginary frame of reference, hoping that a clear pattern would emerge. As the winter wore on, his clandestine groping became more important to him than his work on the communications desk, for it was not the war that concerned him, only the ungovernable tides of the war. Any operation which might conceivably carry him back to England was infused with magic.

That whole winter he had found himself interpreting the war in terms of Valerie. In early December when the British had raced to the last hills before Tunis and AFHQ made ready to roll its headquarters eastward, he had felt himself hopelessly trapped in the currents of the Mediterranean war. Then the rains swept down and the Germans counterattacked boldly at Djedeida and the move eastward had been cancelled. Though his conscience bade him be wretched for his countrymen dying in the Tunisian mud, he was content that he had not been drawn farther away from Valerie. And now Overlord, mysterious and provoking, had materialized to nurture his hopes.

He had come to hate Algiers quickly and violently. It was hardly possible, he thought at first, that a man freshly footloose from Connecticut should find the place unbearably dull and he tried to revive the urges of his boyhood when the mere mention of Algiers would have conjured fabulous dreams. He tried but it was no use.

In his dismal view the casbah loomed neither romantic nor mysterious; it was a depressing slum, merely older, filthier, and more leprous than American slums. The city itself which gleamed so magnificently from its surrounding heights turned out, on closer inspection, to be rundown, discolored, and crowded. The civilians they had liberated from the Nazi yoke proved neither gallant nor joyous; only cynical, dejected, and disgustingly commercial. Exotic African pleasures were cunningly organized into a commodity that could be measured out and sold by the yard to roving bands of troops on leave from the front. It rained most of that winter, and when it didn't rain a pneumonic wind swirled columns of dust up and down the streets. It was a city of whores, petty thieves, dysentery, repellent beggars, black markets, murders, and various unhappy intellectual pastimes among which America-hating stood primary and chronic.

Even his duties fitted miserably into the pattern of that winter. The section was an integrated British-American group commanded by a happy, dissolute British colonel called Robey, who knew a cushy job when he had one and gloried in it. The section lacked spirit and challenge, and despite daily preachments from the top command the Americans openly resented the British and the latter suffered their parvenu brethren with a sort of tight-lipped condescension. The officers' clubs, dedicated to the ideal of inter-Allied brotherhood, soon splintered into national anthills of malevolent gossip. When the Tunisian front bogged down after the American setback at Kasserine, the gossip became loud and barbed and an occasional fist fight enlivened the long nights, cutting deeply into the fiction that officers, even British officers, were of necessity gentlemen.

Almost at once Brad divorced himself from the rumbling unhappiness and withdrew into a secret existence of his own. He was billeted in a murky building called the Pension d'Alsace and here, after duty hours, he fell into the custom of drinking by himself, not to excess but so regularly that his monthly ration of two bottles of whisky and three of Algerian brandy scarcely met his needs.

The whisky rarely lasted more than a week and for the rest of the month the brandy, harsh as it was, became a necessary companion in the long evenings. The atmosphere of his room was cold and peculiarly sickly and the massive furniture, chipped relics of an outmoded colonial prosperity, glowered at him from every wall. When he had made himself sufficiently warm and heady, he would dip his hand into a bureau drawer he had reserved for Valerie's letters, select one blindly, and settle down to read it as if it were newly arrived. He played the little lottery almost every night and felt properly foolish, but the liquor helped a good deal. There was always something in her letters—a paragraph, a line, a phrase—that brought her wonderfully into the room.

"My thoughts are yours," she had written. "Keep me near you wherever you go, no matter how far . . ."

"I hate the war," she had written, "and yet I find myself fearing it will soon end and then, my darling, we shall be face to face with a strange, quiet reality. I wonder how it will be and I dread it. What the war has done to us all! . . ."

"Lately I have felt a longing for India," she had written. "It really isn't as inexplicable as it sounds. India to me means childhood and childhood means escape—coward that I am! Escape into escape itself, into the big, the teeming, and the lost. But it's only a child's dream. Alas, we are grown up . . ."

This last letter was his favorite. He would count himself lucky on the night his groping fingers picked it out of the drawer, for he too suffered a dream which wasn't really a dream. It came out of memory and cut on his mind with the hardness of a copper engraving. He would see again the early days when he was sure he was in love with Janie, their drives to Lake Whitehead in the spring of their courting, and then their wedding trip and the wonderfully touching abundance of her happiness.

Often he tried to divert the memory before it could burgeon in his mind, but his New England conscience, which was savage and sadistic, would not abide the cowardice and he would be forced to argue it out inside himself.

He had not been dishonest with Janie. Their romance had been right and their marriage right. Everything about it had been blindingly right; his mother's secret pride, the quiet affection beaming out of Damien's gray, rich man's face, and the future stretching out like a thick, soft carpet to the end of his life, and above all, Janie's full-flowing contentment. He would think of all these things which were so right, but now he knew there were fiercer fires and he had never really been in love with Janie.

He wondered how long he could continue the deceit. The time would come when all the raid sirens and church bells and engine whistles and human throats would scream shrilly, it would all be over, and he would be left alone with the decision. His mind would try to leap forward to the time, to taste the steel of the decision, but it was useless to try, just as it is useless to try to embrace the moment of one's death, knowing it is approaching, because the moment is too vast or too infinitesimal to comprehend beforehand.

Thus the winter passed in anguish and loneliness and surreptitious pursuit of the meaning of the operation code-named Overlord.

On an evening balmy with the afterglow of an early spring sun, his telephone rang and a voice in an outrageous falsetto began, "Ees zeess you, Brad? Zeess ees Claire, cherie. You 'andsome Americaine, you 'ave been 'iding from your pover petite Claire. I 'ave 'ad zee police searching for you everywair in belle Algair, cherie . . ."

He listened with mounting annoyance and then suddenly, delight-edly, he recognized the voice of Dan Stenick.

He had taken only a step or two into the overcrowded café at the Hotel Aletti when Dan's stubby body fairly lunged at him from across the room. Dan was clearly mellow and smelled overpoweringly of bad cognac but there was no question of the genuineness of his wel-come. He thumped Brad's chest, threw an arm around his neck, and loosed a flood of affectionate profanities. Brad had to struggle free.

"Dan! I'm delighted to see you. What are you doing here and how the devil did you find me? Let's go get a drink."

Dan remained athwart the doorway. "Why, you good-lookin' bastard, you haven't changed a bit! Get this pot of mine. Nine days on a trooper out of Baltimore and I ate like a pig. How's the staff business? Jeez, I figured you for a general by now. Get *me*, bud."

He pretended to polish the captain's bars on his epaulet, but Brad had noticed something else. A Silver Star led off his row of territorial ribbons.

"That?" Dan cackled. "Between us, boy, it's a fakeroo. You heard, eh? We jumped on Adak. What a frost! The Japs skedaddled couple weeks ahead and the colonel's got a face as long as your arm. So me and my boys we get sent out on patrol just to make sure they're gone and we have a dust-up with a few who were left behind. You never saw such scared little yella fellas in your life. We bring back six alive and kickin' and the colonel is so goddamn proud he's in a war he hits me with this here Silver Star. Do I care? It's the moolah that counts, boy." He made another gesture of polishing his captain's bars. "Remember Martinez? Well, he gets hung up in a tree and breaks a leg in three places comin' down and I get the company. What a racket! I tell you it's a swell goddamn war. I——"

Brad clapped a firm hand over his friend's mouth. It was like old times. Dan's exuberance had already begun to pump animation into his flagging existence.

"Hold it, boy! I've got to get a word in here. I want to know how you are and how a guy gets from Adak to Algiers. Okay. Talk."

"Talk he says! Who wants to screw around Adak? So I get me a transfer to the Rangers and they ship me all the way to here and to-morrow I move up. Place called Tunisia. Ever hear of it? Cap'n Stenick, sir, of the Rangers reportin' for duty." He fashioned a clownish salute. "You know what? The way it sounds I feel like I'm Nelson Eddy. Cap'n Stenick, sir, of the Rangers reportin' for duty. Right off the cob."

Brad said, "You go up tomorrow?"

"Yep. In the mornin'. They're flyin' a bunch of us out to Bône."

Brad felt certain he knew the operation. It was a small affair code-named Transact, the details of which had recently moved across his desk. Three Ranger companies were to sail from Bône to seize an out-flanking bridgehead east of Tabarka as a cover assault for the spring offensive. He remembered the naval liaison arranging follow-up ships to provide for twenty per cent casualties the first day and eight per cent for every subsequent day until the link-up.

He said, "What the hell are we standing here for? Let's go get a drink."

Dan whirled around. "Holy God! I left my girl alone in this snake pit. Come on, boy!"

The large café surged with the roistering soldiery of three nations. The British and French were grouped around their separate tables, drank mostly *vin rouge,* which was the cheapest item on the tariff, and amused themselves by watching the fearsome traffic at the stand-up bar. Here were the affluent scotch drinkers, largely young American officers, a sprinkling of war correspondents, and a bizarre assortment of Frenchwomen with hard, appraising eyes. The black-out curtains flapped loosely against open windows and on the street outside French raid wardens blew on their pea whistles and shouted indignantly that light was showing. No one inside seemed to bother about them.

Dan led the way muscularly through the smoke-filled confusion. "Jeez, I'm glad to see you," he said. "Missed you like hell, 'specially up in Adak. Ain't this a town, though! Minute I hit the place I—uh, uh, trouble ahead."

A gangling young air force major, wearing pilot's wings, was sitting at Dan's table, talking to the girl who was there. He looked up through half-closed eyes and drawled, "Hi, Cap'n, I like this babe."

Dan pushed in between the major and the girl. "Screw, flyboy. She's been drinkin' my drinks."

The major smiled lazily into his glass. He was sodden, slow, and happy. "Tell you what, Cap'n. Let's you and me go outside. Guy that comes back gets the babe. Okay?"

Dan said, "You're out of your mind, bud."

"You don't look yella t' me. How about it?"

The matter was quickly settled. Dan cuffed the glass out of the major's hand, grabbed his thumb, and bent the top knuckle inward. It required only a sudden twist to send the man writhing to the floor. His eyes stared upward in shock and pain. Dan increased the pressure. He said, "You been flyin' too high, bud. More oxygen down there?"

"You son of a bitch, you're breaking my firing thumb!"

Dan gave it another twist for good measure, then lifted the man by his armpits, and shoved him toward a phalanx of waiters that had gathered around.

"Jerk," Dan mumbled, winking at Brad. "Where were we? Oh yeah, this is a great town. Look what I found."

The girl, who had sat through the encounter languidly nursing a pony of cognac, was small and slim except for the violence of her bosom line. She had auburn hair and a narrow, hooked nose set upon a cunning but disinterested face. She wore a silver-fox stole too proudly, like a newly earned medal.

"Zeess ees Claire," Dan announced. "Baby, zeess ees Brad, my pal from America. You see the resemblance, eh? First cousin to Clark Gable, but watch it, baby. He's married, see? Wife in America. Beautiful wife. You comprennay?"

She smiled indifferently. "I unnderstan', honey."

"Okay," Dan sang out. "Let's order up." Peering about for a waiter, he spotted his recent adversary, who stood at the bar rubbing his injured thumb. He chuckled. "Learned that twister out in Omaha back around '36 when I was a company cop in a packin'-house strike. Felt sorry for the poor bastards who were strikin' but I had to eat too. Hey there, waiter! What you drinkin', Brad?"

"Scotch. Tell me, Dan, is there anything you haven't been at one time or another?"

"Not any more," came the happy reply. "All my life I'm a bum and suddenly I'm an officer and a gentleman with medals yet. It's a great war. Full of democracy. Wouldn't miss it for a million." He leaned over and gave the girl a smacking kiss on the cheek which she accepted passively. "We been in love two days. Who knows? We might get married yet. Eh, cherie?"

She smiled a tired smile. "Kood be," she said dubiously.

"Damn right, could be."

When the waiter arrived with the drinks, Brad swallowed his quickly and ordered another round while the waiter was still there making change. "You've got a head start on me, Dan," he apologized. It was a strange thing for him to do, drinking before the others. He didn't know what made him do it.

Dan chortled, "That's the idea, tootsie. This got to be a big night. Who knows when we get together again." He said to the waiter, "Make this one a double for my son's benefit here."

It was a good atmosphere in which to drink for the purpose of getting drunk. Corks popped, Americans argued and occasionally scuffled, and there was the obscene laughter of easy women. All over the café waiters debated indignantly with their clients about the size of the tip, and the raid wardens outside continued to shout their futile threats about the curtains. A lance corporal from a Scottish regiment sank to the floor in a corner, his balmoral hanging over his eyes, and played a lament badly on his bagpipes. When a Scots officer came in, the piper's friends lifted him to a chair from which position he played louder but no better.

For a while the drinks and Dan's rough, happy face filled Brad with a warm and wonderfully nostalgic feeling, especially when Dan told him about the Adak drop.

"Say, that Bellenger turned out okay," Dan related. Lieutenant Bellenger had taken over Brad's platoon at Fort Harrison. "Real good. Goddamn colonel cited him for platoon efficiency but some of the guys figured you had a finger in that pie. I remember askin' Ryan if he missed you and he says, 'Sir'—you remember the way he talks, chin up at you like a pistol barrel—he says, 'Sir, the platoon commander I got is always the best I ever had.' That Ryan! Still the best top kick in the business. If the Japs don't get him he's gonna wind up with service stripes up both sleeves and down his back and around his rump."

Brad drank steadily and the liquor opened his memory to names that had long lain neglected. He asked how Artie Claverack had worked out. Artie, a full-blooded Sioux, had been the best natural jumper in the outfit.

"You kiddin'? How you think I got this medal? Artie! He can smell a Jap five miles away if the wind is right. Led me right to 'em." Dan gulped at his drink and put his arm around his girl by way of keeping the franchise. She put her fur piece on her lap so he wouldn't ruffle it. He said, "Say, you remember Bossin?"

Brad remembered Jerry Bossin, a big shaggy man with the face of a prophet, full of courage and hate for the enemy. He didn't have the reflexes to make a good jumper and he always needed Brad's intervention to save him from being washed out of the force.

"Comin' down on Adak he broke two legs. Not one. Two! Squealed like a pig when they shipped him back. Never forget the way he kept hollerin' from his stretcher, 'I'll be back, fellas, just hold everythin', I'll be back,' like we can't win the war without him. And young Allen. Sure you remember him. Gene Allen. Cute baby-faced kid. Well, he got himself a Bronze Star . . ."

Dan went on and on, and Brad found his warm and wonderful nostalgia turning into bitterness. Dan had an exasperating way of waving his freedom like a flag, at least that's the way Brad felt about it. He was free to live the war, free to fight and to make an ass of himself and even to die. He had always envied Dan his freedom but never as much as now. He looked at the girl with her cunning face. Algiers was full of girls like her, former shopgirls clinging to the belief that it wasn't whoring if you didn't walk the streets. Dan was even free to marry a cheap bitch like her.

Dan said, "You're gettin' sad, boy," and wildly snapped his fingers for a waiter.

"I was thinking about Adak," Brad lied. "I'd like to have jumped with the outfit. At least once."

"I should've kept my goddamn lip buttoned."

"You're nuts. I wanted to hear all about it."

"Still should've kept my mouth shut. Say, you want Claire to get you a girl? She's got swell friends."

"No."

"There's one that's a beaut. What's her name, baby? You know, the tall dark one."

Claire said, "Dragitsa. You want I telephone?"

"She's a Pole or somethin'. Smart as a whip and she's got what it takes. What do you say?"

Brad said, "To hell with it. Thanks anyway."

Dan said, "What's wrong, boy?"

"Nothing's wrong."

"You know I love you, you bastard. Now tell me what's wrong."

"Nothing particularly. It's been a lousy winter."

"Got the brass ridin' you?"

"No."

"Then what the hell is it?"

Brad thought a moment. Then he said, "How did you work the transfer from Adak to the Rangers?"

"Why d'you want to know?" Dan was drunk, but he asked the question cagily.

"Just curious."

"You don't lie well, tootsie. High-type guys are lousy liars."

"I'm collecting material for a book called *The Legend of Dan Stenick.*"

Dan winked at the girl. He said, "You got to love this guy. Honest, Brad, there wasn't anythin' to it. After the first dust-up, Adak was dead. Strictly an occupation job and brother, you can have it. Coupla Eskimos, fog, and the lousiest USO shows you ever saw. So I put in for the Rangers. Thing to remember is the army never refuses a transfer from a non-fightin' job to a fightin' job, 'specially the Rangers. They figure if you're crazy enough to put in for the Rangers, you got it comin' to you. How you doin', Claire baby?"

The girl had been quiet. She didn't seem to mind being ignored, and when Dan began paying her extravagant attention, touching her about the neck and ears, she accepted it with a certain inner amusement.

Brad was glad enough to lose Dan for the moment. He didn't want to explore the point any further.

A scuffle flared up in the corner of the room where the bagpiper had been playing and a lot of waiters and people from nearby tables converged on the scene. There was a crack like the breaking of a chair and a flood of oaths shouted in white anger. When order was restored it was found that the bagpiper hadn't been involved at all. He was still slumped in his chair, playing mournfully off key. The antagonists turned out to be the same gangling air force major and a captain of the Free French.

"That flyboy is sure lookin' for trouble," Dan said. "I should've bust him in two. Still," he said, "I wish he'd smashed the chair over that Scotchman. Those bagpipes are killin' me."

The tumult in the room bore in on them now that the first flood of their talk was spent, and Dan suggested they go to another place, the Bar Georgette. "It's a real nice saloon," he said, "piano and singer and anyway it's Claire's hangout. She gets a cut off the drinks. Eh, baby?"

"Yes," the girl said.

Brad got up. "I'm shoving off, Dan."

"You nuts?"

"It's your last night," Brad said, blinking at the girl.

Dan said, "Over my dead body, boy. The three of us are goin' and we're goin' together. I break my neck two days tryin' to find him and he wants to shove off."

Having made the proper gesture, Brad was quite willing to remain with them. He was drunk but not drunk enough. There was part of a bottle of scotch in his room, but drinking with Dan was better. He always suffered a gutter feeling about drinking alone.

As they left the café they saw the air force major teetering over a table and leering at somebody else's girl.

"You know what?" Dan chuckled. "Bet he's been grounded. I've run across guys like that. Get a desk job and they think they're lucky and then they get the miseries and after that they go around fightin' in bars tryin' to prove somethin'. Like that bum." He nudged Brad. "Think I'm talkin' about you? Goddamn right I am. Always remember they put you where they need you. So don't go off the deep end."

They decided to walk. The night was soft and the sky, low and dazzling, cast a wonderfully silver sheen on the palms that lined the boulevard. The girl conducted them across the boulevard and into a tangle of shadowed alleys. They passed through a narrow street which was thronged with groups of American and British officers. The men were congregated outside a huge dwelling of Moorish design and there was much banter and three military policemen regulated traffic in and out of the dwelling. The girl made a spitting noise and hurried her two Americans through the street and into a wide thoroughfare where there were tramway tracks and many cafés.

The Bar Georgette was a small place decorated with threadbare velvet drapes, dim lights, an ancient grand piano, and other evidences of faded elegance. As soon as they entered it became clear that Dan was a celebrated client. The *patronne*, a fat stern-faced woman, came from behind the cash register, which was mounted above the bar like a pulpit, and embraced Dan and also the girl. A bald-headed pianist plunged fortissimo into the "St. Louis Blues."

The service here was prompt (the only other clients were a warrant officer and a girl who sat in a motionless embrace as if their mouths were glued together) and the drinks came up as fast as they could drink them and sometimes a little faster. It wasn't necessary to order; Dan was that kind of celebrated client. Drinking was sheer pleasure. The piano tinkled out some pleasant, unfamiliar melodies. With the *patronne* looking on, the girl fussed tenderly over Dan but not enough to intrude on the drinking and the talk.

Dan said, "Stick to your guns, boy. It's going to be fine. Fine war."

Brad said, "Feeling no pain right now. None what—so—ever."

"That's great. Great. What time's it? Anybody know what time's it?"

The girl said, "One o'clock and twenty minutes. Much time."

Dan winked. "Don' worry, Claire baby. We'll run up a plenty big bill. That's what I like 'bout this girl. Square shooter. She gets a cut and that's okay with me. Okay with you?"

"Okay with me."

"Okay. We got lots of time."

"What time's your plane?"

"Got to report at seven."

"Where?"

"Transport Command. Don' ask me where it is. I don' know. I don' know my way around here at all without Claire baby. You goin' to get me there, eh, Claire baby?"

The girl said, "Don' worry, sweet'eart."

Brad said, "You know, Dan, you could've knocked me over with a feather when I heard you on the phone. I've been meaning to ask you. How did you find me?"

"Claire."

"What do you mean—Claire?"

"Knows everybody. Got on the phone to some guy in the provost marshal's office and he had you taped one two three. Great gal this gal." He gave her a smacking kiss.

Brad said, "I mean, how did you know I was here?"

"How did I know?" Dan rubbed his chin. "How *did* I know? Jeez, I must be gettin' drunk." Suddenly he exploded. "Holy jumpin' Jerusalem! I must be outa my mind! I got a message for you!"

Brad put down his glass and tried to focus on his friend. "What message?"

"Jeez, I got a real good message. Almost forgot too."

"Ready to receive message. Roger and over."

"It's a pip the way it happened. I'm in Baltimore this one night 'cause we're sailin' in the mornin' and there's a dance at the big canteen they got over near the burlesque house and——"

"What's the message, boy?"

"It's comin', tootsie, it's comin'. Well, a lot of balloons float down from the ceilin' and we're supposed to grab 'em for prizes and what d'you think I draw? The one thing I got no use for at all—a free telephone call anywhere in the U.S." He chuckled and drank part of his drink. "Would you believe it? Here I get a free telephone call, California if I like, and there ain't a soul I want to call. Then I say to myself I'll call the doll and see where that bum is, so I get put through to Malton and I get the doll on the phone and she seems pretty happy to hear from me and we talk awhile and she says 'Where you off to?' and I say 'North Africa' and suddenly she's cryin' or somethin', anyway she's all choked up, and I say hello hello and then she tells me you're in Algiers and she says 'Will you do me a favor, Dan?' and I say 'Sure, doll' and she chokes up again and then she says 'Tell him I love him' and that's the message except I can't tell you the way it came through over the wire, kind of got me right between the eyes the way she said it, 'Tell him I love him.' I tell you, boy, that gal sure goes for you. We better drink to the doll. Here's to the doll. Bottoms up on this one for sure."

Brad pushed back his head and drank his drink. The ceiling spun about, but his mind was startlingly clear.

*So she knew.* It wasn't possible, but she knew. It couldn't be, but it was. She knew. *Tell him I love him.* Janie wouldn't say that to her closest friend. She wouldn't say that to her own father. Not quite like that. Not emotionally. Janie's proudness was a hard proudness. It was old Everett Bolding's hardness covered over with a terrible sense of aristocracy. *Tell him I love him.* She would never say such a thing to Dan Stenick. To Dan of all people. Her terrible sense of aristocracy rejected Dan. *But she did.* That's how he knew she knew. Now he could see perfectly why she knew. The letters he had sent her riffled through his mind and of course it must have been perfectly obvious to her. He had tried to hide it, but the way the letters riffled through his mind he could see them all at once and of course she knew. She knew because she loved him.

There was another drink placed on the table and he reached for it. He wondered if it was good or bad that she knew. He made a snap decision. It was bad. It was bad because she was hurt. He shuddered to think she was hurt. He loved Janie in a very special way. Hell, one couldn't live three years with a girl as fine as Janie without shuddering to think she was hurt in the most vulnerable way a girl like Janie could be hurt. It was a bad thing because the time hadn't yet come. Perhaps the time would never come. Perhaps she need never have known. He might even be killed. *The war will make it right. God alone knows how, but the war will make it right.* It was a bad thing that Janie knew.

Dan said, "Got you, eh? Got me too."

"Thanks for the message."

"Perfec'ly okay. Here's lookin' at you."

They drank and after a while Brad said, "I've been thinking of asking for a transfer to some other outfit." He was lying. He had just thought about it.

"What outfit?"

"Outfit like yours."

"Nuts. With the doll and all back home you got to be crazy to go stickin' your neck out."

"I'd like a shot at a fighting outfit again."

"It's the liquor talkin', boy."

Brad thought, It's the liquor talking all right, and then again maybe it isn't. *The war will make it right.* But I'm not in the war. I'm not gambling. I'm getting a free ride. There's no balance in this thing. No balance at all. I haven't earned Valerie. I haven't earned the right to hurt Janie. Whatever it was I went to war for, I haven't earned it.

In this single drunken blistering moment it was all perfectly clear. He said, "I'm serious, Dan."

"You're bein' ridic'lous. They need you where they got you."

The pianist came to life, pounding out "I Can't Give You Anything But Love" and somewhere in the room a girl sang the lyrics in French. Claire pulled Dan to his feet and they began to dance. They danced very close and the *patronne* turned off some of the lights. Brad felt like a peeping Tom watching them. He was glad when he found a fresh drink on the table.

He remembered Dan going away with his girl, winking and saying

they'd be back soon, but they didn't come back and after a time the
girl who had been singing sat down beside him.

She was a tall girl, well made, and she had thick brown hair. She
looked like Janie in a general way and when she said she drank only
champagne he ordered a bottle for her and laughed inside him.
Maybe all tall girls with thick brown hair had a sense of aristocracy.
She fed him sips of her champagne and in a little while he laughed
inside him again. Maybe she was Janie's projection chasing him
down. She looked enough like Janie to make it funny and he felt like
the character out of Chekhov, not quite like the character out of
Chekhov because that fellow was tragic and he was enjoying himself
imagining she was Janie's projection and knowing she wasn't. Then
she said she couldn't finish the whole bottle by herself and he
switched to champagne to help her finish it. She told him she was a
refugee from Sarajevo where she had been a *vedette* in the big cafés
and she asked if he wanted to go home with her. He enjoyed this too
because he knew he wasn't going to go home with her. She said she
was sure he had never been with a Slav girl otherwise he would be
happy to go home with her. He laughed inside him because he imagined it was Janie's projection testing him and he wasn't going to
be caught in *that* trap. He settled his bill and gave her a thousand
francs and went out, but not before she kissed him sweetly and said
he was very gentle because she needed the money so badly.

The stark light of morning hurt his eyes and made his head go
around. He wasn't so drunk not to know he was very drunk. He was
unsteady on his feet. He leaned against the steel shutters of a shop-
window.

It *was* the liquor talking. He had no intention of volunteering for
the Rangers. God knew he wasn't a coward, but God also knew he
was in love with Valerie and she was in love with him and all he
wanted was to get back to England. The steel shutters went around
and he retched, and he thought, retching, of the illuminated scroll
in the *Star's* lobby and his name listed beneath the fancy lettering:
In the Service of God and Country. An Arab's *calèche* plodded by
and he hailed it and rode to his lodging.

## 15

WHEN summer came and all of Africa had been conquered, the dignitaries poured into Algiers. They came from London and from Washington and filled the VIP villa in the hills overlooking the city and the sea.

The people from London looked trim, aloof, and omniscient, even in their tropical shorts, and accepted victory as though they had won it handily by themselves. They underplayed the role so well that the American dignitaries, a few Pentagon generals but mostly ebullient congressmen, were made to feel like carpetbaggers. It wasn't that the British didn't partake of the eating and drinking, the luxury of the villa, the honor guards, and the wonderful bargains in the special PX shop for VIPs. That was the trouble. They partook fully but they seemed to accept everything to the manner born, which secretly infuriated the Americans.

Sanford Jaques arrived in the third wave of congressmen toward the end of August.

Brad had been informed a week in advance. The British chief of his section, Colonel Robey, had summoned him into his office.

"I say, Parker," the colonel had said, "are you one of these queer American fish known as a P.I.?"

"P.I., sir?"

"You must be, you know. I've got an order here seconding you for three days next week. Escort duty for a party from Congress. Usually a job for some blighter on Ike's personal staff." Most senior British officers referred to the general as Ike because it sounded American and very cosy.

"I don't know what you mean by P.I., Colonel."

"Don't really? Well, maybe you aren't." Robey screwed up his face, which was swollen red from a lifetime of happy drinking. "Anyway, pop around to Colonel Lessing in G-1. He'll give you the form. And for your information, P.I. stands for political influence. We have 'em in the British army too, only we call 'em DBNs. You know. Don't be nasty to this chap sort of thing."

On his way to G-1 Brad thought bitterly about Robey's remark. Influence! Almost every week individual officers were being detached from AFHQ for duty in England; he hadn't been among the lucky ones. Influence indeed! But he wondered how he had come to be selected for escort duty. When he reported to Colonel Lessing he found out quickly enough.

Colonel Lessing, a careworn American with milky eyes and a nervous habit of puffing continuously on a cigarette, asked abruptly, "How well do you know Congressman Jaques?"

"Reasonably well, Colonel."

"How well? First-name basis? That well?"

"Yes, sir."

"Helps." The colonel puffed jerkily at his cigarette. "I'll be escorting the party. You'll be my aide. It's tricky. Never know what they want. Very tricky." He talked the way he smoked, in short puffs. "Some want to go shopping. Easy. Some want to go up front and look the enemy right in the eye. Got to be talked out of it. Always one who wants to know all the plans from here to the end of the war. Toughest. Got to be handled carefully. Very, very carefully."

He shuffled some papers on his desk. "Trouble is you and I are cleared for top security. They're not. They get very touchy about it. Understandable. They're our bosses. It's a funny situation. But—crazy thing, war."

They discussed the details of the visit. There were six congressmen in the party, and Brad was to concentrate on co-ordinating their daily schedules and seeing that they didn't wander afield during their tour of the War Rooms at headquarters. He was also to check the special PX and make sure it was well stocked with leather goods. "Figure three-four handbags each," the colonel warned. "Got to bring handbags home for the womenfolk."

Brad said, "What about plans and security, Colonel?"

"Coming to that." Lessing puffed nervously until his face was almost screened by smoke. "We've decided to tell them about Baytown. Make 'em feel like insiders." The pursuit of the Germans in Sicily was in its closing stages and Baytown represented the crossing of the Messina Strait into the toe of Italy. "Also," he continued, "we'll brief them on Avalanche. Not everything though. Not the date or the beach. Just the objective—Naples. Got that?" His voice came down to a conspiratorial whisper. "Just one more thing. Not a word about Overlord."

The sound of the word electrified Brad's laggard mind. He had long since gathered up the evidence that placed Overlord where his imagination wanted it. This was the first time he had heard a senior officer mention the operation.

"Play dumb on it," Lessing instructed. "You don't know. It's not this theater. But they'll ask all right. They're sure to find out about the seven divisions. The enemy probably knows it by now anyway."

Brad tried to keep the excitement out of his voice. He said, "I don't know about the seven divisions, Colonel."

Lessing said, "Four American, three British. Being released to train for Overlord. If they ask, tell 'em it's routine, all kinds of people going up to the U.K., rotation, anything." He puffed at his cigarette as if a small electric motor were operating his lips. "But they'll ask all right. Always do."

When Brad left the colonel's office he felt like a small boy about to break open a Christmas parcel. His mind spun with anticipation. Seven divisions! At last the tides of war were beginning to shift. There was a chance, a real chance. He hadn't seen Valerie for nearly ten months.

Driving out to the airport at Maison-Blanche, he began to dread the moment he would meet Jaques. He envisioned a flood of news about Malton, how well Janie looked and how Damien was prospering, perhaps letters from them and even gifts.

It didn't happen that way at all. When the silver C-47 came in from Marrakech, Jaques and the others posed for a battery of uniformed photographers, inspected an honor guard of poker-stiff Negro troops shining under a merciless sun, and stood about chatting with an array of generals that had been ordered out to greet them. Not until the others moved toward their cars did Jaques bustle over to where Brad had placed himself, a respectful distance from the generals. He loosed his widest smile and offered his hearty politician's handshake.

"Grand seeing you, Brad. You look fine—by gosh yes. Very thoughtful of Colonel Lessing to make you available. I'd requested you but

—well, it's very gratifying. You're going to be a real help to us poor
ignorant legislators. A real help and you look fine."

That was all. He squeezed Brad's arm and hurried to join his com-
panions who were climbing into cars. Not a word about Malton or
Damien or Janie. Brad was content but mystified.

The mystery deepened as the party plunged into its crowded
schedule of events. Every minute was accounted for with a precision
only the military can accomplish. The visitors inspected supply
dumps and training areas, they ate kouskous with their fingers in an
Arab village near Blida and were rushed back for a cocktail party at
the French governor's residence, after which they were taken on a
thrilling ride beyond the harbor defenses in a motor torpedo boat.
Then, exhausted, they were taken on a quick tour of the War Rooms
and it turned out as planned; they were too mind-weary to ask any
sharp questions. Brad accompanied them everywhere. Not once did
Jaques mention Malton or the family.

But he paid extravagant attention to Brad himself. As a member
of the Armed Services Committee, he was the group's unchallenged
leader and spokesman. He leaned heavily on the young lieutenant
for guidance, complimented him for arrangements that had been
made by Colonel Lessing's staff, and pushed him so persistently into
the forefront that Brad began to feel that the colonel might be getting
justifiably angry.

Lessing didn't seem to mind. When he dropped Brad at his billet
at the end of the second day, he said, "They're a good bunch. Not
a stickler in the lot. We were worried about Jaques. These labor
congressmen, when they get the bit in their teeth, can make it plenty
tough for the military. I *know*."

They were indeed a good bunch; amiable, diffident, and almost
embarrassingly appreciative. They stood properly aghast at the
beauty of the view from the hills, laughed sheepishly among themselves when they donned GI suntans as protection against the sharp
heat, made fine and profuse speeches of thanks for military briefings
which were ridiculously obscure, and chirped with pleasure at the
leather-goods bargains in the special PX. Brad never discovered the
reason for their trip. If it was to investigate a specific matter, they
came away without an iota of useful information. Every installation
they visited had been alerted, the GI lunch served from a field
kitchen had been especially prepared, and even the soldiers in the

punishment camp clicked their heels and sang out that they had
no complaints.

Everywhere they went the congressmen were photographed by a
motion-picture cameraman from the Signal Corps, an engagingly
brash youth named Sergeant Barkley. He balanced himself on fences,
lay flat on the ground for angle shots, and kept cajoling the legislators
for additional poses, singly and in groups. They readily obliged and
tried hard to look solemn and investigative.

On the night before departure, the enemy conspired to put a final
touch of perfection on the visit. The sirens blew. No bombs were
dropped, but there were several thunderous salvos from heavy anti-
aircraft batteries in the harbor area. This took place during a tour
along the fringes of the casbah, and the congressmen were herded
into a nearby cellar which housed several malevolent-looking Arabs.
The double peril set the congressmen to feeling like scarred old ad-
venturers and they whooped it up a bit when they finally reached
the cocktail lounge of the VIP villa.

Colonel Lessing was a happy man. When he and Brad came away
from the villa after seeing their charges safely retired, he said, "Well,
off tomorrow. Good. Nothing's gone wrong. Turned out fine." He
puffed at the nub of his cigarette until the fire ran up his fingers.
"Nice leather-goods selection you made, Parker. They cleaned out
the lot."

Brad said, "I think Sergeant Barkley tickled them most. He really
puts on a show."

Lessing said, "Barkley's very good. I get him for all these parties.
Impertinent squirt. Wouldn't have him in an outfit of mine for a
minute. But *they* like him. What the Signal Corps does with all that
film I'll never know."

Brad knew. He had asked Barkley and the sergeant had replied,
grinning, "What film? There hasn't been a single foot in this camera.
Makes 'em feel good though to have it turning on 'em."

When Brad arrived at the villa the next morning, Sanford Jaques
suggested that they have breakfast alone. A farewell breakfast had
been arranged at which the chief of staff was to be the host and
Brad was sure that the absence of the ranking congressman would
be a serious matter, but Jaques insisted he had a right to a meal

alone with a valued constituent and Colonel Lessing agreed to make
the necessary explanations to General Smith.

They ate on the terrace after the others had departed for headquarters.

For a time the talk was small and polite. Then the congressman
congratulated Brad on his performance as a guide. He said he was
proud to see how well the army was being run and he could go home
and assure the fathers and mothers of Connecticut that their sons
were being efficiently and compassionately handled. Brad could see
the subject of Malton looming up at last.

He was right. Jaques said, "This is a nice break for me. You have
no idea, Brad, how hard we go at it in Washington, especially on
the Armed Services Committee. Believe it or not, I haven't been to
Malton since election day and that's nearly a year." He looked into
his coffee, stirring it slowly. "So I suppose you're up on the Malton
news a lot more than I am. How *is* Damien?"

The question was tartly asked, its political overtones inescapable
—at least to Brad. He replied, "Last I heard, a couple of weeks ago,
he was fine." He couldn't help adding, "The *Star* was doing well
too."

Jaques said, "Yes, the *Star* moves along, always moves along. And
so do I. Did Damien send you the figures on the election?" The question was rhetorical. He went right on: "I polled a record vote. Better
than three to one over Damien's boy, Jensen. But I don't hold it
against Damien. I honestly don't. I *like* Damien"—he hit the word
with full force—"and I make bold enough to think he likes me."

Brad said innocently, "I'm sure he does."

The congressman nodded solemnly and then both men looked out
on the magnificent view of the sea. The water shimmered blue and
silver in the midsummer heat. Far out, eye level with the terrace, a
pair of patrol bombers banked in the clear sky like gulls at play.

Jaques sighed. "This is so much better than sitting around with generals and making conversation. Come to think of it, it's just a year
ago that I lunched with Damien in the *Star* tower. I remember we
talked a good deal about you. He must have written you about it."

Brad thought how carelessly he had skimmed over letters from
home during the last year. He said truthfully, "I don't recall it, Sanford."

There was a brief silence and then Jaques leaned confidentially over his coffee. "I've been meaning to ask you, Brad. Curious they haven't given you a promotion."

"I'm afraid promotions come faster to the combat people. I guess they should too."

"You haven't been in any trouble, have you?"

"Oh no."

"Then you're happy."

"Reasonably."

"You're not sorry you were transferred out of Fort Harrison."

Brad shook his head. "In the army we like to think they put you where they need you."

"Fine spirit! Just what I would expect." (The politician was beginning to break out all over, Brad thought.) "But I'll be very frank with you. After the impression you've made on me, not only on me but on my colleagues, I'm amazed you haven't had a promotion—captain at least. I've always felt our machinery for evaluating junior officers hasn't kept pace with the growth of our armed forces and I intend to take it up——"

Brad interrupted. "Sanford——" He was thinking of Colonel Robey's ugly remark. "Sanford, I'd like to take my chances."

Jaques said, "I don't mean you particularly. I simply think the whole system needs overhauling."

"I'm sorry."

"Quite all right."

They both looked out to sea, knowing that neither was fooling the other.

After a time Jaques said, "I know you won't take it amiss. It's a perfectly legitimate thing, done every day, and to my way of thinking, not done nearly often enough by congressmen, who, after all, are closer to their own people than the military. I've had a long talk with Lessing. I made clear to him the regard in which I hold your ability. No harm in that?"

Brad mumbled, "It's good of you." He didn't mean it. He was shocked. He thought of Lessing, who was a pitiful character puffing away nervously at the mention of a congressman because his job was to keep them happy. He thought of Damien and how he would react to this. But he couldn't bring himself to say anything more than, "It's good of you."

They talked about General Montgomery, who had caught the im-

agination of the American press, and about a musical called *Okla-
homa!* which had become a curiously fevered success in New York.
It was casual talk in which Brad took part mechanically. His mind
was in England and he felt sick for knowing how easy it would be to
arrange a transfer here and now. Then he heard the roar of the official
cars coming up the driveway and the chortling of the well-fed and
-buttered congressmen. He was glad the time of temptation had
passed. More than anything else in the world he wanted to fly to
Valerie, but not by a congressman's stealthy favor.

At the airport another honor guard, this time from the navy,
awaited the departing legislators. As they inspected the ranks,
Sergeant Barkley turned his camera acrobatically all around them,
and when they climbed into their C-47 he was at the foot of the steps
beseeching a final wave at the door of the plane.

They all looked extremely pleased but no more so than Colonel
Lessing.

"That's it," he said to Brad. "They're gone." He lit a cigarette and
took a long, satisfying draw at it.

As September passed slow panic began to take a grip on Brad.
Everybody knew the war was approaching its climax. Sicily and
south Italy had been conquered; the Fifth Army had won the bloody
battle of Salerno and was spilling over the slopes of Vesuvius into
the plain of Naples. Overlord was no longer a mystery, not even to
the enemy. The movement of seven divisions out of the Mediterranean to England had been accurately evaluated by German Intelligence and the evaluation relayed back to Algiers by allied Counter-
Intelligence.

In Colonel Robey's section, certain officers and non-coms had
quietly disappeared and it was an open secret that they had been
transferred to COSSAC, the planning headquarters for the great
D-day assault. COSSAC was an abbreviation, not a code name; it
betokened the chief of staff to the supreme Allied commander. The
supreme Allied commander hadn't been appointed yet, but everybody figured he was going to be General Marshall.

By the end of the month Brad, torn between frantic hope and a
premonition he might be overlooked, watched for an opportunity to
put his case to Colonel Robey. It came one day after lunch. He saw

the colonel humming contentedly on his way back from A-mess and he followed him into his office.

He felt he had picked the right day. The colonel's wine-stained lips clucked happily as he peered at the solemn young lieutenant standing in a reasonable attitude of attention.

"You look like a very sad owl, Parker. I feel a problem coming on. Don't tell me the Jerries have lifted the code or some such thing. Don't feel I can cope today."

"It's not that serious, sir."

"Oh, good. For God's sake, sit down. Don't be so bloody formal!"

Brad thought the man was feeling extraordinarily good. He made his request for a transfer to COSSAC as brief as possible.

The colonel seemed amused. "None of my business of course, but I can't fathom why the devil anybody'd want a transfer to England. Long on rain, short on beef, no whisky to speak of, old boy. Can't fathom it at all." He spread his mouth in a wide, pleasant grimace. "Girl?"

Brad had long since prepared his reply. "It's Overlord, Colonel. As long as it's coming off I'd like to have a finger in that pie—if it's at all possible. Frankly, sir, the whole conception of Overlord excites me." He felt he sounded shamefully convincing. He was lying well and he had never been a liar.

Robey looked dubious. "Won't be too bloody romantic I can tell you."

"I'd consider it a great personal favor if you could work it for me, Colonel."

"Sure it isn't a girl?" Robey asked the question in high good humor as if he was ready to settle back and gossip about boudoirs.

Brad said, "No, sir."

"You mean, no you're not sure it isn't a girl or no you're sure it isn't a girl?"

Brad nailed down the lie. "It isn't a girl."

"In that case, Parker, I'd better let you in on something. Don't spread it around." He paused to release an obstinate burp. "The chaps were telling me at lunch. The general's decided on the new headquarters. It's going to be Caserta, lovely castle up near Naples. Going to be an absolutely smashing winter. Change your mind?"

Brad realized he had misplayed his hand. He shouldn't have lied. Robey was the kind of harmless scoundrel who might have sent him to England for a girl. The story about Overlord had had no effect. Nevertheless he said, "I'd still prefer Overlord, sir."

"Ever been to Italy?"

"No, sir."

"I spent two damn good years there in the attaché's office. Take it from me, Parker, you'll go batty over the place. Smashing for a young stallion like you. Absolutely smashing." He told a long pointless story about a liaison he had had with a marchesa whose husband was keeping a Hungarian ballet dancer. When he finished he seemed disappointed that Brad declined to withdraw his request. He said sharply, "I'll do what I can," and Brad was convinced he wasn't going to lift a finger.

The westbound troopships moved across the harbor almost every day now. Brad could see them lying at anchor far out beyond the anti-submarine nets as the refueling ships moved among them. It seemed that everybody was going back for Overlord, everybody except him.

Valerie felt the same way. In her last letter she had written, "You'd never recognize London now. Remember how empty the streets used to be when we walked in the evenings and would see only a few air force lads prowling about? It's so crowded now——" (The next line and a half had been scissored out by the censor.) "—and with all those sunburned faces, so strange to see after our desolate summer, I find myself looking for you, my darling. Aren't they ever going to send you back? I wish I could describe the rising tide of excitement here——" (Another line had been scissored out.) "—I sometimes dream you're here and have forgotten me. Almost everybody has come back now . . ."

*Almost everybody,* she had written. He wondered if John Wynter had come back. She never mentioned John in her letters. But every day he could see the troopships, their decks jammed with British and American infantry, all moving west to the strait and north to England. He couldn't imagine that John would not be among these thousands returning to England, returning to Valerie.

One afternoon early in October a lieutenant called Glass, who worked in the code room at G-3, came in from the harbor and made for Brad's desk. He had been distributing a code change among troop commanders on the ships of a Clyde-bound convoy. He said, "Ran into a friend of yours out there, fellow called Stenick. He said to say hello. The convoy's not sailing till midnight if you want to run out. I think I can get you on the cutter."

Brad didn't go out. He didn't want to see anyone who was sailing to England, not even Dan. After dinner at B-mess he went to his room and got out a new bottle of whisky and thought about Dan, who was out there on a ship which would land him in the Clyde. Dan had lived through the fighting in Tunisia and Sicily and now Dan was going to England. He should have done what Dan had done. He should have transferred to the Rangers. He pictured himself, weary and full of battle honors, sailing to England. He pictured Valerie waiting for him on a platform and proud because he was weary and full of battle honors. He drank very steadily that night.

The next morning he went to see Colonel Lessing.

He saluted smartly, trying to show more respect for the colonel than he honestly felt. The man acknowledged the gesture with a nod and reached for a cigarette. It was as though he had been expecting the visit.

"Well now," he said after Brad had stated his business, "that shouldn't be an insuperable problem." He stressed the word *insuperable*. "Tell me though, are you unhappy here?"

"Yes, sir."

"Oh. Anything serious?"

"No, sir. It's just that I've had my eye on Overlord and I'd very much like to be part of it."

Lessing eyed him intently, almost belligerently. "It's a creditable interest but it's not a sound military reason for a request of this kind. You understand that."

"I understand, Colonel, and I'm prepared to give a sound military reason."

"Good. Let's have it."

"I'd like to go combat, sir. I was a platoon commander in the Special Service Force before I was shifted to the staff side. I've never heard of a beach assault that had enough qualified platoon commanders."

Lessing smiled in a distant manner, as if he had just remembered something funny. "I'm glad you said that, Parker, because it makes it easier." He tapped his chest. "Makes it easier here. You can make up your mind about going combat when you get to England. Meanwhile I'll put the request in motion for Cossac. We've been beefing them up on the staff side so I guess they'll approve an officer of your experience."

After the first wave of elation had swept through him and subsided, Brad thought of the gesture and the words. *It makes it easier here.* He looked at the colonel puffing sadly at his cigarette and a lot of questions came to his mind, but he didn't allow himself to ask them. He knew the answers. He knew he was using the specter of Sanford Jaques to force the colonel's hand.

"I can't thank you enough, sir."

Lessing made an empty gesture with his hand. "I'll let you know how it works out."

Brad saluted and turned around. It was a long way across the room to the door and when he closed it behind him he wasn't thinking of Valerie. He was thinking of Damien and of Sanford Jaques, who would assuredly be told about this.

It only hurt for a little while. He wrote to Ray Boyce demanding his room back, and by the time he settled down to write Valerie he had forgotten all about Colonel Lessing.

The orders came through two weeks later. Colonel Robey handed him the stapled sheaf of documents.

"Congratulations, Parker. I see you made it."

"I'll be sorry to leave your section, sir."

Robey laughed. "In a pig's eye but it's decent of you to say so. I see this calls for surface transportation. Apparently your presence at Cossac isn't breathlessly urgent."

Brad felt the hurt and kept silent. He had it coming to him.

Robey said, "It's a long haul after you get on a ship which is God knows when. How would you like to go by aircraft?"

"I'd prefer it, Colonel."

"Good. I've got something to send to the War Office. I'll give you a pouch. Courier means priority one."

"That's very thoughtful of you, sir."

Robey smiled narrowly. "Splendid. I've managed a box of silk stockings for my wife and I bloody well don't want the old girl crawling through Customs. No skin off your nose though. It'll be a sealed pouch for delivery to the War Office. I'll send them a signal."

When Brad flew into the airport at Marrakech there were combat men in the transient huts who had been languishing three weeks for transportation to the U.K., but he was air-lifted that same evening because he was carrying a pouch for the War Office.

## 16

V A L E R I E didn't want to leave the city even for a few hours but there was no way out of it. Viscount Haltram had pleaded with her to come to Smallhill for dinner and had promised it would be perfectly all right for her to depart immediately afterward. Besides, the car would have to return to the city in any case and it seemed a pity, he had said, for her to miss this opportunity of seeing John's home. He had added that it would be a great comfort to him, and this was when she had found she couldn't disappoint the frail old man, not on the proud and tragic day he had received from his King the V.C. his eldest son Derek had died to win.

So, on this gray afternoon in late October she found herself with John's father and his younger brother Bertie riding out to Tunbridge Wells in an ancient Rolls Royce provided by the War Ministry for the parent of the hero.

The trees were bare and there was frost on the fields. She thought bitterly about journeying southward on this of all days. It was not that she suspected for a moment Brad might arrive. Yesterday's cable had merely said he was on his way; of course he wasn't allowed to specify how or when. She knew it would be days at the very earliest, more probably weeks if he traveled by ship. But simply being in London and knowing the telephone *could* ring was exquisite excitement. It was a terrible time to be driving to Kent. And to John's home of all places!

The day had been mournful. Sitting in a gold and crimson hall in Buckingham Palace she had watched John's father clasp his bony hands as he heard a court chamberlain read the citation for a posthumous award of the Victoria Cross to Lieutenant Colonel the Hon. Derek Edward Fothergill Wynter, Royal Dragoon Guards, for valor above and beyond the call of duty. She had thought it was unnecessarily cruel that the old man should have to stand and listen.

Because the V.C. award always came first at an investiture, he had stood at the head of a long line of recipients that stretched from the left side of the dais along the wall and around to the back of the hall.

". . . Despite his grievous wounds Lieutenant Colonel Wynter resolutely declined to be removed to the rear, knowing that the outcome of the battle might depend on holding the salient near Battipaglia. Though a strong and determined enemy assault had reached the immediate area of his battalion headquarters, he remained actively at his post . . ."

She had kept looking at the old man with his clasped hands and wondering if the citation would ever end. And she had stolen a glance at the King, the neat, slim King standing alone, his face harrowed by the words.

". . . a third grenade explosion bereft him of the use of his legs and he clawed across the ground to a gun post. He took the place of a wounded trooper and directed such accurate and authoritative fire that the enemy finally fell back. Lieutenant Colonel Wynter died of his wounds before the stretcher-bearers could reach him . . ."

Bertie had whispered to her, "Must be wretched for the governor. He's been in a spin ever since it happened, but you see, Val, he never did know how Derek bought it, never wanted to know. Didn't bother much with John and me but he was awfully keen on poor old Derek."

At long last it had come to an end. The King handed the medal to the trembling old man and as they stood conversing gravely together, Bertie had said, "I do hope he's not giving George an earful on Roman roads. The governor's a bug on the subject. I say, Val, you *will* come back to Smallhill with us. Please, for my sake. I'd hate to be alone with the governor the rest of the day."

It had struck her as odd that John's young brother should call her Val. They had never met before, but he seemed to take it for granted she was already part of the family. Perhaps, she had thought, it was his youthful flippancy. He was a flying officer and full of that blend of modesty and happy bravado which was the hallmark of the R.A.F. Even in the presence of the King he had worn the top button of his tunic loose in the arbitrary fashion of all fighter pilots.

Now they were speeding along a country road, capriciously it seemed, in the rich high-bodied old Rolls Royce with a stubby corporal immobile at the wheel.

Viscount Haltram hadn't spoken since leaving the palace. He sat almost lost in the car's lush upholstery and his face, pinched but ruddy as if years of wind had nipped at it, was exceedingly sad. He held the tiny brown box containing his son's medal in both hands ceremoniously. It might have been an urn containing his ashes.

The car passed through Tunbridge Wells and made a sharp turn into a side road and then another into a tree-lined lane.

Viscount Haltram said, "John is well."

She said, "Yes. I had a letter yesterday."

"I had one too. Quite a time ago though. I think it was when he heard about Derek. A very good letter."

Bertie said, "These old Rollses do stand up, don't they? Think of the petrol though. Awful splurge for the good old War Ministry. Chaps won't believe it when I tell them."

The old man said, "Is he still in Sicily?"

Poor John, she thought. He had left Sicily a month ago. His Commandos had fought through Potenza and Foggia and his father didn't even know. She said, "He's on the east coast of Italy."

The old man said, "You'd think they'd send him home—now."

As soon as the car turned into an old stone gateway she understood violently a great many things she had not fully understood before. The great sweep of lawn was covered with dead leaves, lying over paths, at the base of bare linden trees, against a garden house where the wind had whipped them into untidy mounds, floating thickly in a pond, and imbedded in the neglected shrubbery. The mansion itself looked gray and cheerless. The windows were crevices in heavy stone walls, almost all of them boarded over.

She looked at the remote old man and the strewn lawn and the gray building and she remembered how John would come to "Darjeeling" on his leaves, his shy little boy's attitude, and his strange hunger. He was the elder son now, heir to all this cheerlessness. She wanted to weep for poor, sweet John and for herself because she was faithless to him.

It was as if she had spoken aloud. Bertie said, "It does look rather crummy, Father. Can't old Elson do up the leaves at least?"

The old man nodded in a confused manner. "I must remember to ask him."

"Bother asking! Tell him."

When the car pulled up, the great front door was opened by a tiny girl who could not have been more than fourteen. She was bundled up like a char in an incongruously long dress and soiled apron. She squeaked, "I do hope it's been lovely, m'lord." The old man said, "His Majesty was very sympathetic," and the girl said, "Wouldn't that be just like him, m'lord," in the manner of a mature woman. The man they called Elson came and helped Lord Haltram off with his coat. He was bald and old and enormously fat. He wore an apron too and he breathed hard as though the carrying of his great weight was an overwearying burden. Lord Haltram opened the box and showed him the medal. They both stared at it without saying anything.

Bertie said, "Come now, Elson, drink and a fire, that's what we need. Oh, this is Miss Russell. Wager she needs a sherry but I could do with a whisky. No whisky, is there?"

Elson said, "There's a fire in the study, Mr. Bertie."

"I see. No whisky."

"It's this way, Mr. Bertie. The provisioner hasn't had a single bottle in months."

"He's letting you down."

Elson seemed disturbed by Valerie's A.R.C. uniform. "He says it's all going to the American forces."

"Quite. He couldn't be righter. We raf types don't drink the stuff. Strictly lemon squash in the mess."

Elson murmured, "That's after the hymn singing, I'm sure."

"Dead on! How'd you guess?"

Viscount Haltram, still gazing at the medal, said, "Bertie, take Miss Russell into the study, or show her about if she's not too tired." He snapped the box shut. "I'll be down after I've put this away." He walked uneasily, like a man lost, across the dank, dim hall to a staircase which curved upward into utter gloom.

Bertie said, "You really don't want to see the old place, do you? There's nothing historic about it except that not a stick of furniture's been changed since Ethelred the Unready."

She was miserably cold. She said, "Perhaps we'll look about later. At the moment I think I'd like a fire."

"Good-o. So would I."

The study proved a pleasant relief. It was a good-sized room made warm and intimate by shelves of books lined solidly along the walls and by a fire which snapped with fresh kindling. There were deep, comfortable chairs with frayed and hollowed seats, as if they had been sat in by generations of enraptured readers. A set of french doors looked out on a clump of elms standing askew over a swift, narrow stream.

"They're lovely old trees," Valerie said, and then the girl brought in a sherry tray and brusquely drew the blackout curtains. "Fog's coming in," she explained in her old woman's way. She had put on a clean white apron in honor of the guest, but the char's dress still trailed at her heels.

When she had gone, Bertie poured the sherry. He said, "Isn't she something though? A child harridan. Best Elson could get with the war and all. Well, here's to you, Val. Decent of you to come out. Damn good turn."

"Bless you, Bertie. I'm glad to be of some use."

"Father was keen on it," Bertie said. He lit a cigarette and blinked his eyes at the fire and said, "Now that Derek's bought it I rather imagine he thinks a bit about John. Can't think of Derek dead. Not because he was my brother, mind, but he was splendid. Had it all."

She said, "V.C.s don't come along every day," but she was thinking of Bertie's easy familiarity. She wondered what John had written them over the last year that they should take so much for granted.

She looked about the room and she heard Bertie say, "Oh, it's not that bad, Val. The place could do with a bit of fixing but you'd be amazed how cheerful it can be in summer." She felt as if she had been caught cheating.

"I wasn't thinking about Smallhill," she said, and she added brightly, "I'm only now beginning to thaw out. Do tell me about the lads at Biggin Hill. They're quite legendary, you know."

"Grand bunch," Bertie said. "Of course our lot are pretty much parvenus. The old chaps, the Battle of Britain boys, those that are left, are pretty much scattered now. Full of gongs and rings up to their elbows." He poured another sherry and said carelessly, "God, I hope John makes it nicely. I mean, I'd hate to have all this shoved at me someday. Not my cup of tea at all. John's made for it. He'll never be Derek of course, but he's awfully settled—you'd know about that better than any of us. Isn't the war a mess though? Here I am all geared up to spend the rest of my life in absolute sin and squalor,

preferably in Soho, and suddenly Derek buys it, poor chap, and John
is still out there with the Commandos and being used as shock troops
of all ridiculous things, and honestly, Val, I get into a blue funk
thinking about it. Do write him to be careful. Tell him to think of
dear old Bertie and keep his head low. I say, I do talk a line of tripe,
don't I? Must be the sherry."

He smiled the sort of shy, introspective smile that reminded her
of John. He said, "The sherry or maybe it's the old house. Always
get morbid in the old house. I much prefer my leaves at the Mapleton
right on Leicester Square. Honestly, Val, the fun we've had there——"

Relief came to her with the opening of the study door. Viscount
Haltram took a sherry and went to a chair which was clearly his, for
it fitted him perfectly. His face became relaxed and he seemed
able to coax a little brightness into it.

He said, "I suppose Bertie has been chipping away at your patience."

"She's been grand, Father. Super."

The old man glanced at his son. "I haven't heard a proper English
sentence from him since he joined the air force. Super, gen, prang
—it's an absolute threat to the language. I gather however that
Bertie approves of you. May I call you Valerie?"

That's the way it was through another round of sherry and then
at dinner. She was being clearly appraised as the next Lady Haltram.
There was nothing she could do about it, not with these lonely men
in this great lonely house which gasped for the voice and touch and
presence of a woman.

They dined in a large square room which gave the impression of
being dusty, probably because it was so empty. The table, chairs,
and a sideboard were lost in the vast expanse. She was reminded of
her childhood days when her father transferred from one command
to another and they would dine on a card table in the new quarters
until their furniture could arrive.

They had tomato juice, fried cod, Canadian cheddar, and a superb
sauterne, all of it served by Elson, who wheezed continually and
snapped instructions to the girl who was helping him at the sideboard.

Viscount Haltram applied himself studiously to the food while
Bertie chattered about a German spy, parachuted in, who had been
picked up at Luton and how the silly fellow had given himself away

in a pub by offering the barmaid a cigarette from a packet of Wood-
bines wrapped in tinfoil. Even the barmaid knew that tinfoil had
disappeared from cigarette packings in 1939 and informed the authorities of her suspicions.

"The chaps in our mess couldn't let that pass, you know," Bertie
went on. "We managed to dig up a sheet of tinfoil and we cut it up
and did up our Players packets and on signal we went around the
pubs offering cigarettes to barmaids. Had M.I.5 doing loops for a
whole week. What a froth!"

Viscount Haltram didn't appear to hear. At least, his small well-
bred mouth continued to nibble at the cheddar as if Bertie were
a child who had to be suffered with infinite patience, and then he
conducted Valerie to the study for coffee.

Somewhere in the journey between the dining room and the study
Bertie had made off. She knew it was no accident when the old man
began to talk about her father and how much John respected him.

Then he was suddenly sad. He said, "To say I am grateful to you
is to put it poorly. It is much more than that."

"Grateful for what, Lord Haltram?"

He closed his eyes a moment as if it was a hard confession to
make. "It would be easier for you to understand if you had known
Derek. He was not at all like me. He was strong and he had the
face and bearing of a leader. I had always looked to him to give
the line new vigor. It's a fine old title, you see, and a hundred years
ago it produced fine men for England and I was certain Derek would
restore something of its glory."

The old man looked away remorsefully. "But Derek is dead, and
now I see a great many things clearly that never occurred to me
before. I used to wonder why John joined the Commandos and how
he came to win his decorations. Now of course I know. I think he
must have resented Derek——"

"Lord Haltram, he loved and admired Derek."

"Perhaps. I never quite knew how fine a lad he is and how unfair
I must have been. I sometimes think he went to war in order to die,
and if he is not dead it is because you, my dear Valerie, have given
him a reason for living."

She thought, Oh God, why did I let myself come here? Brad—
Brad—not by ship, please not by ship. Come by air—come quickly

—come rescue me from my own country that is torn and sad. I don't want to live for the past and die for the past. Come quickly and bring your strength and your love to help me fight the dust and ashes and barren urges. I am a person, not a nation. A life. A being. Come quickly, Brad, with your strong American face, your vigor, your joy. Quickly, Brad, quickly!

The old man was saying, "I understand that certain privileges accrue to a parent who has a V.C. as a substitute for a son and I have suggested that John be transferred to some less hazardous duty. He was never robust. God alone knows how he gathered up the strength and courage to carry on as he has."

There was nothing she could say. She watched the old man turn abruptly and take a long time at the coffee urn. Finally he said, "I promised I would let you go after dinner. I'm sorry, Valerie. I think I've said all there is to say. Not very well."

Then Bertie mercifully knocked on the study door, opened it a crack, and said that the Rolls had to report back at the Ministry before 2300 hours.

"You'd better get cracking, Val," he said, and she was glad that the light in the hall was dim because it made it so much easier to say good-by.

The air was chill and heavy with fog, but she opened a window of the Rolls and breathed deeply and listened to the wheels singing on the damp pavement. From the deep seat of the Rolls it seemed as if the corporal up front were steering through pitch-blackness. It didn't matter. Nothing mattered as long as Smallhill was left behind.

The fog swirled around the open window and she thought Brad's plane couldn't land anywhere in the south of England even if he *had* taken off from Africa. But he couldn't have taken off. She had listened to too many Americans at the club recount the weary days of waiting at Algiers for a ship or at Marrakech for a plane.

The corporal said, "I think you'd better put up that window, ma'am. Fog's comin' in good and heavy."

He turned on full headlights and slowed the huge car. After a time he said, "I couldn't help noticing, ma'am, how hard his lordship took it. Still," he ventured, "it's a V.C. A wonderful thing a V.C.—of course not for the laddie who gets killed." He chuckled. "I guess my mum and dad would be good and satisfied. It's a wonderful thing for the family."

She thought, In war it's the V.C. and in peace it's the Ashes or climbing Everest or making money. It's all a game, a whim of the moment. Only one thing counts, is constant and eternal, and that is what happens inside you.

The fog grew thicker.

Suppose he had already arrived. Suppose he had emplaned when he sent the cable. He would have flown overnight and would have landed today. It was impossible. Only generals and cabinet ministers flew immediately. The others waited. But suppose he *had* emplaned yesterday?

The Rolls barely moved on the road. It would be hours before they would reach London.

The corporal said, "I'm sorry, ma'am. It's impossible to see. I'm afraid I can't go faster."

She hadn't complained. Everybody seemed to be able to read her mind. She felt naked.

After a time they saw a red light up ahead weaving frantically from side to side. The Rolls pulled up before a roadblock formed by two jeeps at the entry to a traffic circle. There were four American military policemen standing athwart the road and behind them a convoy of trucks moved around the circle and took the fork westward.

One of the policemen looked at the War Ministry markings on the Rolls Royce and came forward. He took no chances on the person who might be inside so distinguished a vehicle. He gave a stiff-armed salute as he opened the door.

He said, "Sorry, lady, this is a night convoy exercise. We should be clear of this point in ten minutes or so." He saluted again and closed the door.

The discipline of the convoy was superb. On such a night full headlights were used and each truck roared through the swirling mists with unbelievable precision, two or three seconds apart. They were troop carriers. A glint of helmet linings and rifle barrels could be seen from the interior of each truck as it made its turn and caught the headlights of the truck behind. When the troop carriers had passed, a succession of open trucks piled high with kit bags swung around the circle.

The corporal said, "This is no convoy exercise. They're moving to a new bivouac. I guess the balloon's going up. They say it can't be much longer."

It must be more than ten minutes, she thought. Now the field guns were passing through, scores of them, each pulled by a 600-weight. And when the guns had passed there was a new convoy of supply trucks, and then the engineer equipment trucks, the field kitchens, the command cars; then the tanks, huge rumbling monsters coming out of fog and disappearing into fog.

The corporal said, "Do you mind if I smoke, ma'am?"

"Of course not, Corporal."

He turned off the ignition and lit up. "Rum luck running into this, ma'am."

She took a torch out of her purse and looked at her watch. It was almost eleven o'clock. "Do you know where we are, Corporal?"

"I'd say just past Sevenoaks, ma'am."

She said, "Can't we turn around and take a detour?"

"I wouldn't risk it, ma'am, not in this soup if you don't mind. There's the ammunition lorries. Must be near the end."

A succession of heavy steel monsters screamed around the curve of the traffic circle and the hollow sound of their exhausts shook the countryside. A line of jeeps carrying four men each scampered impertinently in their wake.

"I think we're on our way, ma'am. That was an armored division. Throws you, doesn't it? Cor, these Americans!"

The last were the dispatch riders. The military policemen gathered up the red lamps they had strung across the road, hopped into their jeeps, and pulled away.

As soon as the car began to move gingerly through the fog she found herself fighting down panic. She could see him standing somewhere in shrouded London waiting for her. But she knew better. It was a whole year of dreaming that was playing tricks with her. After all, he had cabled only yesterday. It took weeks to come up from Africa. But suppose he *had* arrived!

The corporal said, "I think this is Bromley, ma'am. Where would you like to be let off in London?"

"Eaton Square at Elizabeth Street if you don't mind." She was a householder now. During the summer she had found a flat in a con-

verted Victorian town house and had brought Mala down from Burlingham.

"I don't mind a bit, ma'am. I guess I can find London. It's a big
enough target even in this soup."

In the open country the fog had swirled and spun in the gleam
of the headlights, but now it hung low and thick and dirty yellow.
They were in the city. The car barely crawled along and from time
to time the corporal stopped, looked about, and pushed forward
again.

She looked at her watch. It was eleven-thirty. She said, "Do you
know where we are, Corporal?"

"We're well in the city and I'm pretty sure we're on the Old Kent
Road, ma'am. I haven't turned off. We'll know when we hit one of
the bridges."

Again the panic rose inside her. She fought it down with all the
power her mind could muster. Even if he *had* arrived it wouldn't be
disastrous. He had been away a year, a whole wretched, lonesome,
ridiculous year. A few more hours wouldn't matter. He would be
exhausted from the trip, happy to get to a billet and drop off to sleep.
They could wait till tomorrow. They weren't children. They could
wait. Anyway he hadn't arrived. Questions and answers and argu-
ments tumbled about in her mind; conclusions came and went
without leaving a trace of what had been concluded. Only panic remained. Suppose he *had* arrived. *Oh God, what is happening to me?*

"Look at that, ma'am. I'll have you home in a jiffy."

The car was crawling past an Underground and the station name
shone fuzzy in the dense fog: Elephant & Castle.

"Please wait a moment, Corporal!"

She was out of the car and bounding down the steps of the Underground, rummaging in her purse for three pennies, and when she
got into a booth her trembling fingers dialed a wrong number twice
before Mala's voice came on the phone.

Mala said, "I'm so glad you called. I was worried about the fog
and how you'll ever get in." There was a pause. "A post-office telegram has arrived."

It was as if she had known it all along. "From whom?"

"It arrived about an hour ago. Perhaps a little more."

"From whom? What does it say?"

"I haven't opened it."

"Oh, Mala!"

The servant was an interminable time. At last a rustle of paper came on the line and Mala said severely, "I think you'd better read it when you return home," as if it was something obscene.

"Quickly, Mala!"

"It reads *Happiest landing of my life* and then it says, *At last darling arrive Euston Station 10:57 tonight all my love,* and it's signed by someone called Brad."

"Look at it again. Does it say ten fifty-seven? Have you got your glasses on?"

"I don't need my glasses. It's quite clear."

"Ten fifty-seven?"

"Yes, and since it's nearly a quarter of midnight now there's no use fidgeting about it. I would suggest you'd better——"

"He hasn't called?"

"Most certainly not."

There were so many questions she wanted to ask. Where was it sent from? When was it handed in? But there was no time. She closed the phone and was almost at the ticket booth when she remembered the Rolls. She flew to the stairs and up into the street and for a confused moment she couldn't see the Rolls but there it was at the curb all the time. She couldn't think of what to say, so she said, "Thank you very much, Corporal," and dashed down the stairs.

An American soldier stood at the wicket fingering a pound note. He asked the ticket seller, "Can you change this, mister?"

"I think so."

"You're a sucker if you do, brother. It don't look worth a plugged nickel to me."

"We rather like them."

"Tell me, you honestly believe it's worth four bucks?"

"The banks are the people to tell you that, laddie."

"Tell you what. You give me fifty American cents——"

Valerie pushed in front of the wicket and handed in a shilling. "One to Euston, please."

The soldier said, "Now wait a minute, lady——"

"I'm in a terrible hurry."

"I know, lady, but I'm talkin' a big deal with this here fella——"

She appealed to the ticket seller. "Won't you please give me one to Euston?" She snatched her ticket and ran for the escalator.

It didn't descend fast enough nor did the train go fast enough, and she couldn't remember ever waiting so long at Charing Cross for a Northern Line train. But it came at last and she closed her eyes and counted between stops because it seemed to make the train go faster. She thanked God for the fog. Railway trains were always late in the fog, often two or three hours late, especially the trains from the Midlands. She couldn't bear not being there when he arrived. She looked at her watch. It was nearly midnight. She prayed for the fog to come down heavy and the train to be late.

The next stop was Warren Street and the next would be Euston. She could hardly believe she would see him this very night. If the train had already arrived surely he would wait. *She* would wait. Surely he would wait. But she didn't want to find him waiting. She wanted to be there on the platform when the train pulled in and to see his face before he saw hers and to read what his face said when he caught sight of her. *Please God, make the fog thick and the train late.*

It seemed a long way from Warren Street to Euston. The Underground train roared on and on and she listened for the sound of the brakes being applied, but it roared on and on and she knew it was her imagination that was making it seem long. She stood wedged between an Australian air force officer and a fat civilian waiting to get off at Euston. The Australian's lips were thin and chapped as if he had been drinking and smoking too much. She glanced at the civilian. He wore a narrow black Homburg which was soiled and frayed and he had flaked eyelids and his jowls shook to the rhythm of the train. She thought of Brad's face and she couldn't believe she was about to see him. The train roared on and now she could have sworn it wasn't her imagination. She closed her eyes and began counting and then she heard the wheels squealing on the curve of the rails turning into Euston and the brakes being applied.

She dashed ahead of the others across the concourse of the dun-colored old station to the arrival bulletin and she saw at once that the train due at ten fifty-seven (from Manchester, Crewe, and Dunstable) had not yet arrived.

She stood there panting, her eyes glued to the magic words in chalk *Retarded—due about 1 A.M.* and she felt indescribably fine and wanted to laugh out in triumph.

From the snack bar she couldn't see the length of the concourse. Only a few blue lamps hung from the curved roof and fog obscured even this sparse light. The place was deserted save for an occasional late commuter trudging toward the train gates. A woman's voice rasped over the loud-speakers: "Train for St. Alban's and Luton leaving from gate four in exactly one minute. Please hurry along now . . ."

She drank coffee which was bitter and the milk lumpy, but it was warming. She thought there was nothing sadder than a railway station late at night and especially this station which was old, scarred, and fogbound. But this was England, she thought. It was all of a piece with the war and with Smallhill, even with the crimson and gold hall in the palace which was not scarred but nevertheless inexpressibly sad. She remembered the eyes of the neat, frail king listening to the bloody details of how his people died.

It had been this way for four years and she could scarcely remember it differently except for the precious months with Brad. She looked at the platform ticket, a bit of cardboard she had bought for a penny. Then she squeezed it until the corners dug hard into her skin.

Now it was approaching one o'clock and she was no longer alone in the snack bar. She had watched the girls drift into the station, cast a practiced eye over the arrival bulletin, and walk saucily to the snack bar. There were seven or eight of them drinking coffee and chattering animatedly. They wore silk print dresses and nylon stockings and most of them had the skimpy fur jackets which were the trade-mark of the profession. Some of them were extremely pretty. Frequently they turned to eye her as if wondering whether she would like to join them.

She was amused and she imagined how Brad would be amused when she told him about them. She listened to their loud, happy chatter and suddenly it occurred to her that Brad had a wife somewhere across the seas. She had scarcely thought about it during the whole year of waiting, but now it came forcibly into her mind.

Then she heard the rasping voice on the loud-speakers: "Train from Manchester, Crewe, and Dunstable now arriving on platform six . . ." and as she got up she felt terribly chilled and frightened.

She saw him the moment the doors all along the train burst open. He stood framed in a door in the second carriage back, a kit bag slung over his shoulder and a suitcase in his hand. Then the pas-

sengers, mostly troops, spilled out over the platform and she lost
sight of him. She didn't know quite how she found him in the swarm
of people moving in a counterdirection to where she wanted to go
and jostling her and she them in her flight. She didn't know anything
except that she felt his hard, strong body pressed against her. They
kissed blindly and she dug her chin into his shoulder and her cheek
was against his.

After a time he said, "I haven't shaved since yesterday morning."

"I don't care."

"It's a tough stubble. It'll scratch your face."

"Let it."

"I didn't expect you here this late."

She said, "You're not serious."

"No. I'd have died if you weren't here."

"Suppose I was out of town or sick."

He said, "I'd have died anyway."

"It could never happen."

"What could never happen?"

"That I wouldn't be here to meet you."

"But if you were sick."

"I'd have crawled here."

"Are you sick?"

"I feel wonderful."

He said, "I can't tell. You won't let me look at you."

"Not yet. I want to feel you. I don't want you to get tired of looking
at me."

"It's because you're ugly."

"That's exactly how I feel. Ugly."

"Let me look at your ugly face."

She said, "Not yet."

He drew her away from his shoulder and held her off at half arm's
length. She blinked her moist, shining eyes and his mouth went a
little open in wonderment of her face. They kissed and he caught
her up again, hard. He said, "I'm home, Val. I'm home, I'm home."

She said, "Of course, my darling, of course. You're home."

They held each other and then he released her and heaved his kit
bag over his shoulder and picked up his suitcase. The platform was
deserted. The gateman who was counting tickets grumbled because
he had to open the gate for them. "You'll have a time finding a taxi,"

he growled at them. They didn't mind. He was a very old and very ugly man.

They walked through the great, empty, dun-colored station and out into the black street. They didn't care a hoot about the thickening fog.

## 17

IN ALL its long history London had never been as crowded as it was at the festive season of 1943. More than a million troops, it was said, had taken possession of the south coast between Beachy Head and Plymouth, and they all seemed to have taken simultaneous leave in London. They jammed into the blackout of Piccadilly Circus, shuffled along Coventry Street in a great company of perplexed shadows, spilled overflowingly into pubs, cellar cabarets, and ridiculously expensive clubs called bottle parties. Green troops and veterans alike entered freely into the revelry as if victory had already been won. Black marketeers, once furtive and frowned upon, became popular figures because London wanted desperately to celebrate. The urge was a contagion crossing every threshold.

It had been a great year. Africa and Sicily had been conquered. Italy had surrendered and Allied armies bestrode the peninsula from Naples to Foggia. Air raids were sentimentally recalled and roof-watching, once an intrepid duty, had become a drudge. Bombers flew overhead in their thousands, but they were American by day and British by night and their bombs were shattering Berlin. Music-hall comics donned Hitler mustaches for the first time since 1939 and the people laughed. A London newspaper speculated in a headline: "The War's Last Christmas?"

The gaiety was of course spurious. D-day was approaching and no one was blind to the trials and tragedies that awaited over the bend of the new year. But trial and tragedy had long since become a bore. People thought less about men, more about armies, and still more about manpower. It was inevitable. After four years of blood and tears only victory counted. The freshly uniformed youngsters laughing and shuffling in Piccadilly were so many bodies in a calculation of brute strength.

It was a time neither of hope nor of foreboding because these bespoke the future. It was a time of the present, of happy defiance, of sudden love racing sudden death, of excitement, of rapture and ruin. It was not London's finest hour but certainly its maddest.

"Is that you, Val? I've got great news——"

She said, "I can hardly hear you, darling. There's a terrible row here."

He cupped his hand over the phone. "I said I've got great news. I'm off at eight."

"Oh, splendid. How ever did you manage it?"

"New boy arrived fresh and innocent from OCS. I got to him before the others and handed him my night duty."

"You're wonderfully clever, my pet. Can you hear the noise?"

He said, "Sounds like a football rally. Are they drunk already? In the Red Cross?"

"Not yet but most of them will never see the midnight in. They're feeling quite happy and it's not even six."

"It's our first New Year's Eve. We've got to make plans."

"Let's not. Let's wander."

He said, "We've got to have a drink at my place. Promised Ray. He scrounged some champagne from the Free French—if there's any left by eight. You know Ray's parties."

"All right, and then we'll go to my flat and have a drink with Mala. I must have a drink with the poor dear."

"And then?"

She said, "We'll wander. A real old pub crawl. It's been my life's ambition. Before the war I always managed to get stuck at a stodgy party. Do you mind terribly, darling?"

"I mind terribly but what can I do?"

"Oh, splendid. I've always wanted to be a bully."

He said, "Pick you up at eight."

"Lovely."

"And watch out for those air force drunks."

She laughed. "These lads have given up on me ages ago. I don't get the slightest tumble except from some colonels and they're all married—oh, Brad darling, I'm sorry. Do you hear me, darling? I'm sorry."

He said, "Terrible noise on the line. Sorry about what, Val?"

She said, "It's too hard talking in this racket. See you at eight."

He had heard her all right and he didn't care. Neither of them cared. The sharp edge of their concern had long since been blunted by the time and the atmosphere, and the small voices that occasionally gnawed at them when they were apart simply fell away in the sight of each other.

Nothing normal mattered any more. At Val's Red Cross club the terrible casualties of daylight raids over Germany had become merely figures. If there were eighty-seven planes missing one felt disappointed, but only twenty-two planes missing was cause for high spirits. The bright fresh faces of the young fliers who were shattered in the skies over Hamburg and Leipzig could be quickly forgotten. At COSSAC in Norfolk House, Brad worked in the liaison section. The estimate of twenty-two per cent casualties among the nine divisions of assaulting troops on D-day was a logistically comforting statistic; only the rate of production of landing craft was disconcerting.

There wasn't any future except when they were apart, and then the future consisted of the moment they would meet again.

He managed to extricate his girl from the teeming, frothing lobby of the Park Street club. A slight ground haze gave the cold an extra bite at the neck and ankles, but the sky was clear and a diffident moon poured enough light into the haze to give the careening drunks on Grosvenor Square a middling chance of avoiding one another.

Hurrying across the square they were serenaded by a huddle of American air force youngsters singing "White Christmas" and the silver haze that lay on the street and the earnestness of the singing, though the men were nipping from bottles contained in paper bags, made the listening very sweet and touching.

Val said, "It's going to be a lovely evening, my darling. If I had known you were going to be off early I'd have put on my party dress."

This gave him a chance to stop and kiss her. He said, "I never know what you're wearing."

"What a dreadful thing to say!"

"It's true. The face is too much."

"I can change when we go home."

He said, "Mala doesn't like me."

"Of course she does. She doesn't trust foreigners, that's all. She thinks they're all dangerously good-looking."

"She's a foreigner herself."

"Don't be silly, darling. The English aren't English any more. Only people like Mala are. She's Clive's immortal triumph."

He said, "Do *you* trust foreigners?"

"Definitely not."

"No?"

"I don't mean you, my darling. I always think you're that first Parker of Devonport come home at last. Did they play *Berkeley Square* in America? Leslie Howard was wonderful in it."

He said, "We're in Grosvenor Square."

"Are we? I never know when I'm with you." She kissed him lightly. "Oh, it's going to be a lovely evening."

They stayed at the apartment only long enough to savor a glass of pink champagne, although Ray Boyce's Free French colleagues, who were drinking cognac, scoffed at the stuff. One of them demonstrated by shaking a few drops of the champagne in his hair and rubbing vigorously. The party seemed well behaved as Ray's parties went, all except Ray, who was in rare form (he had that day been promoted to major) and insisted on toasting the French and the British and Val and his wife and the coming victory. "We'll win all right," he exclaimed, "but here's to winning not because we're strong and getting stronger but because we're right and getting righter!" Brad decided Ray was a born diplomat because he could see the Frenchmen were very happy about the toast.

Middleton, the hall porter, came in for a New Year's drink. He apologized for being a bit merry, explaining that he had been visiting his other tenants, and it was clear that his two-year contact with Americans had caused some dilution in the dour reserve which had been his hallmark.

Ray protested vigorously when Val and Brad left. He followed them down the hall and bellowed, "You're anti-social you two. Anti-social, anti-foreign, and dammit, anti-democratic! You're a couple of Philistines! That's the trouble with love. There's no fun in it——" By this time they had fled into the elevator.

When they got to Valerie's flat, she disappeared into her bedroom for a long time. She finally came into the living room, flushed and shimmering and lovely in her beige Paris frock. The changing hues from the wood fire in the hearth danced on her light hair, and the half-sweet, half-anxious smile played on her mouth. He thought she was the most beautiful woman on earth. She sat on the carpet beside his chair and said, "It's going to be a truly lovely evening, my darling."

Then Mala came in, stiff and unyielding as she always seemed to be in Brad's presence, never quite looking at him but always respectfully attentive, and they had their drink.

They started at the local just around the corner on Elizabeth Street, and there in the public bar they found a taxi chauffeur having a mild and bitter. He agreed to drive them to the 400 on Leicester Square. Val protested that the 400 was much too swank for a pub crawl but they danced all the dances until eleven-thirty and Brad was sure that everybody in the elegant room was looking at his girl because she was so beautiful.

They went out into the dark crowded street and walked toward the Strand. As they passed the Nurse Cavell monument she tugged at his arm and led him down into Trafalgar Square. "We can hear Big Ben from here," she said. "Please, Brad."

On this night the street revelers of London rallied at two distinct points as if it had been so arranged. The troops, Americans, Canadians, and young apple-cheeked British, frolicked into Piccadilly Circus, brandishing flasks and bottles and surging around the bare pedestal from which the statue of Eros had been removed. The Londoners foregathered at the foot of Nelson's column in Trafalgar Square and there waited quietly to hear the chimes roll up on the heavy night air out of Westminster.

Valerie and Brad stood on the museum steps overlooking the square. In his uniform he felt like an intruder in a family gathering. And yet not so much an intruder. He held close to Val and he was part of her and she was part of this, and so in a way he belonged.

For a time the square was quiet, as if the people resented the faint sound of revelry from the foreigners in Piccadilly. Then there was a mass shuffling among them and everybody linked hands cross-armed and they began to sing "Auld Lang Syne" not loudly but sweetly and sadly as British crowds always did their singing. They swayed as they sang and their linked arms made the whole crowd sway like a great wave back and forth. It seemed a long time after the song died away that the chimes of Big Ben penetrated the night air.

The last stroke of midnight lingered over the square. A woman standing close by said, "I guess 'arry's thinking of us," and someone rejoined, "It's an hour gone in Italy and 'arry's probably drunk." Then

Val kissed him. She said, "Happy New Year, my darling. Now let's run to the Savoy for a big wonderful warming drink and then on to the pubs. It's a lovely New Year's Eve."

It was about half past the midnight in the American bar at the Savoy when they heard that John Wynter had been reported missing in action.

A covey of young R.A.F. pilots had plunged out of the men's bar, making for the lobby. They were self-possessed youths with wings and multiple decorations on their tight-fitting tunics and one or two of them sported handle-bar mustaches which looked silly on their boyish faces. Almost everyone in the room had turned to look at the noisy, happy young heroes and that's when Val had caught sight of Bertie Wynter.

"Happy, happy!" he had called out as he came to their table. He was flushed and a little drunk.

She had introduced him to Brad and it was a waste of effort because Bertie paid no attention to the American beyond a limp handshake.

"I say, Val, you're a stunner tonight. Isn't it a grand night?"

She had said, "You watch yourself, Bertie. Your eyes aren't as clear as they should be."

"We've been tearing like mad," he had said proudly. "We've got a hansom outside. Actually a hansom, Val. One of the chaps dug it up God knows where, driver and all, and we've been galloping all over the old town. Simply tremendous fun."

One of Bertie's friends had dashed back for him. "Come on, Bertie, we've got to find oats for the dobbin and then we're going to crash the dancing on Tottenham Court Road."

"I thought we were going to prang the Dorchester."

"Bobby's keen on impressing a *refeened* parlormaid."

"Be with you in a minute."

"Well, hurry it up. Dobbin's hungry."

Then Bertie had said, "You haven't heard, have you, Val?"

"Heard what?"

"About John going missing."

Brad watched her closely. Her head went a little askew and she looked at the floor. Then she turned to him and her eyes were wide

open as if she had no lids at all and he didn't know what to read in
them, shock or grief or penitence or even accusation.

"When did it happen?" Her voice was flat and calm.

Bertie said, "It's a shocker, I know, but it's really not that bad.
There's always the chance he's in the bag. It happened on the Sangro
and John apparently was hit so there's a chance he's in the bag——"

"When did it happen, Bertie?"

"We got the telegram yesterday."

"And you didn't call me."

"Oh, Father talked about calling you but we didn't really know
much and it seemed silly——"

Bertie's friend was back. "Come on, lad. You're holding up the
bloody parade."

"Be right with you." Bertie looked at her and squirmed. "I do have
to go, Val. I—I guess I shouldn't have spilled it."

Now her eyes began to glisten. She said, "Why aren't you at Smallhill?"

"On New Year's Eve? God, Val, you've been to Smallhill. The old
boy moping about and all that. Anyway I've had a beast of a week.
Sweeps every day and four chaps in the squadron bought it. That's
the trouble with the Spit. Grand plane and all that but the damned
fuel tank's in the wrong position and if it catches fire you can't even
jump. You've got to flip over on your back and by then it's too late—
anyway four lads didn't get out—oh, damn, they're going without
me." He stood guilty for an irresolute moment. "I've really got to run."

They sipped at their brandy for a time without speaking and then
she said, "I'm sorry, darling. It's not really your affair and now it's
gone and spoiled your New Year's Eve. I'm most dreadfully sorry."

He said, "It's not your fault. It's not anybody's fault."

She said, "I think I'd better go home. No—let's have one more
brandy. May we?"

They finished the new drink quickly and left. There were others
waiting for a taxi and they stood a long time in the darkness of the
court while a porter went out into the Strand to snare one.

She said, "It's not the shock, darling. I've expected it so long that
there isn't any shock left in me. I think it's Bertie tearing about the
town that's saddened me. And yet you can't blame Bertie. It's a
disease. It's the war. And the worst is yet to come. Of course you

can't tell me, my darling, but you know it, don't you? The worst is yet to come. Don't mind me. It's not John, really it's not. I love you, and you *will* go home to Ray's party and have a grand time. Promise me you will."

A taxi finally came into the court and he drove her home. There was nothing to say except, "Tomorrow?" And she said, "Of course. Tomorrow."

Walking to Grosvenor Square, he thought the English were the most emotional people in the world. The façade, the stiff upper lip, was a pretty obvious gambit if you knew the English.

The party at 37 Grosvenor had grown to enormous proportions. The apartment was filled with people he didn't know. He shouldered his way to his room and went to bed.

## 18

I T  W A S late on a cold gray afternoon in January and the sirens had just wailed an alert which created not the slightest disturbance among the crowds leaving the shops and offices of the West End. Everyone in London knew that plans for the greatest sea-borne invasion in history were being fashioned within the solid granite walls of Norfolk House in nearby St. James's Square; the Germans knew it too, and with the approach of almost every dusk their bombers swept up the Thames estuary in an operation which came quickly to be known as the Little Blitz and which interested no one except those unlucky people who chanced to be hit and the deep thinkers in the Psychological Warfare section who evaluated these blind, ineffective thrusts as evidence of the enemy's nervousness.

In the huge room which contained COSSAC's liaison sections, a room filled with steel-gray desks like the clearinghouse of a bank, the siren had had no effect. Its wail had merely overridden the clatter of typewriters and mimeograph machines being worked by uniformed girls in a fenced-off segment outside the private offices of the generals and the admirals.

When the siren died out, the captain at the desk next to Brad's said, "Damn! It'll be hell getting a taxi and I've got to pick up a gal at the Embassy. Ever see some of those gals in the visa section? Brother!" He was a man called Fox, a national-guard officer who had seen his first action at Salerno and after a week of it had been sent back to England for reassignment to a non-fighting job.

Brad turned around to make a rejoinder and that was when he caught sight of two men coming down the aisle between the desks toward the private offices.

One of them was Dan Stenick.

The other was a tall, big-boned British captain of marines. The two men strode with quick, muscular precision and their cleated heels rang out on the hardwood floor as if to advertise to the desk-bound, paper-fighting soldiers that a couple of combat men had arrived in their midst. An A.T.S. corporal from reception who was conducting them had to trot to keep up.

Dan's face was stern, his chin high, and for a moment Brad thought he was going to pass right on through. Then, as if nudged by a telepathic signal, he turned his head impulsively and his mouth dropped open in delight and amazement.

Brad saw that his temples had become flecked with gray, his face had lost some of its roundness, and his eyes seemed deeper and more meaningful. An oak leaf gleamed on his Silver Star and two new battle stars had been added to his African ribbon.

But he apparently hadn't changed inside. He whipped his hand into Brad's with a smack which caused heads to be raised all over the huge room.

"It's the printer! Jeez, boy, I'm glad to see you. Imagine runnin' into you like this. How long you been here, you bastard?"

They talked for a moment or two and then Dan turned to glance at the British marine, who was already inside the gate near the private offices and motioning him to hurry. He said, "Got to get in there, boy. Wait for me, hear? Won't be more'n a couple minutes. Jeez, this is great, kiddo." He hurried to rejoin his companion and both men followed the corporal into the office of Commodore Turner.

Brad dropped his paper work. He reflected on the gray at Dan's temples, on the oak leaf and the battle stars, and the hard, firm-fleshed, wind-burned handsomeness a man's face takes on when he's conditioned for combat, and it occurred to him that Dan was a symbol of the war he had left home to fight and of the warrior he had set out to be.

They remained in Commodore Turner's office a good deal longer than a couple of minutes, as Brad guessed they would. He felt sorry for them.

Commodore Minton Turner, an officer who had grown gray in the depression navy of the thirties, was notorious at COSSAC for being chronically unable to explain anything to anybody in less than twenty minutes, and when he had to refuse a request it usually took a full hour. He still suffered from the pre-war military malady of avoiding the slightest offense to anyone, even emissaries as lowly as army captains.

His problem was landing craft. At the dawn of 1944 people back home envisioned the year of decision in terms of immense armies driving the foe relentlessly across the hedgerows of France, but the field commanders dreamed their rosiest dreams in terms of ugly little ships which could drop a ramp on a hostile beach. Landing craft were in short supply; all the shipyards in America and Britain working around the clock couldn't keep pace with the tempo of the war rising rapidly to its climax. Landing craft were the bottleneck in every plan, the chip on every general's shoulder, the stickler at every high-level conference. The problem was so acute that Allied HQ in the Mediterranean exchanged a formal mission with Allied HQ in Britain for the purpose of spying out and reporting any fancied unfairness in the allocation of the snub-prowed little ships.

In these circumstances, Commodore Turner, who was in the chain for allocation of landing craft to units in training, was even more long-winded than was his bent. He had no craft to allocate to American, British, and Canadian units that were ripping up the south coast in vigorous rehearsals for D-day. When unit commanders or their deputies came storming at him with the irrefutable argument that they couldn't rehearse assault landings without landing craft, he spoke slowly and precisely of production complications in the shipyards and of the troublesome problem of supplying craft for Operation Shingle, which was the forthcoming assault at Anzio. He was the perfect man in his job. His entrapped listeners, bored beyond belief but unable to become angered at this earnest, plodding man, usually fled his office determined never again to try to jump the gun on rehearsal craft.

Now it was more than an hour. The outer office was empty except for Brad and the men who had drawn night duty. The alert still hung on. Distant and sporadic anti-aircraft fire (a good ten miles away, he figured) faintly penetrated the blackout curtains. He found himself unable to concentrate on his current job which was to summarize into two pages a thirty-page study of the weight of Sherman tanks in relation to the stress limit of French bridges between Utah beach and Carentan. He put the reports away and fell to thinking about Valerie.

He wouldn't see her until late. It was her first free day since the news about John Wynter and she had gone to Smallhill to spend it with Viscount Haltram. He loved her all the more for it, for the quick, intuitive compassion that made her true and lovely, inside and out. But he missed her, even for the few hours. He hoped she would take an early train back.

Once more a sound of distant cannonading came into the room. He found it a comforting sound. *The war will make it right* she had said. The war had made it right, at least for her. They had always shared the gnawing hurt of conflicting loyalties; though it was unspoken it intensified their dependence one upon the other and added a sense of clandestine magic to the simple joy of being together. Now she was free. Their delicately balanced little world had gone off balance and the duty of putting it right was his alone. That duty was coming up to challenge him sooner than he had expected.

Damien's letter, which he had received that morning, had come from Fort Lauderdale in Florida.

". . . The big news," he had written, "is that I may very well be seeing you in about two weeks. Mr. Stimson has invited a small group of publishers to make a brief inspection tour of Britain (because, I suspect, he wants us to see there really *is* going to be a second front) and he has been kind enough to include me. You know my reluctance to accept a government facility under any conditions, but the itinerary calls for a few hours in London and my immense anxiety to see you supersedes, I'm afraid, the *Star's* stout traditions.

"Janie is here at Lauderdale with us, an achievement for which we must thank Dr. Bloch, who resolutely ordered the holiday. She was terribly run-down, and small wonder! I never dreamed anyone (especially Janie!) could work as hard as she has during this past year. She seemed deliberately to plunge into duties that wouldn't allow her a moment's respite. In addition to the Red Cross work and the hospitality hut in Revere Square which she runs almost single-handedly, she has organized a transport corps to run relatives to military hospitals as far away as Boston—but here I am telling you things she has probably written you a dozen times. What she hasn't written, I'm sure, is about her illness. It apparently isn't all pure physical exhaustion. She is emotionally ill, nerves tight as a drumhead, Bloch tells us, and I can believe him. From where I write I can see her, resting on a beach chair, and I have the impression there is something extraordinarily melancholy about her attitude toward life.

"I guess she misses you. For that matter, I miss you too—and badly. There's a tremendous job of reorganization to do at the *Star*. We're simply growing out of our skins, despite the war. Circulation and want ads have been pushed out of the tower and are operating out of two floors in the old Chartman warehouse we were lucky enough to lease. We're going to need two new presses, including color, which advertisers are beginning to demand, and it all adds up to a clear need for building an annex to the tower. I wouldn't dream of going ahead with plans until you get back, and from the way the war is moving I imagine that won't be too long.

"Did I tell you that Sanford Jaques called in when he was in Malton last month? Probably mending a few fences for the autumn election. He seems to have grown terribly fond of you. Whatever did you do for him in Algiers?

"Your mother arrived down here yesterday and looks wonderfully well. We're happy to have her, of course! She's extremely proud of you, as we all are . . ."

There was a postscript:

"Grace has just looked over my shoulder and has asked me to say —please write Janie more often. Dr. Bloch says it will help a great deal."

He listened to the sound of cannonading. It was closer now but still far down the estuary. He listened to it with all his senses. He liked the feel and the sound of war. He remembered a cocktail party he and Valerie had attended on Boxing Day. A colonel's wife, a pretty baroness who also worked for the American Red Cross, had said brightly on the urging of several gins, "You know, darlings, one of these nights, Lord love us, the war is going to end and I can only think a great big gong will crash and a supernatural voice will say, 'Time's up, ladies, everybody back to their own husbands.' What a traffic jam *that* will be!" The gay company had laughed, for she said it crisply and well. He had glanced at Valerie. She wasn't laughing, nor was he.

A battery of heavy anti-aircraft shattered the night. It was close now, probably just about over in Green Park, and the light bulb on his desk shuddered. After a time he wished Valerie hadn't gone to Smallhill.

"Holy jumpin' Jerusalem! Another minute an' I'd go clean off my rocker! This guy'd be the champ in an old ladies' home. He's a secret weapon. He'd drive Hitler nuts. He your boss, boy? How you stand it?"

After an hour and a quarter with Commodore Turner, Dan had come staggering toward Brad's desk, feigning abject weakness. "I need a drink, boy. A commodore yet! Imagine this guy in action. The gun'd be obsolete before he pulled the trigger. Where's a drink around here? Anythin', arsenic, anythin'. Jeez, I'm glad to see you. How long was I in there? Couple months?"

Brad said, "You were lucky. He sometimes goes twice as long. You shouldn't come nuzzling around for an LCI."

"Who said anything about an LCI?"

"That's what you saw him for, isn't it?"

Dan scratched his head. "Maybe. Got a bar in this morgue?"

"Top floor."

"Say boy, this is Captain Waller." The British marine captain had come up behind Dan. "Call him Jeff. Brad Parker—old buddy from way back. Okay, let's go get a quick one."

The Britisher, who wore two rows of decorations on his battle-dress jacket, gave an appearance of such bruising toughness that Dan seemed almost delicate by comparison. He was tall, his long neck heavily muscled, and the disordered contours of his face made it difficult to guess his age. He had small, thick ears lying flat against a close-cropped head; his cheeks were lumpy and his nose twisted, and the hand he offered Brad was huge and had an angry grip. Brad noticed that both men wore the same sleeve patch, the rifle and anchor design of Combined Operations.

He asked, puzzled, "You both in the same oufit?"

Waller said, "Yas," in the peculiar cockney pronunciation which sounded much like the Negro mess boys back at Fort Harrison.

Dan said, "Betcha. We're gettin' up a real outfit. Breakfast time Jeff pours a bag of nails in his cornflakes so he can chew good." He chuckled. "Where's the drink, kiddo?"

"Wait a minute. You fellows are kidding me. What do you mean— the same outfit?"

Dan glanced at the Britisher. "I'm not kiddin'."

"You're still with the Rangers, aren't you?"

"Sure," Dan said carelessly. "Come on, boy. One drink. We got to get goin'. We got a colonel who burns your back teeth if you don't report."

Brad took his coat and cap and led the men up a staircase to the top floor. After their passes had been scrutinized, he brought them into COSSAC's pride and joy.

What had once been the austere board room of Lloyd's Bank was now an officers' club dominated by a fancy bar and complete with the irreverent accouterments of a happy drinking place. It was crowded with chattering men and women of all services in the D-day triumvirate, and though waitresses ran their unceasing errands between the bar and the tables, the talk was uninhibited, much of it about the most priceless and dreadful secret in all the world. Words like *Neptune, Mulberry, Juno,* and *Omaha,* hallowed words in the D-day hierarchy, were spattered about in the lively conversation. The anti-aircraft fire outside could scarcely be heard.

Dan and his British comrade, their faces tweaking with incredulity, sipped at their whisky and kept looking about the noisy room.

Finally Dan said, "Hey, Jeff, a buck against a shilling the colonel don't believe it."

Waller seemed dazed. He asked, "What's the form, Parker?"

Brad was enjoying himself hugely. "You fellows feel you can talk freely now?"

"I'll tell you, boy," Dan said uncertainly, "we got an outfit you won't find listed in the order of battle. It's a special force."

"Oh, one of those." Brad knew of all kinds of specially trained and semi-independent units being organized for D-day. There were the air-borne scheduled to drop inland six hours in advance of H-hour, marine engineers going in at H-hour minus thirty minutes to remove submerged obstacles from the beach approaches, and certain small units assigned the task of making a furtive visit to the D-day beaches a full week in advance in order to scoop up samples of sand for technical study by the tank people. He said, "What's so mysterious about it?"

Dan said, "You got your security system. We got ours. What about these waitresses? They staff officers in disguise? Set up a conference for me, boy. Any time."

"Yas," Waller said. "Pretty bloody poor show, I'd say."

Brad explained COSSAC's security system with a certain appetite. All COSSAC personnel were proud of the experiment made by the shrewd, cheerful, and daring British general who organized the head-quarters, pending the arrival of the supreme commander.

"The general called together everybody who works in this building. And I mean everybody—cooks, waitresses, janitors, window cleaners, as well as the brass and all the rest of us and spilled the works about Overlord. Simple as that. Any questions?"

An uneven grin spread across Waller's knobbed face. "He's got a nerve."

Dan said, "How's it workin'?"

"So far perfectly. Everybody's on their honor. And we can come up here and blow off steam."

"In our mess," Dan chuckled, "we can't put a calendar on the wall 'cause it says 1944 and that's a breach of security."

Brad asked, "Are you H-hour?"

"Ahead."

"Jumping?"

Dan shook his head. "Uh—uh."

Brad whistled. "One of those."

"Yas," Waller grunted, looking about with a derisive grin. "Ours is a proper do."

It was a proper do all right, Brad thought. The estimated casualties for pre-H-hour operations on the beaches ran as high as seventy per cent for the marine engineers and only slightly less for certain special units assigned to destroy heavy German emplacements which had already been photographed and pinpointed.

Waller swallowed the last of his drink. "Fine whisky, Parker," he said, and then to Dan: "Come on. Get cracking."

"Jeez, boy," Dan said, "we're movin' outa town tomorrow. God-damn trainin' area." He turned around to Waller. "No reason why he can't come down to our mess for a drink."

The marine shrugged. "Your responsibility. No skin off my fanny."

Brad said, "I'd rather not, Dan." He had felt warm pleasure at see-ing Dan, but now something akin to resentment was taking its place. He thought perhaps it was Waller he didn't like.

Dan said, "What do you mean—you'd rather not? You got somethin' better to do? Hell, boy, we're leavin' tomorrow."

Brad was conscious of his own resentment and fought it down. "All right. Let's go."

They went downstairs and signed out. In St. James's Square it was cold and drizzly and black. The cannonading could scarcely be heard. The searchlights tracking the sky were several miles distant.

Dan said, "These raids give me the willies. I'll take a nice foxhole hollerin' distance from the Germans any time. Here I feel like a fish in a barrel."

Waller drove the jeep. He was all elbows and knees in the shallow seat as he gunned the vehicle around the square and tore through a complex of narrow streets into Piccadilly. His eyes were superb, for he handled the jeep with daring and whisker precision though the night was impenetrable. Brad decided he was making a small demonstration for the benefit of the chicken-livered staff officer.

They screeched around Hyde Park Corner and drove along deserted streets deep into Kensington. When a fire truck suddenly swung wide out of a cross street, Waller jammed on his brakes. The jeep skidded crazily on the wet asphalt. Then he straightened out and gunned the vehicle once more.

Dan said, "If it's a fire you're goin' to, Jeff, you're goin' the wrong way. If I got to croak, it might as well be in the war."

The Britisher chuckled. "You're not scared, are you, Parker?"

Dan cut in. "Listen, Jeff, that's no scout badge he's wearin'. I saw this guy jump at eight thousand feet in a twenty-mile wind. He was operatin' when you'd be pukin' your guts out."

Brad listened to the talk. He didn't know which he resented more, the marine's attitude or Dan's defense of him. Then a burst of antiaircraft fire thundered all around them in the black drizzle.

Waller made a sharp turn off Old Brompton Road and came to a halt near a dwelling which even in the darkness seemed to stand whole amid the burned-out ruins of its neighbors. It had not, however, escaped punishment. A pathway to the door ran through rubble and in the hall the wall plaster had crumbled to the floor. There were no light fixtures; only a dim bulb hung from a wire strung across the ceiling. What was once a living room contained only an unpainted wooden table and a few chairs. The window frames were roughly boarded over on the inside.

Dan called out, "Carson!" and a soldier wearing a white houseman's coat over British battle dress clattered into the room. "Carson, any whisky left?"

"A bit, sir."

"Three then. Mark it up to me."

"Yes, sir."

"The colonel still here?"

"Yes, sir. He's been asking for you and Captain Waller."

"Okay. Get the drinks." Dan turned to Waller. "Why don't you go in and tell the old man?"

"We were both sent."

Dan said, "What the hell. There's nothin' to report. We got the ol' run-around. Tell him I'm entertainin' a hostage from Cossac."

Waller thought it over dubiously for a moment, then walked briskly to a door off the far wall of the room, knocked on it, and entered. The sound of his heels clicking as he saluted was like a rifle shot.

Dan motioned Brad to a chair. "How you like this setup? Crummy, eh? We been here three weeks organizin' the outfit. Three weeks in this dump's enough. I'm glad we start trainin' tomorrow. You know you're a real son of a bitch for not tellin' me you're in town all the time."

Brad said, "I'd like to know about the mission, Dan."

"It's a beaut. The best yet. Where you been hidin' out? Bet you got a gal."

Brad said, "What's Waller doing in it?"

"We're going to have some Canadians too. It's a three-way deal, this one. A beaut."

The soldier called Carson, a short, blond youth, came in with the drinks and an extra tumbler of water. After he set them down, he said, "You're all packed, sir, all except your bedding roll. I'll do that up in the morning."

Dan watched him march out of the room. He said, "A guy like that almost makes you wish you were a limey. We got no batmen in our army, not like him."

Brad said, "If it's a pre-H-hour deal, it must be cleaning out beach obstacles."

"Here's to you, boy." Dan lifted his glass. They drank and then Dan said, "Don't mind Jeff. He acts tough, only with him it's no act. That's one thing I found out about the British. Most of 'em aren't as tough as our guys, but when they come tough—brother, they're tough."

They sipped at their drinks. Brad said, "You don't want to talk about the mission."

Dan grimaced. "I can't, tootsie. You got your security system and we got ours, and the guy who laid down the law he's real buggy on the subject——" He thumbed toward the colonel's door and clapped his mouth shut. Waller was coming out.

The marine grabbed his drink, waved it around, and took a big swallow. He said, "The old man wants to see you *and* your friend. Better hop to it. He's burning."

Dan said, "What you mean he's burnin'?"

"The old story."

"He's nuts. You tell him Brad's from Cossac?"

"I told you way back it's no skin off my fanny."

Dan put down his glass and winked at Brad. "Give him the old spit and polish and we're outa trouble. He's a real good head only he's got this bug."

"American or British?"

"American. Okay, boy, like the old days at Fort Harrison. Hup! One two three!"

The two men swung into quick firm step and marched across the room. They made sure their heels rang out in unison loudly enough to be heard behind the closed door.

He should have known, Brad thought. There could only be one such colonel in the whole of the Allied Expeditionary Force. It fell into his laggard awareness even as he was clicking his heels at the threshold and saluting. A pot of coffee sat steaming on the desk. There spun into his mind a distinct association with the pair of enormous shoulders, the muscular neck, and shiny black hair, and before the colonel twisted his scowling face around Brad knew he was Alex Timmer.

The scowl melted on the hard, handsome face and reappeared instantly, but it wasn't the same scowl; now it was tinged with surprise and small traces of pleasure.

Timmer said, "Talk to you in a minute, Brad," and then the face stormed up again. "All right, Dan. You know the orders. What have you got to say?"

Dan said slowly, "You know Lieutenant Parker, sir?"

"Do you know the orders?"

"I figured, Colonel, an officer from Cossac was safe enough."

"Nobody's safe enough!" The sound of the gruff monotone filled Brad with nostalgia as if 1942 had transpired in his far, far youth. "I thought I laid that down in orders. Nobody's safe enough and I don't give a good God damn who it is. How do you figure you know who's safe enough? There's a cover operation in circulation. Maybe he's been told about *that*. How do *you* know? Maybe ours is the cover operation. Ever think of that?"

Dan looked extraordinarily contrite. "I guess you're a hundred per cent right, Colonel."

"I lay down an order. One simple specific goddamn order. This headquarters is secret. No talk. No visitors." Timmer bounced a finger hard on the desk to punctuate his words. His face grew red and fierce. He was feeding on his own choler. "By God, I'm not sure I shouldn't kick you out. We've got months of training ahead of us. Security's going to get tougher. We're not even started and here you waltz a man in just because he's wearing a uniform. I tell you, Dan, of all the crazy, dumb, dangerous plays, this one takes the grand prize——"

He ran out of words and reached for his coffee. Brad said, "I've got to take some of the rap, Colonel. Our security setup at Cossac——"

"I like my own setup. As long as I'm commanding this outfit it's going to be run my way." He glared a long time at the captain. "This is your last goof, Dan. Next time you won't know what hit you till you land up at a court-martial. Understood?"

"Yes, sir."

The hard, square face relaxed abruptly. "You're a lucky soldier. If you had to fumble, you fumbled with the one man I know I can trust. But it doesn't excuse you. Now get out and let me have a word with Lieutenant Parker."

Dan heeled and toed a precise turn, gave Brad a hidden thumbs-up sign, and marched out of the room.

The colonel put his hands over his eyes and rubbed them gently. "Sit down, Brad. Have a smoke. I'm damned glad to see you."

Nothing had changed, Brad observed. Having played the hard-bitten professional, Timmer had now fallen back on another old stand-by, the careworn commander. Nothing at all had changed, not even the silver medallion on his epaulet.

Timmer must have noticed the same thing about Brad. He brought his hands from his eyes and said, "No promotion? How long have you been at Cossac?"

"I got back from the Med end of October, Colonel."

"Still wrestling paper, eh? That's the way it goes. It's murder unless you're from the Point. Got to explode yourself out." He brought an extra cup out of his desk drawer, filled it with coffee, and pushed it across the desk. The same wide, mirthless grin spread across his resolute mouth. "Remember my little job at Dieppe? Well, it finally paid off. Took a long time. They had me in Movement Control and when the section doubled in size and the T.O. called for eagles in my job they whistled up a young squirt from the Point and shifted me to Supply. For a couple of months I was in command of every toilet bowl between here and Salisbury. But I hammered. By God, I hammered! And finally somebody remembered Dieppe——"

The rich high tone of the all-clear swarmed into the room. Timmer listened to it. There was a glint of excitement in his small, stabbing eyes.

"Remember me telling you Alex Timmer would go home a general or a corpse? Well, this is it. Took a long time but I've got what I want."

He lit a cigarette and snorted two sharp streams of smoke from his nostrils. "This is one they can't take away from me. It's an independent force. No higher echelons around here. No generals to grab the credit. When the balloon goes up this outfit will be playing for keeps. And when it's over I'll be right up there with the best of them or I'll be dead." He chuckled. "No wonder they gave me the job. Only a crazy coot like Alex Timmer would go for it."

Brad saw an opportunity he had been looking for. He said, "If Dan Stenick is typical of your outfit, you're in the clear, Colonel. They don't come better than Dan. He's a born fighter. We trained together at Harrison."

Timmer said, "Clowns a lot but he's all right. Not the best but all right. I've got a Canadian who gave up a majority to come in with us as a captain just because this is his kind of a fight. And there's Jeff Waller. You met Jeff. Twenty-three raids with the Commandos and he's never killed a German with a bullet. Always a knife or his bare hands. Got a couple more good tough officers reporting tomorrow at the training area. Interviewed hundreds. All I've been doing for eight-nine weeks and I'm still at it."

Timmer went on in his gruff monotone, detailing the bloodthirsty qualities of his officers and making vague references to the suicidal nature of the mission. A well-remembered fever played behind the eyes of his otherwise impassive face. Brad sipped at his coffee and wondered when the exposition would end and the challenge would come. He knew Timmer too well. There would be a challenge.

It eventually came but not quite in the way he anticipated. Timmer looked squarely at him and said, "I'll say this for myself. I don't kid any of my men. I lay it right on the line. I tell 'em you don't have to be crazy to join this outfit—but it helps."

Then he got up and walked Brad slowly to the door. He said, "I don't know if you barged in with Stenick because you knew I was in command here or if it was just an accident——"

Brad said, "Strictly an accident, Colonel."

Timmer smiled as if he knew better. "Hell, Brad, you're a good man. Back on Grosvenor Square I figured you the only officer I had with real stuff on the ball. But this thing here—this is the real war. It's a different world. This is for the type of man who wants nothing except to get in there and fight, and the hotter the better. You know what I mean."

He had been used this way before, Brad told himself. He remembered the man at Dieppe. This was merely Timmer on the road to a greater Armageddon convincing himself that everybody else lacks his courage.

He said, "I'm happy where I am, Colonel, but all the same I'm sorry you don't think I would qualify."

Timmer gave him a friendly tap on the sleeve. "Nice seeing you again, Brad. Tell Stenick to give you a set of co-ordinates for the training area and be sure to drop by if you're in the neighborhood. Always glad to see you."

In the outer room Dan had another drink ready. "Lucky thing you knew the colonel, boy," Dan chuckled. "He's sumpin', eh? Old woman about security but he's one hell of a soldier."

Brad thought, I know him like a book too and he's something less than one hell of a soldier.

But on his way home by Underground he reflected on his interview with Timmer and discovered he liked him for all his weaknesses. He knew that Timmer in his curious, inverted way had offered him a job in a tough, fighting outfit. He had no intention of volunteering for the job but the offer made him feel better about himself. He couldn't wait to see Valerie.

She telephoned as soon as the train from Tunbridge Wells had pulled into Victoria Station. He met her at the Green Park Underground and they dashed through the drizzle to a small French restaurant off Curzon Street.

Each time he beheld her face was a brand-new adventure, and especially this night, and he didn't notice until long after she had taken off her mackintosh that she was dressed like a young widow just out of the first stage of mourning. The suit she was wearing was black, buttoned high, with only a trace of her white blouse showing at the neck. He had never seen the suit before and he wondered if she had bought it on account of John. Then he remembered with relief that she had recently been in mourning for her father.

The waiter was slow bringing her a gin and orange. When it came she drank it eagerly, speaking not a word until she had finished it. She put down the glass and reached across the tiny table for his hand.

She said, "Better, darling. Much better. I'm coming out of it now. I feel I've been away for years."

"How long?"

"Two or three years at the very least."

He said, "You're stingy. It felt like ten or twenty to me."

"I'm glad. Could I have another?"

"I'm not sure. Fill out a requisition in triplicate and I'll take it under advisement."

She play-acted a pout and when he ordered another drink for her she uttered a sigh of huge relief. The black suit set off her face wonderfully. Her un-English lips seemed redder and fuller against her English complexion and her eyes were indescribably adventurous.

He said, "I wish I could kiss you."

"I kept wishing you would all the way from the Underground. Why didn't you?"

"It was raining."

She smiled pensively. "I think about it each time it rains. It was raining the first time I saw you."

"You didn't see me though. I saw *you*."

"You only think I didn't. I'm very well brought up."

He said, "I wonder what would have happened if I'd jumped out of the jeep and kissed you there and then."

"I'd have kissed you right back."

"You'd have stalked off insulted."

She said, "But I wouldn't. I love kissing you in the rain."

The waiter placed the new drink before her and she looked down into it and suddenly her hand tightened over his. She cried, "Don't let me go back to Smallhill. Ever. Please, my darling—even if I want to, please forbid it. Don't let me go back ever again."

Her head dropped lower and though he couldn't see her eyes he knew she was fighting back tears. "It was a dreadful nightmare. Gray, sad, deserted, bare. Please never let me go back. The poor old man keeps wandering about the place as if he's lost in a woods. My visit wasn't a good idea, it wasn't at all."

Her fingers pressed hard into the palm of his hand and she kept her head askew so he couldn't see her eyes.

He said, "They've had no definite word."

She gave a brief shake of her head. "Nothing. His name hasn't come up on a PW list and the Red Cross in Geneva is a blank. But of course the raid was over a river . . ." She didn't complete the thought. They sat in silence for a little while and gradually her fingers relaxed.

It was past ten o'clock and the after-theater people streamed through the blackout curtain into the little restaurant. There was a red-haired movie actress, one of those whose face was familiar but whose name didn't come quickly to mind, and they took to guessing who she might be and thus spent the time over their supper resolutely avoiding the subject of Smallhill.

*But of course the raid was over a river,* she had said. She who had lived with death all around her since 1940, even she couldn't bring herself to finish the sentence. There had been no PW report (he knew what she had been trying to say) because the body hadn't been found; it was lying in the Sangro. Walking home through the black and drizzle on Park Lane, he wondered about it, about the body at the bottom of the river, and about Timmer and Dan and the man Waller who had never killed a German with a bullet.

He thought, Some die and others live and when it's all over who

are the heroes? John Wynter? Not this John Wynter nor all the John
Wynters. He remembered as a boy standing with his mother in the
lobby of the Waldorf and feeling an intense excitement as General
Pershing came up out of his private railway car which had been
shunted to a private siding underneath the hotel. People pushed forward and there was a lot of hand clapping interlaced with cheers
and he had been thrilled to see the frail, hollow-cheeked old man
who was the hero of the war. He thought, This time Eisenhower
and Montgomery and MacArthur will be the heroes of the war, traveling to the end of their days in private cars and planes, and receiving
honorary degrees from learned deans, and having men walk fore
and aft to make sure that no one so much as jostles them. Who will
care that John Wynter was killed? Or that I was killed? But for the
luck of the draw I might have been killed and he would have been
left with Valerie. Lovely, compassionate Valerie. But *he* was killed.
That's the thing about getting killed. It's nothing and nothing and
nothing, and in a couple of years they don't even remember you.
But if you live you have what you have.

## 19

O N  J A N U A R Y 17 of that year of hope and glory, a new sense of purpose surged through Norfolk House. General Eisenhower arrived to claim his command and by the very act of his arrival, in the manner of a royal standard being hoisted over a great hunting lodge, COSSAC became SHAEF: Supreme Headquarters, Allied Expeditionary Force.

The supreme commander, walking briskly through the offices of Norfolk House by way of showing himself to all hands, failed fortunately to notice that one officer in Liaison remained seated during the brief inspection. Brad hadn't heard the sharp command heralding the arrival of the party, and it wasn't until an unaccustomed scuff of many boots clattered past his desk that he looked about and found himself the only person not standing stiffly at attention. By that time it was too late. The supreme commander and his staff had already moved into another section.

He hadn't heard the command because another event far more important to him had burst in on that startling day.

A few minutes before, a Captain Rouse of Public Relations had reached him on the military line. The War Department's party of newspaper publishers was on its way and one of them, Damien Lakelock, had asked that he be informed. The estimated time of arrival, Rouse said with a slight lisp, hadn't been buttoned up but it would probably be late in the afternoon and the party would be staying overnight at Claridge's.

The distance from his billet to Claridge's hotel was less than fifty yards along Davies Street. Brad walked it slowly. When he reached a mews at the back of the hotel he paused to light a cigarette. The night sky, which glowed with stars and a half moon, lit up the street and set him to wondering how London would be when the war was

over. This is the way the streets would look, he thought; perhaps a
little brighter with the help of lamps but not much. It was hard to
imagine London with street lamps and without blast walls, with traffic jams, without the wonderful intimacy and warmth that develops
in a besieged city.

He flipped away his cigarette and reached into his trench coat
for another. It wasn't that he didn't know exactly what he had to say
or that he quailed before the duty. On the contrary he was content
that it would be done and over soon, and the long months of com-
promise and furtiveness which were foreign to his character would
be at an end.

He lit a new cigarette and told himself it was merely the abrupt-
ness of Damien's arrival that had brought him to linger this way.

He had scarcely arrived at his apartment when the phone had
rung. He had recognized Captain Rouse's lisp and then Damien had
come on the line, his voice shot through with joyous excitement.

". . . I'm only here till tomorrow morning, Brad, so let's not waste
time on the phone. Are you on duty? . . . Oh, good. Then get over
here and let me look at you, my boy. You're not too far away, are
you? . . . My God, that's convenient, and better bring a kit bag. I've
lugged over a raft of presents. Socks, sweaters, chocolates, even
brought a couple of lobsters, live and twitching, at least they were
the last time I looked . . . Come on right up—323 and 324, a suite no
less. I've just cabled Grace I'm not sleeping in Buckingham Palace
but the next thing to it. She was worrying her head off that I'd be
on a cot in a shelter or something—oh, and Jane is a bit better. You
got my letter, I hope. Florida was a real lifesaver. And your mother's
fine . . . Say, you can't arrange a harmless little air raid, can you? I've
waited twenty-five years to get near a war and now that I'm here it's
as peaceful as a Sunday afternoon back in Malton . . . I can't wait
to see you. It's over a year and a half . . . Come on, get that pretty
nurse off your knee and get over here . . ."

It wasn't only the suddenness of Damien's arrival, he thought; it
was Damien himself. He had almost forgotten how deeply fond he
was of Damien, how their relationship was close as brothers. It was
a pity Damien had to hear it first, Damien who enjoyed the even
flow of life as much as life itself. Poor Damien! *Get that pretty nurse
off your knee.* His conception of a wartime romance was as traditional
as Malton itself and as meaningless as a chorus of "Mad'moiselle

from Armentieres." He wished he could muster the deceit to post-
pone the painful hour. He couldn't. He had made all the compromises
he intended to make.

, He walked the last few yards briskly, cut around the blast wall,
and entered Claridge's lobby, which, despite the war, exuded a
tight-lipped air of meticulous luxury.

Damien hadn't changed save possibly that he was more thoroughly
Damien than ever. His Florida tan set off the gray hair with distinction, his lean face fitted perfectly in the handsome Regency sitting room of his suite, and (after the excitement of their first greet-
ings had worn off) the fond smile with which he contemplated his
son-in-law seemed to Brad fonder than ever.

Nor had the deep sense of rapport between them deteriorated.
Brad felt its warmth when, after they had settled down, Damien
said, "I'm almost as surprised as you are to find myself here. The
*Star* has always disapproved government junkets and I fought
against it to the last minute, but it was the only way I could get
here quickly." He looked thoughtfully at his son-in-law. "I felt it was
necessary for me to get here quickly, Brad, so I could make some
contact with whatever it is that's happening between Janie and you.
Not that it means a great deal in the light of what's going on in the
world, but we're all a bit selfish about our own."

At least the shock would be cushioned, Brad thought.

He said, "I want to hear about Janie. Was she very bad?"

"She's regained some weight but now that she's back in Malton
she's going at it harder than ever. There's no stopping her. Motor
corps, canteens, Red Cross, from morning till very late at night. It's
beyond all reason. Dr. Bloch is afraid she'll go under again and this
time, he says, it might be serious."

"But she's always had a good, solid mind. Doesn't she know what
she's doing to herself?"

Damien smiled out of memory. "It's a pity you never knew old
Everett Bolding. He was the most aggressive, purposeful man in
all of New England. Those around him bent to him and there was
no escape. My own Grace inherited nothing of this character. She's
been sweet and pliable all her life. But the genes were there all the
time, they often skip a generation, and Janie has them in full measure." He paused and contemplated his finger tips. "I thought of it

when Janie moved heaven and earth to get over here as the *Star's*
London correspondent. Of course I could control that situation but
Janie wasn't stopped. She switched to something I couldn't control—
the Wacs. The only reason she isn't a Wac officer is the regulation
that forbids a married Wac from being sent to the same theater of
operations as her husband. That's Janie," he said wistfully, "and I
imagine all of old Everett in her cried out in frustration. So she's
doing the only thing she can do to work off the frustration and that's
to drive herself into a breakdown. She loves you, Brad."

He got up and walked toward the window. He stopped short
of the drawn curtain. "I've done it a dozen times already," he said. "I
keep forgetting about the blackout."

He came back slowly to his chair. He said, "Something's happened,
Brad. What is it? Did you two have a quarrel on your last night in
New York? Or has there been something fundamentally wrong in
your marriage I've never suspected?" He didn't wait for a reply.
He went on: "A woman of Janie's self-will is difficult. She resists
diagnosis. Bloch's no analyst of course, but he's known her since she
was born and he's sure it's an emotional matter."

Brad thought he had never seen Damien so nervous. It was a well-
bred nervousness, but it came through his pleasant features.

"Our marriage was always happy, Damien. We had no emotional
disturbances——" He suddenly remembered her outburst on the train
to New York that last night. "Not of any importance."

Damien stared into space for a time. Then he said, "It isn't only
Janie. I don't think I would have come if it were only Janie acting
up. She's so fundamentally sound I'm sure she can survive this emotional storm, or whatever it is. It's also you, Brad. You seem to have
lost interest—at least your letters or the lack of them indicated as
much. There was also something Sanford Jaques said to me a couple
of months ago. Not something he said exactly; it was his attitude.
He said you were a smart young man—harmless enough, but the fat-
cat way in which he said it hurt me. It really hurt. It didn't sound like
you. And the thought struck me that perhaps you're having a difficult
time. Right now I seem to feel you are. You can tell me, Brad. We're
very old and very good friends."

It was going to be hard, Brad thought. Desperately hard. He said,
"Is that all Sanford said? That I was smart?"

"He said you'd arranged your own transfer from Africa to England

like a very smart young man, and smart in Sanford's context is a very
disturbing quality to me. It was strange to find it applied to you of
all people."

"He's not quite accurate, Damien. There was nothing smart about
it. I used Sanford Jaques to poleax a timid colonel into transferring
me back to England. I'm not proud of it."

He watched for Damien's reaction. There was an almost imper-
ceptible wince which left his face quickly.

"There must have been an urgent reason for it," the older man
said indulgently. He peered into Brad's face as though he were looking for signs of battle fatigue. "Let's do this, Brad. Captain Rouse has
left a car and driver downstairs for me. I'm particularly anxious to see
St. Paul's and some of the badly bombed places. There's enough
moon, I think. How about it, Brad? We can talk in the car."

Brad shook his head. He said, "Damien, I used Sanford Jaques to
get myself transferred back here. I wanted to get back here for a very
specific reason. The reason concerns my relationship to Janie and
through that, naturally, my relationship to you." Hearing himself
speak he thought it sounded oddly like the numbered paragraphs
of a military communication.

Damien continued to search Brad's face. "Are you sure you want
to discuss it now?"

"I've thought it through. I——"

"Just a moment, Brad. Before you go on, let me say this. I can remember a few instances in my own life, which on the whole has
been a placid one and certainly hasn't included anything so traumatic
as war, when I've wanted to speak out. I've never regretted that I
stopped short of it. Let me put it another way. There are two stages
in any personal crisis—first, when you feel the crisis rising inside you,
and second, when you put it into words. The first is something every
intelligent married person experiences a great many times in his life.
If he put it into words each time, if he brought it irrevocably into
reality, I'm afraid life would be infinitely more complicated than it
is. Time and thought have a wonderful way of dissipating any crisis.
But once it's put into words and openly expressed, it's trapped and
must be challenged and engaged. The trouble is, the sound of your
own voice makes it much more critical than it really is."

He smiled reassuringly though his eyes were anxious. "How about
it, Brad? Shall we go down to the car and see what's happened to

people who've really had the roof fall in on them? I assume you're being unfaithful to Janie."

Brad remained in his chair. "I wish it were that easy, Damien. It isn't." He looked squarely at his father-in-law by way of a brief and tortured preparation for what was to come. "You've got to know, Damien. It's my duty to tell you. I'm not going back to Malton after the war."

The shock was greater even than he expected. Damien's face was racked as if it had suddenly headed into a chill, rain-swept wind, as if the man had expected a confession of mere fickleness, as if *Get that pretty nurse off your knee* had been the extreme limit of his preparation.

Even now he didn't quite believe what he had heard. He said incredulously, "Where do you intend to go?"

"I haven't thought about it. I can't go back to Malton."

"But—but *after the war* is pretty far off in the future."

"No, Damien. Not for me. The war doesn't make that much difference. I'm not a soldier in the same way that a man leading a platoon at Cassino is a soldier. My job is about as dangerous as crossing Pentland Street against the lights. It's the luck of the draw. Unless my luck changes I can see the end of the war."

The older man sat quietly and after a time the storm passed from his face. He said, "I'd like to hear about it, Brad."

"I feel I should tell you."

Damien shook his head. "Not on that basis, Brad. If you feel you want to tell me, let me hear it as your friend, not as an aggrieved party. I've always been your friend. Most of the time I've felt like your father rather than Janie's, as proud of you and as necessary to your life. I don't know how a boy grows up without a father, as you have, without being left with some scars, emotional scars. Let me be your father in this instance, Brad. Your father and your friend."

He didn't want to believe it, Brad thought; he didn't want to accept it. He was struggling against the bad moment. It would have been easier to face up to Janie. She was willful and resistant; she would fight back. It was hard to hurt this man.

Damien said, "Tell me, Brad. How did you meet her? When did you meet her?"

There was a fireplace in the sitting room handsomely faced in marble. Brad leaned on the mantel above it. The day in Burlingham seemed very long ago.

"It was no sudden thing. Make no mistake about this being an infatuation, an affair. It's nothing like that. We've known each other for a long time, almost from my arrival here, and we've fought against anything like this happening. I've had a whole year in Algiers to think what it means—what it means to Janie and to you and Grace and to my own mother. But there's nothing I can do. Of course I could go back to Janie. It would mean both of us living in a prison of our own misery the rest of our lives. I can't do this to Janie and I can't do it to myself. I wish it weren't this way, Damien. I wish I could view this, even remotely, as an adventure, a soldier's comfort gone a little mad. I can't."

Damien leaned forward in his chair, his elbows propped on his knees. He looked at the floor. "Tell me about the girl—if you want to."

"She has other loyalties too, and she feels bitterly about them. But she's as helpless as I am——"

"Do I gather she's married too?"

"No."

"American?"

"English. She's a brigadier's daughter. At least she was. He was badly wounded at Dunkerque and committed suicide in 1942. The man she's engaged to, morally not formally, is a Commando. He's missing in Italy. She's had a bad war, a really bad war, but that's beside the point——"

Damien looked up thoughtfully. "I don't think it's beside the point, Brad. If you're going to tell me what happened why don't you begin at the beginning?"

"It's useless, Damien. There's really no beginning, no middle, and certainly no end. We didn't meet in an air raid. I didn't save her life. She didn't nurse me back to health. There was no one event, no dizzy melodrama. The war had nothing to do with it. We just crawled deep inside each other and we can't crawl out again. We can't crawl out again, Damien."

"Does she know you're married?"

"Yes."

"How does she feel about it?"

"I can't speak for her. She feels a terrible guilt about her own loyalties. But she's helpless too."

The older man, studying the carpet, nodded slowly. "I don't know the girl of course and I may be all wrong about this, but she's obviously fine and honorable, and I think I can see her in my mind and I can't help wondering if she's as sure as you are about this matter——" He held up his hand as if to cut off a swift rejoinder. "I'm thinking in terms of you and not of Janie or myself."

Brad said, "There isn't a doubt."

"Not a doubt?"

"None."

A silence fell over them. The older man came painfully to his feet and walked to the window. He stared at the blackout curtains as if they were transparent.

He said, "This isn't a long story, Brad. I've never told it to anyone before. I want to tell it now. You've heard Grace talk about how a long time ago I rushed home from Paris to marry her. It's her favorite reminiscence and she's embroidered it here and there as the years passed.

"This is what really happened. I was engaged to Grace when I got out of Yale. That was in 1913. My father, who had worked all his life, wanted me to have a year in Paris. It was a fetish with him. He had made shoes from the time he was twelve and he wanted me to have everything he didn't get out of life—education, luxuries, but most of all a year in Paris. To him it was the dream touch to his son's upbringing—he was a wonderfully unselfish man."

Damien turned around and he was smiling faintly. "I met someone in Paris. It was the only time I've ever been unfaithful to Grace either before or after our marriage. The girl was beautiful, beautiful in depth. If ever a man was adored, I was. She defied her family—they were upper-middle-class French and more chary of their daughter than any New England family would dream of being—and she gave herself to me fully, honestly. We would look at each other, and I still remember how we would shake our heads slowly as if we couldn't believe an emotion like this could ever exist. It grew worse. We kissed on the street because we couldn't wait to get behind a door. And she was a shy girl, not at all wanton. My happiness was her life. Then, after two months, I became frightened—suddenly, unreasoningly frightened. I lied to her. I said I had to go to London for a few days but I sailed right back home. I never saw her again, nor heard from her, except one letter which arrived months later, for-warded from London. I wept over it.

"For years after that—years, Brad—she would come suddenly into my mind, sometimes at the office, sometimes at dinner, I never knew when the thought of her would strike. Even now when I think of her I feel a chill. Ever since then, in the occasional moments when a man thinks over his sins, great and small, I think of her and count what I did the one sin for which there is no forgiveness. I never doubted punishment would come. It had to come because what I did was to transgress against a pure human emotion, and pure human emotion is as close as we can get to God. But I never dreamed it would come like this after all these years."

Brad watched the older man's fingers lock in anguish, unlock and lock again. He felt a great outpouring of love for him and searched his mind for something he could say. There was nothing.

Damien said, "I can only think this is the perfect retribution, a work of art by the hand of God. I've been punished of course. The punishment has been inside me down through the years, the wretch-edness of thinking on what I did and what became of her, and I've accepted the punishment. But I belonged in Malton and I be-longed to Grace. The years that have punished me have also proved that I was right. And that brings me to you, Brad. I would have staked my life on your devotion, if not to Janie then to the simplest kind of duty a man must face. This isn't you, Brad. It may be the war that's worked this wretched miracle, for God knows none of us, no matter how far from the fighting we are, can be normal in this kind of world. But it's not you, Brad. You can't be faithless no matter how deep, how preposterous, or how exalted the emotion."

He looked up and a strange, fleeting smile passed across his face. "I don't believe it. You've told me and I still don't believe it."

Brad said, "Don't blame the war, Damien. The war had nothing to do with it. Janie has nothing to do with it. There are some emotions you can't fight. I can't fight this one."

The older man nodded. He turned out the light and thrust aside the blackout curtains. Moonlight hit sharply into the room. He said, "It's a good night to see the ruins. But you needn't come along, Brad. I imagine you've seen them."

They went down into Brook Street. An olive-drab Chevrolet was standing at the curb, and the driver, a stick of a youth who wore his overseas cap stabbing into his left eye, saluted them. Damien said, "The party leaves for the Midlands first thing in the morning. Would you like to have an early breakfast with me? Seven?"

"Seven, Damien."

They shook hands, each averting his eyes from the other.

Brad walked slowly down Brook Street and along the north side of Grosvenor Square.

He hadn't expected to feel a sense of accomplishment; only of relief that at last he had cut himself free from the deceit. Even this was lacking. There remained fixed in his mind the look on Damien's fine, rich man's face, the look of helpless anguish from one unaccustomed either to helplessness or to anguish. He imagined how it would be when Damien arrived home and he saw the scene so vividly he shut his eyes impulsively, trying to cut it off. He heard a click of heels. The MP on guard at the entrance to ETO headquarters saluted him as he passed. He quickened his pace and turned into Park Street.

The Red Cross club was unusually quiet though a score of officers, mostly young fliers, stood about the lobby and there were several clustered around Valerie's desk. He dropped into his usual chair near the entrance to the reading room. After a little time she caught sight of him and waved.

A Red Cross girl he knew only as Edna, an ungainly American girl with a hairy mole on her cheek, came out of the reading room and paused at his chair and said, "Isn't it awful? The place's been a morgue all day."

He said, "I haven't heard."

"The Dixie Rebel crashed on take-off this morning. After fifty-nine missions. And this was only a training flight."

"The Dixie Rebel?"

"That was the name of the Fort. They were all Southern boys— Clay Binns and Jack Drury and the rest. They've been coming here since the day we opened, like part of the family. We should be used to it by now but—gee, they were nice kids. You've seen them around here."

Brad said, "Nobody got out?"

"Got out? Ashes maybe. It's awful."

He looked across the lobby toward Valerie. She had turned out her desk light and was putting on her cap and combing back her hair. Watching her, he felt better, almost altogether better. Damien had run away from this. Poor Damien! No wonder he couldn't understand it.

She didn't smile when she came across the lobby toward him (he wished that she had on this of all nights), but when they got out into the street she took his arm and held it firmly against her body. He could feel her warmth even through the heavy cloth of her coat, and her eager sense of possession. They walked to Park Lane.

She said, "We had a terrible shock today, my darling."

"I know. Edna told me."

"I kept hoping you'd come early. I wanted so much to see you sitting there. Whenever anything happens I'm terrified and I keep looking for you."

He said, "I was kept late on something important."

"Of course. Everybody seems to think it's getting close. They say huge stretches of the south coast are already evacuated—but I shouldn't bring it up. You can't talk about it. As long as you're here everything is fine. Let's promise not to think about the future."

They crossed to the Hyde Park side of the street. She said, "Isn't it light? I don't think it's ever been so light in winter."

He said, "There's no news about John?"

"None."

He said, "What would happen if he did make it after all? And came home?"

"Have you been thinking about it?"

He said, "Yes."

"Why?"

He stopped short. She looked up at him and her eyes were deep and ardent and unwavering. He said, "I can't lose you, Val. I'll never be able to lose you."

She said softly, "Don't you understand? You're in my blood. You're in my blood, my darling. I've never loved before. I love you, Brad."

They walked on a little way and then she stopped him.

"I feel something has happened. What has happened? What is it?" She kept searching his face and when he didn't reply she said, "You haven't had orders? You're not being transferred to another unit? You're not, are you, my darling? You *would* tell me."

He said, "What put that in your mind?"

"Tell me you're not."

"I'm not."

"The truth?"

"The truth."

Her mouth quivered. "That's all I want to know. I don't think I could bear it."

She took his arm again, holding it tightly against her. They walked the rest of the way to her flat, cutting through a corner of Hyde Park where the moon was bright enough to cast the shadows of guns across the heaped-up sandbags, and through Belgrave Square where great dead houses stood bleakly against the bright sky.

He felt wonderfully fortified against any challenge Damien might offer in the morning.

Clearly Damien hadn't slept at all. His face, in the uncertain light of a winter's daybreak, looked fearfully lined and his Florida tan had turned overnight into something yellowish and patchy as if he hadn't shaved properly. But the fine disciplines which were implicit in him rallied to his aid. He greeted Brad with easy grace and when the floor waiter came in for the breakfast order he managed a smile. He said, "We didn't have a raid last night but I'm having powdered eggs for breakfast which they tell me is almost as terrible."

Brad wished he hadn't been asked to come. It wrenched hard to watch the man being casual, yet scarcely touching his food, making conversation, yet unable to interest even himself in what he was saying. A burst of anger would have been a relief.

There was nothing like that. While the eggs and sausages were being nibbled at, he went on talking about his tour of the city, how he had had tea with a fire-watcher whose son was a prisoner of the Japs, and of a woman, an ambulance driver at a post in Whitechapel, who thought he might know her sister because she also lived in America, in Jersey City. He betrayed the strain only occasionally, sipping at his coffee and not noticing that it had turned stone cold, or studying the gathering light at the window for brief, thoughtful periods.

Suddenly he glanced at his watch. "Good heavens! They told us to be packed and ready to leave by eight." He faced his son-in-law with unreserved sadness. He said, "Is there anything else, Brad?"

"No, Damien."

The older man nodded. "I'm glad of one thing. I thought of it last night after you left. You might have spent the evening with me without saying a word about this. It would have been easy but dishonest. I want you to know I admire your honesty and, in a way, your courage."

Brad said, "No courage is required—not between us, Damien."

"Brad——" The gray man's brow creased fiercely. "Brad, I'm not going to tell them at home."

"Whatever you feel is best."

"I think it's best. Janie's in no condition to be told—not now. Besides, I think she's entitled to hear it firsthand. After all, it's her life and yours."

The big step was behind him, Brad thought. At long last there was nothing more to say. He watched Damien make a slow, thoughtful turn of the room and station himself at the window. Full light had broken over the city, but it was a gray light. The sky was overcast. Damien peered up into it.

"Brad, when you saw Sanford Jaques in Algiers, did he tell you that your transfer from the paratroop force was no routine matter, that he had deliberately arranged it in Washington?"

"It's not true!"

Damien turned full around. "I'd hoped I'd never have to tell you, at least not until Sanford came around someday for the return favor and by then you'd be safely home. It's true, Brad. He had you yanked out of the special force because he wanted the *Star* to owe him something possibly as valuable as your life."

"When did you find out?"

Damien evaded the younger man's stare. "Shortly after you left for overseas."

"Why didn't you let me know?"

"Because, frankly, I was afraid of what you might do about it. I thought, the harm can't be undone except through a foolhardy and impulsive act. But now I feel you should know. I feel, Brad, there isn't very much danger of you being foolhardy or impulsive."

The remark cracked across Brad's mind like a bull whip. He took an involuntary step forward, staring at his tormentor.

"For God's sake, Damien, what are you trying to say?"

The older man came away from the window and dropped into a chair. He studied the carpet.

"I didn't sleep much last night. I tried to sort this thing out in my mind. It didn't make sense—like a jigsaw where all the pieces fit but the picture on top comes out a hodgepodge. You haven't changed, not in any fundamental way, Brad. You proved to me all over again last night that you're still sensitive and honest, and there's lots of moral courage in you. Even this new emotion—I'm sure it isn't tawdry. I don't know this girl but I imagine her as a magnificent person. She must be because you couldn't be in love with any other kind of person. You haven't got a tawdry bone in your body.

"So there was the jigsaw I kept puzzling over all night. Every piece fitted perfectly and yet the complete picture was absolute madness. It certainly wasn't you. I tossed the night trying to find the explanation——"

"Please, Damien——" Brad wanted to weep for this man who had never known adversity and couldn't face up to it. "There *is* no explanation—at least, none that adds up like a balance sheet. Don't try, Damien."

It was as if the older man hadn't heard. He went on, his voice growing stronger and harder. "My mind kept going back to the time you rushed off to war, how much I admired and understood you then, and I couldn't match that Brad with the man who used a scheming politician to get himself out of the Mediterranean and back to a girl in London. That cut to the heart of the puzzle and then, suddenly, the jigsaw became very clear."

He hesitated and when he began to speak again his voice became even harder and it was challenging. He said, "I can be frank with you, Brad. Some men rush off to war with all the courage in the world and when they get into it, they find they hate it. It's a dirty ugly business and they hate it. They want to get away from it. They're not so much scared. They're shocked. They won't admit it to themselves, perhaps they don't even know it, but they're shocked and they do foolish things to cover it over, to justify themselves.

"That's what's happened to you, Brad. You say this decision has nothing to do with the war. I say it has everything to do with the war. The war has shocked you, Brad. You're searching for justification—justification for escape from the war—and you think you've found it in this emotion of yours, in this girl. That's what's happened, Brad. And I dare say that's what's happened to the girl. She's finding her escape in you, as you are in her. I hate to throw this at you, Brad, but it's the truth. There's no other explanation. You can take it from there."

He glanced at his watch, averting his eyes from the young man who stood staring at him in shock and disbelief. "It's almost time," he said. "Think it over, Brad. This emotion is part of your war, so let the war work it out before you destroy yourself and all of us back home who love you."

Brad watched him snap the locks on his suitcase. He thought, A good try, Damien. But it isn't true. It's ridiculously untrue, but I can understand why you tried it. You would like it better if I were killed in the war. Anything would be easier for you than this. It just isn't true and I'm sorry you tried it because it shows me you're deeply hurt, and God knows I don't want to hurt you, Damien. Not you of all people. It isn't true but you wouldn't understand.

There was a knock on the door and a valet came in with a passkey. He said, "Pardon me, sir. The others in your party are downstairs. Can I take your baggage, sir?"

Damien said, "Can you come back in a minute?"

"Very well, sir." He went out.

The two men faced each other and their faces were filled with compassion and anguish.

"Good-by, Damien."

"Good-by, Brad."

Brad searched the older man's face and he thought it had brightened a little. It was a good time to leave. When he got out on the street he remembered the presents and he wondered what Damien would do with them.

When he arrived at Norfolk House an urgent message to call Valerie awaited him. Her voice on the telephone sounded tearful and excited. A stick of type in the *Daily Telegraph* (though the bulk of the reportage from Italy dealt with the fierce battle for Monte Cassino) described how a patrol of the 4th Indian Division, reconnoitering an abandoned farmhouse near San Leonardo, had found the surviors of a missing British raid party and among them its commander, Major the Hon. John Wynter. They were wounded and wasting but still alive and the Indians carried them back through three miles of disputed territory into British lines.

## 20

THE day the challenge came was damp and gusty, as what day isn't in London in February, and only occasionally spattered with rain as if the winds in their rough passage across the skies had accidentally torn some moisture from the overcast and whirled it down to the streets. The people, noting the unaccustomed quiet of the raid sirens, listened to the wind slapping against the windows and many of them chuckled a little proudly that even the Germans couldn't bear English weather.

Approaching along the corridor to his apartment, Brad gained the impression that one of Ray's spontaneous parties had erupted, but when he opened the door he found it was merely that Dan had come to London on leave and had dropped in unexpectedly. He had often wondered how it would be when two happy extroverts like Ray Boyce and Dan Stenick were brought together. Now he knew. The sound it gave off was loud and lusty, like a clash of broadsword against shield.

There were bottles and glasses distributed about the living room, the radio churned with "Waltzing Matilda" by a muscular choral group, and a girl sat laughing at Dan's side, a startlingly bright-eyed, country little creature who could not have been more than seventeen, but the disorder derived principally from the discovery of each other by Ray and Dan.

"Say, boy," Dan called out in lieu of a greeting, "Ray here and me, we're arguin' about Timmer——"

Ray cut in. "There's no argument. He's a bum."

"Tough—sure. But there's nothin' he asks us to do he don't do himself. In our outfit they give with the orders at five in the mornin', butt-freezin' time, and he's always right there with the rest of us. Yesterday we did a five-mile hike with big pack and he was up front on his two hind legs—not in a jeep like some colonels I know. You go find me a colonel like that."

Ray said, "He's still a bum."

Dan winked broadly in Brad's direction. "This guy's murder. How you been livin' with him I don't know."

"I know Timmer from way back," Ray went on relentlessly, "so let me get a literate word in here——"

"Insultin' too," Dan grumbled.

"Here's why he's a bum. He's out for personal profit and that's no way to go to war. Might have been in 1744 and maybe 1844 but not in Anno Domini 1944. You see, back home he's an auto salesman and there isn't anywhere to go in that business except sideways. But if you come home a general—hell, they give *you* cars and you take the salute on St. Patrick's Day and the Fourth, and the boss who used to bawl you out makes you a director of the firm, and you might even get to be superintendent of the state police, and maybe Legion commander. That's for Alex Timmer. He doesn't give a damn about the war. He's the closest thing to a mercenary. He's in it for the gamble and that's why he's got to be a lousy leader of men because most of our guys fighting this war hate to fight but they think it's kind of important to win. With Timmer it's profit and loss and therefore he's a bum but he'll make general, more's the pity. Now pour me a drink and pour one for our melancholy friend who's just come in out of the storm."

"I don't get it," Dan said, heating up a little. "Don't they all want to be generals just as bad as Timmer? I don't get it at all."

The girl with Dan said, looking at Brad, "I'd like a drink too, Dan, and I haven't been introduced."

Ray said, "Sure they want to be generals. But most of all they want to win. I'm talking about the good professionals—the Ikes and the Bradleys. They believe in what they're doing. In a word, they're not Prussians. *Sieg heil.*"

"*Sieg heil!*" Dan bellowed.

Both men sprang to their feet and clicked their glasses and Ray for no apparent reason began to sing "*Deutschland über Alles.*"

Brad, who had been standing in the archway leading from the vestibule, said, "How long has this been going on?"

Ray reached for a bottle and sighed, "He arrived about an hour ago and I've been taking refuge in gin ever since."

"Yep," Dan said ruefully. "I come lookin' for you and I run up against this crazy major and he's been hackin' at me ever since. We got nothin' in common except gin."

Ray said, "Good gin drinkers are most uncommon."

Dan said, "So are crazy majors."

"You see," Ray said, "it was love at first sight."

The girl said, "Really, Dan, I haven't been introduced." She was trying to promote a measure of ladylike indignation, but she was much too young and there was no authority in the voice that came out of her thin frame.

Anyway Dan didn't respond. His attention had been drawn to Brad, who had tossed his coat and cap over a chair and was reaching among the bottles for one that contained whisky. Dan said, "Pour yourself a good one, boy. What's troublin' you?"

"Do I look troubled?"

"I dunno. Ever since you left the outfit back at Harrison, I meet you and you're draggin' your fanny."

"Maybe I shouldn't have left the outfit."

"You can say that again, tootsie. Drink hearty."

Ray said, "A little old-fashioned elegance, Dan. Brad hasn't met this little charmer you brought along."

"Oh, sure. I'm for elegance." Dan took a swallow of his drink and introduced the girl. Her name was Binny Cabot, but everybody, he explained, called her Bright-eyes.

"Skinny but she'll grow," he said, appraising her shamelessly. "I guess I'm in love this time for sure. Ever see such saucers goin' for eyes? And the complexion's no fake." He passed a finger down her apple-red cheek to demonstrate.

She said, obviously pleased, "You shouldn't, Dan."

"I figure I could buy a house and lot with the money this gal is gonna save in lipstick and rouge. Her old man's the butcher down near our trainin' area——"

"He's the provisioner," she said severely.

"Anyway he's handy with a cleaver so I guess I better watch my step. She had a hell of a time gettin' away this trip. Never been to London. Can you imagine? Hundred miles away." He gave her a one-armed hug. "Like it, Bright-eyes?"

"It's marvelous," she said, in a way that encompassed her vast girlish happiness.

Ray poured a set of drinks and had scarcely passed them around
when he and Dan plunged recklessly into a new argument, this time
about the British monarchy. Dan thought it was a lot of foolishness
and Ray countered by saying that it was government by a pure
nostalgia, stronger and more binding than law, and no one not born
under the Crown could understand it and therefore couldn't argue
intelligently against it.

Brad scarcely listened. He sat in a corner, clear of the cross fire,
and his drink warmed in his hand. Twice over the din of the argument he thought he heard footsteps in the outside corridor, but when
he went to the door he found it was his imagination.

Valerie had gone from the Red Cross club by the time he called
there for her. She had left a message with the girl called Edna that
she would come directly to the flat as soon as she was free. He wondered where she could be.

More than a month now had passed since the news of John's rescue. In a field hospital near Bari he had recovered from the worst of
his wounds and he was being invalided home full of honors—a bar
to his D.S.O. and promotion to lieutenant colonel having been the
rewards for saving himself and the remnants of his raid party. Brad
wondered if he had already arrived, if this was why she had left the
club unexpectedly.

It had been a sensitive month for her, he felt. She had spoken very
little about John. Their nightly meetings had continued gay and
ardent, but there were moments when her mind seemed to drift (he
thought) to the inevitable rendezvous in the future and he knew
she was troubled. He prided himself on having become expert at
penetrating the fabled English façade, yet he often wondered if he
understood all the emotions that played behind the lovely and fugitive mold of her face.

Only once had he asked her what would happen when John came
back. She had pressed her finger across his lips before he could complete the query and had said, "Let me find the way. I promised him
a long time ago I would wave him welcome when he came home. This
I must do, my darling—and afterward, let me find the way. You do
understand. Tell me you understand."

Of course he understood. He hadn't become so calloused he
couldn't understand that a man coming home from the war should

be met and have matters explained. But, if she had really left the
club to meet John, he wished she had told him.

The music on the radio faded out and a precise reading of the six
o'clock news began, creating a temporary armistice in the battle between Ray and Dan. They all listened to the reports which seemed
as cheerless as the weather and just as unchangeable. The bridgehead
at Anzio was being deepened in stiff fighting, but enemy artillery
still raked the beaches; the Germans atop Monastery Hill held on
stoutly in the face of furious attacks by the Polish division; near Kiev
the Russians were rounding up enormous numbers of the enemy and
gargantuan quantities of his supplies, and there was the usual ad-
dendum about air strikes on Truk and Rabaul in the Pacific.

Then, as the news was succeeded by Glenn Miller's band playing
"Tuxedo Junction," Brad thought he heard footsteps in the corridor.
He darted to the door. This time they were real and they were
Valerie's.

"Did you wonder, darling?" she said. She kissed him and shook
her dripping umbrella in the hallway. "I hope you did. I've just spent
the most wonderful two hours at Brown's Hotel. And with a man.
I know it does sound dreadful. Did I ever mention Mr. Tamarga to
you? Anton Tamarga. He was my grandfather's solicitor in Calcutta
and he's just come to London. A delicious little old man, half brown,
and he speaks the most beautiful English and he knew my mother.
That's the wonderful thing, darling. He knew my mother and he
spent the whole teatime telling me about her and I couldn't have
been more excited. He even had some letters she had written . . ."

Inside the living room Dan twisted his stubby frame sideways so
he could see what was going on in the vestibule.

"What's this, Ray?"

"This," Ray said, lifting his eyebrows significantly, "is it."

"You mean—overboard?"

Ray nodded glumly and took a swallow of gin. "Both of them.
No life jackets. Can't swim either."

"You're kiddin'!"

"I wish I were."

Dan strained for a closer look. "Is she real?"

He whistled a low, meaningful whistle and rose slowly as they
came into the room. He had been drinking since morning, he remembered, and perhaps his eyes were playing tricks, but he thought he

had never seen a more glowingly beautiful woman, Red Cross outfit and all.

The gusts that beat through the streets of London also buffeted a hospital plane holding to the strict approach pattern for the southwest coast of England. The heavy, four-engined craft shuddered in the wind traps and its engines labored and made strange, variable noises as if they were human. A nursing sister, who was seated near the tail end, unbuckled her safety belt and walked slowly along the narrow passage between bunks which were lashed by chains against the fuselage. She paused at each bunk and said something to the man who lay in it and smiled at those who could see her. She was a wiry, gray-haired woman with a fearless, efficient face which clearly had never been touched by a cosmetic.

The plane was bumping hard when she got back to her seat and she dropped into it and pulled the safety belt taut.

There were only two seats near the tail end of the plane. The other was occupied by John Wynter. He was bundled up in a heavy scarf and a British warm.

She said, "It's a horribly long trip from Gib. I hate it."

He nodded. "Longer by ship though." He looked through the porthole into a blanket of wet, swirling mist. "Pity about the weather. It would be nice to see the old country stretched out below."

"Have you been away long, sir?"

"About twenty months."

"Seems like forever, I suppose."

He smiled and nodded and kept looking for a break in the mist. "Amazing it's still light. It's past five."

She said, "You've forgotten we're on double daylight at home."

He leaned his head against the back of the seat and closed his eyes. The nursing sister frowned as she studied his face, which was thin and sickly yellow. She said, "We've still almost forty minutes, Colonel. Hadn't you better go back and take a lie down?"

His eyes came open abruptly. "Don't mention it, Sister. Don't you dare. I'm not going to encourage some miserable M.O. to bung me off to a hospital for the weekend. Not this weekend anyway."

One of the stretcher patients was coughing hard enough to be heard over the racket of the engines. The nursing sister drew a cup of water from a canteen in the tail of the plane and went on another trip along the aisle. When she returned she glared at John and said, "I hate having colonels as patients. Other ranks are so much easier. They do as they're told."

He smiled and passed his hand over the insignia on the epaulet of his British warm. "I'll say this, Sister. I'm the newest lieutenant colonel you'll ever nurse. I think they handed me this extra pip as a sort of going-away present." The smile faded gradually from his pallid face. "I *will* get past the M.O. at the field, won't I?"

She said, "I know why they gave you the extra pip. For the same reason they gave you a bar to your D.S.O. If you do as I say you *might* get past the M.O. at Croydon."

"You sound desperately interesting."

She handed him a pill and a cup of water. "This has codeine. It should give you a nice lift by the time we land, especially if you relax as much as possible."

He swallowed the pill. Then he said, "You're really very good to me. I suppose there'll be transport at the field."

"Transport to where, Colonel?"

"The West End."

She said, "If nothing else is available, I'm sure one of the ambulances will drop you off. Most of the lads are bound for East Grinstead. But don't forget, you've got to get past the M.O. first."

"I'll get past the M.O. Better give me another of those pills."

"One will do," she said decisively.

After a time the plane steadied itself and he tried to doze as the nursing sister had instructed. She thought he was the youngest lieutenant colonel she had ever seen, but then they were getting younger all the time, she reflected bitterly, and the biggest slaughter of the war hadn't even begun. She leafed through the medical charts until she came to his. He had taken a land-mine burst in the back, had been down with dysentery and jaundice, and there were symptoms of shock after almost four years of continuous combat. After all this, he at least would be spared. She watched him dozing. A furtive little smile played on his well-mannered mouth. She thought he looked absurdly gentle to have led a company of Commandos.

The plane made a shallow turn and came down under a cloud bank. She nudged him.

"There's England, Colonel," she said, "and I think I'll let you have another codeine."

She didn't know why she had done it. Codeine was in terribly short supply and she was always very strict with her patients, but she found herself wanting this young lieutenant colonel to get past the M.O. and on to whatever he had been daydreaming about.

The ambulance let him off at Marble Arch. The last thing the nursing sister had told him was to keep out of the wind as much as possible. The driver had offered to detour the vehicle and take him exactly where he wanted to go, but he thought the man had been kind enough, what with four stretcher cases in the rear. Besides, a short walk would do him good. He knew he looked ghastly and the cold air might nip some life into his face.

She was right, though, about the wind. It was really howling down Oxford Street and he found himself breathing hard before he had passed a single turning. He slipped behind the blast wall of the Cumberland for shelter and, feeling unsteady, he thought he had better go inside the hotel and rest a bit.

He managed to get one of a row of chairs at the entrance to the tearoom and sat listening to the swift rhythm of a dance band. He could scarcely believe he was back in London; it seemed unreal after the fighting and the last horrible weeks on the Sangro which remained very real. A long line of soldiers and their girls stood waiting at the gates to the tearoom which were guarded by a headwaiter. The soldiers were American except for one close-cropped Polish officer and a party of noisy Canadians. He remembered this room when a string trio played the music from *Chu Chin Chow* strenuously so the few old ladies at their tea wouldn't hear the racket of the daylight raids. He liked it better this way but he wondered, oh Lord, will London ever be English again?

He looked at his watch. A quarter past six, time to get on. It was a damned silly idea, but he had planned it this way ever since the moment they had told him he was emplaning for home. Val had written that she worked until six-thirty every evening and he had dreamed up the wonderful idea of getting into a queue of Americans at her desk. At least it seemed wonderful thinking about it during the flight, but now it struck him as absolutely mad. He pushed himself to his feet for there was no time to make a new plan.

The wind whipped at his face but he didn't mind now that he had struggled to Park Street and made the turning. It was a good idea

after all, he thought, getting into a queue with the Americans. He
hoped she wouldn't spot him until he was absolutely in front of her.
He tried to think up a nonsensical query, something like "I'm just in
from Chicago and I'd like to meet a nice English girl," as an opening
gambit so he could see her laugh. Much better than a sticky, sentimental show. On the other hand, he wouldn't be able to kiss her,
not in the club, and from this point of view it was a bad idea.
There would be time to kiss her, years of time he hoped, though he
couldn't quite believe it.

He knew the exact location of the club. It was on Park Street, she
had written, just near the corner of Upper Brook. He had pinpointed it in his mind a thousand times during the flight. Now he
heard the sound of American voices in the harsh night and as he
came closer he saw the glow of their cigarettes and caught sight of a
dimly lighted sign *A.R.C. Officers' Club.* He paused to catch his
breath. His legs felt a little unsteady, but it didn't matter now. He
had arrived at his long, long journey's end.

"How's for chow, fellas?"

"Okay but not Willow Run. It's got me bushed."

"Let's knock back a few first."

"How 'bout that jitter joint on Wardour Street?"

"You mean the one with the B-girls, lover boy?"

He listened to the loud, cheerful talk, much of which he didn't
understand, and he thought again how much London had changed
from the quiet, deserted place of the bad summers early on. He
found himself trembling and though it may have been the walk
against the wind, he was sure it was the excitement.

He pushed through a blackout curtain and blinked in the bright
lights. He couldn't see her on his first look around. There were groups
of American officers all over the main hall and he walked gingerly
around them (though he felt terribly conspicuous in his British warm
and green beret) and he shifted his eyes furtively one way and then
the other because he wanted to catch sight of her before she saw him.

She wasn't there, at least not in the main hall. He had walked the
full length of the big room and back again to the entrance and then
back once more. She wasn't there.

He thought it was an utterly childish idea in the first place. He
should have telephoned from Croydon as any reasonable man would
do. They were all looking at him now. He was making a ridiculous

spectacle of himself, a British officer wandering about an American club and not too steady on his pins at that. They must think him drunk or a madman. The British warm seemed lead-heavy on his shoulders. He was hot. There were no empty chairs about. He wanted badly to sit in a chair for a bit.

"Looking for anyone, Colonel?"

He wrenched off his beret and he was conscious of sweat pouring out on his forehead. He saw that the girl who had asked the question was looking anxiously at him. He saw that she had a mole on her cheek and long hairs growing out of it and he wondered why she didn't have it removed. It seemed a silly thing to think of but he was a damned silly fellow and he wished he could find a chair. The British warm was terribly heavy.

"Sure you're not sick, Colonel? You look sick."

"I'm sorry. There—there isn't a chair about I—I can sit in for a minute. I'll be all right then."

She said, "Sure there is. You just come along with me."

She grasped his arm and led him into the reading room at the back of the main hall. There was a big leather couch strewn with magazines and paper-covered books. She gathered these up with a single, efficient sweep of her hand.

"You can stretch out if you like."

"A sit will do, thank you."

She said, "Don't be shy. It's been stretched out on an awful lot. Why don't you take off your coat?"

He was sure she thought he was drunk. He said, "I'm quite all right now." There was a round leather arm on the side of the couch and he leaned his elbow on it, trying to look as proper as possible. "Quite all right," he said. He wished she wouldn't stand over him. "I'm sorry—barging into an American club."

"It's all the same war," she said. "How do you feel now?"

"I'm fine."

"No you're not. You're a sick boy."

He thought it was funny, remembering how the nursing sister on the plane had called him sir. There was something very kind about this American girl but he wished she wouldn't stand over him as if he was going to faint. At least she had stopped thinking he was drunk.

He said, "I came looking for Miss Russell. Do you know——?"

"Val? Sure I know her. You a relative?"

"Is—is she here by any chance?"

The girl said, "I thought she didn't have any relatives. Her father died about a year back. I heard he was the last relative. Sweet girl, Val."

He wondered how they had got sidetracked into the topic of Val's relatives. He couldn't see the girl's face because she was standing so close over him. He wished she would stand back or sit somewhere.

He said, "I was hoping to meet her here. She does work here?"

"Bet your life. Only she took an early weekend. That's what we call it around here when you go off Fridays a couple of hours early. She had it coming. She's worked plenty nights till ten, eleven. So it's Val you were looking for out there. You know, Colonel, at first I thought you were drunk. We once had a British colonel—gee, I guess he was a brigadier—anyway he wandered in here drunk as a lord. Gave us plenty of trouble. You say you're a relative of Val's? I thought she didn't have any relatives."

*That* again. He didn't have the strength to cope with this girl. He shouldn't have deceived the M.O. at Croydon. He should have gone straight to a hospital. The whole thing was a damned childish idea.

He said, "No. Just a friend of the family."

"You should really be in bed, Colonel. You want me to call your unit? I'll be glad to."

She was still standing over him. He was tired of looking at the waist buttons of her jacket. He said, "Kind of you, but it won't be necessary. You say she's gone away for the weekend?"

"I don't think so. She doesn't go out of town weekends any more. Not since her father died."

"Then—then I think I'll call her flat." The coat was heavy on his shoulders. He wondered if he could muster the strength to get up.

The girl said, "Hold it a minute, Colonel. It's just possible she's in the neighborhood. I'll see if I can locate her. Just hold it a minute."

She moved away from him at last and he could see something other than the waist buttons of her jacket. The bookshelves across the room shimmered before his eyes.

She was holding the reading-room door open and the clamor of animated talk broke in from the main hall. He heard her call out over the din: "Georgina, know where Val went? Did she say? . . . Oh, damn. Have we got a note on her boy friend's number? . . . For goodness' sake, Georgina, you know him. Lieutenant Brad something. Brad Parker—that's it. He lives around here somewhere . . . Okay, forget it."

She was back now. "No dice, Colonel. If you take my advice you'll let me call your unit. You're in no shape to go traipsing around looking for Val. You can see her any day next week. I'll tell her a relative called in. I didn't catch your name. What is it again?"

He leaned against the round leather arm of the couch. The whole thing was such a bloody idiotic prank. Anyway it was just as well she had left. He didn't want her to see him, not in this condition. He'd be stronger Monday. A weekend at Smallhill would do the trick. He thought it was an odd remark about Val's boy friend, but Americans used words loosely, especially this girl. Naturally, Val would have made friends among the Americans. Still, it was an odd remark.

He said, "You're quite right. I'm not very well. I'll—I'll be in next week."

She didn't move. The buttons were still staring at him. She said, "Say, what can we lose? I'll try her house. You wait right here, Colonel. I'll be back in a jiffy."

She went out the door. As soon as she was gone he got up and, steadying himself against a shelf of books, he put on his beret. Then he slipped out and dodged as quickly as he could between groups of officers through the main hall. Outside, the turbulent wind hit his face with a shock that braced him momentarily. When he caught his breath he saw, miracle of miracles, that a taxi had slid to the curb and three Americans were frolicking out of it.

He fell heavily into the seat and said, "Victoria, please, driver." He thought it was clever of him not to have given the girl his name. He could try it all over again Monday, when he would be stronger.

The telephone rang several times before Ray bestirred himself to answer it. He regarded the telephone as an evil invention along with the submarine and the airplane, and if he had his way he would abolish all three, especially the telephone and more especially when it intruded its peremptory summons into a good party. He got up and shuffled into the hall toward the bedrooms, muttering that no mechanical contrivance should be accorded the power to command a human being.

This one was clearly shaping up as a good party. It had begun in earnest when Valerie arrived. Dan had demanded the right to pinch her arm to see if she was real, vowing he was going to sit around till midnight to see if she disappeared like Cinderella.

After order had been restored and proper introductions made, Dan had prodded Binny to sing for his friends. She sang a Welsh hymn she had learned as a child. Her small, artless voice rang out with sweetness and courage and they all applauded, and Ray, whose sentimentality expanded in direct ratio with the gin, said he hadn't been so touched by music since a Christmas Eve in a Negro mission church near Savannah. Dan thereupon swore he was going to marry Binny and take her back stateside and make a fortune with her on the radio.

On this happy premise Ray had produced a bottle of armagnac (he had been saving it, he said, for the victory, but he couldn't allow gin to defile such priceless vocal cords) and Binny, flushed and pleased, had eagerly volunteered another Welsh song. That was when the telephone had intruded.

It was for Valerie.

The girl was singing when she came away from the telephone. Brad watched her aimlessly as she entered the room. He thought he would never weary of watching her, the way she moved with easy grace, and then their eyes made contact and he darted to her.

She gathered up her coat and cap wordlessly, and all the time her eyes burned into him. He remembered the look on the New Year's Eve when she heard John had gone missing. It was the same look of mingled shock and grief and accusation.

He went with her to the door and when they were out in the corridor, he said, "John?"

She nodded. "Will you ask them to forgive me and tell Dan I think his girl friend is sweet and quite lovely." This was one of the times he hated the ways of the English. Her mouth quivered for wanting to weep and she insisted on polite talk.

He said, "Was that him on the phone?"

"Mala."

"For God's sake, Val! Talk. What is it?"

Now tears sprang out of her eyes. "They just called Mala from the club. He's come looking for me, at least they said a lieutenant colonel in a green beret, and he's so ill and weak he can't stand on his feet and—oh, my darling, I've got to run. I've got to run quickly."

"I'll take you there."

"No! Please not."

"I mean just to the door."

"No, my darling. Let me go now. It's nothing to do with you."

"Will you call me?"

"Of course."

He said, "I mean soon—tonight."

"Yes."

She half ran along the corridor and down the staircase, not waiting for the elevator, and long after she had gone he still heard the diminishing clatter of her footsteps and the frantic way she had said *Let me go now. It's nothing to do with you* and he was sure this was the first time she had left him without kissing him even lightly. The thought plunged into his mind that he should have told her about Damien's visit and what he had done. He wondered now why he hadn't told her. Then he remembered how quick she was to compassion and this was merely a compassionate gesture and nothing else. He felt better but only for a passing moment. He hated going back inside to the others.

Dan said, "What's wrong, boy?"

"Nothing."

"Not what I read on your kisser."

"She had to go for a little while. Back to the club."

The girl said, "I do hope she comes back. She's just wonderful."

Brad said, "She'll be back."

Ray squirmed deeper in his chair and said, "Better pour yourself a drink."

The spirit had gone out of the party. A fresh round of drinks, generously poured, failed in its purpose. For a time they pretended to listen to the radio. Dan tried to encourage Binny to sing again but she said she was a bit dizzy from the strange, brown liquor Ray had poured for her. The radio droned an endless succession of Bing Crosby records.

Then the clock struck eight and a few moments later the telephone rang. Brad flew to it and had the receiver off the hook before the first automatic ring was completed.

"Mr. Parker?"

"Yes."

"This is Mala, Mr. Parker." Her enunciation was slow and precise and she waited infuriatingly to be acknowledged at every pause.

"Yes, Mala."

"Miss Valerie asked me to telephone you——" Again the pause. "Yes!"

"She'll try to telephone you from the railway station but when she left here she didn't quite know whether she would have the opportunity before the train went off and she asked me to telephone you just in case—are you there? Are you there, Mr. Parker?"

A great many questions tumbled into his mind. He didn't ask them because he didn't want to hear the answers. He said, "How is Colonel Wynter?"

"We don't know."

"But she met him at the club!"

"We don't know, Mr. Parker," the servant said firmly. "He somehow disappeared from the club. That is why Miss Valerie is going to Tunbridge Wells and she asked me to call you just in case—are you there?"

He said, "Thank you, Mala," and closed the phone.

Ray, who sat deep in his chair turning his glass in his hand, and Dan and the girl watched him put on his coat and cross the living room. They heard the click of the snap lock as the door was pulled shut. The only sound in the room was Crosby singing *Every little breeze seems to whisper Louise* . . .

Dan reached over and turned off the radio. "Hate that song," he said.

Brad handed the driver a half crown as the taxi made its turn into Victoria and was out before it had come to a full stop. He hurried through a gothic passage that led into the station and found himself in the midst of a complement of American troops, some fifty of them, their kit bags slung over their shoulders. He ignored a salute from the sergeant who was herding them and looked about, trying to find his bearings. It was a huge concourse with confusing crevices and angles and it was dim and an icy draft cut through like a gale.

Every crevice seemed to harbor a soldier and a girl. The civilians stood in motionless queues before the train gates all along the concourse. He saw a steel-helmeted constable, ambling importantly across the center of the station, and he pursued him.

"The next train to Tunbridge Wells, Officer."

The constable turned about slowly. "Sevenoaks, Tunbridge Wells,

St. Leonard's, and Hastings——" He rubbed his chin. "That would be platform eight. Just where you see that goods wagon, sir."

The gate at platform eight had not yet opened. There were travelers standing before it in an orderly queue and he saw at once she was not among them. He stood apart from them, frantically re-examining the queue, wondering if she could have taken an earlier train, wondering if he should have waited at the apartment for her to telephone, and then he thought she might be at the telephones and he raced across the concourse to the booths. They were all occupied and he peered through the glass door of each one and she wasn't in any of them.

Near the telephone booths he saw a sign *Restaurant-Tearoom*. He made for it as quickly as he could without running and pushed through a frosted glass door and there she was.

She didn't see him until he came up to the table. She had been crying. Her eyes were dry now but red-rimmed and she looked at him completely without surprise as if she knew he would come. He pulled a chair from an adjoining table and sat beside her. He looked at her fingers curled about the handle of her coffee cup. She hadn't touched the coffee and a skin had formed over it.

He looked once more at her red-rimmed, tearless eyes and at her fingers frozen on the handle of the cup and the coffee cold and untouched. The breathless urgency of his search went out of him. He knew all there was to know and they hadn't spoken a word.

She said, "There's only two or three minutes."

"Yes."

"You understand."

He said, "You must go to Smallhill."

"I must."

"When did you know you must?"

She said, "When Edna told me. When she told me he could scarcely stand and they thought at first he was drunk."

"He's had a bad war."

She said, "God help me, he deserves more than I can give him."

After a little time he said, "Then you'll be back."

"You're in my blood, my darling."

"But you must go to him. I can understand it."

"Let's not talk any more. It makes me want to die."

They sat listening to the hollow noises in the concourse beyond the frosted door. A woman's voice on a loud-speaker was mixed up with bells and the scuff of hurrying feet and the high clear toot of a steam whistle, and then they heard the voice say, "Hurry along now for Sevenoaks, Tunbridge Wells, St. Leonard's, and . . ."

He picked up her overnight case and they went out to the concourse where the cold draft hit them.

She said, "I didn't tell you I'm glad you came. I *am* glad. It makes it easier. We're both doing this and it makes it easier. Forgive me, darling. We weren't going to talk about it."

When they reached platform eight the people in the queue had already gone to the train and now the soldiers and their girls were clustered around the gate. They were Canadians and they had haversacks bulging at their hips and most of them were kissing their girls.

The voice said, "Hurry along now."

He handed her the overnight case. She looked up at him with her red-rimmed eyes and he thought this was altogether finer and better and more tender than a kiss. She must have thought so too because she turned slowly and walked through the gate. He watched her until she was lost among the Canadian soldiers far down the dark platform and he found himself standing among the waving girls.

It was a long walk back to Grosvenor Street, but he hardly noticed the distance and the cold. He knew Dan would still be there because this was the way it had to be. There was no other way.

He motioned Dan to come with him into his bedroom.

He said, "Dan, did Timmer ever say anything about me at the camp?"

"In what connection, boy?"

"In any connection."

"He said you'd come into the outfit, if that's what you mean. He was pretty damn sure of it."

"Does he want me?"

Dan said, "You kiddin'?"

"Okay. Tell him to make the request for me. I'm coming in."

"You sure, boy?"

He didn't reply. Sure was an infinitely small word in the press of all the things he felt.

# BOOK FOUR

## Overlord

## 21

T H E wind careened out of the sea and snapped at the faces of the men who lay exhausted on the bluff high above the narrow beach. The ground was damp and colder than the wind. The place was a wild stretch of sand and cliffs west of Studland Bay on the Dorset coast. The day's first light had appeared, a gray and cheerless ribbon on the far line of the white-capped sea, but the Dorset coast where the men lay was still wrapped in darkness.

The men belonged to Special Force 6. There were about three hundred and fifty in all. They lay on the ground in four groups near the four steel and concrete pillboxes which had been the objects of their mock attack. A few had crawled behind the pillboxes for shelter from the whipping wind, but most had simply fallen to the ground on signal that the exercise was over and lay inert in varied and grotesque positions. Those who troubled to unbuckle their webbing had thrown off their small packs and lay face up to the sky. Others lay on their sides, their knees doubled up against their stomachs, because this eased the cramp in their back muscles. These were the men who had lugged the mortars and heavy machine guns up the cliffside and through the defilade that gave entrance to the high ground from the beach.

Out on the far line of the sea the first gray ribbon of light burgeoned with faint shafts of pink. Sailors on the night watches and workmen early afoot on the streets of London and Germans uneasy in their fortifications across the Channel must have watched the dawn come up, for a new day rarely fails in its peremptory demand on the senses.

Not these men who lay on the bluff above the narrow Dorset beach. Their awareness was confined to themselves, to their exhaustion, to remembering how many nights they had rehearsed the same attack across the beach and up the cliffside to the pillboxes, to wondering how many more times they would be ordered to repeat the attack.

Brad too was unaware of the day's new light bounding in from the sea. He walked slowly among the prostrate men of his company, evaluating their exhaustion and their capacity, if an occasion should demand it, to carry on the attack beyond the point of exhaustion. He remembered weeks ago asking Dan about it and Dan had said, "Don't worry about it, boy. Couple hot bullets and you got lungs you never even used."

He was worn out and longed to drop to the ground like the others but he kept moving about, trying to fend off his aching weariness, because he was the company commander and he felt it his duty to show a reserve of strength. But the cold wind howling off the sea sucked under the rim of his helmet and bit at his sweaty neck and he wished he could fall to the shelter of the ground.

Now he looked out over the sea and his eyes blinked against the rising light. Standing on high ground, he traced the ragged edge of the Dorset coast until it fell away into a confluence of sea and morning mist. Beyond the confluence, in Devon and as far west as Cornwall, there were men, scores of thousands of men, drilling and rehearsing and marching. He remembered the days before Pearl Harbor when he listened on the radio to the sound of falling bombs and felt cheated that he was not part of the crimson pattern. Now he was part of it, and this was compensation for his weariness, knowing he was part of it, feeling his own sweat and yet sensing the drama of the whole of it as (he imagined) people reading about it ten or twenty years from now might sense it. He looked around at his men and wondered how many of them sensed it and felt sorry for those who didn't.

The wind came in harder like a herald of the dawn. It came in violent gusts that ricocheted against the pillboxes and made hollow, enraged noises. When the damp in the ground penetrated their rubberized battle dress and the cold became more intolerable than their exhaustion, the men began to sit up. A few lit cigarettes, cupping matches in their hands with a perfect instinct for the vagaries of the wind, but mostly they sat motionless, their heads wilting, staring at the ground.

In the gray light the men of Special Force 6 looked much like any other body of troops training along the isolated south coast of England. They were all sizes and shapes, chunky, lithe, heavily muscled, wiry or fat, and their ages ranged from nineteen to the middle thir-

ties. They groused like any other troops, cursed the dumbness of
the brass, and thought about their next leave, mostly about whisky
and women.

But they were not ordinary troops. They had been selected from
among crack British, American, and Canadian battalions because
they had proved themselves in one way or another to be tougher,
more skillful with weapons, and more resourceful than the average
soldier.

Special Force 6 consisted simply of four undersized companies,
each mustering about eighty-five men. Two of the companies were
American, one British, and the fourth a mixture of British and Canadians. There was also a headquarters company which wasn't really
a company at all, merely a handful of riflemen and aid post, signals,
and beach elements.

The organization was rudimentary because the mission was rudimentary. Special Force 6 had been created for a single urgent action
on another bluff overlooking another narrow beach on a day an ignorant world had already dubbed D-day as if the name had been
freshly coined and was not the commonest term in the lexicon of
military planning.

"Here comes Ironbones," men muttered all over the training area
and they pushed themselves to their feet, picked up their weapons,
buckled their webbing, and began to form ranks before the commands to do so rang out over the howling of the wind.

They watched Timmer stride up out of the defilade that formed an
exit from the beach. When he reached the edge of the bluff, he
stood there, his back to the sea, and made a visual review of the
four companies spread across the training area. He wore a cotton
shirt as if this were summer and the men in the ranks shivered at
the sight of the freezing wind ripping at him, but he stood splendidly
erect, his fists dug into his hips, his pistol belt slung low, his face
scowling fiercely beneath his helmet. He looked a magnificent warrior.

Ever since the attack rehearsals had begun in March, when snow
often swirled off the sea, Timmer had come down to his beach headquarters in a shirt and it was inevitable that the men would call
him Ironbones. They suspected he was showing off and bets were
made that he would come down with pneumonia. He never did and

the men decided he was tougher than any of them. Timmer knew
this and it gave him great satisfaction.

On this morning he stood on the bluff against the careening wind
longer than usual. Then the ritual of report began.

The plateau above the beach was divided down the middle by a
shallow gulley. On the left side of the gulley, companies A, B, and C
were formed up in front of the pillboxes they had in theory captured
and destroyed. On the right side of the gulley, more than a hundred
yards distant from the nearest of the others, there was a single pillbox and before it stood company D.

The ritual never varied. As Timmer strode across the rough terrain
toward company A, its commander moved out to meet him. They
exchanged salutes in the open ground and began a comparison of
notes on the exercise.

Captain Peter MacEwen, a Canadian, was commander of Abel
company, which was made up of British and Canadian elements.
In the stripped down organizational plan of the special force, he was
also second-in-command to Timmer. Even if protocol had not dic-
tated that the 2IC of the international force should be a non-Ameri-
can, MacEwen would have been by popular consent the logical
choice. He was of middle age and middle size, an intense, meticulous
man who spoke slowly as if every word had been fiercely thought
out before he uttered it. He didn't act tough; indeed, he didn't act
at all. He possessed that rare balance of character which allowed
him to approach soldiering in the same grave way he had lived his
civilian life. He had been a mining engineer in northern Ontario and
it was rumored around the camp that he was a millionaire but no
one really knew. Millionaire or not, the men of company A were
grateful for him. They had long since gathered from the nature of
the exercise that company A would make the climactic assault against
the deepest of the four enemy fortifications and they felt confident
MacEwen would lead them where they had to go. Defying penetration, he inspired trust and an abiding respect.

He conferred with Timmer for several minutes while the four companies stood stiffly at attention. Then he turned with formal precision to face the companies. The command rang out:

"Special Force 6—Stand at ease! Stand easy!"

The command was drowned out by the noise of the wind, but the
men knew what it was. This was the signal, according to Timmer's

ritual, for the commanders of B, C, and D companies to come forward and join the colonel for a briefing on the results of the exercise.

Jeff Waller, whose British company B held down the left flank, and Dan, who commanded company C, set out from their respective posts and converged on Timmer at almost the same time.

From company D, which was isolated on the right side of the gulley, Brad had a much longer march. He struck out with gusto. After the rest in the cold wind, it was pleasant to move quickly. Moreover he suspected that decisions of the gravest importance to him were being made in Timmer's huddle and he was anxious to know what they were.

He had been with the force for nearly seven weeks and for the last two he had led company D, supplanting Lieutenant Moore, who had been switched to the headquarters platoon. Rennie Moore was a husky young West Pointer and the demotion had surprised everybody except Brad who retained a lively recollection of Timmer's prejudices. But both his company command and the captaincy that went with it were provisional. He wanted desperately to nail down the job. He had worked hard for it. He had spent his nights reclaiming the almost forgotten routines and techniques of the infantry officer and his days rigorously matching the physical fitness of men whose bodies had been hardened by months of route marches and inhuman obstacle courses. He had fought off muscle weariness and had refused to report sick on mornings when he could scarcely crawl out of bed. He had foregone his leaves and had put up enthusiastically with the spit and polish demanded by Timmer. He had driven himself mercilessly. He had felt a clean, hard purpose in what he was doing. He couldn't bear the thought of failure.

He reached the gulley and ran down its near side and shinnied up its far side and when he came on the flat again he saw that Timmer and MacEwen were watching his approach and talking together. He knew they were talking about him.

Timmer returned his salute and said, "That was a nice move off the beach, Brad. Fast and quiet. You got up there on the nose."

"Thank you, sir."

"We've been wondering if you can handle it. MacEwen thinks so."

"I'm sure I can, sir."

Timmer was feeling good. He was playing it cute. He said, "Well, if MacEwen thinks you can and you think you can, I guess that buttons it up. Dog company's your baby from now on. Take damn good care of it."

Brad broke into a smile and saluted his acknowledgment of the promotion because he knew it would please Timmer, especially with the whole force looking on. The man in the ridiculous cotton shirt returned the salute carelessly and peered into Brad's face. Brad could have sworn the man was wondering what he was so happy about.

Special Force 6 was bivouacked in a clearing bulldozed out of a wooded area three miles from the beach and half a mile from the village of Mortrain. The camp, a collection of weather-beaten frame huts interspersed with a few bell tents and one marquee tent, had been hastily thrown together in 1940 for use by a British battalion which had been rushed to the area in the lively expectation of a German assault against the coast. It lacked minimum recreation facilities for in the frantic summer of its construction no one cared. When the invasion threat faded, the camp had been abandoned to the elements and was subsequently downgraded by the War Office as unsuitable for further use. Timmer was permitted to reoccupy it not only because the nearby coastal formation closely resembled the problem he would face across the Channel but also because he insisted a tough formation required tough quarters, thereby establishing his reputation at SHAEF as the sort of determined commander the task at hand required.

The result was that Mortrain became the recreation area for the force. The village was almost as cheerless as the camp. Before the war it enjoyed a permanent population of 600 which, in summer, swelled to about 1000 with the addition of landscape artists and other queer city people who found the bare, rugged coast somehow stimulating for a holiday and one or two of whom rarely failed to lose their lives over the cliffs. Now, with travel restrictions and the call-up, the population had withered to less than 400, mostly fisher families, the folk who worked a nearby quarry, and a few merchants.

There were also several apple-cheeked girls in the village, not nearly enough to go around even if they were not so zealously watched by their parents, and a pub called The George.

It was in the saloon bar of The George that the celebration took place on the night of Brad's permanent elevation to captain and company commander.

"Big night tonight, boy," Dan Stenick had chortled whenever he got within earshot of Brad during the rest of the day. "We'll fall off the wagon real good." On the firing range he had run over to Brad with eager news. "Al's holdin' back plenty of gin for tonight," he had panted. Al was Allisham Cabot, proprietor of The George and an uncle of Dan's girl friend Binny. Dan, recklessly playing the role of an incipient member of the family, had already initiated Allisham into clandestine ways of tapping military supplies of bottled goods.

Brad hadn't wanted a party. His satisfaction wasn't the kind that called for a celebration. He cared about the company command and the captaincy only because he had proved to himself he could once more rise to a challenge and, rising to it, he had reclaimed the logic of his life. Clearly it was not an occasion for carousing, but Dan had insisted with such happy vehemence that to refuse would have been like denying a child his birthday party.

So the three of them sat at a table in the dim light of kerosene lamps in the saloon bar of The George, he and Dan and Binny, and the girl's face glowed as it always did in Dan's presence. She sat respectably separated from her beloved. The public bar was crowded with village folk and their dour, corrugated faces were quizzically absorbing the fact that she sat with not one but two officers and both American at that. The social outlook of the village remained persistently Victorian and a young officer was inevitably an aristocrat and a libertine.

Eventually a darts contest got underway in the public bar, much to Binny's relief, and Jeff Waller and some platoon leaders came into the saloon bar and the atmosphere warmed up considerably.

Dan lost no time getting mellow on gin and orange. "Tomorrow's Sunday," he kept reminding Brad. "Sleep till eight. So drink up, Cap'n Parker. Mighty shiny couple brand-new bars you got on your shoulder, Cap'n Parker. How you feel, Cap'n?"

Brad said, "Are you surprised?"

"At what, boy?"

"That I made it."

"Look, tootsie, you're talkin' to a guy knew you when. If anybody figured you'd make it, I figured you'd make it."

Brad said, "I'm not sure. You didn't want me to come into the outfit."

Dan frowned. "Jeez, boy, I thought you were a real smart cookie.

I didn't want you to make company, that's what I didn't want. You've done okay so far in the war. I don't believe in a guy pushin' his luck. I figured you for the admin side, maybe the beach element, but not for company. That's for slobs like me and Waller. Love that gamble. But you went for it, you made it, and there's nothin' I can do except be happy for you even if I still think you're nuts."

"You think I haven't got what it takes."

"You made it, didn't you?"

"I mean when the balloon goes up."

Dan said, "One thing you got to learn around here. We don't talk about when the balloon goes up. We're real happy slobs. How you doin', Bright-eyes?"

Brad said, "You just talked about it. What makes you think I don't love that gamble as much as you?"

"You got too much brains, that's the difference. How's with you, Bright-eyes?"

The girl said, "I think it's wonderful, Brad being captain."

"Swell," Dan said.

"And I think it would be just lovely if Brad's girl friend was right here to be happy with us. I liked her."

No one spoke for a time after that. The girl looked inquiringly at Dan and Dan looked toward the bar where Waller was drinking a quart-size glass of mild and bitter. There was silence even in the public bar where the villagers were gathered on three sides of a leathery old man who was poised to make a climactic shot in the darts contest. Then she looked at Brad and her eager young face with its wind-blown complexion seemed harassed as if she were about to be spanked and knew not why. He smiled to reassure her.

The days of embitterment had long since passed. A succession of Val's letters over the weeks had reassured him that he could fairly claim her loyalty in addition to her love. His headlong flight into the combat army, though he hadn't reasoned it at the time, had been true and instinctive and had righted what had been wrong. The thought of Val was sweet and warming to his mind.

So he smiled and said gently, "It's a nice thought, Binny, and I'll tell Val when I see her that you remembered her."

Dan came to life. "When's that?"

"On my leave."

"You put in for it?"

"I couldn't until now. I'll do it tomorrow."

Dan said, "Take my advice and put in quick."

Brad didn't pursue the point. Having worked at SHAEF, he knew what Dan couldn't possibly know. The supreme command had long since laid down the minimum conditions for the great assault: full moonlight for the air-borne drop and low tide at dawn for the run in against the beaches. The earliest these meteorological requirements coincided was during the period between May 30 and June 6. Here it was only the fifteenth of April. He felt there was lots of time for his leave.

He said, "I'll get to the colonel tomorrow."

"Better, boy. He's gettin' awful stingy about leave."

It grew late in the evening by Mortrain's standards, almost nine o'clock. The public bar was almost empty. Most of the officers had departed the saloon bar. Binny's Uncle Allisham was wiping the last of the beer mugs.

A draft swept through the place as the blackout curtains parted and a young British lieutenant wearing a reasonably clean trench coat came into the saloon bar. "Good evening," he said pleasantly to no one in particular. He had a slim, boyish figure, not very tall, and he wore the blue sleeve patch of the Second Army and an artillery badge on his service cap. "A whisky, please," he said to Allisham.

The publican didn't move. He looked uneasily at Jeff Waller, who had put down his glass and had turned full around to examine the interloper. The half dozen tipplers in the public bar edged toward the partition for a better view of whatever might transpire. The village and particularly The George had come to be claimed as the exclusive preserve of Special Force 6. Soldiers of other units were not tolerated. This canon had been laid down not only because the special force lacked recreational facilities in its drab camp but also because of a carefully nurtured sense of superiority over ordinary soldiers. Men who were going to die in larger percentages hated and resented those who were going to die in lesser percentages. The canon had no official sanction of course, but it was well known all over the area and the one effort by neighboring troops to transgress it early in February had resulted in a bloody roughhouse in which the special force had been clearly victorious. Colonel Timmer had let it be known albeit unofficially that he highly prized the spirit of the special force.

"I say, old man, a whisky please," the lieutenant repeated.

Allisham put down the beer mug he had been wiping and looked inquiringly at Waller. The latter walked slowly toward the lieutenant.

"What is it you want?"

"Whisky—with water and of course your kind permission, Captain," the newcomer said crisply and with twinkling good humor.

Waller said, "You with the field battery?"

"Good guess," the lieutenant replied. "I'm with the 19th Field Battery and I drink whisky and water. Now you know everything except possibly my serial number and I was saving that for the Jerry in case I went into the bag."

Waller said, "You know a lot, Lieutenant, but you don't know this village belongs to the special force."

"Oh, I'd heard that bit of nonsense." The lieutenant turned to Allisham. "Come along now. A whisky and water."

Waller's massive fist smashed hard against the lieutenant's unprotected face. It was a short blow, savagely propelled, and the sound it gave off was sharp and unpleasant. The gunner staggered back a few short steps. His knees gave way and he grabbed the edge of the bar for support. He remained uneasily balanced, one hand clinging to the bar, the other on the floor. Then he came up slowly and when he was on his feet he said quietly and deliberately, "We'd better go outside, Captain."

Waller's reply was another blow. It was a harder blow than the first, for Waller's fist had been cocked and ready and the target was wide open. The smaller man went off balance and all the way down. He lay sideways, his face bloody and incredulous and his head turning from side to side as if he were trying to shake himself out of a bad dream. His service cap had rolled across the floor on its wire hoop and a cat bounded out of a dark corner and sniffed around it.

Brad hadn't seen the first blow but he had heard the lieutenant's challenge and had turned around in time to see the second split the man's mouth. He felt Dan's arm on his shoulder, decisively keeping him down in his chair.

Dan said, "Forget it, boy."

Brad stared at his friend, then at the other officers who were drinking their beer, and at Waller. The powerful marine stood with his back to the bar and his fists were turning small, impatient circles.

Dan said, "Drink your drink. Forget it."

"What the hell's going on?" He tried to shake off Dan's restraining arm but there was no mistaking its pressure and its firmness.

Dan said, "Let it lay, I tell you. You're still green around here. Don't screw yourself up in the outfit."

The lieutenant had lifted himself to a crouching position. He gazed fascinated at the untidy smear of blood on the floor where his head had lain. His tongue passed across his split lips. Suddenly he was on his feet, his fists high, rushing blindly at Waller. The marine side-stepped with lazy grace and dealt him two crushing punches to the face and a third to the side of the head. The young gunner swayed, pawing at the air. Waller said, "Still the fighting cock?" and hit him flush on the mouth where he had been bleeding. The gunner went down slowly on one knee, then sank forward on his hands and knees, and it was hard to know whether it was blood or vomit dripping from his mouth.

Dan, still pressing hard on Brad's shoulder, called out, "Okay, Jeff. He knows now."

"Think he's had the course?"

"Yep."

Allisham came from behind the bar carrying a wet rag and slapped it against the gunner's mouth. His arm reached across the fallen man's chest and supported him.

"Come on, Binny, look sharp," Allisham called out and the girl darted behind the bar and brought out a freshly wetted cloth and took back the bloody one. She did this two or three times. Then Allisham dragged him to a chair and positioned a table so he could rest across it.

Waller finished the last of his beer, dropped some coins on the bar, and went out.

Dan said, "Hell, boy, what did you expect? Caviar on toast? Don't look so goddamn sad. I been tryin' to tell you. You should've stuck with the staff side or maybe a division with high-class officers and a general who went to college. We're pros in the special force, we're tough slobs and that's why they picked us. I been tryin' to tell you but you wouldn't listen, you been so goddamn busy learnin' your job. Now you know."

Brad had nothing to say. He was sick with anger and his own

indecision. He knew the pressure from Dan's arm hadn't stopped him from going to the gunner's aid. This is the way it had to be. He was determined to get used to it.

Dan said, "Anyway, the kid's not hurt bad. You should see what an MG slug can do to a guy's face. Let's have a nightcap."

Binny said, "I never did like Captain Waller. He's a bully."

Dan laughed derisively. "Sure, Bright-eyes. And when he comes back from the war covered with medals for killin' nice German kids, all the gals in town will be rushin' to take him home for a pet. Boy oh boy, I could write a book about what people don't know about fightin' a war."

Allisham brought a last round of drinks and Dan waved his glass and said, "Here's to us, boy. We sure come a long way since Fort Harrison."

By the time they left the bar the gunner had managed to raise his head from the table. His face was lumpy, dazed, incredulous, and unquestionably drained of fighting spirit.

## 22

BRAD had slept the heavy sleep of the exhausted. He wouldn't have remembered it was Sunday. Someone in the signals truck, searching for an early news program, accidentally tuned in on a church service and organ music boomed over the area and penetrated the open window of his room. He lay in his cot and contemplated a startlingly bright shaft of sunshine streaming across his khaki blanket. The organ music was joined by a company of shrill voices and his drowsy mind extricated some words out of the blatant singing . . . *and the mercy of our Saviour* . . . and he said aloud to himself, "Gee, it's Sunday morning."

He moved his shoulders gingerly to see how sore the muscles were. Then he moved them abruptly. They weren't sore at all. He lay back and enjoyed a sense of wonderful well-being. He could remember not many Sundays ago when the slightest move of a muscle after the long Saturday-night sleep brought him excruciating pain. Even the gins he had drunk with Dan, and they were a good many, might have been poured down a well for their effect on him. He felt extraordinarily fine and hard, ready for anything. It was a grand day to boot. Spring had come at last to this Godforsaken coast.

His batman, Sorensen, clattered into the tiny room.

"Quarter to eight," Sorensen said in a flat voice. He was carrying a basin of steaming water and he placed it on Brad's foot locker. He was a thick Nebraskan youth with a look of perpetual unawareness on his wide, flat-featured face. He was surly but as good a batman as any American officer could find. MacEwen and Waller had English batmen who were the best. He poured a little of the hot water into an old mess tin and placed it on the window sill next to a fragment of mirror. Then he gathered up the captain's boots and went out.

Brad shaved out of the mess tin and sponged himself with the clean water in the basin. There was a shower hut in the camp, but it operated only two mornings a week and Sunday wasn't one of the mornings.

When Sorensen returned with the polished boots he said, "Captain MacEwen told me to tell you there's a small O group with the colonel at 0900."

"You sure, Sorensen? An O group?"

"That's what Captain McEwen told me to tell you."

An O group on Sunday was unprecedented in Brad's experience with the outfit. Under the staggered leave system there was always a company commander away over Sunday and Timmer was rarely present. He usually left early in the morning for parts not completely unknown; a platoon leader had once reported seeing him in a hotel in Reading with a good-looking V.A.D., both pretty drunk.

He was definitely in camp on this Sunday. By the time Brad hurried into A-mess for breakfast, he was eating voraciously in his place at the head of the U-shaped table. The mess was where Timmer enjoyed himself thoroughly. He enjoyed having the only armchair in the mess, his own heaping plates of bread, butter and cheese, his own condiments, and his own pot of coffee (the other officers passed these items up and down the table among themselves), and he enjoyed most of all being in a position to patronize his officers in what he considered a jocular and generous way. He was still pursuing the image of the *grand seigneur*.

On this Sunday morning he was unusually cheerful and expansive.

"All right, all right," he said as Brad came briefly to attention inside the door. "Sit yourself down, Captain, and dig in." He emphasized the word captain. "Did you celebrate last night?"

"Modestly, Colonel."

Timmer laughed heartily. "Not what I heard but that's all right. Remember when I made captain. It was something in those days. The army was a stepchild, nobody gave a damn about defense. I went down to Minneapolis and they tell me I tore the town up by the roots. Personally I can't remember."

Laughter rippled up and down the table and Timmer beamed.

After he had lit a cigarette, which served as a signal that the others could smoke, he said, "I'm afraid, gentlemen, I've got to issue a reprimand. Real stiff one."

His voice was mockingly stern and everybody looked expectantly at him.

"Yes, gentlemen, I had a telephone call from some old woman over at the 19th Field Battery. Says one of his officers got beat up at The George last night. What do you think of that?" He clucked his tongue deprecatingly. "He said it was a vicious attack and his officer will be unfit for duty for two whole days. Now, gentlemen!"

Everybody sought out Waller, who had been caught with his mouth full. His knobby face was alight with innocence.

Timmer said, "I asked him how many of my men beat up his officer and he said 'A captain' and I said 'A captain? One captain?' and he said 'Yes and it was completely uncalled for' and he said I should bring the man to book. That's exactly what he said—bring the man to book." He chuckled. "Must be a book writer or something. And I said 'I will certainly bring him to book' and that's the story, gentlemen. The question is, who's going to be brought to book?"

Waller raised his hand. "I'm your bloke, sir."

"Not you, Jeff!"

"Yes, sir. I'm afraid, sir."

Timmer clucked again. "Did you use a club?"

"No, sir," the marine said, grinning.

"A pistol butt?"

"We don't carry side arms off duty, sir."

Timmer nodded gravely. "That's what I always thought the orders were. Don't tell me you used your fist."

"Both of 'em, sir."

"Well now, Jeff," Timmer said, "you know you've got to be brought to book." His massive face aped a hanging judge. "That's what the man said. How in hell do I bring you to book?"

"I'm sure I don't know, sir."

"Maybe Captain MacEwen knows." He turned to his 2IC and said, "Peter, I've heard tell a Canadian sometimes gets into a fight. Not often, mind you, but sometimes. How do you bring 'em to book?"

MacEwen, who was sitting on Timmer's right, would have no part of the farce. He was the only man in the force who could be uncompromising when Timmer was having his fun. He said, "We throw 'em in the jug, sir."

The shadow of a frown passed Timmer's face but he picked up the old thread quickly.

"There you are, Jeff," he said. "It's a pretty damn serious thing making a poor gunner unfit for duty for two days." He cut a piece of cheddar from his plate and nibbled at it. "Tell you what. Consider yourself brought to book. But next time you hit a gunner and I hear he's unfit for duty for two days I'm damn well going to throw you in the jug. Any man of mine who can't put a gunner away at least a week raises some grave doubts in my mind. Understood?"

"Yes, sir. Sorry, sir," Waller sang out.

Timmer's dead-pan face made a turn of the table. Apparently satisfied with the reaction to his wit, he nibbled at another piece of cheese and grumbled, "These damned coffeehousing gunners. Don't know a war from a pink tea."

Brad had sat through the performance with mounting shame and disgust. He recalled his parting picture of the lieutenant's face, not so much the blood and pain, rather the look of puzzled and helpless outrage. He wondered again why he hadn't intervened and then he became aware that Dan was eying him from across the table as if to say, "See what I meant last night, boy."

The scuff of Timmer's chair as he pushed it back was a signal for the officers to come to their feet. Timmer stood there a moment. He said in an unusually low voice, "Sit down, gentlemen. Remember, the small O group at 0900. MacEwen—Waller—Stenick—Parker. That's all."

The look of the man as he called the roll of his company commanders sent Brad's mind spinning back to the day of Dieppe. The quiet voice, the bravado, the stabbing excitement behind the eyes, all were terrifyingly familiar.

Clearly the O group was going to be a momentous event. The men of the special force, accustomed to Timmer's security precautions, had never seen anything like this. Sentries had been posted around the hut which was Timmer's headquarters. They stood outside a twenty-yard radius marked off by a rope strung on stakes. Blackout curtains had been drawn over the windows. The encampment thought the colonel had finally gone off the deep end.

Inside the office, Timmer waited, arms akimbo, until his company commanders had settled in their chairs. Then he brought out a bulky gunny sack, placed it on the desk before him, and leaned his elbows on it.

"I think myself it's a little early in the game," his monotone began, "only April 16 today. But the people at Force G with the approval of Shaef have issued the orders and I don't intend to argue the point although God knows we've had pretty lousy security on other operations from this island. Anyway, they feel company commanders should be put completely in the picture before we begin the last series of rehearsals with the navy. So here goes, gentlemen."

He broke a lock on the gunny sack and brought out a map which he carefully unfolded and spread across his desk.

"Gather around," he said tersely. "Feast your eyes. This is the baby they've been working on for two years. You're looking at the Normandy coast from the mouth of the Orne river, right here—" his finger moved swiftly along the line of the coast—"to the neck of the Cherbourg peninsula, right here. That's the whole front, about sixty-five miles. All right, let's break it down. The British Second Army with Canadians under command goes in on the left. Most of it pretty damn good beach, towns well separated, level country behind for quick exploitation. It's roughly a twenty-five-mile front, the British front, from the mouth of the Orne to this place, Arromanches. Clear?"

MacEwen, who stood fascinated, said, "Clear, sir."

"Okay. Let's move to the right. Here's where the American First Army goes in. The front starts at Omaha beach, place called Colleville, and stretches around to this place, La Pecheris." Timmer's finger traced the curve of the jagged coastline. "Altogether, a thirty-five-mile front. Couple of bad spots of beach and some land the Jerries can flood but nothing serious."

Timmer brought up his head from the map. His lips were spread across his face in a mirthless smirk. "Well, does anybody see a gap?"

The captains kept staring at the map. They all saw the gap.

"It sticks out like a sore thumb," Timmer said. "Between the British right flank at Arromanches and the American left flank at Colleville, there's a hell of a gap. Five miles of it. And there won't be a link-up, not on D-day. Reason? It's impossible to make an assault landing in this five-mile gap. In most places there's no beach at all. And where there is a beach it's a narrow one and the cliffs are too steep. And even if we could make an assault landing it wouldn't do us any good. Landward of the beach there's nothing except forest, hills, and gulleys. A midget on a bicycle couldn't get through."

The captains were still staring at the map when Timmer abruptly pulled it off his desk, folded it, and returned it to the gunny sack.

"That's the big picture, gentlemen. The British on the left, the Americans on the right, and a five-mile gap in between which can't be assaulted from the sea. Shaef would like nothing better than to leave the gap strictly alone but it happens to have a piece of high ground sticking up like a star on top a Christmas tree. It's called Pointe Ange. And if there was a coastal gun sitting on that high ground it could raise hell with our run-in at Omaha beach and at Arromanches."

Timmer paused to light a cigarette. He drew deeply on it, coughed, and chuckled inexplicably.

"There happens to be a coastal gun sitting on that high ground, gentlemen. It's a 155 enclosed in a bunker. And that's not all. There's a combined observation and signals post and two defense casements and it all adds up to what the fancy guys over in Shaef G-2 call a *Stuetzpunktgruppe.*

"As I said, this thing can't be assaulted like the regular beaches, behind DD tanks and under navy guns and in daylight and on a divisional front with two brigades up and one in reserve and a fighter wing zooming in for close support. This thing has got to be taken by a small force, landing in the dark and getting up to the high ground before the enemy knows what the score is. And it's got to be taken just before H-hour. Tactical surprise is absolutely essential, otherwise there isn't a hope in hell of reaching the high ground. And once the high ground is reached the Germans will be sitting behind concrete. And gentlemen, no ifs, ands, or buts, it's *got* to be taken."

An off-center grin played on Timmer's heavy lips. "I needn't tell you that the force is us and the job is what we've been training for. How do you like it?"

Brad glanced around at the others. Dan winked at him; it was a strangely comical and reassuring wink. Waller bore a puzzled look as if he didn't quite understand. MacEwen pulled at his lower lip and his eyes were thoughtful and placid.

Timmer's monotone shot out again. "Well, how do you like it?"

MacEwen, who never seemed to deny his literal mind, said, "It's not a question of liking it, Colonel. The question is, what's the enemy strength?"

Timmer's crooked grin grew wider. He rummaged inside the gunny sack and came up with a document.

"This is the latest G-2 appreciation, dated March 25. It says, 'The enemy garrison holding the Pointe Ange station is made up of army and Luftwaffe ground personnel, most of whom did not originally form the garrison but who were brought in after special training within the last six weeks. At the present time it is estimated that the troops number from 115 to 130, but this includes signals technicians. Morale is reported high due to realization of the impregnability of their position. Agents have been sent into the area and a more detailed report may be expected about D minus 10.'"

Timmer put away the document, rubbed his hands briskly, and glanced around at his captains as if to see if there were any weak sisters.

"All right. You know how we operate in the big picture. Now let's get down to our own picture and I promise you it's rugged, plenty rugged."

From under his desk he drew a huge canvas map case. He unbuckled the flap and let it fall, revealing a detailed operations map of Pointe Ange. The general features, especially the location of the four bunkers, were similar to the maps they had been using in exercises.

Timmer said, "This shouldn't be news to you. It's practically our old operations map, but I want to point out a couple of important differences. The high ground is one hundred and twenty-five feet above the beach, twenty feet higher than we've been climbing. And this depression in the middle is precipitous. You can't move across it. This means that you, Brad, you'll be on your lonesome over here on the right. Not too bad though. The bunker is the smallest of the four —not more than fifteen-twenty men, nothing heavier in it than MG. And when you take it, you're through. You can't move over to support the others.

"On the left though it's more complicated. Once Baker and Charlie companies take their objectives, they've got to organize covering fire for Abel company to move through to the final objective—the signals post. It's a tricky one for you, Peter. You've got a deep penetration to make and you can't make it unless Dan and Jeff give you maximum cover fire. And of course, if you need extra help I'll be holding the headquarters platoon in reserve. Got it, men?"

The captains studied the map long after Timmer had finished. It was clearer than ever that A company had drawn the toughest job of all. MacEwen would have to lead his men into the deepest penetration and against a fully alerted garrison in the signals post. The unasked question hung heavy over the quiet room. Each man knew what the other was thinking. What happens to MacEwen if Stenick and Waller fail in their missions?

Waller finally broke the silence. He said, "Don't worry, Pete. Dan and I will clean up quick and give you plenty of fire support."

"Betcha," Dan said.

MacEwen, rubbing his chin thoughtfully, said, "I'm sure you will, but willy-nilly I've got the proper lads for the job."

He had quietness and quality, Brad thought. He was the real leader of Special Force 6. Looking at the man hunched over the map, he knew that MacEwen's company would go in and the signals post would be put out of action.

Timmer said, "All right. Forget the map and let me have your attention."

The captains nodded blankly. In the light of MacEwen's tranquil acceptance of Abel company's suicidal task, the colonel's brusque air of authority seemed singularly hollow.

"Supreme headquarters has issued two orders to insure maximum security. The first, gentlemen, you will note almost immediately. All officers not authorized to be in the picture are being issued with white tabs to be worn on their epaulets. This will be a constant reminder to you men who are in the picture that you carry a heavy responsibility in your daily association with other officers.

"The second order from Shaef becomes effective fifteen days from now. At 2400 hours April 30 every camp on the south coast will be sealed off from the remainder of the country. There will be no passage in or out except on the most urgent official business.

"We in Special Force 6 have an added responsibility. We can't take the slightest chance on a security leak. As I told you, we need complete tactical surprise on Pointe Ange or we're stone-cold dead on the beach. I don't know about you men but I intend to come out of this thing alive.

"Therefore, gentlemen, I have advanced the Shaef order as it applies to personnel of Special Force 6. Effective immediately, all leaves are canceled.

"That's all, gentlemen."

The encampment was extraordinarily quiet that afternoon.

On Sundays, especially on such a balmy Sunday, the men would be playing handball or would strip down to shorts and sun themselves around their huts and tell loud, irreverent stories about past leaves and future intentions. The radio in the signals truck would be tuned in full blast on the Forces network and inevitably a poker game would draw a large and noisy gallery.

Not on this Sunday. The order canceling all leaves had been posted. The men foregathered mostly in the wet canteen, and over innumerable glasses of beer they grumbled about "the old man." Some went to their bunks and wrote letters. The camp atmosphere was quiet and morbid as if this were the eve of battle.

Brad lay on his cot. He counted the slats on the ceiling and the strips of tar paper where the leaks had been stopped up. He thought about the battle and about Valerie, whether he would ever see her again. Now it depended on the battle.

Despite his Unitarian upbringing he had never felt fully a believer. He regarded himself as an unconvinced believer though he had never relinquished the habits and forms of devotion. His mother believed unquestioningly in God. In her last letter she had written of her conviction that her prayers had brought him safely through the war thus far. Her prayers might have helped, he thought blasphemously, but until now Sanford Jaques had helped a good deal more. Jaques couldn't help him from here in. He felt somehow easier for knowing that his mother was offering up prayers for his safety.

He thought of Abel company and the terrible field of penetration it had to cross in the face of a fully alerted enemy. He wondered what Pete MacEwen was thinking of at this moment. It occurred to him suddenly and decisively that he wasn't going to die in the battle. Pete MacEwen might die but he wouldn't die. He had no doubt that tens of thousands of men just like himself were resting easy along the south coast on this Sunday afternoon and all of them musing about the beach across the Channel and all deciding they weren't going to die there and a lot of them would die there. This was the notion, he reflected, that sustained soldiers going into battle. They thought about death but always in relation to the next fellow; it was one of those stubborn miracles that resulted in *esprit de corps* for which the high command took a ridiculous degree of credit.

Then he thought of Valerie. She would be at Smallhill now. She was at Smallhill on every Sunday afternoon and she wrote him every Sunday night when she got home.

"Someday I shall remember this spring," she had written in her last letter, "and I shall hate it. I hate it now. I was at Smallhill this afternoon. The fields are growing deeply green and there has never been such a year for roses and the wisteria is running wild and lovely. But the rumble never ceases on the road leading down to the coast and the dust never settles. If I were God I would forbid battle in the spring.

"John seems to hear the rumble of the convoys a great deal more distinctly than I do. That's, I'm sure, because he listens for it. He rarely talks about the war, at least about himself in the war, but this afternoon he said quite suddenly, 'You'd think, Val, they'd call me in. I'm fit enough. After all the little parties, it would be damnably silly to miss the big one.' He reminds me of my father. I wonder what it is about war that makes men so utterly lonely when they come out of it?

"I hate to hear the convoys because I have the most terrible premonition that you are riding in one of them and I want to run out to the main road and look inside each troop carrier on the chance of a glimpse of you. I wish I could be sure you are still on the staff side. I'm terribly frightened. Aren't you ever going to get leave?

"It's mad, isn't it, my darling? I sit with John, admiring him because he is gentle and sweet and has gone through so much; we both hear the convoys and he wishes he were a part of it and I pray you are not a part of it.

"Do you remember how it was when we first met? I told you all about John and you talked a great deal about your wife Jane and we were both so splendidly honest. And even later on, we still wondered about them and about ourselves. It was easy to blame the war then, the great restless war, flinging us together and tossing us apart, and we fell into the habit of drifting with the war. On a clear day, standing on tiptoe, one can almost see the end of the war now. And I die for you and long to see you safely back. What will become of us? What, my darling? . . ."

He dropped the letter on the cot and now, thinking of her and of the battle, he was content with Timmer's order. He didn't want a leave. This is the way it had to be. He could see it clearly without anger and without bitterness. The war was the blind matchmaker and had to be paid in its own currency. First he must pass through the battle—not because Damien had challenged him, not because John had already passed through the battle a hero, not because he had torn up the roots of his life. He must pass through the battle in order to reclaim himself, and then clean and tempered, he could reclaim Valerie.

He lay back on the cot and looked out the window into the sunshine. He felt strong and good; he was reminded of the time he lay in the plane flying over the Atlantic in violent anticipation of the morrow.

Timmer didn't show up in A-mess for supper that night. His batman brought word that the officers needn't wait, that the colonel would be eating in his quarters.

Until then the atmosphere had been morose. The officers had foregathered for their customary evening drinks in the mess bar, which was merely a space curtained off from the dining room, and their behavior had been brittle. They didn't know whether to be gay and hell-bent or quiet and sober. They had been groping for an attitude.

The news about Timmer broke the tension wide open and after extra drinks the officers tumbled into the dining room and they were jocose and uninhibited like boys in a schoolroom when the master has been reported sick. The *pièce de résistance* came when Dan slipped into Timmer's armchair and gave a wonderful mimicry of the colonel freezing in a shirt and instructing them, while munching on cheese, how to murder gunners who wandered into Mortrain.

Then Lieutenant Moore, who doubled as facilities officer, reminded them that a movie was showing in the wet canteen, Gable and Crawford in *Strange Cargo,* and they all rushed through their coffee and frolicked across the encampment to the big marquee tent where the troops were already shouting profane demands for the film to begin.

Brad slipped out after ten minutes. He had been thinking about Timmer. He felt he knew the man better than the others. He had seen him wide open on a summer's night back in '42. He knew the misgivings as well as the bravado, the strain no less than the ambition.

It was pleasant walking in the balmy night air. The moon diffused by a cloud bank invested the camp site with a spurious softness.

He stopped at the orderly room and asked the corporal on duty if he knew where the colonel was.

"Last I saw him, sir, he was driving down toward the beach. That was a good three hours ago. If he's come back he hasn't called in, sir."

Timmer's jeep was parked outside his quarters. Brad paused a moment and wondered if he should go in. He had nothing to say and yet he felt urged to pay a friendly call. It had been a fateful day.

He knocked on Timmer's door. He thought he heard a grunt and let himself in. Timmer lay heaped over his desk. His massive head was buried in his arms and his muffled snores droned through the room.

Brad said, "Sir——" and then he saw that a tumbler had shattered on the floor and near it an empty whisky bottle, lying on its side, as if Timmer had flung them away in disgust before he had passed out. He was lying over his map case and the narrow chain attached to the handle was looped around his wrist.

Brad thought he had better get out.

The next morning the four companies were on the bluff rehearsing holding attacks against the concrete pillboxes, one platoon firing with mortars and MG while another positioned itself to press a two-pronged assault with grenade and bayonet.

Timmer stood on the edge of the bluff in his cotton shirt, scowling and roaring and cutting easily the bravest figure on the whole of the south coast.

## 23

L O N D O N was all waiting and whispering. It was a conspiratorial city. Its people awoke each morning and thrust aside the
blackout curtains and peered out as if the news might be emblazoned
in the sky. They turned on the wireless and listened for the voice of
Churchill telling them that this was the day. They went out into the
streets and business places and exchanged rumors. They said, "Mrs.
Frangeon's boy Harry is in it, you know. He was supposed to come
home on leave but he didn't and they haven't heard a word and you
know what *that* means." They said, "Any minute now. The war correspondents have absolutely disappeared from Fleet Street." They
said, "At Dover you can't see the water for the ships."

And each morning there was nothing in the sky except the glinting
sunlight of a lovely May and nothing on the wireless except news of
the advance on Rome and nobody cared about men dying on the
terraced vineyards that led to the Eternal City. In Trafalgar Square
the band of the Royal Scots Guards played selections from *Bitter
Sweet,* but the voices of rumor persisted. "There isn't a blade of grass
growing between Beachy Head and Land's End. All tanks and heaps
of ammunition." At night they drew the blackout curtains and said,
"Four years ago we jolly well knew what was happening. It was
happening to us. Cor! What a change!" The fine days of May passed
and the people could scarcely sleep for wondering if it would be tomorrow. And then tomorrow.

All over the world all kinds of people wondered, and some wondered and prayed.

In Malton too there were rumors. Letters from the troops in England had stopped abruptly, as Brad's had stopped just after he had
written, briefly and hurriedly, that he had been promoted to a company command. The atmosphere of foreboding had drifted across the
Atlantic and as the last days of May passed people listened to their

radios until very late at night and turned them on again promptly in the morning.

Janie was one of those who wondered and prayed. She had run herself out. Her attempt at willful escape into countless home-front services had failed. Her mind would not be diverted from a growing agony over Brad and she learned to hate the long Connecticut twilights for it seemed to her that time also stood still, holding its breath in anticipation of the great and dreadful day. She didn't care any more about herself, about the fierce instinct that prodded at her and convinced her that she had fallen away from his thoughts. She cared only about him now, about his life. She wanted him back within the orbit of her mind and body so she could use her own limitless energies to blot out whatever had transpired in the long years of separation. But first he had to stay alive. This was the agony and she prayed.

But nowhere in the world was it quite like in London. Here they could feel the drama, feel it physically, it was so close to them, only an hour's train run to the south coast. They could see Coventry Street and Piccadilly Circus bereft of uniforms and they felt a loving warmth for the faceless men who once shuffled about these pavements looking for fun and were now only a little way off on the south coast facing across the Channel. They could see the dispatch riders hurtling through the hushed streets from one secret headquarters to another, and in staff cars they could glimpse the faces of generals and admirals, grim, as if something had gone tragically wrong at the last minute.

They went to their local pubs to pass the endless evenings and here it was worst of all. The pubs were filled and deathly quiet and people wondered why this should be. They could remember when London lay defenseless and alone awaiting the enemy onslaught. The pubs fairly exploded with defiance and laughter. Now not even the barmaid had a merry word. It was the waiting, they told themselves, but it was the death on the beaches they were thinking of.

Into this foreboding city Alex Timmer rode on the last Saturday in May.

He had been summoned to a final conference of small-unit commanders called for the purpose of checking and confirming their

movement to the marshaling areas and of briefing them on the latest
Intelligence reports relative to their assault points.

His staff car sped along roads which were shadowed for miles by
thousands upon thousands of parked trucks, tanks, bulldozers, ex-
cavators, amphibious vehicles called ducks, and more complicated
armored monsters called avres and priests. The fields behind overflowed with gray mountains of ration and ammunition boxes.

At a check point which gave exit from the sealed-off area, his
orders were examined and he was saluted with immense éclat and
waved through. The orders were important. He was important. He
felt exceedingly buoyant.

He sat back relaxed in the staff car and reminded himself that he
deserved it all. He remembered the high-school boy trudging
through the Minnesota winters to the drill hall three nights a week,
the youth studying for his commission while his friends cut up at the
Jardin de Danse, the young man spending every summer vacation at
training camp, and all through the depression his wife nagging at
him, demanding to know why he couldn't sell more cars and how
this silly soldier-boy stunt was going to educate the kids when they
grew up.

He wished she could see him now. Hell, this was only the beginning. There would certainly be decorations for this job, British as
well as American and even the Canadians might kick in. It was one
of those great spots a man gets himself into in war if he's lucky
enough and tough enough. They would have to give him a full battalion after this. It was an easy jump from battalion to regiment and
that meant brigadier general. He wondered what his wife would
think of that. And the boys in the auto agency. General Timmer!

The conference was held in a school in suburban London, in a
huge room with rising tiers of desks. Timmer glanced around and
could see only full colonels and brigadier generals and a few major
generals. It confirmed everything he had been thinking. He was right
up there knocking on the door. He scarcely listened to the nasal voice
of the little British general who looked like a shopkeeper. "Don't
worry about your flanks," the man was saying, "don't try to mop up
on the beaches. The idea is to break through the crust and push on
inland. That's the idea," he droned repeatedly, "break through and
push on inland." Cheerleader stuff, Timmer thought. It didn't apply
to him anyway. His was a clean operation, clean and rugged, and he

didn't have to worry about pushing inland. But the man went on and on and finally invoked the blessings of God and dismissed them.

Upstairs in Movement Control, Timmer examined a map of the marshaling area on the outskirts of Southampton, checked the site reserved for Special Force 6, and put in a few stout complaints about the amount of transport allotted to him.

Then he went to Intelligence.

"Not too happy news, I'm afraid, sir," a bespectacled British major of Intelligence said cheerfully. He swung his head from a map of Pointe Ange to a document and back again incessantly. "Our people in the area suspect the old Jerry has thickened it up a bit. Lots of activity around the point, they report, but they don't really know, do they? Sometimes send the most awful rot. Anyway, what they're sure of is this: Extra platoon, probably LMG, has gone into the signals thingamajig—that's your Abel company objective. Makes it quite a tough nut really, not happy at all, not at all. They've strung extra clumps of wire in front of all four objectives. And they've been spotted fiddling around your beach. Probably obstacles. Not very pleasant but there you are. Otherwise very much as previously reported."

The major continued to swing his head back and forth between the map and the document and then looked up brightly.

"Envy you, sir. The point should give you a bloody fine view of the show on the beaches. That's after you take it, of course. Bloody fine view. Absolute ringside seat. Give anything to be up there with you, sir. Oh—and good luck! Damn good luck!"

When Timmer left the building he thought he had better go up to his old club on the Haymarket and get a drink.

Shortly after midnight a staff car cleared the check point of SHAEF's advanced headquarters at Bushey Park and accelerated swiftly on the dark, deserted highway toward London. It contained a very angry brigadier general whose name was Ulysses S. Backhouse. Wasn't he entitled to *some* sleep, he muttered to himself, a *little* sleep? He had been trying all evening to clean up his desk and get to bed, but one problem after another had kept skimming in. With thirty-nine divisions and over four thousand landing craft being jockeyed into position in the narrow sea and land spaces of the south coast, there was no end to the problems, and toward midnight he had told himself, to hell with it, he had better get some sleep.

That was when his aide had come in with the message that Norfolk House required him immediately for an emergency meeting.

He tried to nod off in the back of the staff car. He couldn't; he was too angry. What sort of blazing emergency could it be, he asked himself savagely, that called for a meeting in the middle of the night? The rubber and canvas dummy fleet at Dover gone up in smoke? A German agent get hold of our plans? A surrender offer from Berlin? It was none of these or they'd have yanked Ike himself out of bed. It was these damned rear-echelon types trying to throw their weight around, he decided, and the violence of his anger reached a fine, tingling pitch by the time his car swept into St. James's Square.

When he stepped into Major General Pike's office, his anger became laced with disgust. He was never fond of Marcus Pike, who had been pompous even when they were classmates at West Point, and he positively disliked Major General Mellinsbeck who was Pike's British opposite number. Besides the two generals, the room contained a Canadian colonel he had never seen before and two provost-marshal captains. This cast of characters confirmed in his mind that there was no real emergency.

It didn't help at all when Pike said, "Sorry to get you down here, Backhouse. We simply couldn't take action without Bushey Park being represented."

"What is it, General?"

"Just pure bloody murder, that's all. It's about Special Force 6."

"What's wrong with Special Force 6?"

"Not a thing," Pike said tartly, "except that its commanding officer, a fellow called Timmer, was picked up tonight in a doorway in the Strand. He was dead drunk and he was talking——"

"A drunk?" Backhouse groaned inwardly. "Is that what you called me in for? God, General, I haven't slept in twenty hours."

Pike held his fire a moment. Then he said, "He was talking, General Backhouse. To an audience. On the street. About the operation."

"Oh God!"

Pike enjoyed a flicker of a smile.

"I'm afraid *we'll* have to play God in this matter." He turned to the two provosts. "You needn't stay. Let Colonel Timmer sleep it off and have him report to me in the morning." When they had gone, he

said, "Well, gentlemen, we have two specifications to decide—
quickly. One, is Colonel Timmer fit to remain in command and, if
negative, two, where do we go from here? I needn't remind you
every hour counts."

The Canadian, whose name was McNeil, said quietly, "We dropped
a valuable officer less than a month ago under similar circumstances.
Our man didn't talk, thank heaven, but we have a firm policy about
alcoholics remaining in control of troops."

Mellinsbeck chimed in. "It's a shocker, Backhouse. He's got British
under command as well."

Backhouse nodded. He was sick with chagrin. He said, "I'm thinking about security. What did he say? Anybody know?"

Pike thumbed a document he had been holding. "We've got the report of the police constable who picked him up. Damned lousy writing but I'll try to make it out. He says, 'I was proceeding up the Strand
on my regular rounds when at 11:08 approx I noticed several persons, eight or ten, gathered about a cobbler's shop just down from the
Savoy. I proceeded to investigate the cause. When I pushed through
the crowd I saw the lieutenant colonel in question sitting in the doorway. There were indications he was very drunk. In my judgment he
was semiconscious. He was speaking very indistinctly. He seemed to
be referring to military matters. I cautioned him against speaking
and I also requested the people to move along. I shook him and
said *Are you ill, sir?* He tried to hit me——'"

Backhouse said, "Let's get to the point, General. What did he say?"

"I want you to get the picture," Pike said, and continued to read:
"'He was still speaking as I lifted him. I can't remember everything
he said on account of the difficulty in taking notes while supporting
him. After Corporals Jarriman and Fairchild of the Provost Corps
reached the scene, which I estimate was five to six minutes later, I
jotted down what he said to the best of my recollection. According
to my notes, he spoke in my presence the following remarks: *See the
gap? Sticks out like a sore thumb. Smack between Gold beach and
Omaha. Good old Pete MacEwen.* I remember he mentioned the
name *MacEwen* several times. Then he said *Not very happy news.
The old Jerry has thickened it up. Takes guts to give the order.
Good old Abel company. Smack between Gold beach and Omaha.*
Then he said *Angel Point. Good old name. Good old Pete. Good old
angel.* I managed to quiet him down and he snored until the vehicle
arrived.'"

"That's it, gentlemen," Pike said.

After a silence, Mellinsbeck said, "Has a copy gone to Counter-Intelligence?"

Pike nodded. "They've got it in hand."

Backhouse said miserably, "Who's MacEwen?"

The Canadian said, "His 2IC. Also his Abel company commander. Grand type. He gave up a majority to join the special force."

"I remember meeting Timmer once," Backhouse said slowly, as if he were recounting a bad dream. "Remember it well. I could have sworn he was the most fearless man alive. I wonder what happened."

"Oh, he's fearless enough, I imagine," Mellinsbeck said airily, "but if fearlessness was enough for command, great generals would be common as grass."

Pike said, "Nobody's accusing him of cowardice. I'm beginning to feel sorry for the poor bastard. He'll be lucky if he's only cashiered. The tragedy is, he'd probably have made a great private, maybe sergeant."

"We've not here to try Timmer," Mellinsbeck reminded them, "we're here to decide what to do about the special force. They move to the marshaling area tomorrow night, you know."

Three pairs of eyes fixed on Backhouse. He drummed his fingers on the arm of his chair. Although he was not the senior officer, he represented supreme headquarters and the responsibility rested heavily on him.

He said slowly, "God, what a vicious thing to do—even drunk. Let's settle Timmer first. Does he operate?" It was an unnecessary question. The three faces he looked into were stony. "All right, he doesn't operate. Then I suggest we go by the book. The 2IC takes over, this fellow MacEwen, and everybody moves up a notch. The reinforcement pool can whistle up a good smart platoon leader for the bottom slot."

Mellinsbeck shook his head. "Won't wash, old man. We can't take MacEwen off Abel company. It's the heart of the operation. Look at it." He handed over the operations order and a map trace of the final phase. "He makes a pure frontal assault over open ground and without surprise."

Backhouse glanced over the documents and nodded his agreement.

"Well," he said briskly, "at least we've decided something. Timmer's out and we need a new O.C. And for God's sake, let's get somebody who's been through this sort of thing. Good Ranger or Commando type who can control the show from the beach end without getting into an uproar. Shouldn't be hard."

He beamed as if a happy thought had suddenly struck him. "The Personnel people will just be about comfortably asleep. Let's get 'em up and over here. Yessirree. General Mellinsbeck, you get hold of yours and I'll get hold of ours and we'll drop it in their laps. Right now!"

Special Force 6 broke camp toward dusk on a warm and pleasant evening. By the time darkness fell its convoy had merged into an endless line of traffic moving slowly toward the marshaling area on the outskirts of Southampton.

Brad thought he would always remember this night's journey, the glint of weapons and helmets everywhere in the gloom, the smell of the exhausts relieved every now and then by a sudden cross breeze redolent of freshly cut grass, the wretched quiet when traffic came to a halt, and the strangely soft and contemplative look on the stubbled faces of the men.

Captain MacEwen rode at the head of the convoy. He rode in a station wagon reserved for the commanding officer. He had been told that Timmer had been relieved, though not why, and that a new commanding officer would take over when they reached the marshaling area. He passed the journey wondering how they had found out about Timmer and who the new O.C. would be. But mostly he wondered how they had found out about Timmer.

Shortly after midnight the convoy rolled through a gate into a tented area. The men dropped off the trucks, stretched themselves, and lined up by squads. They could see little except the tents to which they were assigned and the ones immediately neighboring, but they heard commands echoing over a great distance and they felt there were many thousands of men around them.

The morning was clear and warm. When the men formed a long line at the field kitchen the word spread around quickly that a new commanding officer had arrived and that he was a lieutenant colonel of the British Commandos and his name was John Wynter.

The date was the thirtieth of May.

## 24

A L L during the night and morning, truck convoys rolled south to the marshaling areas on the outskirts of the ports from Southampton to Plymouth. When the assault troops spilled out at their sub-areas in the great tented cities enclosed by barbed wire and heavily guarded against the slightest contact with the outside world, they fell quiet. It was as if they had come to realize for the first time that the gate through which they had entered was a one-way gate, that the break with the world they had always known was irrevocable, that the only path they could beat back to that world was funneled through another gate that led to the docks and the ships and into the organized fire and mathematically calculated death on the beaches.

At Southampton, in the huge, sprawling area of field and forest and gently rolling hills, they called it "the sausage machine." The men, vehicles, and machines rumbled through the gate by the thousands and without apparent design, but in reality the control was precise and when the time came to make the journey to the docks, they would be organized in neat, tight packets for loading on the ships of the assault fleet.

It was natural the men should dub the place "the sausage machine." For the first few hours they felt like so much meat packed behind barbed wire for future disposal. They could see the life of Southampton passing beyond the wire, people in civilian clothes strolling and riding in trolley busses and girls who looked wonderfully fetching, and everyone peering at them in a melancholy way as if they were condemned or lepers. No one was allowed to approach within twenty yards of the wire on either side or to exchange so much as a word of greeting, and after a time the men turned their backs to the wire and shut out from their minds the strange people who weren't going to fight on the beaches.

Gradually the atmosphere of the marshaling area changed. The recreation staffs began operating, the weather turned warm and pleasant, and a holiday lightness came into the camp. There were three oversized marquee tents in which movies ran continuously. Loud-speaker units were positioned in each sub-area and men lay in the sun as on a picnic and listened to happy music. With the arrival of each new convoy, they discovered buddies they hadn't dreamed of seeing and loud, buoyant shouts of "Hi, sucker!" and "They sure are sending boys on a man's errand!" were heard all over the camp. Occasionally the music was pulled off the loud-speakers for an announcement: "Will the 2nd Tanks orderly room send a nice motherly sergeant to cinema No. 3 and collect a trooper who can't find his way back."

But the gaiety was spurious. What the men felt was written in long, intense letters home and was reflected in the enormous stakes at the poker tables and was etched on the faces of those who lay on the grass and stared at the sky as if in quizzical contemplation of the long road that had led from their homes into this funnel which would spill them out on the beaches.

With the exception of Captain MacEwen, the officers of Special Force 6 had not yet seen their new O.C. He had arrived during the night. Very early in the morning MacEwen had been summoned to his tent and here it was nearly noon and they hadn't emerged.

The remainder of the officers, the three captains and the platoon leaders, lolled on the grass a short distance from the O.C.'s tent and speculated on what might have happened to Timmer.

"Maybe they made him a chicken colonel and gave him a full battalion. He's been bucking for it."

"Naw. I heard he was sick."

"Who told you?"

"His batman. Says he was sick for a couple of weeks and didn't let on."

"What does his batman know?"

"Nothing else would keep him off the operation."

"It sure is a mystery."

Dan Stenick, who was lying on his back blinking into the sun, said, "I got it, fellas. He collapsed from heat prostration. Goddamn cotton shirt was too heavy for London."

There wasn't much laughter.

A lieutenant called Norden, who was one of Brad's two platoon leaders, said, "This new guy is pretty snooty. I'm beginning to hate him already." Norden was a moody youngster from Timmer's home state of Minnesota and from the beginning had been an especial favorite of the colonel.

Someone cracked, "Bet he's got buck teeth, a monocle, and says splendid every second word."

Waller said, "Don't worry, laddie. If he's a Commando colonel, he's tough."

"Tougher'n Timmer?"

Waller said, "Tougher'n Timmer."

The conversation idled between Timmer and the new O.C. and then Dan called out, "Hey, Brad. You been keepin' awful quiet. What you heard?"

Brad had scarcely thought about Timmer. He had been watching the O.C.'s tent all morning, wishing the flaps would open. He was wildly curious about John Wynter, what he looked like, how he would react when they met—if he reacted at all. He felt he knew the man intimately but only as a wraith, as a shadowed person whose sole purpose was to stand between him and his complete happiness with Valerie. At first he had tried to argue himself into the notion that this couldn't be the same John Wynter, that there must be two John Wynters in the British forces, but now he felt a sense of foreordainment in the whole affair. This was the pattern; there could be no other for the last short violent journey to fulfillment. The fates that had crossed and crisscrossed so many paths to bring Valerie to him had played a last, logical prank. A good one, he thought.

Dan said, "Speak up, boy. You been holdin' out on us?"

"I don't know a thing, Dan."

Dan said, "Jeez, I wish this guy would hurry up. Then we can go catch a movie. I hear there's a beaut. Alan Ladd licks the whole goddamn Jap army with a rusty schmeisser and a couple rocks. Maybe we can learn somethin'——"

Waller said, "Hold it, men. Here he comes."

They all scrambled to their feet, adjusted their caps, and stood easy.

He was slighter than Brad had pictured him and his face pleasanter though by no means handsome. His lips were thin and tightly

pressed against his teeth as if made so by a lifetime of listening a
great deal and talking little, and his eyes were pale blue and too
thoughtful to command quick attention. His battle dress, though
clean and neatly pressed, had seen years of service and fitted too
snugly around his narrow chest. His green beret was badly faded. He
carried no side arms, only a swagger stick which he hit lightly against
his leg as he came forward.

He didn't see them at once. His head was bowed, listening
thoughtfully to what MacEwen was saying as the two men came
across the short piece of ground, and when he looked up he seemed
genuinely surprised.

He said, "I'm sorry, gentlemen. I hadn't realized you were waiting."

MacEwen said, "I had them stand by, sir. I thought you'd want
to meet them."

"I most certainly would."

Brad glanced at the others. He wondered if they were as puzzled
as he was. The man moved and talked with a certain finely grained
awkwardness which was the quintessence of shyness. He was the
perfect antithesis of Alex Timmer.

As MacEwen introduced him down the line of officers, he returned
the proffered salute loosely but lingered over the handshake. It was
as if he was trying to say, There isn't much time for the military
niceties; we've got to know each other quickly and well and learn
to trust each other; we've a big job.

Brad was third in line. John repeated his name and shook his hand
firmly and looked at him honestly as he had done with the others,
but there was an extra moment of hesitation in the handshake and
a look of sharp appraisal in the Englishman's pale blue eyes, and
Brad thought, Valerie has told him. Then John passed along the line
to the lieutenants and Brad thought, No, he doesn't know. The reaction was too slight, he told himself. No man, not even an Englishman,
was that good an actor.

When the introductions had been completed, the officers broke
ranks and gathered around their new commander. He looked at the
ground and bent his swagger stick back and forth and said, "I'm
sure you're most anxious to know about Colonel Timmer. I'm afraid,
though, I can only pass on what I was told in London yesterday. Your
colonel has been taken ill—not seriously, I'm given to understand—

but he'll certainly be unfit for this operation. Pity. I'm sure it's as great a disappointment to you as it must be to him."

He shoved his swagger stick under his armpit, locked his hands behind his back, and continued to look at the ground.

"As for myself, I'm delighted to be back in action, particularly with so fine a body of men. I should have thought that Captain MacEwen would be appointed to the command; I feel it's quite unfair that he wasn't, but of course I'll do my best as I'm sure you will. We have a neat operation, plenty of hard fighting but nothing complex, and if we all do our jobs I see no reason in the world why we shouldn't have maximum success.

"That's about all. If you don't see very much of me before we move on, don't feel I'm being exclusive. It's just that I have a good deal of boning up to do—but of course please feel free to barge in on me at any time."

He flicked at a blade of grass with his swagger stick, looked at them all thoughtfully and walked slowly to his tent.

It was clear from the spate of conversation that he had made a deep impression on the officers. The combination of his slightness and reserve and the multiple decorations on his well-worn battle dress had been powerfully effective. Not a word about Timmer was uttered as the men broke up into small groups and gave voice to their reactions. It was as if Timmer had never existed.

Dan nudged Brad. "Say, boy, he's all right. Knows his fightin'. Funny thing how you can smell it a mile away when a guy's got it. Let's go eat and catch that movie. This is the life, eh? Come on, boy, snap out of it. What you seein'? Ghosts?"

Brad kept his eyes glued on the flaps of the tent into which John had passed. The man was good, no question of it. He was the sort of Englishman one heard legends about but rarely met. Then he thought of Valerie's last letters and he was prouder than ever that she loved him and he couldn't wait for the battle to prove to himself he was as good a man or better. Better, God damn it!

Toward dark on Friday, the second of June, a leisurely life of eating, sleeping, poker, movies, and letter writing came to an abrupt end for the men of Special Force 6.

The music cut out of the loud-speaker in their sub-area and in its stead came a series of sharp instructions. Officers and non-coms added their stern voices to the cadence of commands and the city of slate gray tents came alive with hurrying men. Troops turned in their blankets and cots to QM stores; they paraded at the pay office and received shiny little bills which represented French francs and didn't look like money at all; they drew emergency rations and medical kit; they donned heavy underwear, specially issued, and rubberized battle dress and their bulky equipment; they filled their water bottles and cleaned and oiled their weapons which were already thoroughly cleaned and oiled; and at the day's last light, when the sergeants called the roll, the sub-area which had frolicked with music was grim with erect figures suddenly grown faceless in full battle array.

At 2230 hours, as an ominously black night rolled over the south coast, the air cold and heavy with a threat of rain, the men of Special Force 6 climbed into trucks and rode through the south gate of the camp toward the docks.

It was the slowness of the journey that made it miserable and memorable. The narrow Southampton street along which they moved was clogged with a double line of traffic. Tanks with flail chains were tangled with troop transporters and bulldozers and self-propelled artillery and jeeps. The awkward paraphernalia of war made a confusing cavalcade and one wondered how these unwieldy instruments would ever be sorted out and unleashed on the beach across the Channel. The great mass moved slowly, a few feet at a time, and then waited endlessly. It was cold and cramped inside the trucks and many of the men climbed down and paced restlessly in the verges of the road. They smoked, holding the glowing tips of their cigarettes inside their cupped hands, and peered ahead. There was nothing to see except more steel monsters standing motionless in the gloom.

There were dwellings on both sides of the street. The windows were blacked out but here and there among them the curtains had been pushed aside and startlingly white faces were pressed against the glass.

Brad rode in the cab of his company's lead truck. He looked up at the white faces pressed against the windows of the dwellings and thought, I wish they wouldn't look at us. I wish they'd go back to their comfortable beds.

They reminded him of home. He didn't want to be reminded of home. A light rain began to fall. It was one in the morning and they hadn't moved a mile since leaving the marshaling area. It would be seven in the evening now in Malton. He could see Janie and her mother sitting on the open veranda at the Country Club, overlooking the eighteenth green. They would be waiting for Damien to come in from the course. Damien usually golfed on Fridays in summer and they dined at the club. He didn't want to think about Janie. He hopped out of the truck and walked about in the rain. There were a lot of men walking in short circles in the rain. They shuffled past one another and didn't talk. It was a long, miserable, cold night.

A British military policeman wearing a heavy canvas coat came by. Brad said, "What's holding us up?"

The MP said, "Bloody tank transporter made a bad turn and sideswiped a post. Bloody turret gun clipped a trooper's head clean off."

The way the man said it reminded him of John. The British were good at this kind of thing. They fought the war as if it were the normal course of life. He liked the American way better, American bitterness and impatience and the sense of adventure, the way Americans hated war and loved it in a peculiar but honest confusion.

He had met John for the second time that morning when he had been summoned into the O.C.'s tent. The conference had been crisp and routine, merely a check of the signals Brad would transmit back to beach headquarters and the flares he would fire to denote the completion of each phase of the attack. He had watched for some sign, some quick unguarded reaction that John knew who he was and what he represented in his life. But there had been none.

Toward the end of the conference, when the signals had been checked and confirmed, John had looked up pleasantly and had said, "We're squared away, Captain. Just one last word of advice. The essential thing is a good quick eye for ground when you get up top. Everything depends on how you position your covering fire. There's no happier man than a machine gunner in good ground shelter. Then if your rifle platoon presses the attack firmly you should winkle them out in a jig. It's all quite neat."

All quite neat. He remembered Timmer saying, "This is the real war, Brad. This is for the type of man who wants nothing except to get in there and fight, and the hotter the better." He thought he preferred Timmer's way. It was less British but more honest.

Presently traffic began to move. The men walking in the verges wouldn't believe it was really underway and they shuffled through the rain alongside their vehicles and waved with mock gaiety at the white faces peering down at them from the upper story windows. After about half a mile the convoy halted once more.

Brad climbed back into the cab of his truck and tried to doze off. He couldn't sleep. His mind was too angry and alive thinking of the quiet Englishman who rode in the station wagon at the head of the convoy. There was something strongly appealing about the man's demeanor, something he admired and quickly deplored. *God help me, he deserves more than I can give him* Valerie had said. Now he had inherited a part of Val's dilemma and he hated it and was afraid of it. Traffic began to move once more. An immense tank alongside roared thunderously in his ears and he was reminded of the battle that lay ahead.

He awoke with a shudder. The rain had stopped and the wind came in colder than before and it had a peculiar feel of the sea. It was nearly six. He climbed down from the truck and peered ahead in the dull gray light. Above the tops of the forward vehicles he saw the rigging of ships and above the rigging he saw barrage balloons straining their cables in the wind.

They waited another hour. Then they rolled down to the hards and the men formed up on the windy dock and eventually they marched down a cement ramp to the broad open deck of a ferry. The men stood sullen and shivering on the deck of the broad-beamed little ship as it cast off and moved slowly into the Solent. The wind howled pitilessly. Low black clouds skulked across the sky and in the open patches between them there was only solid gray overcast.

Out beyond the hards the invasion fleet rode at anchor on the sheltered water, hundreds of gray-painted ships of all sizes and shapes waiting to accept a complement of men and machines and to sail out over the Channel to the most massive amphibious assault in all history. But the drama was for those who could not see, who could only imagine, for the people at home who dreamed in terms of their singing, stalwart, invincible warrior sons. The men who would do the fighting waited motionless and bedraggled in the cold wet of the open deck until the ferry hove to against the belly of a rusting old ship that had assault craft hanging from davits over her sides. Then they lugged their gear and weapons across a weaving gangplank and dropped asleep in whatever open space they found between the hatchways below decks.

## 25

I T W A S the third day and they had not yet sailed.

Life aboard the *Great Wallsend,* an ancient 3000-tonner that had once run the North Sea passage between Harwich and Flushing, had deteriorated from excited vigil above decks to abject boredom below. The view from the rails had become an eyesore, a few deserted boathouses on the Isle of Wight and the ships close at anchor, an LST, two LCIs, and an old destroyer with three upright stacks. The men had already used their daggers to carve their names on every free wood surface from stem to stern. The rumors that had swept the ship had run the gamut down to cancellation of the whole show, and by the afternoon of the third day, a cloudy, windy day, almost everyone lay below decks and had long since ceased to care whether the ship ever sailed.

Then it happened.

The harsh squeal of a straining winch penetrated into the tiny cabin where Brad lay on a narrow steel hammock lashed against the wall. He dropped the paper-backed book he had been reading and glanced across an eighteen-inch space between the hammocks to see how his cabin mates were reacting. Lieutenants Norden and Urquhart, his platoon leaders, had been writing letters on pads propped up against their knees and now they too looked about and listened.

For three days the only sounds had been the hollow slap of the wind against the hull and the creak of the cables which supported the twelve assault landing craft on their davits. This was a new sound. It was harsh and grinding and vibrated the ship so vigorously that shreds of white enamel broke loose from the ceiling and fluttered down on them.

They couldn't look out to see what was happening. The only porthole was permanently sealed by an iron ring. They could scarcely move. The cabin was minuscule, seven feet in depth and five-feet-

six-inches across. Norden had measured it. He kept a diary for his
wife's benefit and this, he thought, would be one of its most interesting entries—three full-grown men, their gear and weapons, existing
in a cabin in which the only open space was an eighteen-inch passage between the hammocks.

Suddenly the winch was silent.

Urquhart, a thickly built, happy youth from New Jersey, said, "Say,
men, I guess——"

"Shhhh!"

From above decks they heard a crisp Scottish voice call out, "Skipper to *ferrst* lieutenant—shorten in!"

"Aye aye, sir."

"Bridge to fo'c'stle—weigh!"

The winch started up again and the three men in the cabin swung
their legs down from the hammocks.

The voices above decks cried out more powerfully than the racket
of the winch.

"Five shackles on deck! . . . Four shackles on deck! . . . Cables
up and down, sir!" Then came a hard, buoyant yell: "Clear anchor,
sir!"

Now a new sound, a deep rich rumble from the bowels of the ship,
came into the tiny cabin. The three men leaped down from their
hammocks and made for the door. Urquhart reached it first and
effectively blocked the passage.

He said, "What's today, Norden?"

"Monday. The fifth."

"Gee," Urquhart exclaimed, "I'm rich!" He reached into his blouse
pocket and pulled out a slip of paper and waved it under Norden's
nose. "I got it. I won the pool. I drew the sixth of June!"

The three men scrambled out of the cabin and joined scores of
others loping through the hatchways to the decks.

There was no question of it. The invasion was underway. The
creaky old *Great Wallsend* was sailing steadily through the Solent
and hundreds of other ships that had lain stodgily at anchor moved
in concert with her and all seemed suddenly to have developed
leanness and swiftness and were driving forward, breasting the gentle swell of the sheltered waters, eagerly aimed in the same direction
like well-trained pointers padding over a wide expanse of field. It

was a thrilling sight and the troops crowding the rails laughed and
prattled as if this were a race.

Brad leaned against a port rail, clear of an overhanging assault
craft. A strip of English coast which had been green a few minutes
before was turning gray in the distance. A high overcast arched the
sky and the wind was chill. On the receding land there were patches
of sharp brilliance where the sun, invisible from the ship, had broken
through the overcast and was shining on English fields.

He remembered the eve of Dieppe, how he had stood on the
shore and watched the ships disappear into the curve of the sea.
He had studied the men crowding the deck rails to landward and he
remembered how he had thought tomorrow a lot of them would be
dead and then he remembered the scuffed boots jiggling from out of
the closely wrapped blankets. He thought there must be people on
the shore watching the ships, pitying the men in them, knowing tomorrow would be D-day. He glanced at the man next to him, a
chunky, beady-eyed British corporal with a stolid face, his helmet
at a rakish angle. He felt sorry for this man but he was pretty sure
he himself was going to survive the dawn.

From the moment of sailing the ship's loud-speaker had been
droning a series of instructions about smoking on deck, about the
method of inflating life belts, about defacing the property of His
Majesty's Navy, about the removal of light bulbs from passageways
at night. Now, after a few moments of silence, the speaker announced:

"Attention! All officers of Special Force 6 will proceed immediately to the wardroom on A deck forward. Officers only. Immediately,
please."

An operational map of Pointe Ange with the phase lines drawn in
had been pinned against a wall in the wardroom. John Wynter and
Captain MacEwen stood before it, studying it with deep concen-
tration.

When the officers, fourteen all told, had seated themselves loosely
around a huge, leather-covered table, John turned about.

"All here? Good. Let's get cracking." His voice was soft but crisp
and authoritative. Unlike the day in the marshaling area when he
had taken command, there were no awkward hesitations. This was
the first time Brad had seen him without his beret. His blond hair

needed cutting, especially around the ears where it curled thickly, and it made him look youthful, almost boyish. But there was no question of his command and incisiveness.

He said, "I've two bits of news you can pass on to the troops. First is that the met people assure us we'll have heavy overcast which means our chances of getting ashore undetected are very good indeed and we'll be able to run in to the beach closer to our objectives than we planned.

"Second, the beach at Pointe Ange is not mined. I had this from the navy when I visited headquarters on Wight this afternoon. A party of marine engineers stole in on the Pointe Ange beach three nights ago, actually tramped around it for nearly ten minutes, and brought back samples of sand and some gradient soundings. As a result our skipper assures me his men will give us a dry landing from the assault craft, so I think we can go right ahead and mark up the exact location of the beach HQ . . ."

He drew a circle on the map and called out the co-ordinates. In the review that followed, the men began to understand why they had seen so little of their O.C. His knowledge of the operation was meticulous for every phase down to platoons and squads and the manner of his instruction bore an imprint of complete confidence. Dan whispered, "Tell you one thing, boy. Compared to this guy, Timmer's way out in left field. This guy's an operator."

Then, as his review drew to a close, he made an announcement that caught up his small audience sharply and incredulously.

He said, "At this point, gentlemen, I think I should tell you of the only radical change I've made in the plan. With Captain MacEwen's consent which I obtained, I must say, over his very vigorous objections, I am taking command of Abel company——"

He paused to allow an impulsive murmur among the men to subside. His face grew stern, as if to remind them he was still commander and would brook no dissent, but his voice remained soft.

"It was the only course. If you think it over, I'm sure you'll agree. I've been with you quite long enough to realize that Captain Mac-Ewen has a more thorough grasp of the whole operation than I could possibly have. And not only of the operation. He knows each one of you and the non-coms personally, your strong points, your weaknesses, your reflexes, and I'm sure he can make a wiser decision, certainly a prompter one, on where and when to commit the reserve. He also has the necessary qualities. In my opinion, he should have succeeded to command, but that of course was not my decision to make. However, here we are out at sea and the wireless is quite dead, so I have taken completely unfair advantage of my rank and have nominated myself to lead Abel company."

He looked about to see if there were any unconvinced faces. The room was full of them.

The slight, blond Englishman went on quickly. "This last word, gentlemen. Remember to commit yourselves quickly and boldly. Hesitation won't save casualties, it will cost casualties. Look at it this way. Speed and boldness are the keys to this kind of operation. We've a certain number of lumps to take, but remember, you'll give better than you take and in the long run more lads will be alive when it's over.

"That is really all. I've always found it a good idea to put the operation completely out of mind for the last few hours to zero. Shall we, gentlemen?"

They didn't follow his advice. After he had left the wardroom their minds were filled with the operation though, for a time, not a word was uttered. The old ship was making speed through a light swell and the creak of her beams was the only sound in the room. Each man understood what the decision entailed and was shocked no less than captivated by the casualness of the O.C.'s announcement, but the eve of battle was no time to put such thoughts into words.

Presently MacEwen did it. He jammed a cigarette into his mouth, looked hard at the leather on the table, and growled, "There's no one else who'd ask it——" He paused and added savagely, "And no one else I'd let have it."

Brad fled the wardroom and went up on deck. The ships of the invasion fleet had spread out on all sides, ahead and behind, tugs and cruisers and pleasure ships and landing craft, even an old paddlewheeler wheezing along grotesquely and churning great heaps of foam into the bow of a lithe destroyer. In the failing light they made a picture of immense power.

He took his last look at England. The coastline was only a dark ribbon against the deepening purple of the night, and he thought of Valerie who was somewhere behind it. He thought of her in anguish, and for an intense moment he prayed. No words occurred to him. It was an obscure and tortured emotion and it clutched at his whole being and passed quickly.

Gradually the night closed in on the sea and the ship was alone, and then it closed in on the deck and each man there was alone.

The commissionaire on night duty at the Park Street club shuffled down the stairs to the main hall and drew the blackout curtains over the windows and the doorway. The light from the main chandelier was dim but Valerie didn't turn on her desk lamp. There was no need; not a single visitor had entered the club. Edna had also failed to turn on her lamp. Valerie looked at her across the hall, wondering if she also knew. Their eyes met and Valerie saw that she knew.

This was the eve. No one had told her but she knew as surely as if she were standing atop the white cliffs watching the ships move over the bend of the darkening sea. The foreboding had developed slowly as the torpid day wore on and now at dusk it drove into her fully and relentlessly. This was the eve and tomorrow was the day.

The music of a concert orchestra filtered meaninglessly out of the radio and then the voice of a newsreader came and it was flat and maddeningly casual. There was more music. The girls looked at each other and then at the curtained doorway. If only someone would come in! No one came in. The evening was lifeless as the day had been lifeless.

The clock chimed eight.

Edna came across the hall and said, "What's wrong, Val? Why are you staying?"

"I don't know. Why are *you* staying?"

The American girl made an unhappy face. "Do you feel what I feel?"

"Yes."

"Tomorrow's the day, I guess."

Valerie said, "I'm afraid so."

"So am I." Edna stood uncertainly at the desk and then she said, "Let me sit down here with you."

"Do."

They sat silently like two small girls in a dark house and after a time Edna said, "It's a funny thing. I've got nobody in it but I want to cry all the same."

Valerie thought, My whole life is in it. She hated herself for being

English, for having been taught not to cry. Crying was for lesser breeds. She had so much to cry for. She had known for almost a month that Brad was in it, ever since his last letter had come with a censorship seal over its flap and he had written, ". . . Don't misunderstand if you don't hear from me for a little while . . ." These were the most hateful and heartbreaking words ever written in war by husbands and lovers, and women all over the world were weeping over them. If she could only misunderstand. She couldn't. The meaning was terrifyingly clear. And now John had gone too—John who was sweet and undemanding. "Temporary duty," he had told her on the telephone, "back soon." She had been suspicious of the unaccustomed briskness in his voice but she couldn't believe he was on the assault. He wouldn't be on such short notice. Yet she couldn't be sure. It was more than a week and he hadn't come back and tomorrow was the day.

She said, "It will be a dreadfully long night."

Edna said hopefully, "Perhaps we're wrong."

"Perhaps."

She knew they weren't wrong. She walked home through streets that were dark and unnaturally silent and the few people she saw seemed to be hurrying as if to get home before a terrible storm broke. The air was dank and still. There was no storm brewing except within them.

When she arrived home she wept. She wept out of a great sense of guilt no less than a great sense of prayer, for the dilemma that racked her had now passed beyond her brief control. She wept, and Mala, who had taught her never to weep, held her close as if she were a child in India once more and tried to comfort her.

Inside the ship the troops slept everywhere, on tables and floors in the mess decks, in the passageways, and in what had been the main lounge. They slept fully dressed beneath the single blanket that had been issued to them. Only a few were kept awake by the creaking of the old ship and these lay on their backs and stared at the dim yellow lights on the ceiling. Infrequently a man gave up trying to sleep and rolled up his blanket and stepped gingerly across the bodies of his comrades and went up to the deck, but most of the troops slept solidly in their bulky clothes and the bells of the watch failed to disturb the calm on their wind-burned faces.

When the bells sounded two o'clock, Brad was on deck. The ship had entered a new current of the Channel and was pitching heavily and the wind blew strongly across the forward deck where he stood. It was ominously quiet, he thought. In half an hour, according to the navy schedule, they would reach the rendezvous area seven miles off the Normandy coast. It seemed hardly possible that this immense armada could have come seventy miles across the Channel without being tracked. Surely the Germans knew by now. And yet the sea was black and soundless except for the slap of waves against the hull.

He hadn't been able to sleep. He envied Norden and Urquhart, who were snoring contentedly in their hammocks in the tiny cabin below decks. All night his mind had bounced wildly with memories of Malton, mad, inexplicable memories of picayune incidents, of his first dance with a girl whose name he couldn't even remember, of his tenth birthday party, which had been canceled because he had come down with a cold, of the time he got horribly drunk at Dartmouth. He thought he had better come up on deck and take the air, but even here he couldn't get Malton out of his mind and he wondered how Damien would react when the news broke, as it would in a few hours, that the D-day assault had been launched.

"Starboard lookout to bridge! Aircraft approaching starboard bow, sir!"

He peered through the darkness and could barely see the sailor who had shouted the warning.

The skipper's Scottish voice wafted down from the bridge.

"Very good."

He hadn't heard anything. Now, listening intently, he could make out the faint drone of airplane motors. The sound grew louder, then receded, and suddenly the air immediately overhead was turbulent with the thrum of pistons.

"Starboard lookout to bridge! Sounds like enemy aircraft, sir."

Again the deep highland voice: "Very good."

The invisible aircraft screamed as if it was making a wide turn. A flare dropped. It was a single orange flare and it struck a small circle of light over the sea and revealed a line of perhaps ten ships plowing through the whitecaps. Brad could almost read the reaction of the plane's pilot in the sound of the plane's motors. It was as if he couldn't believe what his single flare had revealed. The motors roared abruptly, climbing steeply, and then a series of flares dropped out of the black sky, orange and yellow and red, and the area was ablaze like a giant Christmas tree sitting above the Channel.

From where he stood Brad could see scores of ships stretched out over the water. He wondered why the anti-aircraft guns weren't firing. High above the flares, the plane's motors screamed shrilly and roared away into nothingness.

"Starboard lookout to bridge! Aircraft retiring, sir!"

The voice on the bridge said, "All right, lad. A happy trip to him."

The flares hung low in the sky for a few moments, then dropped slowly one by one into the sea and the ship was alone as before and the only sound was the deep throb of the engines and the slap of the waves.

After a time Brad became aware that someone stood at the rail beside him. He saw it was John Wynter.

The Englishman peered down into the water.

"Spotted you from the bridge. Can't sleep?"

"I'm afraid not, sir."

John chuckled mildly. "If you feel drowsy later on, take a benzedrine. There'll be a bottle of them on the breakfast table. Should carry you through nicely."

Brad said, "What about the plane, Colonel? Bad break for us?"

"Oh no. Our air-borne divisions landed in France over an hour ago. We'd been expecting that visit. It's all quite in order."

"Won't it alert them?"

John said, "They can't do anything about it. They can't regroup in four hours."

They stood together silently. Brad wished he would go away. He wanted desperately not to have to talk to this man. They peered down from the rail and watched a white sheath of water thrashing away from the hull.

John said, "I take it this is your first show."

"Yes."

"It's the best, Captain. The first is always the best."

Brad thought the man was patronizing him. He turned to look at him and met a faintly apologetic smile.

"I do mean it, Captain. The first is really fine. It's new and challenging and you have all your luck riding with you. That's important. A lot of men have chipped their luck away bit by bit until there's only a little left. But when you've got all of it, you're in great form. I rather envy you."

Brad knew he was talking about himself. The anger that had lain deep within him ever since John had arrived to take command surged into his mind. He faced the Englishman squarely.

"Why did you take the job, Colonel?" It was an impertinent question and he didn't feel he should ask it, but they were standing on the deck of a ship three hours before the assault and he was filled with a hard, compulsive sense of equality.

John said, "You mean the special force?"

"Yes."

"Why did I take it? It's a strange question."

Brad said, "I'm sorry, sir." He emphasized the word sir.

John said, "Do the officers resent it?"

"They have the greatest confidence in you."

"And Captain MacEwen. Does he resent it?"

Brad said, "He has no pretensions. He wants to win."

"That was exactly my impression. He's first class."

There was another silence. A few feet below them a wave rose precipitously out of the choppy sea and crashed against the hull.

John said, "Why did I take the job? It's hard to say, Captain. They were up a tree for someone quite suddenly and I'd put in for a post on the show and I got it—but that's not the answer. I suppose it's because I know this sort of thing. It's the only job I do know. I was never much good at anything before the war and I imagine I'll be a rank failure after it's over, so a chap does what he can when he feels he's of some use."

Brad's anger fell away. He said, "You didn't mind me asking?"

"Not at all. I'm sure you must have been wondering." He added quietly, "It's an odd place for us to be meeting."

Oh God, Brad thought suddenly. *He knows. He's known all the time.* He thought, *Damn the English. Damn their façade. He's known all the time.*

A thrum of aircraft flying very high and in great number filled the air. The two men waited until it had passed out of their hearing.

Then John said, "Ever been to France before?"

"No."

"Pity seeing it this way the first time. It's a lovely land."

Brad said, "How many of these have you been on?"

"Off the sea? About half a dozen. Some duds. Some fairly good ones. I'm sure this is the best."

"I wonder how it will be."

John said, "Busy and noisy mostly. And when it's over you can't remember half of what happened."

There was another silence and Brad said, "How is Valerie?"

"Lovely as always."

A wave struck the hull amidships and a curtain of spray was flung up. The wind whipped it into their faces.

John said, "Treacherous old beast, the Channel."

Then bells sounded on the bridge and the ship's loud-speaker called out: "Attention all personnel! Attention all personnel! The mess decks will be cleared. Breakfast in ten minutes. Clear the mess decks! Lively now!"

John said, "Here we go." The two men walked a short piece along the deck and pushed through a double set of blackout curtains. Inside the ship the bright lights had been turned on and the men who had been sleeping fidgeted on the floor and came slowly to their feet and rolled their blankets.

The loud-speaker came on once more: "This is the skipper speaking. We are approaching our launching station. Everything is going well. Don't mull over your breakfast. Launching will begin in exactly forty minutes. Good luck to all of you." The loud-speaker clicked off and the men who had been rubbing their eyes leaped to their feet and made for their company stations. There was a confusing cross-traffic at the hatchways but hardly any talk.

John studied his watch. Then he looked at Brad brightly and pleasantly and said, "I think I'd better shave. Good luck."

The assault craft were lowered into a choppy sea and the moment they hit the water they bounced and snorted away from the mother ship. The sky was black and the sea was black. There were thirty men to an LCA. They huddled one against the other at the sides of the small craft, shielding themselves and their weapons from the spray that lashed all about them. Only two men at the helm stood erect. They were the navy men, a sub-lieutenant and a petty officer. They stood on a platform which elevated them above the line of the forward ramp.

The sub-lieutenant commanding Brad's landing craft looked

ridiculously like a boy, fresh-faced and eager, his duffel coat open
and flying in the wind and his helmet carelessly perched on the back
of his head. His was the leading craft of a column of four. There were
three columns, each of four craft, and they held steadily to formation though the swells were treacherous and the spray blinding.

Brad sat in the forward end, his back against the ramp, and he
could feel the thump of the sea crashing against the ramp, fighting
and twisting and almost overturning the small craft. It had never
been as rough as this in their rehearsals off the Dorset coast, Brad
thought, and he wondered if they would make it. The waves thundered deafeningly against the thin steel sides as if eager to splinter
through the impertinent little challenger. He looked at his men
huddled against the sides. Their faces were grim and tight-lipped
and terribly white. They were men who knew how to use their
muscles and weapons on land. They were helpless in the wallowing
sea and they kept looking back at the young sub-lieutenant, seeking
to reassure themselves that he knew what he was doing and where
he was going. The spray came over the sides regularly now. Water
surged along the bottom of the craft and slopped over the men's
boots. But the face of the youth at the helm had not lost its eagerness
and his body inclined gracefully to the thumps and shudders of the
craft.

Some of the men were sick. Brad could hear their retching in the
brief silences between bursts of wind and spray. He made his way
aft.

"How are we doing?" he called up to the sub-lieutenant.

"Coming nicely, sir. We're dead on—or nearly. Perhaps a minute
or two late. Nasty swell."

"How long to go?"

"Oh—twenty-five minutes, I'd say." The youth looked down and
said saucily, "In a hurry, sir?"

There was something vastly reassuring in the way the youth said it.
Brad went back to his place at the ramp. His mind spun over the
time schedule. In twenty-five minutes they would land. In an hour it
would all be over—one way or another, all over. Thinking about it,
he checked his equipment. Two 77 grenades, two 36s, his pistol, com-
pass, dagger, and his field and shell dressings. His Sten gun was
cradled on his arm, the spare clips in the long pocket on the right
thigh of his trousers. And he had his luck, all of it, unchipped as

John had said. He was grateful to John for having said it. That had helped more than anything else. He felt wonderfully calm and confident. He couldn't fail.

The craft suddenly quivered as if it had been struck by a giant wave and it bounced high in the air and fell with shattering impact. For a long moment it remained at an alarming list. A burst of water poured in over the low side before the craft righted itself. The men cursed miserably and more of them were sick.

Then a sound of faraway thunder drove in over the lashing of the waves. The huddled men came alive. They were wildly sensitive to every new sound. The thunder increased in frequency and intensity and reached a violent, unceasing pitch. There was an uneasy shuffling in the craft.

The sub-lieutenant shouted, "Those are our navy guns. They've started beating up the beaches!"

Then a new sound, a distant roar of planes, swept in and added a bewildering complexity to the thunder of the guns and the waves slapping against the craft.

Brad glanced at the luminous hands of his watch. It was five forty-five. Landward to the left a line of briefly flickering lights leaped up out of the darkness like anvil sparks. Flares hung in the sky miles away and looked like tiny candles. Here and there a plume of green flame burst forth and burned fiercely for a few moments. The bombardment of the beaches had begun on schedule. These were the flat, fortified beaches where the full divisions would land after dawn. Straight ahead, the gap of Pointe Ange was cloaked in darkness and it was toward this strange patch of gloom in an otherwise desperate fairyland of fire that the LCAs of the special force beat their way through the rough seas.

The sub-lieutenant came forward, his duffel coat still flying open in the wind. His face was bright with elation, like a boy on a wonderful party.

He said, "You may alert your men, sir. We're a mile off and forming up for the final run-in."

The men didn't have to be told. Shielding their weapons, they crept to their places facing the ramp. The craft moved at reduced speed, stealthily it seemed, and the resistance of the sea slackened. It was very dark. The naval bombardment reached a new and terrifying pitch and though the sound was miles distant its immense power was transmitted through the night and the sea fairly shook with the punch of the great cannon. The men looked about with reborn interest. The feeling of being alone on the wretched sea had dropped away. Someone made a falsetto like an old woman: "Can you tell me, mister, when we reach Paducah, Kaintucky?" A little forced laughter died off quickly and left the compulsive thunder of the warships and the thrum of planes and the lapping of the waves.

"Kedge anchor!"

"Kedge anchor ready, sir."

The engines cut out and the craft floated free and aimlessly a few moments. There was a thump as if it had hit a rocky bottom, then a sickening lift and another thump and the ramp skittered down and a new wind, a soft, land wind, hit the wet faces of the men.

## 26

T H E men of Dog company stood hidden by the starless night beneath a rocky outcropping on the narrow beach. Waves rolled up and lapped at the boots of the men on the outside flank. They waited for the signal that would propel them into action, that would send them scurrying eastward along the beach for sixty-five yards where, according to the map, a defilade opened a way to the high ground. They were restless. Like athletes champing at a starting line, they tested the footing in the soft wet sand and pushed aside clumps of weed the receding tide had left on the beach. They could see only ten or twelve yards ahead and they were uneasy about the debris they might stumble into on their way to the defilade.

They were panting though the run from the ramps of the landing craft to the shelter of the outcropping had been a short one. It was the deadly excitement of waiting that made them pant. The three other companies and the HQ platoon had landed farther down the beach and had to be given time to form up at their starting points which were almost half a mile west of where Dog company stood.

Far out on the sea to the east and west, tiny tongues of flame spurted out of the dark and the deep, full-throated roar of 16-inch naval guns raced across the water and echoed in wave after wave against the shelf of rock where the men stood. The thrum of hundreds of bombers flying high over the coastline was ceaseless. The men didn't look out to sea or up into the black sky. They peered at the limned figures of their platoon leaders, and the platoon leaders kept their eyes glued on the company commander, waiting for him to give the signal.

Brad studied his watch. He was scarcely conscious of the distant thunder of the naval guns and the ceaseless thrum of aircraft. He counted the seconds ticking off and listened for another sound, a sound of small-arms fire. This would be the signal that one of the other companies had been intercepted on its way to its starting line. If this happened, the zero hour for the synchronized attack they had rehearsed for so long would be jettisoned and he would, in the words of the operations order, "act independently to the capture and complete destruction of D company objective."

It hadn't happened. Not yet. The luminous hand turned slowly around the face of the watch, so slowly he suspected something had gone wrong with the mechanism. Now there were three minutes remaining before the move to the defilade would begin. Three minutes seemed terribly long. He wondered how he could pass three whole minutes standing motionless and quiet. There was a foul smell coming off the cliffside, a smell of feces and rotting food. The Germans had been tossing their waste pails over the cliffside. The tide had carried the stuff out to sea, but the smell clung to the rocks and the brush just above where he stood.

Now the arc of the sky had turned from black to murky purple and a thin line of light was rising out of the sea. The beach where he stood was still cloaked in impenetrable darkness. He wondered if the navy people who had set the timing of the operation to coincide with an exact degree of first light had made a mistake. He glanced at the watch. Two minutes to go and there wasn't enough light, not nearly enough light for sure footing on the climb up the defilade. Perhaps the timing was all wrong. Perhaps a clerk in the navy met office had made a simple mathematical error.

He checked himself. There were eighty-five men peering at him and he was their commander. A few were close enough to see the expression on his face. He forced his clenched teeth apart and moved the hand that held the watch in a small circle to show that he was relaxed. He tried to gauge his fear. There was some, perhaps a lot in him. This was his first battle. He had no way of knowing how much fear he was entitled to feel. He remembered Dan saying once, "You're scared all the time, boy, but you're too busy to know it." He wasn't busy now and he was scared. He could feel his sweat on the helmet lining pressing against his forehead. He turned to look into the faces of the men nearest him. He was sure they could smell the feces and the rotting food so he put his fingers to his nose and winked at them. He thought this was what Dan would have done. There was one full minute to go.

One minute to go and there had been no rifle signal. This meant that the other companies had reached their starting lines without interception. The Germans would be alert of course. The bombardment of the beaches to the east and west would have alerted them. They might even know there was an enemy on the beach below making ready to storm them. This possibility had always figured in the planning. The fact that there had been no rifle signal didn't necessarily mean the Germans were unaware of the impending attack. It depended on the commander of the *Stuetzpunktgruppe*. If he was cool and clever, he would preserve silence and meet the assault from his positions of strength behind concrete fortifications. A nervous commander might send his men to the edge of the high ground and attack the assaulting forces coming up the defilades.

But there had been no signal. Either the German commander was cool and clever or the landing, shielded by darkness and the diversion of the distant bombardment, had been undetected. The forecast of the planning staff was that they would land undetected. He prayed they might be right. He would know soon enough. The second hand on his watch passed the thirty mark. The men were shuffling with impatience.

The navy people hadn't made a mistake. The light *was* coming up steadily over the line of the sea, a hazy purplish glow that was neither daylight nor night. He could make out a wooden ration box half buried in the sand about twenty yards ahead. He hadn't seen it before. This was the visibility they had been planning on. By the time they reached the wire on the edge of the high ground, the light would be good enough for sure footing but still too poor for the Germans in the pillbox to see them setting the bangalores. The navy people were wonderful. Right on the nose.

The second hand came up to the sixty. He raised his arm and the men like eager, stealthy animals moved swiftly along the narrow stretch of wet sand.

The light that had appeared hesitantly on the edge of the purplish sky was a welcome sight for a young *Oberleutnant* of signals in the Pointe Ange station. He had been on duty in the big underground casement all night, a terrible night of telegraph keys clicking without a moment's respite and telephone bells ringing with wild impatience and the *Oberst* pacing about in a foul mood. He had never experienced a night of such utter confusion.

He himself was confused. He admired the Wehrmacht. He thought it was the finest human instrument created by the Reich. Yet the generals couldn't make up their minds whether or not a full-scale assault was being aimed at the Normandy coast. Not a single troop movement had been ordered, even in the face of the shelling and bombing of the coastal positions and authentic reports of massive parachute drops behind the fortifications. This was the height of stupidity and he hated to think of the Wehrmacht as stupid.

He welcomed the dawn because it would bring an end to official stupidity and a beginning of visual truth.

He remembered clearly when the confusion had begun. It was at exactly 0145 hours. The Intelligence section of the 709th Infantry Division at Cherbourg signaled urgently that a mass of American parachute troops had dropped in the vicinity of Ste. Mère Eglise. But not more than five minutes later, the same Intelligence section corrected its previous report and indicated that the occurrence was merely an arms drop to the FFI and was being investigated. Then the 716th Infantry Division at Caen signaled a British parachute drop at the mouth of the Orne. Headquarters of the Seventh Army at Falaise immediately asked for clarification. Was it a raid or an arms drop? And was it at Ste. Mère Eglise or at the mouth of the Orne? Nobody seemed to want to say definitely. Then the navy confounded the already terrible mess. The navy station at Courseulles signaled that radar findings showed a great mass of ships approaching the Bay of the Seine, but this interpretation was overruled by Naval District Headquarters at Le Havre. It reported to Seventh Army that sea and weather conditions were clearly unfavorable for an assault and what the Courseulles station had reported was a diversionary maneuver at best. Then Seventh Army contacted the Calais station and the latter reported that the enemy assault fleet based on Dover-Folkestone had definitely not put out to sea. Then the Luftwaffe at Carpiquet airdrome signaled that their night patrols had observed a mass of assault ships in mid-Channel. This launched a new spate of messages between Cherbourg, Caen, Calais, and Seventh Army. The messages were angry and confused and by 0545, when the bombardment of the beaches began, not a single headquarters would make a formal declaration that the long-awaited assault was underway, and Seventh Army was still asking for clarification.

The *Oberleutnant* concluded sadly that this was a perfect illus-

tration of what was called the fog of war. He handed over his duties
to his deputy, slung his field glasses over his shoulder, and came up
out of the casement.

In a few minutes it would be light enough to see the warships
that were bombarding the beaches on the flat beyond Port-en-Bessin.
He thought it would be amusing on his next leave to recount to his
wife how the generals, the Luftwaffe, and the navy had argued
back and forth whether there was or was not an assault coming in
across the Channel and he had merely walked to the edge of a bluff
and seen for himself. It was really quite amusing, he thought. Everybody knew what was happening except the generals.

He climbed the cement steps and nodded good morning to a major
of infantry who sat and smoked below the slits where his men stood
at their machine guns. Then he climbed another short set of steps
and emerged in the cool, breezy air.

It was not quite light yet. He could barely make out the rounded
tops of the pillboxes to the right and left which defended the signals
station though each was only a hundred meters distant. He looked
behind him across the gulley and couldn't see the third pillbox at
all. It was at that peculiar time of morning when the light was ex-
ceptionally deceptive to the eyes.

He walked down the open ground between the two pillboxes, moving carefully in the uncertain light because the ground was pitted
with shallow bomb holes. He listened to the salvos of naval artillery
and the drone of the planes and he thought it would be something
to see when the light became good enough.

He kept on walking until he reached the wire on the edge of the
bluff. New wire had been looped over the old wire and it rose to
a height above the line of his sight, so he moved away from the
wire to a clump of low-growing bushes over which he could have
an unimpeded view of the sea and the beaches.

He reached down at his hip for his field glasses. Then he paused.
He thought he saw a heap of loosely strung wire lift into the air as
though by unseen hands. Fascinated, he watched it for a few moments. He saw the glint of a helmet. Someone was trying to crawl
up from under the wire.

He let his field glasses fall back quietly into the case on his hip
and reached instead for his pistol. He flicked down the safety pin
and waited. When the figure crawled clear of the wire and began

to look about, he saw that the helmet was American. He lifted his pistol and waited until the figure had crawled forward a little more. He took careful aim and fired.

The shot that killed Dan Stenick also set off the battle for Pointe Ange.

Across the gulley, a good three hundred yards distant, Brad heard the shot. He was lying in a culvert a few feet beneath the wire that hung over the lip of the high ground. He heard the single pistol shot despite the racket of the naval bombardment because his mind had become animal sensitive and was alert to any sound that would affect his safety. He wondered if the Germans in the pillbox had heard it. He calculated they were eighty yards farther distant from the shot and would not have been listening for it.

He watched the engineers of Urquhart's platoon push three lengths of bangalore pipe through the wire. They were the first men to reach the lip of the high ground; below them were the MG squads and still farther below were Norden's rifle squads. The engineers needed a few more seconds to set the fuses on the bangalores while men below struggled to position their 2-inch mortars that would fire smoke bombs into the open area in front of the pillbox and provide temporary cover for the men who would crash through the gaps blown in the wire.

They didn't get the few additional seconds they needed. In the wake of the single pistol shot across the gulley came a shattering cacophony of rifle, Sten, and machine-gun fire, of bursting grenades, of screams and shouts of command, of wild inhuman yells that pierced the deafening clatter of automatic weapons.

The men of Dog company had rehearsed for such an emergency. On command, the men below abandoned their 2-inch mortars and let fly with their smoke grenades, the 77s, tossing them high over the wire. It seemed an excruciatingly long time before the grenades landed and their smoke billowed up on the open ground. Then the engineers put fire to the fuses of the two bangalores that were primed and ready. There was a wretched, tearing explosion and flame and choking smoke leaped wildly from the gaps flung open in the wire and the men scrambled up over the lip of the high ground and crashed blindly through the gaps.

There were some, confused by the black billowing smoke, who

failed to judge the gaps properly. They found themselves entrapped on the wire and tried to pull themselves free and smashed frantically at the wire with their rifle butts and screamed for help from the men beside them who were racing freely through the gaps. A squad leader, a bulky sergeant, paused to work the entrapped men off the wire, working desperately on the wire and bellowing and cursing and commanding the others to get through inside the wire. A sudden gust of wind caught up the smoke and the men on the wire were trapped naked in the rising light. A new hail of 77s fled through the air to give smoke cover to the men caught on the wire and the others who were scrambling over the lip of the high ground lugging the heavy equipment, the mortars and machine guns and the beehive charges. But the new smoke didn't come soon enough. The German machine guns at the slits of the pillbox swung swiftly into range and their bullets crashed and whined and ricocheted in the clumps of wire and the men screamed as they were hit and some didn't scream but fell face forward across the wire. The bulky sergeant who had been trying to pull the men free of the wire continued to bellow and beseech the others to keep moving up the defilade and through the gaps and then a burst of 50-caliber MG ripped across his chest and punched him back over the lip of ground behind the wire. The bullets cut him almost in two and he lay half over the lip of ground, his mouth agape and his head and chest unrecognizably bloody like a butchered calf. He dangled there.

The men scrambling up from the defilade heard the screams of the men hit on the wire and they saw the bloody dangling head of the sergeant. They waited for the smoke from the new hail of 77s to cloud the half light and they knew this was the time to get through to the high ground. This was the only time, for a mortar was working out of the pillbox, in addition to the MG fire, and was dropping anti-personnel shells into the defilade and was taking a terrible toll of the men who were hesitating below the lip. So they scrambled past the dead sergeant and through the gaps. Some were hit but most got through and plunged blindly to the right on the inside of the wire, as they had done in rehearsal, until they made contact with their platoon and squad leaders, those that were left. The teams that carried the Brens and LMGs, Urquhart's teams, hurled themselves into the shelter of the merest bulge of ground and set their sights on the pillbox which loomed gray and hazy in the shifting, smoky, uncertain light and on the slits which were punching orange tracer into the gaps in the wire.

The newly organized fire from the Brens and the LMGs concentrated on the slits in the pillbox and the enemy gunners swung away from the gaps in the wire and sought out the men who had broken through.

Now Norden's riflemen flung themselves through the gaps and took up their positions for a right encircling assault on the pillbox. Norden scrambled among his men. A bullet had ripped open his cheek and he was bleeding badly. He cursed. He could count only about twenty men out of the minimum of thirty-five he expected to reach the position. He didn't know if he could make the assault with twenty men. He tried to make another check. He had to keep his head down. The Germans had widened their field of fire and bullets were ripping the ground all around him. The wind was brisk off the sea and was lifting the smoke too quickly. He thought if he didn't get the signal quickly for phase two he wouldn't have even twenty men to make the right encircling assault.

Brad had crashed through the wire with the leading squad. He was on the ground now, crawling like a wary animal behind the men of Urquhart's platoon who were maintaining the covering fire on the slits. It was hard to estimate how many had got through the wire. The light was a thinning, uncertain purple and the waves of smoke stung in his eyes and the inhuman racket of the automatic weapons blunted his brain. He could hear the screams of the wounded piercing the clatter but this did not touch him except as an estimate of how many men he had left for the final phase. He crawled about behind the perimeter of Urquhart's platoon until he found Urquhart, who was firing a Bren. Urquhart shouted over a body that lay crumpled between them. He shouted, "Go ahead. We're all right. We'll keep their heads down." And Brad shouted, "Watch for the yellow and give us everything."

He crawled around farther to the right where Norden's platoon was positioned. Norden's face was dripping blood and he shouted, "We only got twenty men. I don't count more. Only twenty. Do you hear me? Only twenty." Brad saw that Norden was badly wounded and hysterical. He kept shouting, "Only twenty, God damn it, only twenty. Either we go or we don't!" Brad shouted, "We go. Fire the yellow!" and Norden shouted, "Fire the yellow!" and then someone shot a yellow flare and it seemed to hang for a long moment in the smoke and dust.

This was the signal for maximum fire from Urquhart's men and for smoke bombs to be set off from the mortars below the lip of high ground. The air was convulsed with the clatter of every weapon the men could lay a hand to, even piats which would scarcely nick the concrete of the pillbox but would have a strong shock effect on the men inside.

When the new smoke rolled over the open ground, Brad gave the signal and Norden's men advanced to the right in an outflanking movement, seeking to come up against the rear of the pillbox and to blast it open. Norden screamed unintelligible commands and his legs were buckling as he stumbled through the smoke. Brad knew he wasn't going to make it as far as the pillbox and he took command of the men. They advanced through the smoke, keeping well separated, and when the smoke began to thin they flung themselves to the ground. Brad saw they were about fifteen yards from a narrow, cement-lined trench which led to a door at the side of the pillbox. He saw that the door of the pillbox was open, that eight or nine Germans were crouched in the trench peering over their rifles as if they knew an outflanking attack was coming around the right and were waiting to slaughter the attackers when the smoke cleared. He saw that two of his men who were lugging the beehive explosive had gone ahead blindly just as they had rehearsed it and he shouted to them to hit the ground.

The Germans in the trench fired and the men lugging the beehive fell back screaming. In the interminable moment between the time they were hit and the time they fell back screaming, a brutal, chilling, panic-stricken moment, Brad saw that he and his handful of men were trapped in the open, hopelessly trapped, and he thought, This is the way it ends and this is where it ends, here on the pitted ground, and all the things that have gone before are erased and don't count, and all the exercises and the toughness and the unchipped luck, nothing counts. This is the end, the way it's got to be and God! I don't want to die but I'm going to die on this pitted ground and I wonder how it will be. He thought, It's a lousy break having to die like this in the racket and the smoke and the smell, a lousy break first time out. He thought these things in the terrible moment between the time the men lugging the beehive were hit and the time they fell back screaming. He could see clearly they had no chance against the Germans crouching inside the concrete trench, but he was the leader of the men lying on the ground around him, and a leader must do what he must do, but it was hard, so terribly hard to get off the ground and plunge forward knowing he would be cut down, but he had to do it and he got up off the ground. He saw Norden staggering up from behind, his face stark and bloody as if he had crawled out of a grave, and he screamed, "Hit the ground, Norden!" but Norden didn't stop and he plunged forward together with Norden, and all the men, those that were left, shouted crazily and charged the trench.

He was almost at the trench, not more than three or four yards from it, when he was hit. He could see the face of the German who fired the shot, a pair of young, terrified eyes in an ashen face beneath a helmet, and for a lucid and singular moment the war was between him and the young, terrified German.

It was a moment wrenched out of time, removed from the gun clatter and the animal cries, from the fever of the attack. He had been hit. He knew he had been hit. The bullet punched him back as if he had been struck a powerful blow in the belly. He wondered why he didn't feel pain. His whole body vibrated with the kickback of the bullets sputtering out of the Sten he held thrust forward in his two hands. His eyes telescoped on the frightened eyes of the youth who had shot him. He felt a dizzy elation for knowing he had been hit and didn't feel pain, and for his animal awareness that he was stronger, more vicious than the frightened youth, that he was going to kill the frightened youth. He saw the bullets from his Sten strike across the neck and chin of his enemy and he saw the youth's mouth open in an intensely human attitude of indignation. He thought it was a strange expression, that of indignation, at the instant of death. And then the moment was flung back into time and reality and he was shattered by the racket of the automatic weapons and the shrieking and a convulsion of pain poured through him and his elation turned to agony. He couldn't feel his legs for the fire in his belly, no legs at all, and he toppled as from a great height and was a long time hitting the ground. He saw heavy boots leaping over him and around him and he heard screams of animal rage and terror mixed with the deafening vibration of automatic weapons. A grenade came looping through the air and bounced along the ground away from him. He pulled his arms around his head and tried to burrow into the hard ground. There was an explosion. He felt he was being lifted as if by a hurricane wind and the scorching pain in his belly was over-whelmed by a new anguish as if a thousand hot needles had struck into the side of his body. He couldn't see for the smoke pouring up all around him and the fumes of burning cordite brought vomit chok-ing into his throat.

He was afraid to move, afraid to discover how badly he had been hit. He lay still but his mind was frantically alive and he listened to the rattle of fire, calculating its direction, and then he heard the thud of a great many boots racing up to him and past him into the trench. Suddenly the firing and the screaming stopped and he heard only deep sobbing moans and he knew the battle was over.

After a time he tried to bring his arms down from their shielding position around his head. Only his right arm would respond. He couldn't feel his left arm except as part of a great area of pain that throbbed and stabbed and was sickeningly warm. He rolled over on his back. The first thing he saw was the sky. It was at half dawn, gray and shimmering with a haze of thinning purple. He turned his head and looked along the ground and he saw Norden's bloody face star-ing at him. Norden was lying flat on his stomach, his legs spread wide apart, and his head was twisted on its side in grotesque juxta-position to his body. Norden was dead. He tried to lift himself by his good arm. He couldn't. He felt the strength running out of him and he thought he had better lie still.

He spent a little time convincing himself he was alive. He watched the clouds scudding across the purple-gray sky and listened to the soft moans of men around him and to the clatter of the battle across the gulley. He wondered why the battle there wasn't finished. He tried to remember the time schedule for the battle across the gulley but he couldn't remember it. His mind was numb. All he could think of was that he was alive and that he should fire three red flares to signal to the beach that the battle was over. He moved his good hand along his wounds and it came up warm and dripping blood.

Urquhart leaned over him.

"How is it, Brad?"

He said, "Did you fire the three reds?"

"Yes. What hit you?"

"Everything."

"I'll get a medic. Does it hurt?"

Brad said, "Norden's gone."

Urquhart looked over at Norden's body. He gathered up the dead man's helmet and placed it over the bloody face.

Brad said, "How many more gone?"

The lieutenant grimaced and said, "Christ, I don't know. I just don't know. About thirty."

"Oh God. Thirty."

Urquhart looked as if he wanted to cry. He said, "We made it."

A medic, panting and frowning, ripped away the cloth on Brad's left side, cut open a bag of sulpha, and sprinkled the powder over the blood and the bits of cloth stuck in the blood. Brad said, "What is it? Bad?" The medic said with sharp anger, "There's lots worse'n you, Captain." He applied a shell dressing and powdered it with more sulpha.

Brad said to Urquhart, "What happened? At the end, I mean."

"They stopped firing when you hit the trench. They turned their gun barrels up out of the slits and we charged over and collected what was left of them. About a dozen—old men and kids. Christ, they were scared. Worse than us."

The medic bandaged his left arm against his side, over the shell dressing, and said, "We'll get you down to the beach soon as we can," and hurried away.

The sulpha burned on his naked wounds. His head whirled with pain and nausea came in waves and was worse than the pain. He wondered if he was going to die. The medic wouldn't have handled him so angrily if he was going to die. Even on a battlefield there was some pity for a man who was going to die. The medic had shown him no pity at all. That was good. He thought, God, the luck! It wasn't chipped away. I had all of it.

The rattle of automatic weapons and the crump of mortar shells came from across the gulley. The sound seemed to him remote compared with the compulsive clatter of his own action, but he listened to it with a heightening sense of terror for the men who were still in the midst of battle. He thought of John and of Dan and now an awareness of what was happening drove thunderously in on his mind.

"Urquhart!"

The lieutenant was standing against the scorched and blackened pillbox peering across the gulley.

"Urquhart!"

This time the lieutenant heard and came to him.

"What's happening across there?"

Urquhart said, "Take it easy. You're not supposed to move. It'll start the bleeding again."

"What's happening across there?"

"Christ, Brad, we can't do a thing about it. They're in trouble and we can't do a goddamn thing."

A wave of nausea passed through him. He felt terribly sick. He thought, Oh God, it isn't over. I thought it was over but it isn't over. If they don't win across there, it's all wasted, everything is wasted. He said, "What kind of trouble?"

The lieutenant said, "Bad trouble. Charley company didn't make it. They're pinned down." He was trying hard to remain calm. "Baker company made it but Charley didn't. They're pinned down! Christ, what'll happen to Abel?"

Brad thought it was impossible that Charley company was pinned down. Charley company was Dan's company. Dan couldn't be pinned down.

The lieutenant said, "There's nothing we can do. They'll make it. They got to make it."

Brad listened for a little while to the terrible clatter of heavy machine guns. He said, "What's happening now?"

"It's hard to see. We're laying down smoke." Then the lieutenant said, "I think Abel company's starting to come up. Christ! They're starting to come up!"

Across the gulley the automatic weapons opened up in a new pitch of fury. Brad shuddered. He held out his good arm and called to Urquhart: "Pull me around and turn me on my stomach."

The lieutenant said, "There's nothing you can do, Brad. You'll start bleeding."

"Please, Urquhart. Do as I say."

"Christ, Brad——"

"Do as I say."

The lieutenant turned him over slowly and pivoted him around in a quarter circle. He could feel the bleeding starting up again from the movement of his body. He lifted his head and rested his chin in the crook of his right arm and looked across the gulley and he could see the battlefield. Not all of it. But enough.

The gulley was a good sixty yards across. The opposite ridge was several yards lower than the height of ground on which he lay and beyond the ridge he could see the dome of the pillbox which was Charley company's objective, only the top curve of the dome, and beyond that was the field of approach. He couldn't see the signals casement. It was deep to the right of where he lay and well below the ridge on the opposite bank of the gulley. He knew where it was from the tracer that was pouring down the field of approach.

Mortar smoke billowed thickly over the field. He could see streams of orange tracer driving into the smoke. The tracer was coming from two directions, from the signals casement and from the pillbox that Charley company had failed to capture.

Then a gust of wind from the sea whirled the smoke off the field of approach and laid bare the men of Abel company moving up the middle of the rising ground. He saw John out ahead of his company, a tiny figure in the distance and the drifts of smoke, but he knew it was John. He couldn't mistake the posture of the man, the narrow line of his shoulders, and the way he moved steadily a few yards in advance of his men as if this were the Indian wars and not 1944. He thought, The man's gone out of his mind, he's gone out of his mind like Norden went out of his mind. He's forgotten his assault tactics. You don't walk straight into fire, not this kind of fire. He thought, Where's the smoke? Why don't they lay down more smoke? Where's MacEwen and the reserve platoon? He thought, John is going to die.

Now a new agony seized him and it was like no other agony he had ever known. He thought he had already passed through the ultimate agony, the agony of his own battle, and had triumphed over it and had come away the warrior, the victor, the hero brandishing the prize of life. It wasn't the ultimate agony. He watched John advancing along the rising ground into the streams of tracer and this was the real agony, beyond recognition, beyond control, and there were no weapons he could use to fight it, no muscle, no courage, no paroxysm of fury to fight it and overcome it.

Orange tracer enfiladed the field of approach. It was impossible for a man to walk into this stabbing fire. John kept coming on, now running, now weaving, now walking steadily forward up the slope of the ground, and the men of Abel company moved in concert with him. There were those that fell forward or dropped slowly to their knees with the punch of the bullets that hit them, but the rest came on.

Brad watched and the agony stirred afresh inside him and prayers tumbled in and out of his mind and he didn't care any more whether he lived or died. He thought, No man can be so brave. He thought, It's not bravery. He doesn't know what he's doing. It's madness, it's Norden's kind of madness. He thought, If he dies now—oh God, he mustn't die because if he dies, everything dies. He thought, Oh God, don't let him die. Make him stop. Don't let him die.

A salvo of screaming mortars looped over the field from the direction of the signals casement. John fell flat and the men behind him fell flat and black smoke rose in billows all over the field of approach. Oh God, Brad thought, and he shut his eyes and he felt the sweat from his forehead drop down over his face and he struggled with himself not to open his eyes for he couldn't bear to see. He opened his eyes. The smoke of the mortars had cleared and John was on his feet in a crouch, but the men behind still lay flat on the ground. John looked back at them and drew himself erect and still the men lay flat on the ground. He took off his helmet and waved it over his head and moved forward, and now the men, those who were not cut down by the mortar and the bullets, scrambled to their feet and charged wildly to the crest of the high ground.

Brad dropped his head into the curve of his arm. The battle had passed out of the line of his vision, beneath the opposite ridge of the gulley. He heard a new surge of clatter from the automatic weapons and he thought, He's going to die and everything will die with him.

The clangor of battle came across the gulley in convulsive waves. The cries of men intermingled with the crump of grenades and the sputter of small automatic weapons. Brad crushed his face into the ground. This was the terrifying sound of the climax, the last paroxysm, the moment when the ugly gods separated the lucky from the unlucky, the determined from the faltering, those who must die from those who would live. He knew the moment. He had lived it. He quivered with a terrible agony wrought out of guilt and helplessness and despair and great love.

He heard Urquhart cry out, "Charley company's moving. And Mac-Ewen's coming up with the reserve. He's coming up fast! They're going to make it, Brad! God Almighty, they're going to make it!"

The sound of savagery rose up from across the gulley. Brad buried his face in the ground. He felt his wounds throbbing and bleeding freely. He didn't care. The agony that racked him was deeper than his wounds. This was not what he came to war for, he told himself bitterly, not this agony he had never known and never thought to know or wanted to know.

Gradually the crump and the clatter and the inhuman shrieking died out. After a little time three red flares looped up over the battlefield and Urquhart gasped, "They made it! Holy God, they made it! They made it, Brad!" He repeated it again and again as if he didn't believe it and had to convince himself.

Brad brought his head up from the ground and looked across the gulley to the section of field within his line of vision. He saw thin curls of smoke rising from patches of ground where the mortars and grenades had set the grass afire and men trudging inquisitively among the bodies and some of the men bending down and peering into the faces of the dead. He saw that full dawn had broken and the sky was overcast and darkly gray. He thought, This is the way it should be, gray and sad. He thought, It's over and John is dead. We've won, we've captured the signals casement, we've made it easier for them on the beaches but John is dead. He thought, His luck was mostly chipped away and he must be dead. Urquhart, crouching beside him, still panted, "Holy God, Brad, they made it! They made it!"

A medic came up herding two German prisoners who carried a stretcher. The Germans were bareheaded, their tunics torn and caked with dirt. One of them, a haggard, elderly man with matted gray hair, had lost a jackboot, and blood from his toes was seeping through his stocking on the foot that had no jackboot.

The medic said, "Okay, Captain, we'll take you down now."

Brad said, "Take the others down first."

He lay on the ground, his chin propped in the crook of his good arm, and he watched the quiet, smoldering battlefield across the gulley. Stretcher-bearers were carrying wounded down from the area of the pillboxes, moving carefully over the blackened and pitted ground, avoiding the bodies that lay in the grotesque positions of violent death. He watched each stretcher party until it passed below the ridge. There were a lot of dead but there were also a lot of wounded. He tried to believe John was among those who survived.

He dared not ask Urquhart to find out, for he couldn't bear knowing the truth if it was a bad truth. He thought he had better lie still awhile not knowing. He remembered John saying *I was never much good at anything before the war and I imagine I'll be a rank failure after it's over, so a chap does what he can when he feels he's of some use.* This was part of the agony, remembering how John said it, knowing why he said it.

A flight of P-51s thundered out of the sky behind him and passed over the high ground only a few yards above where he lay. He could count the rows of rockets poised on the underside of their wings. He followed their course as they bore down on the flat beaches far below to the west. He watched their rockets strike a crazy pattern of fire on the casements facing the white, deserted beaches and then he looked out to sea. The dawn mists had lifted from the Channel and revealed the invasion fleet lying about a mile off the shore line and stretching as far down the coast as his eyes could see in the gray, squally morning.

The assault had not yet begun. The mammoth guns of the battleships still hurled their 16-inch shells in a thunderous tattoo against the casements, the pillboxes, and the gray buildings along the shore line. Now in full daylight they were joined by destroyers that tore in landward of the assault ships, raced daringly parallel to the beaches, and ripped fire into the German batteries. The Flying Fortresses, squadron following squadron, dropped out of the overcast and roared low over the beaches. Anti-aircraft shells bit into the sky, exploded into fire, and dissolved in black curls of smoke. But the Forts kept coming in and each wave obliterated the beaches in heavy smoke cut through with searing plumes of multicolored flame and when the pall lifted the German batteries were still firing.

He studied the wretched and fascinating panorama and he thought how hard it was to kill a man, how much fire and steel was required, how tough and resistant was human flesh and human spirit.

The squadrons of Forts dropped down in wave after screaming wave and when the wind off the sea whirled the smoke away, the destroyers wheeled in sputtering fire and this was the pattern over and over again and it seemed impossible for anything to live on the beaches but the German batteries continued to fire. Now the rocket craft swerved in across the shore line. They were swift ships with flat open decks and as they passed across the beach defenses the rockets leaped from their decks like red-hot arrows and struck fire along every tortured inch of the casements. Then, as if on signal, a great convulsive effort from battleships, destroyers, rocket ships, and aircraft smashed at the beaches and the air and the land shuddered with the giant blow and a pall of smoke hung low, defying the winds to scatter it. The small assault craft were launched from their mother ships and came slowly in, hundreds of them, in columns of three and four. The leading craft carried tanks and self-propelled artillery and they began firing long before they hit the beaches. There was an-swering fire from the German batteries and some of the craft ex-ploded on the water but the others came on and the tanks and the self-propelled artillery crawled up the beach like prehistoric crea-tures breathing fire. Now the LCAs pitched onto the beaches and dropped their ramps and clusters of men raced across the sand. Mortar shells rained down among them and many were left lying on the sand but many more advanced behind and beside the tanks and the self-propelled guns.

Brad watched in anguish and in terror though the men were mere specks in the distance far below where he lay. He knew the battle was fierce and men were in agony but in the distance they seemed to be spilling out of their assault craft in eager waves. He let his head drop. He didn't want to watch it any more. He felt a great weariness come into him and he thought it must be the bleeding but he knew it wasn't only the bleeding.

After a time Urquhart came up beside him. The medic and the two Germans were with him. He said, "We're taking you down."

The Germans opened the stretcher and laid it on the ground beside him.

He said to Urquhart, "Were you down on the beach?"

"Yes."

"How bad?"

Urquhart said, "Hellish." He looked away and said, "Charley com-pany. There's no more'n ten-fifteen left of Charley company."

Brad said, "Dan?"

"Dan's gone. We're taking you down. You're bleeding bad."

He thought about it. He could bear Dan being dead. Dan was like a gambling man who wins or loses and when he loses it's bad but you can bear it. He would always remember Dan winking out of his rough, happy face but he could bear Dan being dead. He thought perhaps if Dan was dead, John had made it. There was a rule of thumb about dying in battle. So many lived, so many died. He wished Urquhart would tell him about John. He didn't want to ask.

He said, "What about Waller?"

"Not a scratch."

"And MacEwen?"

"He got creased on the head but he's walking."

Christ, he thought. The rule of thumb was failing him. He was afraid to ask. He wondered why it was so hard to ask and he didn't know, just as he didn't know why it was he wouldn't be able to bear John's death. Dan was his friend and he could bear Dan's death. But he couldn't bear John's death and John was a stranger.

The medic laid a blanket on the ground beside him and said, "We'll turn you over on your back. Don't strain. It'll make the bleeding worse. Relax."

They rolled him over on the blanket and the two prisoners and the medic and Urquhart took hold of the corners and lifted him on the stretcher.

He thought it was no use waiting. He would know when they brought him down to the beach. He said, "What about the colonel?"

Urquhart said, "It's a funny thing about the colonel. He took three bullets, one in the neck, but they tell me down below he might make it. It's a miracle they said down below but he might make it."

He lay loose as jelly on the stretcher and he thought, God is good. Then he thought, God isn't good. He'll play me a dirty trick and let him die. Then he thought, Three bullets and he's still alive. Maybe God will be good to me.

They took him down through the gap in the wire, the same gap he had rushed through. He wasn't the same man who had rushed through the gap, he thought, he would never be the same man. He wished he could be the same man, he didn't want to be different, but he knew it was no use wishing. He could never be the same man and he felt cheated and he hated it.

They took a long time getting him down through the defilade. The medic cursed the prisoners and the prisoners panted and grumbled in German. He lay on the stretcher listening to the faraway battle on the beaches. He wondered if the Germans on the beaches were as old and as sad as this German he could see at the front end of his stretcher.

The medics had set up their dressing station on the sand at the base of an overhanging cliff and they had rigged several sections of heavy canvas jutting out of the rock to break the wind that was blowing across the narrow beach.

They placed his stretcher on the ground between two sections of canvas. There were four or five other stretchers in the same space and one of the men was moaning and sobbing. He couldn't lift his head to see who the man was. He figured he must have lost a lot of blood. Then a medic gave him an injection of penicillin and changed the dressings and made him swallow two big white pills.

This was the senior medic, a W/O called Blake whom he knew well, and he asked him about the colonel. Blake said, "You wouldn't think a skinny guy like that was so tough. Three bullets and he's going to make it."

The pills made him drowsy and he floated through a couple of hours. He remembered MacEwen coming to see him but he didn't know what they talked about.

About noon an LSI came in from the sea and let its ramp down on the beach near where he lay. His stretcher was carried through the gaping mouth of the ship and set down with a lot of other stretchers in a dark passageway below decks. He was very weak and sleepy but he heard the winches drawing up the ramp and the rumble of the engines pulling them off the beach and he suddenly remembered something John had said. He thought this was a hell of a way to see France for the first time.

"I have also to announce to the House," Mr. Churchill said in the hushed chamber of the Commons, "that during the night and the early hours of this morning, the first of a series of landings in force upon the European continent has taken place. In this case the liberating assault fell upon the coast of France. An immense armada of upwards of 4000 ships together with several thousand smaller craft crossed the Channel. Massed airborne landings have been successfully effected behind the enemy lines and landings on the beaches are proceeding at various points at the present time . . ."

The words bounded out across all the world, into every far corner, and there were those who cheered and those who prayed and many who waited in quiet attitudes of anguish for news of their men. The high personages who pondered global charts and issued global orders felt something of what it means to be God, but very little, for they understood only the great cataclysm they had engineered and couldn't know the small, unaccountable miracles that had flowed out of their handiwork.

## 27

HE CAME slowly out of the narcotic. He floated between sleep and wakefulness in that light and lovely mood, suspended in time, when all the thoughts that crowded in on him lacked definition but were nevertheless pleasurable thoughts because neither his bandaged body nor his mind had yet made contact with reality. It was all so fine he loathed to open his eyes. He sensed from the quality of light that came through his closed eyelids that they hadn't lifted the shade on the window behind his bed. Or perhaps it was night. Anyway, he sensed it was a cool, restful light and he opened his eyes a little. His head was twisted, lying on one ear, and he saw the creases of the white muslin on the screen which had been placed around his bed.

He remembered they placed the screen around his bed when they gave him the narcotic and changed the dressings, though he didn't know why the screen was necessary. The men in the beds on either side of him were amputation cases and for days they hadn't looked anywhere except up at the ceiling.

His ear began to hurt, the one he was lying on, and he figured it was bent inward and he had better turn his head upright because he didn't want to have flap ears in addition to the wounds in his side, or anyway one flap ear which would be even worse. So he turned his head.

He thought he saw her. He had often seen her sitting in just that position on the side of his bed, looking down at him with a half-sweet, half-anxious smile which was his favorite way of seeing her, but it had always turned out to be his imagination. The narcotic was still whirling deliciously in his mind and he wondered if she was real this time. He wished the arm that was bound and the wound in his stomach weren't on the side of the bed where she was sitting. If she was on the other side of the bed he could get his good arm from under the covers and touch her to see if she was real this time.

He made an effort to open his eyes a little wider. She was still there and the smile on her face hadn't changed.

He said, "Please take off your cap. The peak covers your eyes."

She said, "Brad——" and took off her cap and he saw the red and gold flecks on her hair. Then she put her hand on his cheek and he felt it cool and soft and he came fully awake and she was really there.

He lay looking at her for a long time, knowing she was really there. He could think of nothing nicer to do than look at her, especially at her eyes which were deep and brown and so shining he could almost feel their warmth.

He said, "Could you come to the other side of the bed?" She did and when she touched his face this time he was able to feel the length of her arm with the fingers of his good hand.

He said, "How long have you been here?"

"About an hour," she said softly as if the sound of her voice might disturb him.

"A whole hour. Doing what?"

She said, "Watching you, the way you slept." She smiled fondly and the way she said it, smiling fondly, made him feel, together with his helplessness, like a child in a crib. He was glad they hadn't taken the screen away.

Now the narcotic was running out and the pain began to throb, not so much in his arm and shoulder, more down at his stomach where the surgeon had sewn up the wound, but his mind was clearing and he didn't care about the pain.

He said, "You've been here before."

"Yes. Yesterday and the day before that."

He said, "I'm sure I saw you."

"You couldn't have. They let me in and I watched you a little. You were asleep."

"I saw you. I remember seeing you and thinking 'She'll be back.' I knew you'd come."

"Of course I was coming back."

Her face was moving rapidly into focus now and he studied her eyes and her mouth and her neck where the Red Cross pin fastened the collar of her blouse and then her eyes again.

He said, "You've changed."

"I haven't changed."

"I mean your face."

She said, "My face hasn't changed, my darling, and I haven't changed."

"I mean from the last time. At the station. Remember?"

"I remember. I must have been terribly ugly."

He said, "You could never be ugly."

"My war began that night. It's over now. That's why I look different to you."

She saw that he was puzzled and she said, "We all fight two wars, my darling. The big war and our own."

He said, "And yours is over."

"The days and nights of not knowing and wanting to die. That's over."

He closed his eyes and tried to surrender to the trace of narcotic that still drifted in his brain. Then he thought it was no use and he opened his eyes. The time had come, the time he had dreaded and railed against and rejected, the time he couldn't believe *would* come. But it had come.

He said, "How is John?"

"He's coming along splendidly."

"Will he be as good as new?"

She said, "Good as new."

"Why are you crying?"

"Am I crying, my darling?"

"Yes."

"It's the way you asked—the way you asked about John."

He looked at the ceiling. He didn't want to watch her fighting back her tears.

He said, "You don't know what happened there."

"John told me."

"He wouldn't tell you. Not John. Anyway, he doesn't know—not everything."

She said, "Then you tell me."

He kept looking at the ceiling. He said, "I saw him going in and I couldn't believe it. Not into that cross fire—not standing up—and I thought *Oh God, he wants to die. He's going in because he wants to die.* That's when his men were pinned down and he waved his helmet and advanced. I remember thinking *No man is this brave. He wants to die. He's asking for it.* And then I remember thinking *Oh*

*God, he mustn't die. If he dies, everything dies.* It was as if I was praying for my life. I didn't see much difference then. You can't understand, Val, you weren't there, you can't know how it was. And when he didn't die—when he didn't die——"

He felt her fingers on his mouth and her face dug into the pillow. The wet of her tears was cold on his cheek.

He couldn't see her. He felt her breath against his face. She said, "And when he didn't die, you thought—let me hear what you thought," and her fingers came away from his mouth.

He gave an anguished shake of his head. "You knew a long time ago. You knew that night at the station."

She said, "I began to know."

After a time she came up off the pillow. Her eyes were glazed and lustrous, sad and yet not sad.

He said, "Am I still in your blood?"

"You'll always be in my blood."

"I won't stop loving you, Val."

"Don't ever, my darling."

They looked at each other a little while and then an orderly barged in and folded up the screens and carried them away. The ward looked like a factory with its twenty-four beds, pulleys and ropes over some of them, and much traffic in the passage between the beds, and a radio playing softly at the end of the passage. A nurse came to his bedside and looked at her wrist watch and significantly at Valerie. She said, "There now, Captain, you look fine. Won't be long now and you'll be away home in a nice, new hospital ship. That should perk you up." She looked at her watch once more and significantly at Valerie and went away.

He said, "You used to say the war will make it right, God knows how but the war will make it right. It didn't."

She said, "We can't know."

Her face became anguished and she said, "Turn your head away." He knew she was leaving and he turned his head away slowly but not for long and when he looked for her she was at the end of the passage between the beds. She was standing there with her back to the beds. He watched her standing there a little time and he was glad she didn't turn around before she walked quickly out of the ward.